RAD SAX   RADLEY, T

THE SAXON BRIDES

First published in Great Britain 2013
by Mills & Boon, an imprint of Harlequin (UK) Limited,
Eton House, 18-24 Paradise Road, Richmond, Surrey TW9 1SR

THE SAXON BRIDES © by Harlequin Enterprises II B.V./S.à.r.l 2013

Mistaken Mistress, *Spaniard's Seduction* and *Pregnancy Proposal* were published in Great Britain by Harlequin (UK) Limited.

Mistaken Mistress © Tessa Radley 2008
Spaniard's Seduction © Tessa Radley 2008
Pregnancy Proposal © Tessa Radley 2008

ISBN: 978 0 263 90451 2
ebook ISBN: 978 1 472 00817 6

05-0113

Printed and bound in Spain
by Blackprint CPI, Barcelona

MISTAKEN MISTRESS

BY
TESSA RADLEY

Tessa Radley loves traveling, reading and watching the world around her. As a teen Tessa wanted to be an intrepid foreign correspondent. But after completing a bachelor of arts degree and marrying her sweetheart she became fascinated with law and ended up studying further and practicing as an attorney in a city practice.

A six-month break traveling through Australia with her family reawoke the yen to write. And life as a writer suits her perfectly; traveling and reading count as research, and as for analyzing the world…well, she can think "what if" all day long. When she's not reading, traveling or thinking about writing, she's spending time with her husband, her two sons, or her zany and wonderful friends. You can contact Tessa through her website, www.tessaradley.com.

For Lesley Marshall,
who is always an inspiration.

One

The annual Saxon's Folly masked ball was already in full swing when Alyssa Blake crept up the cobbled drive.

"Walk tall," she whispered to herself as she skirted the shadows between the rows of parked Mercedes and Daimler cars. "Look like you belong."

The winery's historic homestead came into sight, brightly lit against the dark sky. A triple-storey white Victorian building that had withstood more than a century of fires, floods and even an infamous Hawkes Bay earthquake. With every step the music grew louder, even though Alyssa couldn't yet see the partygoers.

At the top of the stone stairs a large uniformed man blocked the double, wooden front doors. Alyssa came to a halt.

Butler?

Or guard?

She wavered for a moment, her heartbeat quickening as her eyes scanned the building.

Don't panic.

"I've lost my invitation." She practised the timeworn excuse to herself under her breath. It sounded lame. Particularly as she'd never received one of the sought-after silver-embossed, midnight-blue invitations. If the guard took the time to check, he wouldn't find her on the guest list. But would he check?

Perhaps she could sashay past with a smile? What was the worst that could happen? The doorman, guard—or whatever he was—would fail to locate her on the list of invitees and demand her identity? No one would suspect Alyssa Blake, leading wine writer for *Wine Watch* magazine, of gate-crashing the annual Saxon's Folly masked ball. Or at least only the few who knew how much Joshua Saxon, CEO of Saxon's Folly Wines, detested Alyssa after the article she'd done a couple of years ago—and most people's memories didn't extend that far back.

There was a chance the burly doorman would let her in without a second glance. Wearing a long, ruby-red dress and her flamboyant black mask decorated with feathers and diamante studs, it was unlikely he'd suspect her being a gate-crasher. Alyssa hauled in a shaky breath.

She'd made up her mind to brazen her way past the doorman—guard, whatever—when a side door opened and light streaked out into the night. A couple slid out into the embrace of the darkness, laughing. The door swung closed but the latch failed to click shut.

Quickly, like a thief in the night, Alyssa slipped into the enormous homestead. She stood to one side of the entrance hall. Ahead of her, an imposing staircase swept upward.

At the top of the stairs Alyssa stepped into a different world—a world of wealth and privilege where women fluttered like designer-clad butterflies in the arms of men in dress suits and bow ties.

After one glance, she dismissed the dancers. Instead she scanned the vast reception room, searching…searching for the man she'd gone to the lengths of gate-crashing a masked ball to find.

"Have you just arrived?"

She looked up into a pair of glittering dark eyes shielded by a black mask.

"I'm a little late," she managed, her nerves rolling as the realisation sank in that she'd made it to the ball.

"Better late than never."

"Never say never," she quipped, wagging a finger at him.

He laughed. "A woman of strong opinions, right?"

"And proud of it."

His voice was husky, oddly familiar…and terribly sexy. A sweeping glance from behind her mask showed her that he was tall, the broad, hard planes of his body showing to best advantage in the superbly tailored dinner jacket. Dark hair topped his head while a black mask concealed his face. A handsome face, she speculated.

"Dance with me." He stretched an imperious arm out. Mr. Tall, Dark and Probably Handsome wasn't taking no for an answer.

Not that those attributes had any effect on her. She preferred her dates kind, caring and capable…qualities that were becoming harder to find. She stared at the demanding arm.

"I take it that silence means yes?"

Before she could object that it most definitely meant no the arm locked around her shoulder and he propelled her toward the dance floor. She started to object. She wasn't here to celebrate the budding of the new season's vines, she'd come with a purpose…and it wasn't to dance with this sexy, cocky stranger. But nor did she intend to cause a scene and be noticed.

If Joshua Saxon discovered her presence, he'd toss her out before she could even try to explain why she was here. Better not to cause a stir by refusing. At least she would blend in better with the crowd. And she could continue her search from the dance floor.

She let him sweep her into his arms and into the throng of dancers. The covetous glances her partner drew made her reevaluate whether this had been a good idea. Perhaps dancing with him would attract the attention she was so keen to avoid. She assessed him through her eyelashes, measuring what the other women saw: broad shoulders beautifully displayed in a dinner jacket, an uncompromising jawline. She glanced upward into eyes that gleamed behind the black mask.

"Do I know you?" he asked, his voice deep.

She considered that. If he was a member of the wine fraternity, they might have met at a wine show. It was possible he might have seen her during the occasional appearance she made on television, a guest spot on a food show…or perhaps he'd read her *Wine Watch* articles or the column she wrote for *The Aucklander* newspaper. But none of those meant he knew her.

So she shook her head.

"Well, I'm going to enjoy seeing your face when we unmask at midnight—it's a tradition." As a pair of dancers jostled them, he leaned toward her. "Do you have a name, Oh Silent One?"

Alyssa hesitated, transfixed by the way the hard line of his mouth tilted up into a smile. The contrast was intriguing. "Alice," she said finally, using the name on her birth certificate rather than the name she'd reinvented herself under as a teenager.

"Alice?" Those lips curved further, deepening the sensual smile. "Do you feel as if you've stepped through the looking glass, Alice?"

If he only knew.

"A little," she confessed in a low voice.

He bent his head closer. "Does that mean this is the first spring masquerade you've attended?"

"Yes."

"That explains why you're not wearing a costume."

She let her gaze linger pointedly on his dinner jacket. "You're not in costume, either."

He shook his head. "Didn't have time to plan it this year."

A busy man, then. But he didn't need the trappings of a

Robin Hood or a regency rake, she decided. He was commanding enough in his own right.

"Most women live to dress up."

His comment set her teeth on edge. "I am not most women."

He laughed softly. "I'll be even more intrigued to meet you face-to-face at midnight. So Alice, you don't like to dress up, but are you like all the Cinderellas—" he waved a dismissive hand at the beautiful women around them "—here to find a wealthy Prince Charming?" A tinge of cynicism coloured his deep voice.

"Definitely not here to find Prince Charming, wealthy or otherwise." But she shivered at his percipience. She was certainly here to find someone.

"You're not given to much conversation." He sounded far too curious for her liking.

"All these people," she simpered. "I'm not used to it."

His gaze raked her. "I'd peg you as a sophisticated city girl—not someone who'd be nervous around people."

Alyssa glanced down at the plunging V-neckline of her ruby-red dress. She'd better take care…he was altogether too astute. Her pulse pounded in her head. She couldn't afford to be thrown out—this was her best chance. "Perhaps it's the excitement. The music…the beautiful people, the handsome masked man." Her voice was sweeter than syrup. She glanced up through the satin strip of her mask to see how the flattery was going down and caught a white flash of teeth.

"As long as you're not nervous, Alice," he whispered. "That's not allowed."

Alyssa shuddered as his warm breath skimmed her sensitive ear and arousal shot unexpectedly through her.

"You *are* nervous. You're trembling."

She couldn't remember the last time a stranger had had such an immediate effect on her. Safer to say nothing.

"You're the most silent woman I've ever met," he growled, and pulled her closer to avoid a couple dancing with far too much enthusiasm in the mass of bodies.

"Not always." Not when she wasn't watching every word—her normal stock-in-trade—in case she slipped up. This disturbing stranger was far too confident…and she was not in the frame of mind to handle him.

Not tonight.

A flash of red hair caused her head to whip around, and reality came crashing in.

Roland! She couldn't mistake him, not even with a rakish pirate's eye patch. The red hair was a giveaway. He held a slim, dark-haired sprite in his arms. Across the crowded room Alyssa followed the couple's progress over her partner's broad shoulder, saw Roland say something to the brunette and watched her reply.

Alyssa had read that her name was Amy…and she was Roland's fiancée. The two of them slowed and left the dance floor.

Panic surged through Alyssa. She couldn't lose them—him. Not when she'd come so close.

"I'm parched, I need a drink," she said, not caring how abrupt she sounded, and freed herself unceremoniously from her partner's hold.

"What would you like?" Her stranger showed every sign of coming with her.

"I'll find myself something." Alyssa glanced anxiously after her quarry and back to the partner she'd failed to shake.

She mustn't give herself away.

He was much too distracting, too perceptive. She didn't want any third parties overhearing what she had to say to Roland. This was private. Too important. "You don't need to worry about me. I'm sure there are other people you should be mingling with…dancing with."

He wouldn't lack for partners. He danced like a dream… confident…moving with rhythmic grace, a man aware of his attraction and power. She jerked away from him.

His sensuous mouth twisted. "None as interesting as you,

Alice. What would you like to drink? A glass of Saxon's Folly Sauvignon Blanc? I can recommend last season's vintage."

Perhaps letting him get her a drink would get rid of him. "Just water, please."

He beckoned to a waiter who arrived at breakneck speed.

So much for getting rid of him. Alyssa resisted the urge to swear.

"Just water?" His eyes gleamed through the mask. At her nod, he turned to the waiter. "Two bottles of Perrier."

Alyssa forced herself not to look for Roland, but she was anxiously aware that if she didn't find him now, she might lose him again.

"I need the cloakroom," she improvised. "I'll be back in a minute," she flung over her shoulder, and dived into the crowd.

A glance back showed that her Mr. Tall, Dark and Probably Handsome had been detained by two women who each kissed him enthusiastically on both cheeks, the mask clearly an ineffective disguise to the ambitious Cinderellas. Impatience was carved into every line of his tall, muscular body, but he murmured a polite response.

Good, he wasn't following.

Then Alyssa put him out of her mind as she wove her way between men in tuxedos, women in silk and satin dresses, intent on finding the man she'd come to confront.

But Roland—and his fiancée—had vanished.

Alyssa hurried out onto the balcony outside, brushing past Rhett Butler and Scarlett O'Hara flirting in the shadows, and a couple of men smoking alone.

She peered over the white wrought iron railing, through the criss-cross shadows cast by a clump of tall Nikau palms, into the well-lit garden below. Two couples stood under the trees. Her breath caught. But neither man sported that distinctive red hair. Her pulse quickening with urgency, Alyssa hurried along the wide balcony and down a set of steep narrow stairs and slipped through the side door back into the homestead.

Sweeping up the long skirts of her dress, she hurried, peering into rooms she passed. A quick scan of the large dining room with tables laden with finger food failed to reveal Roland.

Roland must've taken his fiancée—Amy—upstairs. Alyssa hesitated, eyeing a staircase that appeared to lead to another wing. The bedrooms must be up there. What if she disturbed them in an…intimate moment?

Her teeth played with her bottom lip. She'd come so far, she couldn't chicken out now. Drawing a deep breath, she moved toward the stairs.

But before she got there, the door on her right swung open and a brunette burst out. Amy. Her colour was high, her hair mussed. Alyssa stopped, and then Roland came rushing into the corridor, his eye patch in his hand, his expression determined.

"Amy, listen to—"

"Roland?" Like a sleepwalker Alyssa reached out and touched his arm. "Roland Saxon?"

She knew exactly who he was but she couldn't help enunciating the name that had been imprinted on her mind for years.

He gave her an impatient glance. "Yes?"

"I'm—" She hesitated, her mind suddenly blank. Everything she'd planned to say withered under the attack of doubt devils. Dare she reveal herself as Alice McKay? He hadn't responded to any of her letters or e-mails, so why should he be any more welcoming now?

He glanced past her to where the brunette had taken the main stairs and disappeared in the direction of the ballroom.

Concerned that he would brush by her and vanish again, Alyssa thrust out her hand and said, "I'm Alyssa Blake. I'm—"

Recognition flared in the eyes that met hers in astonishment. "The journalist who did that hatchet job on Saxon's Folly. Yes, I know who you are."

No, you don't.

Finally, to her immense relief, he took her hand and shook it, before letting it drop. "What are you doing here?"

Alyssa found she was shaking. Roland had touched her. His skin had been warm and solid. Real. She'd met him. At last.

Struggling for composure, she said, "I'd like to arrange to interview you for a feature in *Wine Watch.*"

Now she had his full attention, but his expression had shifted to wariness. "What would the focus of the story be?"

"I'm doing a story on how some of the strongest brands in the industry have been built. As the marketing director of Saxon's Folly Wines, I'd like your comments."

"You haven't been too complimentary about Saxon's Folly in the past, Ms. Blake."

"Maybe I've had a change of mind." Please, God, let him believe it. She needed a chance to meet with him one-on-one. They had so much to talk about.

"I don't know—"

"Please." She was practically begging now. "It will be a positive article. I promise."

"Why should I trust you? Joshua believed you were going to do a feature on the estate. Instead you lambasted his management methods."

"Joshua Saxon had it coming," she said heatedly. "He's the most aggravatingly uncommunicative man I've ever interviewed." The man had refused to see her in person, had given her precisely ten minutes of his time on the phone. And during each miserable second of those minutes his terse voice had made it clear that he was doing her a favour. A very junior cellar hand who'd been in the job for less than a week had shown her around the winery. Alyssa had asked him about his job and discovered that the previous cellar hand had been fired under very hush-hush circumstances. A few calls to the disgruntled former employee and she had a different story from the one she'd planned to do. Now she told Roland, "The facts bore me out."

"Joshua didn't think so."

"I did my job."

He looked her up and down. "Some job."

"I tell the public what they ought to know." She knew that sounded pious. So she drew a steadying breath. "Look, this is getting us nowhere. The piece I'm working on now is different. You can even see the copy before it goes to print." Something she'd never offered but she had to see him privately.

He looked dubious. "Why the change of heart? And why ask me now, here at the ball? Why not contact me by more conventional ways, telephone—or even e-mail—to set up an appointment?"

I tried.

You never responded.

She'd tried as Alice McKay. She'd reveal Alice tomorrow. All she could do now was tempt him with the promise of a great profile. He was a marketing man. Unlike his arrogant brother, he knew he needed the goodwill of the press. "It will be great publicity for you, for Saxon's Folly."

But already he was moving past her. Time to give him an ultimatum. She spoke to his back. "Yes or no?"

"Yes, I suppose."

Alyssa knew she'd lost his attention. "When?" Alyssa switched into the familiar role, closing the escape route. "I'm in the area tomorrow. Shall we meet at The Grapevine—" she named a popular café "—in town?"

He turned his head and gave a slow nod, and her heart leapt. At last! Quickly she confirmed a time. Alyssa wanted to punch a fist in the air and yell, "Yes." After all the years…

But instead she smiled sedately and banished her impatience. Time enough tomorrow to celebrate.

Joshua Saxon was frowning. The fascination that his mystery lady in red held for him was fast becoming a compulsion. He'd been holding the two bottles of Perrier, and positioned himself so that he wouldn't miss the lady when she reappeared. But she hadn't.

Either he'd missed her. Or she hadn't been as desperate to go to the cloakroom as she'd led him to believe.

He made for the balcony on the off chance that she'd passed him and gone outside.

As soon as he stepped outside he wished he hadn't. Roland, no mask concealing his features, had Amy pinned against the balcony rail, trying to say something. But Amy was shaking her head wildly, her mask askew, telling Roland she was going home.

Under the hanging party lights Joshua caught a glimpse of tears streaking her cheeks. Roland growled that she wasn't going anywhere.

None of his business. Neither of them would thank him for the interference.

Then he spotted a flash of dark red in the gardens below and all thoughts about his brother's romantic problems fled. Alice. He leapt down the stairs that led to the garden.

"You aren't leaving already, are you?"

She turned, her rich red dress swirling around her legs, every line of her body revealing her surprise.

"Umm…"

"You were." Outraged, he stared at her. Suddenly it had become critically important to know who the provocative woman was, where to find her. But he couldn't tell her that. Instead he said, "You can't leave before the unmasking." He checked his Rolex. "It's only three-quarters of an hour away. And then the real party begins."

"I need to make this an early night."

Joshua almost laughed. Women rarely used that line on him. "The Saxon ball happens only once a year. No early night tonight."

"I have a big day tomorrow."

"Big day?" His curiosity was well and truly captured.

"Work."

She definitely wasn't the most talkative woman he'd ever

met. And that intrigued the hell out of him. Not that he'd ever admit it.

"Work? On a Sunday?"

She nodded. "Some of us are slaves to demanding bosses."

Her lips curved into an irresistible smile, and Joshua found himself smiling back. He couldn't imagine any boss forcing this woman to work against her will. He twisted the cap off one of the bottles of Perrier he held and handed it out to her. "At least take the time to finish the drink you needed so badly."

She looked startled, and a little embarrassed colour stained the elegant jaw that the mask didn't cover. "Oh, thank you."

"Do you want a glass?" Joshua twisted the cap off his own bottle.

"No, this is fine."

He gave her a reckless grin. "I probably wouldn't get you one—you might disappear again." Tilting his head to one side, he waited for her response. For an explanation of where she'd been.

But she only drew a sip and said, "Mmm, this is good."

The soft hum of appreciation riveted his attention on her mouth; the lips pursed against the top of the bottle were full and lush as she drank thirstily from the bottle. A sudden stab of sexual awareness pierced him.

"Dance with me," he said brusquely. He wanted to hold her in his arms again, feel her body against his.

"Here?"

"Why not?" Joshua moved closer. Out here there were no hordes of dancers to navigate in an overheated room. It was private in the cool intimacy of the gardens.

She didn't resist as he took the bottle from her fingers and propped it with his against the base of a Nikau palm. Nor did she utter a word of objection as one arm slid round her waist and drew her toward him.

His left hand closed around her right. Their bodies caught

the rhythm first, then their feet started to shuffle against the night-damp grass.

She smelled of jasmine and heady notes of ylang-ylang. On a conscious level Joshua found his vintner's nose analysing the feminine mix of scents, scents only a woman confident of herself, of her sexuality and her place in the world would wear. The man in him responded to the rich, sensual aromas on another—much baser—level.

Her hip slid against the top of his thigh.

Desire exploded through him. A rush of heat chased through his bloodstream, wild and unwanted. He resisted for an instant in time, then he shifted, giving in to the heat, his leg brushing between hers as they moved.

She gave a little gasp, and her body softened into his.

Instantly Joshua relinquished her hand and wound his arm around her shoulders pulling her closer. She was slim and soft in the curve of his arms. He bent his head, nuzzled the smooth skin under her jaw, and heard the sharp, telling little exhalation.

"You smell wonderful," he murmured.

"Thank you." She sounded breathless. "You smell pretty good yourself." She gave an awkward laugh. "Goodness, we should start a mutual olfactory admiration society."

He doubted that her sense of smell ruled her life as it did his. While he didn't have his younger brother Heath's highly developed ability, he'd grown up at Saxon's Folly immersed in wine, and smelling was as natural to him as breathing.

He nuzzled again. "You smell of dewy nights and dark, exotic spices." He heard her breathing quicken. This time he pressed a soft kiss under her jaw. She quivered. "So soft," he murmured throatily.

"Oh." A sigh escaped her.

Joshua took that as license to nibble gently, and she arched in his arms, her response unequivocal.

His hands explored the bare skin of her back. Under his fingertips he could feel the electric tension tightening within her.

But she didn't push him away. By the time he slid his lips across hers she was ready, her lush lips parted.

She tasted fresh and cool. Of mint and the hint of lemon in the Perrier. A powerful surge of hunger swarmed through him. Instead of tasting carefully, proceeding slowly, he yanked her close and devoured her mouth.

A wild sound escaped the back of her throat. Then her hands were raking up the corded muscles of his back, across his shoulders, her touch sparking a rush of energy that pooled in his groin.

His feet gave up all pretence of dancing. Behind his head her fingers rubbed against the exposed skin of his neck, before burying themselves in his hair. He groaned into her mouth. His tongue swept across the soft, slick inside of her bottom lip, tangled with the sleek wetness of her tongue, then plundered the back of her mouth.

Her response was instant and arousing. Her body tensed against his, and desire ratcheted up inside him until he felt that his skin was too tight. Restlessly, he ground his hips against her, acutely conscious of the blatant hardness of his erection straining for freedom. She moved, too, equally unsettled, and Joshua felt arousal kick up to the next level, his hormones telling his head there was only one place where this could end.

His bed.

For a moment he fought the savage urge. Too soon. He'd never bedded a woman he didn't know enough about to be relatively certain he'd still like her in the morning.

"God." He lifted his head, his breathing heavy.

"I should go." But she didn't sound very sure.

"Why?" he demanded, and his voice sounded hoarse to his own ears.

"Because it would be the sensible thing to do. And I'm always sensible." But her breathlessness belied her claim.

"Haven't you ever wanted to do something wild? Something totally out of character? Something that might change the rest of your life?" He murmured the inflammatory words against her lips, knowing that was what he was doing now. Allowing his body to rule his brain and letting go with this stranger was the kind of risk he, who liked his odds very carefully calculated, never took.

"Yes, I did that tonight."

He raised his head a little, trying to read the glitter in her eyes behind the mask, in the pale silver light of the crescent moon overhead.

"By coming here at all," she said cryptically.

"Come with me." Joshua reached for her hand and pulled her toward the house, leading her down a dark passage, through the empty hallway to a set of stairs that descended to his suite.

She baulked. "We can't go down there."

"Hush. Trust me."

She trailed behind him as he hurried down the stairs and past the living room that he shared with Roland.

"I suppose there are etchings you want to show me?" But beneath the bite there was breathlessness.

"No etchings." Joshua veered left toward his destination. "Come here, babe." He didn't bother to switch on the lights before he took her in his arms.

"But—"

He kissed her objections away. And when her hands ran over his back, Joshua groaned out aloud. He couldn't wait for this. Couldn't remember ever wanting a woman this much. He tore off his mask. The expensive Italian-styled dinner jacket landed on the floor, and Joshua yanked the snaps of the dress shirt open.

The touch of her fingertips on the bare skin of his chest was electric. Joshua bit back a curse of pure ecstasy. She drew her palms across his pectorals.

Joshua shuddered.

He drove his tongue deep into her mouth and shifted his hips, knowing she must be aware of how incredibly turned on he was.

But she didn't flinch. Instead her fingers teased, exploring the ridges of his abdominal muscles, brushing his lower belly.

"Woman, you're killing me," he said hoarsely.

She gave a little throaty laugh.

That was enough. His senses on fire, Joshua drew her to the bed and came down on the cover beside her. In the darkness he cupped her head in his hands, her hair soft and silky between his fingers. The ties of the mask tangled in his fingers and he tugged them loose. He kissed her cheeks where the mask had rested…her neck…and moved his lips to where he guessed the V-neckline of her outrageous dress would be.

She wasn't laughing now. Her body arched beneath him, and the swell of her breasts brushed his arm.

"*Alice.*"

She stilled.

Then his hand closed over the fabric-draped softness of her breast. He heard her gasp out loud.

"Ah, Alice, this is going to be good. I promise." Impatiently, he peeled the dress down over her shoulders—and discovered she wore no bra. He bent his head to taste the skin he'd exposed.

"*Joshua.*"

The call jarred Joshua back to reality an instant before the bedroom door burst open. He rolled in front of her, shielding her from the intruder.

Dim light backdropped the figure who stood in the doorway. Joshua snarled, "Dammit, Heath. Can't you knock?"

Two

The bedside light clicked on. Brightness spilled into every corner of the room, hurting Alyssa's eyes.

But she didn't blink. She couldn't take her eyes off the half-naked man on the bed beside her. The high, slanting cheek-bones and black eyes were all too familiar. She'd studied photos of him, wondering how someone so utterly beautifully and flagrantly male could be such an arrogant swine.

Joshua Saxon.

No wonder his voice had sounded so damn familiar. She pulled her knees to her chest and yanked the bedcover over her nakedness, then buried her head in her hands, humiliation crawling through her.

"What do you want, Heath?" There was an edge to Joshua's voice as he sat up and addressed his brother.

Through the cracks between her fingers, Alyssa peered toward the door. Heath Saxon. The younger, rakehell brother. He'd been featured in *Wine Watch* as a winemaker to watch. In the photo accompanying the profile, he'd been smiling, tanned. Now he hovered indecisively in the doorway. Until, a flush burning into his pasty skin, he said awkwardly, "Sorry, Joshua, but there's been an accident."

Joshua's shoulders bunched under the open shirt. "An accident?"

Alyssa's hand dropped to cover his.

"Roland's been hurt," Heath said. "We need to go to the hospital."

Roland hurt? Alyssa was off the bed in an instant, pulling up the neckline of her dress.

"Roland's my brother," Joshua said to Alyssa. Then his focus returned to his brother. "What kind of accident?"

"A car accident."

"What the hell happened?" Joshua asked the question before Alyssa could.

Heath shook his head. "I don't know, but an ambulance has taken him and Amy to hospital."

That catapulted Joshua into action. He leapt off the bed, started buttoning his shirt and trod into his shoes. "Do the parents know?"

Heath's eyes darkened. "I told them there'd been an accident, that you and I would go see how bad it was. They're telling everyone the party's over."

"Good move." Joshua headed for the door. "If it's necessary, they can come to the hospital later."

Before he could disappear, Alyssa said, "I'm coming with you."

To her relief both men were more concerned with getting to the hospital than arguing with her. Heath gave her a searching look—then glanced at Joshua and raised his eyebrows. Alyssa knew he was making assumptions—assumptions that were totally wrong. He thought she was Joshua's lover. She didn't bother to disillusion him.

Nor was it the time to get into lengthy discussions about her relationship to Roland...a revelation that she suspected might come as a huge shock to both men. Joshua was not to find out who she was. She didn't need a crystal ball to know that she would be unceremoniously tossed out the house.

She couldn't afford that. She had to find out how badly Roland was hurt.

Once in Joshua's Range Rover, the tension became palpable. Joshua drove like a man with a lethal mission, in total silence, his hands clenched around the steering wheel. Beside him Heath made call after call from his cell phone, growing increasingly frustrated when he couldn't get answers out of the emergency staff.

Alyssa huddled down in the back, doing her best to remain invisible lest either man question her right to be here. She prayed that Roland's injuries were minor. Hopefully he'd be discharged tonight. It would be unbearable if, after all the waiting, she couldn't meet with him tomorrow.

The moment the Range Rover braked outside the hospital, the three of them leapt out, hurrying for the glass doors that led to the emergency room.

Inside the smell of urgency and antiseptic injected dread into Alyssa. As Joshua's voice rose, she heard the nurse murmuring "in surgery" and "someone will be with you soon." Alyssa stopped a distance away. Heath asked a series of short, sharp questions and Alyssa strained her ears to hear the reply. She heard "shocked" and "will need supervision" before Joshua replied, his voice cutting. Alyssa felt for the nurse. He'd used that same voice on her in the past after her story had been printed. It had riled her enough to tell him to get lost before she'd slammed the phone down. But now she hoped it would get the answers they all wanted.

When Joshua came back to where she'd settled to wait, his mouth was tighter than before and lines of strain were etched across his forehead.

"How is my—" Alyssa broke off.

Joshua did a double take. "Your…what?" he prompted softly.

Furious with herself for the near giveaway and fighting to keep her face impassive, she asked in an even tone, "How is Roland?"

Instinct warned her that it was vital not to let Joshua Saxon know how important his answer was to her. He detested Alyssa Blake. As soon as he realised who he'd been kissing…touching…stripping…in the dark, he was going to explode.

"He's in surgery. No news yet about the extent of his injuries." The chair scraped against the polished floor as Joshua threw himself down beside her. "Thankfully Amy got off with only some bruising from the seat belt when the car hit a tree."

Hit a tree? A vision of mangled steel and broken glass flashed across Alyssa's mind. The sound of screams and groaning metal rent her imagination. She bit her lip and focused instead on Joshua's drawn features, the beauty dimmed by the savage line of his mouth. For a moment she felt a sense of kinship with him.

"Joshua?"

He lifted his head at the intrusion and the spell was broken. Alyssa felt the loneliness return, stronger and more pervasive than before. There was no bond between her and Joshua Saxon—at least none that wasn't based on sex. She shook away the disappointment.

Heath was heading toward them. "The nurse says they've finished checking Amy out and it shouldn't be long until she's back here."

"It's a relief that she wasn't hurt. She could've been killed if they're right about the speed the SUV was doing," Joshua said darkly.

"Since when did Roland ever drive slowly?" Heath bit out.

Roland had been driving? Alyssa started to shiver with reaction. If only he'd been in the passenger seat…

She thought back to when she'd spoken to him. Had he and

Amy had a lover's tiff? Would he have had the accident if he hadn't been upset?

"I heard them having a fight earlier in the evening. I considered breaking it up, then decided to mind my own business. My mind was on other things." Joshua glanced at Alyssa, his face blank. "A mistake."

So she was nothing more than a mistake. Tightness filled Alyssa's chest.

"Not your fault," said Heath. "No guy would welcome interference in that situation. You probably had it wrong. Amy and Roland never fight."

Alyssa opened her mouth. "When I spoke to Roland—"

"You spoke to Roland?" Joshua interrupted Alyssa. "When?"

"Just before I decided to leave."

"So before I spotted them on the balcony." There was a peculiar note in Joshua's voice. "What did you talk to him about?"

She stared at him, her hackles rising at his peremptory tone. She was a mistake, was she? Well, her business with Roland had nothing to do with him. "It wasn't important."

Joshua gave her a narrow-eyed glare filled with suspicion that told her he thought it was important. But before he could challenge her, a doctor in a white coat entered the reception, ushering a slender, white-faced young woman ahead of him.

Heath was on his feet. "Amy!"

Heath and Joshua both started forward.

"Are you her family?" asked the doctor.

"Yes," said Joshua.

"No," said Heath at that same moment.

There was a confused silence. The doctor looked from one to the other. "I need to see her family. She'll require observation tonight."

"We'll take care of that," said Joshua.

"I'll take her home now," added Heath, frowning as his gaze scanned Amy.

Alyssa flinched as she saw the scraped skin on the other woman's pale face. Her fine-boned build made her look frail.

"She's very lucky. Only one bruise from the seat belt. There's not even a cracked rib or a broken clavicle where the seat belt restrained her. I have a list of symptoms to watch for. We're particularly worried about concussion…or any form of head trauma. If she displays any of them bring her straight back."

Amy stood, unmoving.

"Come on," Joshua said, putting an arm around her, "Heath is taking you home."

Amy blinked. "Where's Roland?"

Joshua answered, "In surgery."

There was a moment's silence. "Will he be okay?" There was fear in Amy's voice. "There was so much blood…and he was so quiet."

"I'm sure he'll be fine," Heath said soothingly. "You know Roland, he always bounces back."

Amy didn't look reassured. "When will I be able to see him?"

"We don't know yet." Joshua's frustration added a hard edge to his voice. "But I'll soon change that."

"I'm not going anywhere," Amy said with a stubbornness that belied her delicate appearance. "Not until I've heard what's happening with Roland. And Heath won't want to leave, either."

"Don't be a child, Amy," Heath sounded exasperated. "You heard what the doctor said, you need rest and observation. There's already one—" He broke off.

"Patient?" Amy's chin lifted. "Don't worry about me, I won't collapse. You can observe me here. I'm not going anywhere until I've seen Roland."

Alyssa suppressed the urge to cheer the other woman on for standing up to the overbearing Saxons. She knew exactly how Amy felt. She, too, wanted to see Roland with a deep, driving ache. She shifted restlessly.

Joshua's gaze flickered to her before returning to Amy. "Can I get you anything while we wait?" His tone was gentle, not hinting at the frustration he must be feeling at Amy's intransigence.

Amy shook her head violently. "I'm fine."

But even Alyssa could see that the other woman was far from fine. How must Roland's fiancée be feeling, waiting to hear the extent of her beloved's injuries?

The waiting was bad enough for her. She'd only met Roland once. Very briefly. The man she'd been seeking for years…

A strand of hair fell forward. She stared at it. It was dark red—thankfully not the bright red that topped Roland's head, more of an auburn shade. But it was something tangible that she shared with him.

There would be more links to discover once they got to know each other. There must be. After all, Roland was her brother and they shared the same DNA.

A stir at the doorway caused Alyssa to lift her head. Kay and Phillip Saxon—Roland's adoptive parents—had arrived.

"How is he? Can we see him?" Kay's eyes were frantic, and the powerfully built, gray-haired man beside her looked shattered. Everyone swarmed around them. Alyssa saw her chance.

She stopped a passing nurse. "Roland Saxon…where is he?"

"What's your relationship to the patient?" The nurse glanced at the clipboard she held. "Are you the fiancée?"

She hesitated, glancing quickly back to where Kay Saxon was bending over Amy, patting her shoulder. It would be better if she didn't lie outright and simply let the nurse assume she was Roland's fiancée.

"My name is Alyssa Blake, I'm—"

"Alyssa Blake?" Joshua had come up behind her, unheard. Now his angry gaze impaled her.

Uh-oh.

"Are you the fiancée?" The nurse looked confused.

"No! She's *not* my brother's fiancée," Joshua hissed from between clenched teeth.

Alyssa's heart crashed to the floor as she read the disdain

and rage in his eyes. Game over. She could kiss her hopes of seeing Roland tonight goodbye.

"So you're Alyssa Blake, the journalist?"

Suddenly everyone was gathered around. Heath, his eyes almost as glacial as his brother's. Kay and Phillip Saxon. Only Amy remained seated, her face cupped in her hands.

Alyssa's gaze flickered from face to face. "Yes, I'm Alyssa—"

"You told me your name was Alice," Joshua interrupted.

"It is—"

"Alice?" Kay Saxon had gone so white that her lips appeared bloodless.

"Don't worry—her name isn't Alice. She's Alyssa Blake, that bloody journalist who—"

Alyssa cut across Joshua's rant. "What does it matter right now what my name is? Roland is hurt."

"You're right! I've wasted enough time on a journalist in the business of telling lies." Joshua's gaze scorched her. "It's my brother who's important right now. Come, Heath." Joshua stormed past her, his brother in his wake.

Feeling sick, Alyssa started to follow.

"Wait." Kay Saxon grabbed her arm.

Alyssa stopped. Maybe Kay would let her see Roland if she told the older woman the truth. That Roland was her brother. That she'd dreamed for so long of this day…of finding her brother…of meeting him. Warily, she searched Kay Saxon's face for a hint of softness.

"Did Joshua call you Alice?" Kay's eyes held desperation.

"Yes."

"But you introduced yourself as Alyssa Blake to the nurse."

"Yes." Where was this going? Alyssa could feel impatience rising in her. She needed to find a way to get to Roland's side. To hold his hand, absorb his pain.

"Does that mean you're Alice McKay?"

Alyssa froze. "What do you know about Alice McKay?"

"You contacted Roland."

"Yes. He told you?" She'd wondered how Kay and Phillip would feel about her contacting Roland. It looked as if she was about to find out.

Phillip stood behind his wife, a solid wall of powerful flesh she'd have to scale to get to Roland. "Darling, the doctor will be here in a minute to talk to us."

"Phillip…" Kay's hand rested on his arm and Alyssa could see that the fingers were shaking. "Didn't you hear? This is Alice McKay."

After one startled moment when everything seemed to freeze, Phillip recovered and in a low voice demanded, "What are you doing here?"

Roland's parents definitely knew who she was. But neither appeared welcoming. A sinking pit opened in Alyssa's stomach. She lifted her chin. "I wanted to meet my brother."

From across the room, she saw Joshua reappear and an ugly frown disfigured his handsome face when he saw her talking to his parents. Clearly he didn't want them talking to the notorious Alyssa Blake.

"Now is not the time for this. We want you to leave," Phillip ordered.

Alyssa stiffened and fisted her hands at her sides. "Now is exactly the time for me to be here—my brother is in surgery. I have every right to be here."

Kay Saxon took her clenched hands. "I understand how you feel, but Roland wouldn't want you here."

Alyssa's throat closed and she felt perilously close to the tears that she'd been fighting. "What do you mean?"

"He never responded to your letters or e-mails, did he?"

With heavy reluctance, Alyssa choked out, "No, he didn't."

"Doesn't that tell you something?"

"That he didn't get them?"

"He did receive them." Kay's eyes held shadows. "He chose not to reestablish contact."

"But I'm his sister." It was as though she'd ventured into a nightmare world, full of blood and death and unhappiness. All she'd wanted was a brother, a taste of family that most people took for granted. "He can't not want to meet me!"

Phillip Saxon looked around, frowning.

Kay's icy grip tightened around her fingers. "Dear, he's a Saxon—the eldest. Not even his brothers and sister know that he's adopted. Roland didn't want it getting out."

"No!" Her stomach churning, Alyssa rejected what she was hearing. She stared at Kay Saxon, hating the older woman for what she was saying. But then she took in Kay's sincerity and the deeply etched lines of pain around her mouth and the hatred evaporated.

"This is hard enough for all of us right now, Alice. Don't force us to reveal the truth…that Roland isn't a Saxon."

The impact of what Kay was saying pounded into her. Roland had rejected his birth sister in case their relationship took away his Saxon status. How could she stay under those circumstances?

Tears stung her eyes. "I just wanted to see him, hold his hand."

"It would be selfish—and not what Roland wants," Kay Saxon said softly, persuasively. "Right now we have to think about Roland."

Blinking back her tears, Alyssa nodded. "All right."

Relief flared in Kay's eyes. "Thank you." The older woman hesitated. "Do you have a cell phone, Alice?"

Alyssa nodded.

"Give me your number, dear. I'll call you as soon as we get an update."

Alyssa dug a business card out of her bag. Kay took it and pocketed it, glancing past Alyssa as she did so. "Now let's all talk about something else—Joshua is coming."

Three

Joshua made his way over to where his parents stood with Alyssa, Alice—whatever her damned name was.

He was aware of the incongruously glamourous, burgundy dress she wore and how it mirrored the colour of her long hair. Against the rich hue her bare shoulders gleamed like pale pearls.

Angrily he suppressed the flare of reckless want. He'd just taken a call from the surgery team advising that his brother was in critical condition—worse than the medical team had originally believed—and here he was lusting after Alyssa Blake, accomplished liar. It was insane.

But even as he drew closer, she gathered up her bag and rose to her feet. He stopped beside his parents and thrust his hands into his trouser pockets, at a loss to convey what he had learned. As Alyssa started for the doors one hand shot out and snagged her arm. "Where are you going?"

She kept her head down and continued to walk. "I'm leaving."

"Wait…I need some answers."

But she pulled free of his hold and marched toward the external glass doors in a flurry of dark red. Joshua started after her, then stopped as Heath came over and murmured, "Have you told Mum and Dad?"

He shook his head.

His parents must come first.

The next two minutes were a nightmare as he relayed what the surgeon had told him. "It's the internal bleeding they're worried about, and the head injury. Roland wasn't wearing a seat belt. He was catapulted from the SUV. The surgeon said they don't expect to be out for hours."

His mother's eyes stretched wide, shocked. His father straightened stiffly. Heath, his brave, bad-boy brother, was still pale under his tan. Joshua knew they all feared the same unspoken thing—that Roland might die.

Through the glass doors he could see Alyssa Blake's back, bare above that killer dress. She must be freezing. Then he put how cold she must be out of his mind.

All this had started with her arrival.

Anger turned his vision bright red. Leaving his parents with Heath, he stalked forward. The doors slid open and cool, dank night air rushed against his face.

The doors hissed closed behind him. Ahead lay the almost-empty car park. Alyssa didn't spare him a glance.

He drew a deep, steadying breath. "You came with me. How do you propose to leave?"

She brandished a cell phone. "I've called a cab—I need to collect my car from your home."

"You can't be intending to drive back to Auckland tonight?"

"Don't worry, there's not a drop of alcohol in my system." She gave him a sideways glance. "But, no, I won't be leaving tonight. I want to stay near Roland."

He drew another, deeper breath and forced himself not to react. Instead he said as calmly as he could manage, "You must be freezing. Here, take my jacket." He started to shrug off the black dinner jacket he'd grabbed before they'd left the homestead.

But she said, "No, thanks. I'm fine."

"You've got gooseflesh." He touched the skin on her upper arms, and she leapt away as if he'd singed her.

"I don't need it. The taxi will be here in a moment."

"You can give it back to me tomorrow."

She stilled. "Okay, thank you."

He slid the jacket off. It sounded as if it had taken a lot for her to accept his offer of help. Contrary damn woman. Watching her wind the jacket around herself, he relaxed a little as the pale tempting flesh disappeared out of sight.

"Where will you stay?"

Her mouth curled. "Don't worry, you won't need to track me down. I'll return it to you tomorrow."

"I wasn't worried about that."

She named a popular hotel in town.

"And you're leaving tomorrow, right?" Part of him wanted her to leave, never come back. He couldn't help the ridiculous superstitious stab of dread that her arrival had heralded Roland's accident. But there was another part of him, the sybaritic pagan part, who wanted to see her again. Touch her again. Kiss her again.

For one reckless instant he considered doing just that. It would be so easy. One tug, and she'd be up against his chest. He'd feel her body warm against his, he'd taste her lips under his mouth. The cold that froze him inside might seep away under her touch…her kisses.

And then he'd despise himself for it. He shook his head to clear it.

Maybe Alyssa Blake was a witch.

"I might leave tomorrow. It depends." Alyssa gave him a sideways glance.

But Joshua barely heard. He frowned as he took in her red-rimmed eyes, the silvery stains on her cheeks where the wind had already dried the tears. "You've been crying."

Quickly she averted her face.

"Why?"

The look she gave him revealed too little. Secrets, he thought suddenly. He glanced through the glass doors and his gaze landed on Amy, curled up in the chair, her face wearing an expression of intense misery.

His gaze came back to Alyssa and narrowed. Instead of drowning her, his dinner jacket simply increased her up-market city sexiness. She was gorgeous, stylish, smart. The kind of woman Roland had always dated before he'd become engaged to Amy....

And Amy had been upset earlier this evening—she and Roland had fought, even though it was common knowledge they never fought. The uncertain suspicion coalesced into certainty.

Alyssa had been having an affair with Roland.

She must have confronted Roland during the evening, and Amy had found out.

It wasn't important, Alyssa had said when Joshua asked her about her conversation with his brother. He'd known from the flicker in her eyes that she'd been lying. The conversation had been very important.

And now Roland was unconscious....

No wonder Alyssa was upset. Did she feel responsible for causing her lover's accident?

Did she *love* his brother?

He raked his hands through his hair as unruly thoughts churned round and round in his overwrought brain. "Who invited you to the ball tonight? You weren't on the list of official guests—it had to be a personal invitation." From Roland?

"I didn't have an invitation. I gate-crashed." There was defiance in her gaze.

Then she turned away. He heard what she had, the sound of the taxi pulling up at the curb.

But all he could think about was that Roland hadn't invited her. Or she could be lying. Again. "Why? What did you hope to achieve?"

She didn't answer and started to move away.

"Tell me, dammit." Without thought, he reached for her. His hands closed over her shoulders covered with the fine fabric of his jacket. He glared down into her blank features, her lashes lying long and dark against her cheeks. "Tell me!"

She shook her head. "It doesn't matter."

Had she tried to break up Roland's engagement? He struggled to read the beautiful, frozen face. "I think it does."

She didn't answer. He slid his hands down and circled her wrists, gave them a shake to get her to meet his gaze.

Wrapped in his jacket, she stood unmoving. And strangely that made him even angrier. He wanted her to object to his hold, he wanted her to struggle, to see her eyes spit fire at him; he didn't like the limp arms in his grasp, the listlessness in her eyes.

So he softened his grasp and said with quiet menace, "What did you want at Saxon's Folly tonight?"

She hesitated. "I'm sorry, I can't tell you."

He heard the taxi door open.

"Ma'am, did you book the taxi?"

He looked over her shoulder. "The lady's not ready to leave yet."

"But I am," she murmured.

His brows drew together. "I want an answer before you go. What did you want?"

What had happened between her and Roland? Had Roland sent her away—was that why she'd kissed *him* out in the garden? To get back at Roland? Was that why she'd landed in *his* bed?

As revenge against his brother?

He didn't like that idea at all. Yet he couldn't seem to bring himself to release her arm. The pain in her eyes damn near killed him.

He'd never envied his older brother, but now he did.

Whatever happened, if Roland survived the hours of surgery that lay ahead, Joshua wasn't going to allow Alyssa to rekindle whatever affair she and Roland had going. He told himself that his resolve had nothing to do with the wild feeling that Alyssa had aroused in him; he had Amy to think about. Sweet Amy who was expecting to marry Roland in two months' time.

Behind him he heard the doors whisper open.

"Joshua?"

He turned and glared at Heath. "What?"

"Mother wants you."

Alyssa pulled free. "I'll get your jacket back to you tomorrow."

"I don't care about the damn jacket." Inside he seethed. "This conversation is not finished. I'll talk to you in the morning."

She wouldn't flee town overnight, not while the outcome of Roland's surgery was unknown. Secure in that knowledge he turned on his heel and followed his brother back into the hospital.

It was going to be a long night.

The sound of her cell phone ringing shattered Alyssa's restless sleep. The compressing darkness of the hotel room lay like a heavy blanket around her.

It would be Joshua calling to finish the conversation he'd started outside the emergency room. Alyssa dragged herself upright. She wasn't ready for this confrontation. Then she spotted the green digital numerals of the clock radio and her heart jolted with fear. Four-thirty in the morning. Too early to be Joshua.

Her hand trembling, she picked up the phone.

"Where are you staying?" Little composure remained in Kay Saxon's voice.

Alyssa's heart slammed against her ribs in fear as she automatically gave Kay the information she sought. "Is Roland okay?" she asked shakily.

There was an ominous silence. Then Kay said, "I'll send a cab. You need to come now." The phone went dead.

It had to be bad.

With few alternatives—the red dress or a pin-striped business suit—Alyssa threw on the pair of baggy sweats and sweater she'd worn for the drive down to Hawkes Bay and was downstairs in minutes. By the time the lights of the cab cut through the dark gray pre-dawn light she was already out on the sidewalk.

Too soon she'd reached the white hospital building. Inside, everything was quiet. She made for the front desk. "Where will I find Roland Saxon?"

"Are you Alice?" A nurse came around the desk at her silent nod. "Come, I'll take you to him."

Sick with anxiety, Alyssa was led through double-seal doors into a unit filled with beeps and a sense of life-and-death gravity. At the sound of hissing as the ventilator rose and fell, fear shafted through Alyssa.

She took in the couple hovering by the bed.

Kay and Phillip Saxon.

On a high bed lay a prone figure wrapped in dressings, attached to the life-support machines, an oxygen mask over his face, so swollen that he was rendered unrecognizable. Only the shock of red hair sticking out from the head dressing revealed that this was Roland.

"You have five minutes," the nurse whispered. "Only family are supposed to be here—and only two at a time. I've already stretched the rules." Then she was gone in a rustle of starch.

Kay Saxon turned, her eyes puffy. She'd aged in the past few hours. "I'm glad you made it."

"How is he?"

"He's unconscious. I'm not sure how much is induced—"

Alyssa said desperately, "But he's going to be all right."

He had to be.

Kay took her hands. "The doctors don't think so. That's why I called you. I couldn't live with myself if—" Her voice broke.

Cold dread suffocated Alyssa. "They think he's going to *die?*"

Kay hesitated. "They told us to call anyone who might want to see him. They warned us to prepare for the worst."

Her world crashed in. Alyssa fell to her knees, stretching her hands to touch the heavily bandaged hands of the man in the bed.

Her brother.

Her brother who was dying.

Kay sniffed behind her, but Alyssa was crying so hard she couldn't think.

This wasn't how it was supposed to have ended.

She was to see him tomorrow. *Today.* She'd been looking forward to reuniting with the brother she'd been searching for since she was eighteen.

"Nooo!" It was a wail of anguish.

Then Kay was holding her and murmuring to her not to cry because it might upset Roland. As Alyssa's tears subsided, Kay pulled away. "Alyssa, the boys are coming, and I don't want them to find you here. Phillip and I don't want to have to answer their questions. Please, for our sakes—for Roland's sake—will you go now?"

Before Alyssa could answer, the nurse was there, waiting to escort her out.

She wanted to beg for more time. Her throat closed. The words didn't come. Finally, she swallowed and managed to speak. "Give me one minute. To say—" her voice cracked "—goodbye."

Kay nodded and waved off the nurse.

Alyssa bent forward, her lips colder than ice as they brushed the forehead of the man in the bed. She noticed a drip of liquid on his forehead. Water? Another splash. No—tears, she realised. Her tears.

Closing her eyes she prayed. For Roland. For herself. For

a miracle. For all the years they'd missed. Then she kissed him and murmured, "Au revoir."

Blinded by tears, she turned for the door, the room a blur.

Joshua hurried toward the hospital elevator, Heath and his younger sister, Megan, flanking him on either side. The panel above the elevator doors showed that a car was already descending and Joshua found himself drumming his fingers as they waited for the doors to open. Hurry. Hurry.

The doors opened. A nurse exited. Then Joshua saw Alyssa coming out. "How did you get here?"

"In a cab."

"That's not what I meant." He turned to his brother and sister. "You go ahead, I'll see you upstairs."

While he waited for the elevator to depart, he inspected Alyssa's features, taking in the hollows under her eyes, the lack of makeup and the way her glorious hair had been pulled back from her face, as though she'd gotten ready in a hurry. In the tatty sweats she looked nothing like the sophisticated woman he'd met…was it only last night?

"What are you doing here?"

Her eyes flicked away from his. "I came to find out if there was any news about Roland's condition."

Joshua's mouth tightened; he suspected she was dissembling. The suspicion of earlier was back in full force. "Why are you so upset? What's Roland to you?"

She shook her head and didn't answer.

Joshua couldn't help thinking about Amy, brokenhearted and sedated for shock. "Heath had to give Amy a sleeping tablet. He's left her at his home, with his housekeeper watching over her. How could you, Alyssa?"

Alyssa let her hands drop and stared at him blankly.

"She and Roland are getting married in two months. Now it's all gone to hell because you couldn't stay away from Roland."

"What?" Her eyes were stretched wide.

Joshua frowned at the shock in her eyes. He'd surprised himself with the outburst. Normally nothing fazed him. He was the boss—people came to him for guidance and advice. Yet right now he felt like raging at her. For sure he was losing it.

And she was the catalyst.

He pushed a hand through his hair. "Why did you have to come to the ball last night and cause trouble? Was it worth it? Was it worth telling Amy about your relationship with Roland?"

"I didn't tell Amy a thing."

Joshua relaxed slightly. So Amy didn't know that Roland and Alyssa were lovers. But surely Amy must have suspected Roland was embroiled in a heated affair with a woman because Joshua certainly had. All the signs had been there. The constant visits to Auckland, the cell calls that his brother took privately while talking in a low, intimate voice. By not denying her clandestine relationship with Roland, Alyssa had confirmed the suspicions he'd had about his brother for months.

"You must know that if Amy found out about you, it would devastate her. Not to say what it would do to my parents to discover that Roland had been two-timing Amy, their goddaughter. Right now they need to think about all the good things he's achieved."

Alyssa's eyes widened. "You think—" She broke off.

Joshua waited for her to refute that she'd been attempting to seduce Roland away from Amy. Deep down, he wanted that denial. Even though he knew it would be a lie. Instead she stood shifting from foot to foot, her eyes reflecting her inner turmoil.

Raking his hands through his already ruffled hair, he sighed. "It would be better if you left now and returned to Auckland."

"I haven't got your jacket here—it's back in my hotel room."

He shrugged. "I don't care about the jacket. I want you gone."

She said flatly, "I'm not going until—" her throat moved as she swallowed "—until it's all over. But Amy needn't worry,

I won't be staying a second more than I have to. I know when I'm not wanted."

Not wanted? Joshua suppressed the urge to groan. He *wanted* the woman standing in front of him more than he'd ever desired a woman in his life. But no good could come out of it. Not only had she assassinated his character in print, she'd been his brother's lover.

And he had no intention of following in Roland's well-worn footsteps.

Four

Alyssa felt terrible.

Joshua thought she and Roland had been lovers. Worse, he believed she'd come to Saxon's Folly to steal Roland away from his fiancée. She bit her lip to stop herself blurting out the truth. How could she refute what he believed without revealing the truth about her relationship to Roland?

Yesterday, just before midnight, his parents had demanded that she leave; now Joshua was ordering her to go, too. A sense of hurt settled around her. The sooner she got away from here, the sooner she could retreat to the solitary comfort of her Auckland apartment and lick her wounds in private.

But for now she had to shrug off the hurt. This morning she would hold vigil for as long as necessary. Because this wasn't about her. It was about her brother.

"Nothing to say?"

The words jerked her attention back to Joshua. He was watching her through dark, suspicious eyes.

"You should go upstairs," she said quietly. "You don't want

to miss what might be your only chance to say goodbye to Roland because you wasted time arguing with me." The thought of her brother lying there with little chance of regaining consciousness was unbearable…heartbreaking…and she sniffed back the fresh wave of tears.

"Do you love him very much?" Joshua's voice held a strange tone.

"Yes, I love him a great deal." Alyssa didn't look at him in case he read the depth of the loss and confusion in her eyes. Instead she stared at her feet and noticed that the laces of her left sneaker had come undone. What was a lace? So unimportant in the greater scheme of things.

"He never mentioned you."

She sighed. How tricky this had all become. Clearly Roland hadn't wanted his brothers to know that he wasn't a Saxon by birth. Now, because of her promise to Kay Saxon and out of her respect to her brother, she couldn't tell Joshua the truth—even though she desperately wanted to. They'd connected on some primal level, she and Joshua. She didn't like lying to him. Finally she settled for, "We hadn't known each other very long."

One brief meeting last night…she'd shaken Roland's hand. And this morning she'd touched his unconscious body.

From the old cuttings in the town's archives she knew he'd played rugby as a boy and captained his team to a regional win. She'd shuddered in fear as she'd watched television footage of Roland as a late teen riding his horse over solid fences with a determination that had won him numerous eventing titles. An article in a wine magazine had said Roland joked that he'd liked fast women and good wine. Alyssa had wondered what Amy had thought about that! A recent appearance on a lifestyle television programme hosted by a pretty blonde had revealed that he wore jeans with panache. Every last fact she could glean about him, she had uncovered.

Yet Roland didn't know her at all.

"Maybe he didn't say anything because he knew you wouldn't be pleased with his friendship with Alyssa Blake, despised journalist." Now, through desperation, she'd cornered herself into an outright lie. Before last night's meeting, Roland had only known her from the letters and e-mails…written in the name of Alice McKay.

"Friends?"

Joshua looked her up and down in a way that made her regret donning the ancient sweats. A disturbing prickle of awareness followed in the wake of his gaze. She shut it out ruthlessly. "Yes, friends. Why not?"

"I can accept that Roland didn't want us to know he was sleeping with you." Joshua's lip curled. "First, because he knows I think you're a hack writer and have no respect for you after that hatchet job you did. And sec—"

"Hack?" She glared at him in outrage. "I only did—"

He held up a hand. "Let me finish. Second, I'm sure Roland didn't mention you because you're of little importance—certainly not worth losing Amy over." Joshua gave her a long, hard stare. "Roland was always a bit of a ladies' man. But I'm not going to let Amy be hurt."

Alyssa drew a deep, steadying breath and counted silently to three before saying slowly and distinctly, "I have absolutely no intention of hurting Amy."

"Good. Then we understand each other." Joshua stabbed the button to summon the elevator. "You're trouble. As long as you keep far away from Saxon's Folly, my family—and Amy—everything will be fine!"

"You should go and see Roland," she said with urgency.

He gave her a snooty look. "My brother has the luck of the devil—he's a survivor."

Alyssa prayed to God that he was right. But his words caused a flare of hope. Joshua knew his brother. If he thought Roland might live…

"And when he's out of here, you stay far away from him."

No chance.

Joshua blamed her for the argument between Amy and Roland last night. She thought about the pretty TV-show hostess who'd interviewed Roland only a month ago. Alyssa had gone to see her. The woman had giggled that Roland was a great lover—and lamented the fact that he was already taken. Not that it had stopped him, she'd added, giving Alyssa a lascivious smile.

Maybe Amy had quarrelled with him over the hostess, but it wasn't up to Alyssa to reveal that scandal to Joshua. It might turn her stomach having Joshua accuse her of being Roland's lover…but no one except she and his parents knew how vile that accusation really was.

She wasn't the troublemaker Joshua had branded her.

Alyssa started as the elevator pinged beside her and the doors slid open. "Think what you want about me—I don't care," she said at last, suppressing the sting of his words.

Joshua strode into the waiting elevator. His gaze swept over her, cool and dismissive. "I'm sure you don't care about anything except yourself."

Alyssa decided that it was just as well she could seethe over Joshua's departing comments while she sat in the hospital café drinking stale coffee. But under her fuming she still fretted about how Roland was faring upstairs in that sterile ward.

Drained of all emotion, Joshua paused in the entrance of the coffee-cum-flower shop in the hospital lobby. His eyes burned. After almost twenty-four hours awake, he needed a shower, a change of clothing and sleep.

But right now there were other things—important things—to which he needed to attend.

His chest expanded as he hauled in a deep breath.

And the first that needed sorting was sitting at a table beside a rack of magazines, staring into a coffee cup, a napkin crumpled in her fist. Some sixth sense must have alerted

Alyssa to his presence because her hand tightened around the mangled, once-white napkin and she looked up.

The vulnerability in her eyes vanished the instant she spotted him, replaced by wariness. Okay, so this conversation wasn't going to be easy. But it couldn't be delayed. He started forward.

"Alice—" No, not Alice. "Alyssa," he corrected himself. He'd kissed Alice. He'd never willingly touch Alyssa. "My mother sent me to tell you…" He broke off and swallowed the burning bile at the back of his throat.

She was on her feet, her hand against her mouth. "Roland…is he conscious? Can I see him?"

He shook his head. An appalling sorrow splintered inside his chest. There was frustration and bewilderment, too.

"Why? Just for a few minutes? Please?"

Her eyes were wide, beseeching. As much as he disliked her, it was clear that she loved his brother, that she'd do anything, even beg, to be with him. Damnation! This was more difficult than he'd expected.

His legs carried him to her without his realising it. He cleared his throat awkwardly. "Alyssa—"

Her hand touched his sleeve. He flinched, and she jerked it away.

"I won't make waves. I won't do anything to cause Amy anxiety. I just want to see my—Roland." She was frantically shredding what was left of the paper towel.

He caught her flailing hands and tossed the napkin on the table, hating what he had to do. "Alyssa, you don't understand. Roland is dead."

"What?" She rocked on her feet, looking as if she was about to faint.

"Steady." He moved closer, shifting his hold to her shoulders, propping her up with his body.

Her eyes were wide, staring. Shocked. Little flecks of black floated in the unseeing smoky purple irises.

"Alyssa?"

"Is it true?" She pulled away from him, wrapping her arms around herself, looking shaken to the soul.

Joshua nodded, swept by a wave of terrible pity. She'd said she loved his brother. Had Roland known the depth of her love? Had he even appreciated it? Joshua doubted it. But he couldn't afford to relent. Family came first.

Alyssa Blake was more than capable of looking out for herself.

Besides, she was too much of a forbidden temptation. "So you'll be leaving in the morning?"

Her head came up. The magnificent eyes flashed. "I'll go after the funeral. Please, leave me alone until then."

And as he watched the tears pool, the foolish and chivalrous part of him wished he had the right to hold her, comfort her and wipe those tears of hopelessness from her eyes.

Alyssa crept in and stood in the back of the church, keeping her head bowed, and stared blankly at the order of service booklet that had been given to her by the usher at the door.

Yesterday she had called David Townsend, her editor at *Wine Watch* magazine, requesting a few days' leave, without giving him any explanations. If she mentioned the word *bereavement,* she suspected that the tears that dammed up the back of her throat might overflow. Once she started, she feared she might never stop.

David had given her two days.

Alyssa had told him she'd be back in the office on Wednesday. But standing here in the crowded church, work…and Auckland…seemed so far away. A numbing mist enveloped her. Beneath the booklet she held, her gray pin-striped pantsuit seemed woefully inadequate. She'd intended to wear the outfit to the one-on-one meet she'd coerced Roland into. A quick glance around revealed that the boutique businesswear was out of place among the designer black and sedate pearls.

She hadn't brought much with her—she'd only expected

to be in Hawkes Bay for the weekend. She didn't even have pins to put her hair up. The dark silky mass lay around her bowed face in a sleek wave. But shopping for mourning clothes and hairpins had been the last thing on her mind yesterday. Roland's death on Sunday had left her reeling.

She opened the order of service booklet and found herself staring at a photo of Roland…a piece about his achievements, a short eulogy where he was described as "the much loved son of Kay and Phillip, brother of Joshua, Heath and Megan."

Of course, there was no mention of his real parents, or the sibling who had been robbed of the chance to know and love him.

The hymns reverberated around Alyssa, moving her until her heart ached so much she thought it might burst. Then Joshua stood and started to talk about Roland, and her heart shattered.

By the time she arrived at the cemetery on the farm where Saxons had been buried for nearly a century, Alyssa was so wrung out by emotion that her legs felt a little shaky.

She'd debated about the wisdom of coming to the burial. She'd known it would be upsetting. The last funeral she'd attended had been her adoptive mother's—and that had been simply awful. But in the end, the need to see her brother— her flesh and blood—laid finally to rest had won out. Perhaps now she might get some peace, too.

The first person she recognised as she made her way through the white-painted picket gate was Joshua.

She hesitated. He hadn't seen her yet.

Alyssa halted a distance off from where the Saxons crowded around the grave and sneaked another look at Joshua.

His arm was around his white-faced mother and on his other side stood his sister, Megan, sobbing into a hanky. Behind them stood Heath and Phillip Saxon, looking solemn. Amy hovered dry-eyed at the edge of the raw grave, her expression bleak.

From her vantage point, Alyssa could see the rows upon rows of vines planted on the hills that lay below the cemetery.

They would only just be starting to bud for the coming summer. It struck her that, unlike the vines, Roland would never see another summer.

Blinking back a fresh prick of tears, she barely noticed the breeze that swept her hair off her face as she listened to the priest delivering the prayer.

"Amen," she murmured with the rest of the crowd as it ended.

"Don't plan on staying," Joshua said very softly from behind her.

She didn't turn her head to look at him. She hadn't heard him approach. But every hair on her nape stood up. "I won't."

"Good." He moved to stand beside her as the final hymn started. "I don't want Amy suffering any more than she already is."

Alyssa stared at the words on the sheet of paper in her hand and stifled an impatient sigh. Amy. His parents. That's all he could think about. What about *her?* "Please believe me, I'm not going to do anything to harm Amy."

He gave her a hard look. "I wouldn't let you." His eyes scanned her face. She could feel the intensity of his gaze, as he examined every inch of her face.

"Well?"

"You're beautiful." His tone was dispassionate. Unmoved. He might have been studying an inanimate block of marble.

"Thanks," she said tersely, her gaze dropping away from his. The knowledge that he considered her beautiful didn't bring satisfaction. Joshua didn't even like *her*—the real Alyssa Blake beneath the veneer—he'd made that clear enough.

A disturbing thought struck her. Perhaps he fancied Amy? And, now with Roland out of the way, did that mean Joshua expected a chance with his brother's grief-stricken fiancée?

She gave him a covert glance from behind her lashes. "Amy's beautiful, too."

He stilled, the skin over his slanted cheekbones suddenly taut. "What the hell is that supposed to mean?"

Her lashes swept up. Her eyes clashed with his frigid ones. "Just that you seem to admire her immensely."

"You think I have the hots for my brother's fiancée?" Darkness moved in his eyes.

"It would be understandable."

Amy would be the perfect wife for Joshua Saxon. She was even Kay's goddaughter. It was a no-brainer. "Amy is vulnerable right now. You'll need to take care that she doesn't view you as a rebound relationship."

"I don't need your pop-psychology advice. I don't poach my brothers' women." His gaze was bleak. "Or at least, I never did. Not until the night I met you."

What was that cryptic statement supposed to mean? A burst of adrenaline shot through Alyssa, quickly followed by a flare of desire.

What would happen if he learned Roland wasn't his real brother. And that she, Alyssa, was Roland's younger sister.

And what was the point of agonizing over it all. It was moot. Because Joshua would never learn the truth.

Despite the pale golden light of the sun, a cold shiver started at the base of her neck and inched down her spine, leaving Alyssa feeling like an emotional wasteland.

He moved away and Alyssa shut her eyes, and let the singing voices swirl around her. After what seemed an interminable time she heard car doors slam, the roar of engines starting.

Her shoulders sagged with relief. Conscious of the careless caress of the wind on her skin, of a tui whistling in a nearby phutukawa tree, Alyssa stood still as the cemetery rapidly emptied.

Finally, she opened her eyes. Only a few people remained. Joshua was gone. But the memory of his intensity as he'd told her that he didn't want Amy suffering any more than she already was, remained vivid. What would it be like to be the focus of all that masculine protection?

She wished....

What was the point of wishing? The connection she'd sensed

with Joshua had ended the minute he learned who she was. She was accustomed to being alone. As the indulged, only child of two older parents she'd grown up curiously isolated. She'd been thirteen when she'd discovered that she was adopted, that she'd been born Alice McKay—not Alyssa Blake.

She'd been so excited at the prospect of finding siblings... more family. But her mother had cried at the idea of Alyssa searching for her birth parents. For years Alyssa had put it off, fearful of upsetting Margaret. But finally she'd been compelled to make a start, secretly. Only after her mother's death three years ago had she been able to focus single-mindedly on her quest.

She'd never tracked down her birth father. But she'd found her vacant-eyed birth mother in an institute for stroke victims and she'd become a regular visitor. But from the moment Alyssa discovered that she had a brother, she hadn't rested.

She'd wanted to find him...Roland.

And now Roland was gone forever.

A cloud drifted across the sky and passed over the face of the sun, blocking out the sunlight and casting a shadow over the mound where Roland lay. Alyssa shivered.

Why? Why had she not forced the issue with Roland sooner, *made* him see her. They could've had a few weeks...months. She sighed. But would extra time have made any difference?

Alyssa supposed it wasn't a big deal to him. Roland hadn't needed a sister; he'd already had a sister—and two brothers. A whole proud, supportive family.

While, to her, finding her brother had become everything.

"Alice...." Kay spoke hesitantly from beside her.

She gave a start of surprise. "Call me Alyssa." Alice was gone. Buried in the ground as surely as Roland was. Alice had existed only as evidence that she had once been someone else...someone with a brother.

Coming to a decision, Alyssa said flatly, "Joshua thinks that I'm Roland's lover." Alyssa still felt sullied by the accusation in his eyes. "I don't like it—especially not since Roland was already engaged. I'd like you tell Joshua the truth, please."

Kay shook her head, and gestured to the raw, new grave. "Roland is dead. Phillip and I don't want the trauma of explaining to the children that he was never their blood brother."

Children? Alyssa goggled at the older woman. Joshua Saxon was no child. "They're adults, not children anymore. Surely they'll understand?"

Kay looked uncomfortable. "It would mean their whole upbringing was based on a lie."

"They deserve the truth."

"It's too late for that." Kay shook her head and started to move away toward the white gate where Phillip stood, his back to them, talking with a group of mourners.

Frustration and despair pooled deep inside Alyssa's chest, setting a heavy lump.

"Why didn't you tell them sooner?" Then Roland might even have come looking for *her*. He'd have had time to come to terms with having a sister, of not being a Saxon by birth.

Kay stopped. "At first we intended to tell them, but the years passed, and then it was too late. Neither Phillip nor I want them to know now. It's not necessary." Kay faced Alyssa, her eyes a cool, implacable gray. "I'd like you to respect that."

Alyssa had known how Kay would react, but she'd hoped…

It wasn't to be. Roland was gone. Yet there was so much Kay could share about her brother. Maybe…

Alyssa's heart started to beat anxiously in her chest at the audacity of what she was contemplating. "Kay, I won't tell anyone. But only if you share your memories of Roland with me. Every day for a week. I want to see the photos of him, hear the stories of what he did, share the places he knew growing up."

"That's not poss—"

Alyssa read the other woman's refusal in her eyes. Thrusting her apprehension away, she firmed her lips into a determined line and stalked past the older woman. "Then I have no reason to give you my promise to keep my relationship with Roland a secret."

"Wait."

She turned her head.

"You can't do that." Kay looked horrified. "And if I do as you want? How can I trust you not to say anything later?"

"I'll give you my word." Alyssa sagged under the weight of the tension. "And I'll never break it, no matter what pressure I'm put under. This is important to me… It's all I'll ever have of the brother I've been searching for since I turned eighteen."

"Okay." Kay wore a peculiar expression. "Come to Saxon's Folly in the morning. You'd better bring your bags. You may as well stay for the week."

Alyssa felt a surge of victory…until she remembered Joshua's hard, judgmental gaze.

Five

Alyssa drove through the curving set of white gates of Saxon's Folly the following morning, nerves tying her stomach in knots. The beauty of the rows of vines stretching away on both sides of the long, oak-lined drive, still bare of the lush green growth of leaves that would come with summer, failed to calm her trepidation about encountering Joshua Saxon again.

At least she had her boss's blessing. She'd called her editor early this morning, telling him that she needed a few more days off. David's annoyance had evaporated when he'd found out she was in Hawkes Bay.

"Why didn't you tell me that last time you called? I heard that Roland Saxon was killed over the weekend. A terrible tragedy. You can do a story on the great loss that he'll be to the industry. Try get the scoop on who'll be replacing him as the marketing man of Saxon's Folly—and how that will impact on Saxon's Folly's place in the industry."

Her breath catching in her chest, she said, "David, I want to take time off."

"Are you ill? You sound strange."

To distract her canny editor, Alyssa announced in a rush, "I've been invited to stay at Saxon's Folly."

There was a short silence. Alyssa could almost hear the cogs turning in David's mind.

"Get a short obituary on Roland Saxon to me ASAP—if I have it by Friday, it can run in the next issue." There was a moment's silence. "You should've told me you were on visiting terms with the Saxons."

She had no intention of explaining about Roland. She'd promised Kay it would remain a secret…and it would.

Alyssa thought about the obituary she'd agreed to write while she walked through the town picking up some toiletries and clothing for her extended stay. She had a horrible suspicion that Joshua would not be pleased when he learned about it.

Typically, as she pulled up in front of the winery, the first person she saw was Joshua Saxon. When she got out of the car, his face hardened, radiating disapproval. Alyssa's gaze locked with his as he approached.

"The funeral is over." His obsidian gaze bored relentlessly into her. "I thought you'd be packed and gone by now."

Alyssa raised her chin. "I brought your jacket back."

"Oh, thanks." He had the grace to look slightly shamed as she got out of the car, popped open the trunk and drew out his jacket.

He took it from her and slung it over his shoulder. "Have a safe trip."

Staring at her overnight bag, Alyssa hesitated. To hell with it. He'd know sooner or later. "I'm not leaving yet. Your mother has invited me to stay for a week."

"You approached my mother?" He replied, openmouthed. "My mother is grieving the loss of her eldest son. She doesn't need an interloper barging in at the moment."

"I didn't 'barge in,' as you so delightfully put it. Your mother invited me." She drew a deep breath. "Inviting" was stretching the truth. She'd given Kay no choice. "Don't worry, Joshua, I'll be very sensitive of her feelings."

He bent forward and hoisted her overnight bag out, then cast her a disbelieving look. "Right."

Her heart started to race and apprehension shafted through her as his narrowed gaze raked her. He'd better never discover the truth of how she'd gotten her invitation. Quickly, she said, "Also, my editor has asked me to write a short tribute to Roland. I'll use this week to research that." No point hiding that.

"Oh, no, you won't! You're not poking around here for dirt on my brother."

She'd expected his reaction. She lifted out her handbag and slung it over her shoulder. "I'm not here to dig up dirt. I'm here at the invitation of your mother. But it's a good opportunity to talk to people about Roland, about what he meant to them, how he enriched their lives. Think about it, Joshua, there's nothing sinister about a tribute in *Wine Watch* to your brother. The wine community is going to miss him." And so would she.

Terribly.

He paused. She watched him weighing up her words, seeking the worst.

"I don't trust you," he said at last. "Don't forget I've been at the sharp end of your poisoned pen before. I want to keep an eye on you, hear the questions you're asking. You're coming with me each day."

Alyssa saw her dream of spending time with Kay, learning about Roland going up in smoke. "But—"

"That's screwed up whatever it is that you want." His eyes had narrowed to black slits. "So why did you gate-crash the ball? What is it that you really want, Alyssa? An exclusive interview?"

His derogatory tone caused her to say heatedly, "No, I came to—" Too late she remembered her promise to Kay.

"To what?" He pounced on her hesitation like a mountain cat.

She tempered her response. "I came to see Roland." Let him draw whatever damn conclusions he wanted from that.

"Why? You still haven't told me what you wanted with him."

"I thought you'd decided that." Alyssa couldn't stop the snippy retort as she slammed the trunk shut.

"To get him to break up with Amy?" He didn't take his eyes off her. "I'm still leaning that way, am I correct?"

"No!"

His eyes held cynical disbelief. "Then what? You had another agenda? Or do you still want me to believe that you and Roland were 'friends'?"

Joshua gave *friends* such a mocking intonation that she flinched. But she didn't give him the satisfaction of a response.

He tilted his head sideways, examining her. "You wanted something from him. Did you think Roland would feed you the story of a lifetime?"

"No, seeing Roland had nothing to do with any story."

"You're trying to tell me that hooking up with my brother meant more to you than the sniff of a story?"

She nodded. "That's exactly what I'm saying."

Joshua fell silent, a frown grooved between his guarded eyes. "You know, I'm starting to believe that Roland meant something to you. That you're grieving for him as much as we are."

Before Alyssa could respond to his unexpected concession, he'd set off with her bag in the direction of the main house.

They found Kay in the library, working at a big walnut desk overlooking the gardens that rolled down to where the vineyards started.

"Your houseguest."

"Joshua—"

"I'm sorry, Mother. I can't stay, I need to get back to the estate." Joshua set down her overnight bag and slung the dinner jacket onto a leather chair. "Don't forget that we arranged to go to see Amy tonight." He glanced pointedly at Alyssa. "It'll probably be better if you stay here."

"It would be rude to leave Alyssa. She can come, too."

"No, it will be too upsetting for Amy—if she ever discovers the truth about why Alyssa was so eager to attend the ball."

Kay blinked, the only sign that she'd remembered what Alyssa had told her in the cemetery about Joshua's belief that Alyssa was Roland's lover. For a moment Kay looked indecisive then she said, "If you think so, dear."

"I do." To Alyssa he said, "As soon as you've settled in, come find me. I'll be in the winery."

"Oh, but…I thought I would get to know Alyssa a little, especially if she and Roland were…" Kay's voice trailed away "…close." Her eyes darted everywhere—except Joshua's face.

But he didn't notice; he was too busy glaring at Alyssa.

"Behave yourself then," he growled.

Which she took to mean that she was not to ask Kay too many questions about Roland for the tribute she was writing.

After Joshua had gone, Alyssa turned to Kay. "I know this must be very hard for you. Rather than talk about Roland so soon maybe we can take a walk around the vineyard."

Kay sniffed but her eyes remained dry. "I want to talk about Roland. It happened so fast. Roland and Amy were due to get married in December. Phillip and I were looking forward to grandchildren—now he's dead."

"Children…I've never thought of children." Or a niece. Or a nephew. Or a sister-in-law like Amy. "I hadn't thought beyond finding Roland. He was the family I've been looking for since I learned I was adopted."

The stark statement hung in the air.

Kay's eyes darkened until the gray had turned almost black. "Oh, Alyssa.…" She hesitated then she opened her arms.

Alyssa walked into them, conscious of the scent of lavender that clung to the older woman. At last she stepped away.

"I feel so…lost."

"What about your parents? Wouldn't it help to stay awhile with them right now?"

"My mother—adoptive mother—died of cancer three years ago. That was when I really stepped up my search for Roland. She'd never been keen on my finding my natural parents—or Roland when she learned I had a brother."

Kay gave her a peculiar look. "Maybe she feared she might lose you."

"How could she ever lose me? She was my mother, she'd raised me. I loved her."

"What about your adoptive father?"

"He remarried last year—his new wife wanted to live on Australia's Gold Coast with her daughter and two grand-daughters."

"So in a space of a few years you've lost your mother, your father has gone away…and now your birth brother is dead." Kay looked quite ill.

"Yes," Alyssa whispered, the pain of it all closing her throat. "But you're going to share a little of Roland with me…and that's so much more of him than I've had before."

Once the Saxons had driven off to visit Amy that night, Alyssa felt strangely deserted. Using the remote to switch off the television, she was plunged into silence and within seconds the vast quietness of the homestead enfolded her. Other than one solitary creak of the beams, the lack of sound was absolute. Picking up the photo album that Kay had shown her earlier, Alyssa started to browse through.

A sharp burst of nostalgia pierced her as she stared at the images. Roland as a baby with only a little ginger fluff on his head. As a toddler, holding a new-born Joshua. A photo of Roland on his first day of school, gap-toothed, his red hair slicked down, with Joshua and Heath in front of him, as different from them as fire from coal. Roland and Heath smiling like little devils while Joshua stared solemnly at the camera, his gaze already self-possessed and direct. No Megan yet. Just the three boys.

The next page showed Roland on a bay horse, grinning as he held a great, big silver trophy aloft while Megan and Joshua stood on either side of the horse's head, looking proud and pleased.

When she'd finished paging through the album, Alyssa set it aside and made her way to the kitchen, which Kay had asked Ivy, the friendly housekeeper, to show her around earlier. There was a tray set out for her. In the fridge was the slice of quiche and bowl of salad just as Kay had promised. But Alyssa didn't bother to nuke the quiche in the microwave. She set the empty wineglass to one side and made herself a cup of cocoa instead and, picking up the tray, made her way out.

At the foot of the stairs Alyssa paused. Her room lay upstairs, along with Megan's quarters, and Kay and Phillip's suite. Downstairs was the wing that housed Roland's rooms—and Joshua's. A wave of shame swept her at the memory of what had so nearly happened in Joshua's bedroom the night of the ball.

Curiosity propelled her down the stairs. At the base of the stairs the area opened up into an airy sitting room furnished with a large plasma-screen television, two brown leather sofas and a pair of armchairs. She'd caught only a glimpse of it on the night of the ball when Joshua had hauled her through.

An immense kauri bookshelf covered one wall that closer inspection revealed was filled with books on viticulture and a couple of rows of crime novels interspersed with classics. The opposite wall was filled by an abstract study of an incoming tide that looked like a John Walker. A narrow arch led to a sleek, streamlined galley kitchen gleaming with stainless steel appliances and beside it lay a cosy dining area.

Leaving the sitting room, Alyssa glanced both ways down the passage that led off the sitting room. At one end, a door stood ajar, at the other, the door was firmly closed. With soft footsteps she made her way to the closed door at the far end. The handle twisted under her touch. As she stepped through the doorway, her throat closed.

Without a doubt this was where her brother had slept.

It hurt too much to stand beside the double bed that he would never waken in again. Through an archway she glimpsed a desk. A few steps took her to what had clearly been his private domain. His trophy room. Two glass-fronted cabinets held an impressive array of silverware. A closer look revealed schoolboy medals for athletics, awards for rugby, while trophies for eventing were prominently displayed, holding pride of place.

She made her way back into Roland's bedroom, and stopped at the sight of a door leading off into a bathroom en suite. An electric razor lay on the marble slab, charging, awaiting its next use. Alyssa picked up the wooden-backed hairbrush. There were short strands of red hair in its bristles. She disentangled a hair, then pulled one from her own head. Laying them side by side, she compared the texture and colour. Hers was darker, his was coarser. She swallowed the lump in her throat and shook the two hairs free.

Closing the door behind her had a certain finality.

At the other end of the corridor the open door beckoned. She couldn't resist the call. Joshua's rooms. She stepped past a study, papers neatly stacked on a desk, past the walk-in dressing room with the bathroom that lay beyond. The instant she stepped into his bedroom, she smelled his scent. Familiar. Taunting. The dinner jacket she'd returned hung draped over a chair, and she lifted it to her face, inhaling the rich, living male scent that had surrounded her outside the chilly hospital. She dropped down onto the navy bedcover and fought back tears. She sat there for what seemed like an age. Finally she rose and returned the jacket to the chair. Collecting her tray, with the now-cold cocoa, from the landing, she made her way upstairs to her own room.

The silence of the empty house was suffocating.

A hollow emptiness pressed down on Alyssa. Here, in the heart of the Saxon family's home, she felt more alone than she'd ever felt in her life.

* * *

Joshua had swept Amy—along with his parents and Megan—off to dinner. It was good for Amy to get out. His eyes rested on his parents—and good for them, too. Yet as they sat at the window table of an upmarket café overlooking Napier's Marine Parade, an unaccountable sense of guilt nagged at Joshua at the thought of Alyssa alone in the great house.

"Why so pensive?" He found Megan staring at him curiously as he set his knife and fork down.

"Just thinking."

She gave him a wicked grin. "About a woman?"

"No comment, wench."

She laughed. Then her cell phone pinged to announce a new message and she looked down at the screen with a secret smile.

"New admirer?"

A slight stain of uncharacteristic colour tinged his sister's cheeks. "Maybe."

"When do we get to meet him?" Kay leaned forward, looking interested, while beside her Phillip shook his head and laughed.

Megan rolled her eyes at Joshua. "See what you've started."

He grinned. "Serves you right for being so secretive." And she wasn't alone. Roland had been keeping secrets, too. A lover who no one knew about, for one. His gaze rested on Amy. She hadn't spoken much, but he thought she was looking happier since leaving her solitary cottage. Joshua had no intention of letting her find out about Alyssa's relationship to her fiancé.

Amy was the reason Alyssa wasn't here tonight. There was no need for him to feel guilty about not inviting her. But nor should Alyssa's presence at Saxon's Folly be kept secret. Amy worked as a PA at the winery. She'd find out soon enough.

"Did my mother tell you that Alyssa Blake, the wine writer, is staying with us?"

"Alyssa Blake?" Amy bristled in disbelief. "Really? After that article she wrote?"

"She wants to write a tribute to Roland for *Wine Watch* magazine." Joshua held his breath, waiting for Amy's—and his parents'—reaction.

To his surprise, Amy nodded. "It would be a nice way for Roland to be remembered."

His mother perked up. "I have some photos she can use… I'll have to find them."

Neither of them had fallen apart at the idea. Joshua started to feel as though he'd overreacted by telling Alyssa he'd be keeping her under his scrutiny…yet, from past experience, he felt he couldn't trust her.

What would she be doing right now? Eating in the salon, settled in front of the large picture windows that overlooked the garden? Or would she be in the bath, soaking out the stresses of the past days? He liked the idea of Alyssa naked in the bath, covered with frothing bath foam. He liked the idea far too damned much.

He shifted uncomfortably in his seat and censored the provocative images. How had this happened that thoughts of the woman could reduce him to a state of hot and bothered?

Restlessness drove him out of the café on the pretext that he had a call that he needed to make. Once outside, he stood on the pavement surrounded by smokers who had come out the restaurant for a quick smoke after their meal.

He fingered the keypad of his phone. He wanted to call home, speak to Alyssa and reassure himself that she was okay. His mother was right. It had been rude to take off and leave her alone. However much he disapproved of her relationship with his brother she, too, must be experiencing grief over his death—much like Amy was. And that disturbed him.

He stared at the phone. What reason would he give for calling her? It was unlikely that she'd even answer the homestead phone.

Finally he pocketed his phone. For the first time in his life he wished that he smoked. It might've helped to ease this unsettling tension inside him.

By the time he got back to the table, everyone was talking about one of the scandals in local politics. Joshua signalled for the bill. He wanted to leave. The feeling that he should not have left Alyssa alone on her first night at Saxon's Folly, with nothing but grief to keep her company, grew stronger.

As they drove up the long drive to the house, Joshua saw that the wing where Alyssa was staying was in darkness. He'd worried for nothing. She was already fast asleep.

It was the siren that woke Alyssa from a restless slumber and confused dreams full of disturbing, disjointed encounters with Roland and Kay and Joshua.

Disorientated by the shriek, uneasy from the aftermath of the nightmare, she swung her legs out of bed.

Men's voices filtered in through her window. Quickly Alyssa pulled on her robe, grabbed her bag and headed for the door. Kay had told her there had been a fire in the past, but the homestead had survived without great damage. Could it be happening again?

Downstairs the house was empty, the doors of the salon flung wide onto the verandah. No smell of smoke. No red haze to signal a fire. But Alyssa could hear the sound of motors. Fire engines? To the left she could see floodlights. Moving outside, she made her way down the stairs, toward the vine-yards where she could hear the commotion.

It took the sound of the helicopter overhead to alert her.

Frost.

Of course. The siren had been a frost warning.

Alyssa glanced at her watch. Four o'clock in the morning. The roar of motors morphed into the drone of tractors. As she came closer she could see the giant fans hitched behind and whirring as the tractors drove up and down between the rows of vines. Overhead the rotors beat the warmer air down, des-perate measures before the frost settled on the vines.

A figure materialised out of the murk.

Joshua.

"Did the siren wake you?"

Instantly she was aware of her hastily pulled on robe, which must look incongruous with her bare feet and the handbag slung over her shoulder. As he came closer she saw that his hair was mussed adding to the impression that he, too, had risen in a hurry.

"I thought it was a fire alarm."

"Not fire, only frost."

Only frost. There was little to be dismissive about frost. She knew the dangers of frost at the delicate budding stage. "Did you catch it in time?"

Joshua nodded. His eyes glinted in the light from the house behind her. "We've got good equipment. And all the local helicopter companies are on standby. Heath usually does a fly-over once he's finished his yards—he's a qualified pilot."

The air beat down on them, Alyssa's hair whipped across her face. She rocked on her feet and almost fell against Joshua.

His hands shot out. "Steady."

Pulling out of his grasp, she pushed her windswept hair off her face and gave a strangled laugh. "Sorry, it's the wind."

"You can go back to bed now, there's no emergency. You'll only get chilly standing out here."

She was conscious of his gaze taking in her dishevelled hair, her sleep-mussed face and the comfortable terry robe that was a world away from the glamorous, sophisticated image she preferred to present.

As the self-consciousness spread within her, she became aware of how isolated they were from the rest…how hidden and sheltered under the cover of night. Her pulse picked up, she breathed slowly, trying to hide her agitation. How could this man have such an effect on her?

"Okay, I'm going." Her voice was hoarse, a croak of sound in the night.

His gaze darted over her wind-ruffled hair, to where the

robe gaped in front. Alyssa yanked the sash tighter. He stilled. She sensed his tension, knew he'd picked up on what she was feeling. He cleared his throat. "I'm sorry you were woken."

"It's not a problem. I should catch another couple of hours sleep if I go back to bed now."

Immediately she wished she hadn't used the word *bed*. It brought an intimacy that she didn't want. And Joshua was aware of it, too. The utter stillness that surrounded him told her that. For one wild moment she felt herself swaying toward him, inching closer. Then she caught herself.

This was madness.

Joshua believed she'd been his brother's mistress.

Spinning away, she hurried back to the homestead, nerves of apprehension fluttering like drunken butterflies in her stomach when she heard his footsteps crunching on the gravel path behind her.

Alyssa set her bare foot on the first step and paused, not daring to look back. "See you at breakfast." She tried for a casual, throwaway tone, and knew she'd fluffed it up when he stepped closer.

"Not so fast."

She froze. Her chest rose and fell, and her toes curled into the cold stone stairs. She was eternally grateful for the fans, for the drone of the rotors. Hopefully Joshua wouldn't hear the thunder of her heart.

He stopped beside her. And touched her face. Gently. His fingertips cupped her cheek, turning her head toward him.

The thunder of rushing blood grew loud in her ears. She caught a whiff of his aftershave, the same scent that clung to his jacket. To her intense horror all the emotion she'd experienced in his bedroom welled up inside her. Joshua grew blurred. The tears she'd been suppressing since Roland died spilled over.

"Hey, don't cry."

"I'm not crying." She wiped frantically at her eyes. "I'm not." She faced him, blinking furiously.

His features softened in the light from the salon behind her. "Come here."

"I'll be okay," she choked out.

"Hush." He reached out and took her into his arms.

The storm of sobs caught her unawares and caused her shoulders to shake and her stomach to ache. His arms were strong and he cradled her against his chest, rocking her slightly. The merino lambswool sweater he wore was soft and warm under her cheek, and she could feel his heart beating steadily under her hand. It was comfortable and safe. Alyssa wished she could stay in his arms forever.

The tears fell faster.

Simply holding her, he let her cry, saying nothing.

The tempest subsided. Her sobs quietened.

And in the silence of the pre-dawn it all changed. Suddenly Joshua's hold wasn't only about comfort. There was something else, too. In slow degrees she became aware that the steady beat of his heart under her fingertips had picked up, that his breathing had become irregular. A sense of expectancy hung over them.

A moment of indecisiveness. To snuggle closer? Or push him away? She was desperately tempted to move closer.

Whatever she did now would change their relationship irrevocably.

But he made the decision for her, easing his grip. "My touch has never had that effect on a woman before. I've never made a woman cry before."

Alyssa knew he was trying to lighten the moment, trying to make her smile. But she couldn't.

She hiccupped. Mortification set in. How could she have dissolved into weak, womanly tears in his arms?

After a little silence, she said awkwardly, "I'm sorry, I'm crying like a baby."

"It's been a hell of a week." He pulled her closer again and rested his cheek against her hair. The unexpected contact was achingly tender. The pulsing sensuality had evaporated. "Cry all you want."

She regretted the loss of whatever it was that had stirred between them. She ached. But his tenderness made the tears flow afresh. Alyssa sniffed, furious with herself for appearing so vulnerable. "You must think I'm so dumb."

His arms tightened around her. "I don't think you're dumb at all." After a moment, he added huskily, "I miss him, too."

Six

A little awkwardness from her emotional meltdown still lingered when Alyssa entered the sunny glass-walled breakfast room later that morning. But she gradually relaxed once she realised the room was empty until Joshua strolled in from the kitchen.

"Oh, you startled me." Her heart started to race and not only from the shock of his sudden appearance. He looked utterly, heart-wrenchingly gorgeous. He'd changed. A black shirt and blue jeans replaced the sweats. The lambswool sweater that had been so soft against her skin earlier was gone.

"Where is everyone?" Her voice was annoyingly breathless as she fixed her attention on his face.

"Working. We rise early. No city hours at Saxon's Folly." His eyes scanned her, making her aware of how out of place her boutique-chic, pin-striped pantsuit and suede shoes must seem. At once she wished she'd worn the jeans she'd bought yesterday morning.

Today's early-morning encounter with Joshua had put her

on the defensive, forcing her to don corporate armour to withstand the devastating effect he had on her. Off balance, she said with a touch of acerbity, "Oh, then what are you still doing here?"

The beautiful bone structure tightened, and his mouth firmed into a sculpted line and all affability vanished.

"I've been waiting for you." There was not an ounce of gentleness in his narrow-eyed inspection.

"Why?" she asked baldly, tensing for a confrontation.

"Have you forgotten? You're accompanying me today. So eat up, I need to get moving."

She *had* forgotten all about it. Her brain had been short-circuited by the nightmare, then jolted by the siren. The crying jag and Joshua's show of sympathy had only deepened her turmoil. She met that granite gaze. "I don't need a guard dog."

"You don't have a choice."

His way or hit the highway. His flinty eyes and the rocklike set to his jaw warned her that there would be no point in arguing. Not if she wanted to stay at Saxon's Folly.

No hint of the gentle pre-dawn Joshua remained. She'd been duped into believing that he was empathetic. Nurturing. Safe.

Mistake.

This was the real Joshua Saxon. Too arrogant. Too sure of himself. Too darn *everything*.

But even knowing all that, she couldn't stop the sensual awareness that prickled under his penetrating regard. What a pity her body was so out of sync with her brain about the kind of man that was good for her.

Alyssa helped herself to toast, scooped on homemade marmalade, and let out the breath she'd unconsciously been holding, "So, what are you going to show me today?" She tilted her head to one side. With Joshua, attack was probably the best line of defence. "More etchings?"

"I'm a pretty straightforward kind of guy. I say what I

want. I don't need those kind of ploys—if I wanted you, I'd tell you." His grim smile held little humour.

So he didn't want her anymore. Alyssa withered a little inside and bit into her toast. Discovering her identity had killed his interest. After a few minutes of eating in silence, wishing she'd resisted the temptation to provoke him with the etchings dig, Alyssa followed him out to the Range Rover.

He took her to the vineyards first. "The vines are the heart of Saxon's Folly." Leaping down from the vehicle, he opened the passenger door for her to alight, then bent and picked up a handful of red soil and let it trickle through his fingers. "And this is the lifeblood."

Some hidden place deep within her responded to the passion in his voice. Standing a little distance from him, she fought it as she'd fought the hold he wielded over her senses. But she suspected this ability that Joshua Saxon possessed to get under her defences, deep into the heart of her, was more dangerous than the way her body responded so wantonly to his.

What was it about this man?

She examined him. Sure, he was tall, dark and dangerously gorgeous. But she'd never been one for looks alone. And, yes, the slanting morning sun struck his almost-perfect features giving his skin a rich, golden glow as he dusted his hands off. But it wasn't that alone that made her heart leap.

"This block was originally planted in 1916. Strange to think about it, isn't it?" He glanced at her. "Men from Napier, a few miles away were going off to fight in Europe during the Great War, and here, on this piece of land a world away from the war, a dozen Spanish monks planted vines. Even during times of death, life must go on."

And just like that he held her captive. Alyssa knew Joshua was talking about more than the vines that he touched with careful fingers. He was talking about Roland. About grief. About life continuing on the other side.

She resented him for it. Resented him bitterly for this uncanny ability to get through to her on the most elemental level, to hold her in his thrall.

In an attempt to break the sudden tension that snapped like a pulled string between them, she said, "What cultivar is that?"

"The monks thought they were planting Cabernet Sauvignon. Only years later when the grapes were ready to harvest did they discover their mistake. They're Cabernet Franc. Too late then to pull them out. They made their wine."

She assessed him. The way his Driza-Bone hat tipped over his forehead, the way he stood with his legs planted hip-width apart on the soil. Master of all he surveyed. "You love it out here, don't you?"

"Who wouldn't?" Pleasure lit up his eyes. A flash of white teeth transformed his face into breathtaking sexiness. Her stomach dropped as desire swept her. "Before Dad decided he wanted to step down as CEO of Saxon's Folly, I managed the vineyards. I never wanted to make the wine. I wanted to grow the fruit that winemakers like Heath and Caitlyn so magically transform into a nectar fit for the ancient gods."

The sheer beauty of the picture he painted touched Alyssa on a primal level. Here was a man with roots, who knew who he was. A man so solid, so confident in his own skin that she couldn't help but admire him…and want him.

Alyssa suppressed the yearning. She couldn't afford the distraction that Joshua presented. Drawing a shuddering breath, she said, "So you miss it?"

He nodded. "I still keep an eye on the vineyards. But I've appointed two vineyard managers. One here, and one for the blocks over at Gimblett's Gravels where most of the grapes for our reds are grown."

After an instant of hesitation, she asked daringly, "Do you miss having Heath to work with since he walked out?"

A frenetic buzz caused Alyssa to pull a vibrating cell phone out of her handbag. She glanced at the caller ID. David. She killed the call.

"Sorry." She smiled sunnily at Joshua. "You were about to say?"

His face expressionless, he said, "That last question sounded a little too much like an inquisition. Alyssa Blake in journalist mode. You should've taken your call."

Heavens, he was perceptive. Thank goodness he had no idea who had been calling. "I'll ring back later." Changing the subject, Alyssa gestured to the rolling vineyards around them. "And how did all this end up in your family's hands?"

"After the Great War the monks decided to move on. The land was sold. My Saxon forefather won it three years later in a poker game. The monks had planted vines for sacramental purposes—everyone laughed when Joseph Saxon said he was going to grow wine in commercial quantities. The land was barren, people told him. But he was determined to prove them wrong." Joshua's mouth slanted wryly. "Stubborn old bastard. The locals called it Saxon's Folly. The name stuck."

"So that's who you get it from."

He raised an eyebrow. "The name Saxon?"

She laughed appreciatively. "The stubbornness. The hard-nosed streak."

He touched his nose. "Soft as butter."

"Sure," she said, smiling up at him. And warmth rose within her as he smiled back at her.

But Alyssa was no longer smiling when, back in her bedroom, she managed to sneak a call back to her editor later that afternoon.

"I've been hearing things about Saxon's Folly…rumbles in the jungle," David said without preamble. "Let me see what more I can find out. I'll get back to you to see if there's enough for a story."

A story about Saxon's Folly?

Alyssa's heart sank. "I haven't heard anything…and I don't want to do a story now. Isn't there anyone else available?" She was no longer certain she could guarantee an impartial perspective. "I'm on leave, David."

"Maybe you won't need to use up your leave," he said cryptically. "I'll call you once I know more. And don't forget to send that obituary through by tomorrow."

Alyssa killed the phone. Oh, heavens, Joshua would have conniptions if he discovered David was considering assigning her a story about his precious vineyard and family. It would be best to say nothing. After all, David's rumbles might turn out to be nothing more than unsubstantiated rumours.

With that conclusion, Alyssa's step lightened. For now, she would put it out of her mind and concentrate on learning about her brother's life for her own satisfaction. Nothing more.

"Jump in," Joshua called to Alyssa late the following afternoon as he throttled back the engine of the Range Rover and drew up behind her.

A quick hello and she clambered into the cab, slinging her handbag at her feet. His rapid sideways glance showed long, feminine legs encased in dark blue denim and a purple T-shirt moulding curves that caused his chest to constrict and heat to shoot downward.

He forced his gaze away from her. "My meeting was unavoidable." His voice was suddenly husky. He cleared his throat. "What have you been doing?" Better, Joshua decided.

"Nothing much." Alyssa paused, pulling a notebook and pencil from her bag. "After you left I took a walk around the winery—Caitlyn kindly showed me around."

Joshua relaxed a fraction. He'd been uneasy about leaving Alyssa alone, uncertain what mischief she might wreak left untended. But he'd had no choice. Work came first. He risked another glance at her. Her hair was blowing around her face and her rosy lips tilted up.

Another surge of lust hit him. Shaken by the force of it, he tightened his fists around the steering wheel and focused on the track leading up the hill ahead.

"That's all?"

"And your mother showed me some family photo albums and told me about the stories behind Roland's trophies." The words sounded torn from her.

All feeling of relaxation vanished. He shot her a brooding look. "I don't want you upsetting my mother."

"I didn't. I promise. She wanted to do it. I think she found it therapeutic."

Was he overreacting? His innate distrust of the woman had him wanting to keep her in his view all the time. But his mother had invited Alyssa to stay at Saxon's Folly. He could hardly forbid his mother to talk to a houseguest. It might even be good for her to talk about Roland to a stranger. God knows he wasn't ready to talk about his brother yet. Certainly not to Alyssa.

They were climbing to the west, the sea behind them.

"Where are we going?" Alyssa broke the silence.

A sudden foreboding closed around Joshua. Perhaps this was not a good idea. "There's something I want to show you over on the other side of The Divide."

"The Divide?"

Joshua pointed through the windshield to where a winding pass cut into the hills ahead, which had they been higher might have earned the label of mountain range.

As they crested the summit of The Divide, he heard her breath catch. He flicked her a look and caught the entranced expression on her face.

Ahead of them lay a valley so beautiful it never failed to take his own breath away. But this time all his senses were focused on the woman seated beside him, a pencil gripped in her fist as she took in the vista of rolling hills, the wide plain, the river running through.

"So, what do you think?" Holding his breath, Joshua waited for her response.

"My God, it's beautiful," she said softly. "Too beautiful to describe in words." She tapped her pencil against her shorthand notebook.

Joshua started to smile inwardly. Satisfaction spread through him. Maybe it hadn't been a mistake to bring her here after all. "On a warm summer's day this is the best place in the world. See that river?"

Alyssa nodded.

"Chosen Valley Vineyard—Heath's home—lies on the other side. There are trout in the river. They lurk under the rocks. It takes time to coax them out."

"What a lovely picture. It's absolutely idyllic. Clearly you love it here and Heath must, too, otherwise he wouldn't live here." Alyssa fell silent for a moment. "What about Roland, did he love it, too?"

Joshua forced himself not to react to the way his brother's name fell so easily from her lips. Yet he couldn't stop the tension that settled between them, destroying the bond that had been forged in the last few minutes.

He gave a short laugh. "Roland didn't have the patience to land a trout. He was drawn to dangerous sports, fast cars…" he cast her a derisive glance "…and equally fast women."

She rose like one of the trout that lived in the stream to a particularly tempting lure. "You're saying that I'm fast?"

Joshua pulled the vehicle off the road and turned his head. "Fast lane? Fast tracked for success? Maybe. When last did you take time to reflect a little? To go hiking? To stand on the edge of a hill and wait for the sunset?"

Then he turned his back on her wide eyes and silky hair and the womanly fragrance that tangled him up in knots. Swinging out of the driver's seat, he slammed the door behind him, and walked to the road's edge, his back to her, his hands on his hips.

He heard a door slam, heard her footsteps crossing the hard ground. She stopped behind him.

His every muscle went rigid.

"You're right." She sighed, a soft, breathy sound that only served to ratchet up the tension inside him. "I've been working so damn hard."

"Why?" He stared blindly ahead, for once not seeing the beauty of the valley. "What drives you?"

"It's so hard to explain."

He swivelled to face her, his eyes searching her features. Her eyes were troubled, her mouth soft. "Try me."

For a moment he thought Alyssa might refuse. Then she said, "I was raised an only child…" Her voice trailed away.

Raised an only child? That was a peculiar way to phrase it. Joshua let it pass. She was clearly unhappy about the subject matter. And waited.

Eventually she spoke and the words were so soft that he had to strain his ears before the wind carried them away. "I was brought up to excel. Special tutoring. Piano. Drama. Art. Tennis lessons."

"Because you were an only child?" He eyed her profile. It would explain some of her hard edges, the ambition that drove her.

She didn't answer immediately. "My parents thought of me as their protégée…their chosen child. Eventually all their expectations became my own. I was expected to become someone. Don't think I was a cipher—I wanted that, too. For a long time I wanted success so much, even though my version was a little different from my parents'. My father was a judge and he wanted me to become a lawyer. It took a while for him to come to terms with my choice of career. I worked like a dog."

"But you got your success." Joshua couldn't help wondering if some of her father had rubbed off on her. "Maybe you're a chip off the old block after all."

Her lips curved into a sad smile. "I was always a bit of a

crusader. And my father made sure I had firm ideas about right and wrong from the time I was very young. Believe me, it's not easy being a judge's daughter. Especially when you're a teen. You can never win." Her eyes had regained a hint of sparkle. "But once I grew up, I realised he was right. The world needs people who stand up for what they believe in. For truth and honesty and all those old-fashioned values."

Joshua decided that this was not the best moment to remind her that trying to break up his brother's engagement was hardly honourable behaviour. But he didn't want to see the desolation return to her eyes.

"At least my mother lived long enough to see me become an award-winning wine journalist," Alyssa was saying. "A television personality instantly recognizable. But it cost me time I should have spent with her—though I never knew she was ill. Cancer," she added as she read the question he didn't ask.

"That would've been hard." There was compassion in his eyes. "She must have been proud of you."

"Oh, she was."

"I've never thought of what it might be like being an only child. About the pressures that go with it," Joshua mused, tilting his head to one side to study her. "We've shared all the responsibilities that go with Saxon's Folly. My life would have been empty without Roland and Heath to fight with, without Megan always wanting her own way."

"You're lucky." There was a wistful light in her eyes.

"Think so?" He gave a chuckle. "Sometimes I want to murder them. But I love them," he added hurriedly when he saw the horrified expression on her face.

"Maybe I was too driven," Alyssa conceded. "But that changed around three years ago."

"When your mother died?"

Alyssa's eyes were bleak. "I missed her." Her gaze focused on him. Direct. Disconcerting. "I wanted siblings…a brother. More than anything in the world, I wanted a family."

Maybe death did that to a person. He knew he would give anything to have Roland back. Pity for Alyssa stirred inside Joshua. Carefully he said, "I'm sorry that you lost your mother. Death is so final."

Emotion flared in her eyes. "I grieved for her."

"And your father?"

"He grieved, too. He remarried last year... He was lonely, I think."

She turned her head and gestured to where the sun had sunk a little more. "Somewhere along the line, I stopped looking for sunsets."

Joshua stood quietly beside her, staring out over the distant western hills at the orange-and-gold streaked sky as uneasiness filled him. He wished that her story had not moved him so much. He wished that the senseless attraction to her would cease.

He should have more sense than to want Alyssa Blake.

"You know, Joshua, I never thought that every splendid sunset means the death of another day—and that time is passing by at an alarming rate." She looked up at him, her eyes a haunting purple that would seduce him if he let them. "Maybe you're right. Maybe my life has become too fast."

A long-waited sense of satisfaction curled inside him. The impulsive words escaped him before he could curb them. "I didn't think I'd see the day that Alyssa Blake might admit that she was wrong."

Her eyes narrowed, the purple depths no longer soft as they shot sparks at him. "You're pretty fast, too. Vineyard manager of a sizeable estate. CEO of Saxon's Folly. Mentor to a full staff. Architect of employment practices that business schools studied," she reeled off his successes. "Are you any better? Saxon's Folly is a big business. You're the boss where the buck stops. Surely you're driven to achieve? Surely you set goals?"

He should've know she'd come back fighting. "Touché. Sure I do. But I'm not obsessed by goals."

"You're implying that I am?"

He shrugged. "You know my philosophy. Here at Saxon's Folly enjoyment is fundamental to the wines we make. How can people enjoy our wines, if the people who work with the wine don't have fun making it?"

She shook her head dismissively. "That's a pile of codswallop. I told you that back when you tried to sell me that line in the ten minutes you granted me for a *Wine Watch* interview."

"I was busy. You caught me in the midst of the harvest with a bad forecast on the way." He paused, not liking how defensive he sounded. "And I firmly believe that the happiness of the staff shows in the finished product."

He could see her fighting to hold her tongue. She wanted to tell him that his concern and benevolence was nothing more than an act. He could see it in her blazing eyes.

Finally she said, "You didn't strike me as the crusading type."

His own anger was rising. "No, you preferred to view me as the type who could dismiss someone arbitrarily."

Alyssa took up the challenge. "So why did you dismiss Tommy Smith? He maintained he was victimised, that you made his life a misery. That your 'happiness' philosophy was a sop."

"You know that's not true, you discovered he was dismissed from his next job only three months after I fired him. I know that the vineyard owner advised you." He'd asked Michael Worth to let her know. Her low opinion of him had rankled. It still rankled.

"That was long after the story was published," she protested. "And it was different. That time Tommy was dismissed for a sexual harassment of a fellow worker."

"And you don't think that I dismissed him for the same reason?"

Alyssa looked at him in horror. "That's why you dismissed him? Why didn't you *tell* me?"

"The last thing the victim needed was the story spilled over the papers."

"So who—"

But Joshua was shaking his head. "Sorry, I'm not at liberty to say. Even off the record."

Alyssa thought back to how dismissive she'd been of Joshua in the story she'd done, how she'd championed Tommy, the underdog. Her stomach rolled over. Had she misjudged Joshua…and Tommy…so badly?

Then her misgivings receded as he said with the arrogance that she'd come to associate with him, "Forget it. It's over and done with."

Any lingering liking for the man vanished.

A cool sea breeze swept over the hill they'd traversed. Alyssa shivered and rubbed her hands briskly up and down her arms, feeling her flesh prickling under the fingers of the wind.

"You're cold. We should go."

But Alyssa didn't move. "I didn't know that he'd harassed one of your staff. And by withholding that essential piece of information, how could I present your side of the story?"

His mouth curled. "I wasn't prepared to break my word to someone who trusted me simply to satisfy your curiosity."

Impasse. "But it cost you and Saxon's Folly."

He slanted her a cynical smile. "And lost *Wine Watch* any respect I'd previously held for the magazine."

"And any respect you might have had for me."

"Yes."

Annoyance—and disappointment—surged within her as he confirmed his poor opinion of her. What had she expected? A denial? Maybe. So when had his opinion become so important? She tried to brush the hurt away with a flippant comment, "So you didn't respect me the morning after the magazine hit the newsstands?"

The brightness of his eyes intensified. "That's what you want? My respect in the morning?" There was a sudden simmering heaviness in the air that hadn't been there a moment earlier.

"Joke," she said hastily, "that was a joke." And, as much as she craved his respect, the crack had not been appropriate.

Alyssa could've bitten her tongue out. "My mouth runs away from me sometimes."

His gaze dropped to her mouth. "Funny, I had you pegged as calculating rather than impulsive. I have the impression that you think rather carefully about every word that comes out of that delectable mouth."

And suddenly he was much too close. Blood rushed to her head, she could feel herself flushing. Alyssa tensed. Yet even as she pressed the lips he'd mockingly referred to as *delectable* tightly closed in annoyance, she experienced another betraying flare of heat.

Joshua's expression didn't change. But a muscle in his jaw tightened, the only warning she had. Alyssa didn't move. His head lowered, slowly, his lips parting. She felt his breath against her mouth and a wave of desire ripped through her. His mouth claimed hers. For a moment he stilled and then his tongue entered her mouth, and Alyssa melted against him.

His body was big and warm and she no longer felt chilled. His arms came around her, pulling her against him. She was fervently conscious of the hardness of his chest beneath his shirt, of the flimsy cotton of her own shirt and her nipples tightening with excitement. So when his fingers slid into her hair, cradling her head, holding her exactly where it was comfortable, all her senses responded and he kissed her with deep intensity.

The tingle started under the touch of his fingers against her scalp and spread down her spine, along nerve pathways she hadn't known existed, until Alyssa felt like every inch of her flesh was electrified.

He lifted his head. "You taste of peaches."

Alyssa opened her eyes, stunned by the emotion that had exploded within her, and stared at him blankly. *"Peaches?"*

"Luscious and sweet like a fine Prosecco." His mouth came down again before she could retort. She couldn't help noticing he tasted of the wind, cool and wild with a hint of mint.

The kiss was thorough, his tongue exploring her mouth, the soft inner skin, the sleekness of her tongue until Alyssa felt that he'd overpowered her senses. She clung to his shoulders, not wanting it to end, not sure whether her legs would support her if he let her go.

When he finally raised his head, her breathing was ragged. He slid his hands down behind her back, linking them, supporting her, their lower limbs touching. Denim brushed against denim. Intimate. A whisper of sound that carried in the velvet silence of the evening.

Alyssa glanced up and found Joshua watching her.

"So, can you respect a woman who responds with such abandon to your kiss?" She tried to sound casual…dismissive… sophisticated. Instead her voice came out thin and thready.

"I respect the honest emotion I discovered," he said throatily.

And her heart flipped over in her chest. Maybe he did want her. Maybe discovering her identity had not staunched the desire.

Even though he fought against it.

Right then Alyssa realised that Joshua was far more complex, far more dangerous to the yearning woman deep inside her, than she'd ever suspected.

That evening Alyssa was the last to arrive at the dinner table in the smaller dining room used for cosier family meals. Her first dinner with the family—last night she'd eaten on a tray in her room. Everyone had already settled in their seats, leaving only one chair empty. Roland's. The place her brother had occupied for years.

Her chest tight, she sank down on the chair where her brother had eaten countless meals. Opposite her sat Joshua with his mother on his right side, and his sister, Megan, on his left. Phillip and Caitlyn Ross, the Saxon's Folly winemaker, sat on either side of Alyssa.

"How was your day?" Caitlyn asked with a polite smile.

"It was fabulous," she replied mechanically, and Joshua shot her a quizzical glance, his eyebrow raised.

Oh, heavens! He was thinking about their kiss. That had been more than fabulous. Earthmoving. Mind shattering. Nothing as mundane as fabulous. Not that she intended him to know any of that.

"I learned a lot," she said lamely, then started to flush as his expression turned incredulous. So she quickly added, "Well, it's so beautiful here."

"Heaven on earth," said Caitlyn.

Alyssa stilled.

Not heaven. Not with Roland gone.

But for the first time she managed to think of her brother without the wild grief and searing regret that had so shaken her. There was still sadness, but the anger and resentment at missing the opportunity to know him was receding and acceptance of his death was starting to settle in. In some peculiar way talking about her mother's death to Joshua had helped.

"If you want to see something special, you need to get the boss to take you to the waterfall," Caitlyn said, with a glance at Joshua. "The best way to get there is by horseback, to hike there takes forever. It's a fantastic ride."

"I haven't ridden much." Alyssa thought back to her childhood, when her adoptive mother had signed her up for two terms at pony club, but with all the other scheduled tuition, she'd never had the time to learn to ride well.

"You can ride Breeze, she's very gentle," said Megan.

"I don't know…" Alyssa hesitated.

"Roland always loved it at the falls." Kay entered the conversation. "He used to beg to go on picnics there as a child. As a teenager he loved to hang out there with friends."

Alyssa started to pay attention. A place that Roland had loved? "Maybe I'll consider it." Perhaps there she would capture that spiritual closeness that she was seeking. Perhaps she'd finally lose the loneliness that lurked inside her.

"Did you know Roland?" Megan was staring at her with a puzzled frown.

Damn. Had she given away too much? Apprehension filled Alyssa. Her gaze shot to Kay, who had stilled at her daughter's question. Then moved on to Joshua. His mouth was set in a hard line.

"Uh…no."

The stuttered denial didn't sound convincing to her own ears. And the force of Joshua's glare told her that he was convinced she was lying.

But thankfully she appeared to have deflected Megan's interest. Alyssa let out a silent sigh of relief. That had been far too close.

Kay turned hurriedly to Joshua. "Do you remember one night you terrified me by arriving back covered in blood? You and Roland had some sort of competition that I never quite got to the bottom of."

Megan glanced from Joshua to her mother. Joshua's mouth tightened. "Teen garbage," he said dismissively.

"For a few years you all thought you were bulletproof." Phillip spoke for the first time.

"We grew up," Megan said quickly.

"Think carefully. You'll be sore if you're not used to riding—it's a fair distance," Joshua murmured as Ivy arrived to collect the dishes.

Looking at him, Alyssa realised that he didn't look wild about the idea. "If you're too busy, we don't need to go."

"I can probably find time to take you on Monday, the winery is closed to the public after the weekend, so it will be quieter."

Had he offered Monday because he knew she was supposed to be back at work then? But if she stayed, that would give her an extra day at Saxon's Folly. Despite his grumbling, David wouldn't mind, she never took leave. And seeing a place that had been special to her brother would be worth a bit of extra stiffness.

"I'd probably survive." She threw Joshua a quick smile, saw his double take and stopped smiling. "As long as I'm back in Auckland by evening. I'd like to do it—if you don't mind taking me."

There was a gap in the conversation. Then Caitlyn said, "I heard that you've decided against attending that European wine show, Megan."

Megan glanced tellingly in her mother's direction. "The timing was all wrong. I wanted to be here, with the family. There'll be more shows next month, starting with the show in Paris."

She'd stayed because of Roland's death. Megan didn't need to say it out loud. But her meaning was clear.

After a short pause, Caitlyn said with forced humour, "That should be fun. Those French vintners can be very charming."

Megan's lashes fell, hiding her eyes, but a small, secret smile curved her mouth revealing a dimple in her cheek. "Oh, I intend to have a lot of fun. I want to taste some of those deliciously sexy wines."

"Frenchmen are supposed to be legendarily sexy, too," Caitlyn responded.

"It's the language," Alyssa said. "Even though I don't speak it, everything sounds so sexy in French."

"Passez-moi votre verre de vin, s'il vous plaît."

Everyone started to laugh as Alyssa stared at Joshua in bewilderment, until Megan took pity on her and said, "He asked for your wineglass."

"No more for me, thanks," Alyssa said, feeling warm and fuzzy inside at the good-humoured amusement on Joshua's face, coupled with an intensity that made her heart melt.

At last he glanced away and the discussion moved onto Chardonnay, becoming increasingly technical—temperature and malolactic fermentation. Alyssa couldn't help noticing how easy the relationship between Caitlyn and Joshua was. Had he ever dated the winemaker? It would be such a sensible relationship, the winery boss and the stellar winemaker, a marriage would truly cement the relationship. She couldn't help wondering whether Joshua had ever considered keeping his winemaker happy forever.

The notion caused her a stab of something like discomfort… she didn't want to label it anything as significant as envy. Or, even worse, jealousy.

On Saturday, David called Alyssa to tell her that the rumours were definitely buzzing and that Saxon's Folly was in the thick of it all.

"It's all about a Chardonnay that was entered in the Golden Harvest Wine Awards. One judge is muttering that what's available in the shops, isn't the same as the wine he tasted in the competition."

"So what happens next?" Alyssa asked.

"They'll give Joshua Saxon the option of withdrawing the wine before the scandal becomes public, I suspect. Although there is a rumour that an investigator has been appointed. But it's all under wraps right now." David was speaking quickly now. "See what you can find out, Alyssa."

"Hey, I'm back in the office next week. Tuesday probably."

"That gives you three days." David didn't say a word about the extra day she'd added on.

"I'm not doing this story, David. I'm on leave." He was still trying to convince her when she ended the call. And the rest of the day passed in a lazy fashion.

The next morning when Kay broke the news that two of the casual workers—students who regularly helped on the weekend with the tastings and cellar door sales—hadn't turned up on Sunday, Alyssa leapt into the fray.

Kay looked relieved. "Thank you, Alyssa. Joshua is there now, he's pitching in, too. He'll tell you what to do and give you price lists."

The car park beside the winery was packed with vehicles glittering in the morning sun. Alyssa couldn't believe the amount of visitors who came for the weekend tastings and tours.

Joshua looked harried. "At least with working for *Wine Watch* you'll know how tasting works."

"Don't be so sure." She gave him a teasing grin. Within minutes she'd settled next to him behind the counter, bottles of wine uncorked beside her, a list of wines with prices. Alyssa scanned the labels of the bottles in front of her out of interest. A Sauvignon Blanc, a Cabernet Merlot and a Semillon. And even a Chardonnay. Could this be the controversial vintage David wanted her to find out more about?

A brief lull followed.

"It's been so busy," said Joshua in disbelief, "now it's gone all quiet."

"Maybe I killed off all the customers," Alyssa joked.

He shot her a dark look. "Maybe."

"Hey, that was a joke."

"It wasn't funny." But his lips curled into a smile inviting her to smile back.

"Why aren't you married, Joshua?" That sounded so blunt. But it had been on her mind since Friday night when she'd seen how at ease he and Caitlyn were in each other's company. "Or at least attached. You're an attractive man—"

"Thank you." He gave her a slow smile.

She felt herself flush. "Don't get me wrong, this isn't a proposition. I'm—"

"In journalist mode?" This time the smile held an edge. "Don't worry, I never did consider it a come-on."

"What a relief," she said, a little barb to keep him from realising how interested she, Alyssa the woman, not Alyssa the journalist, really was. "So are you going to answer?"

"Always the journalist," he said, and the irony was not lost on her.

She didn't respond.

Finally he sighed. "I've never found anyone that I want to

spend my life with." He gave her a crooked smile. "My parents set a tough example to follow. They met each other at a dance and knew from the first moment."

"You expect the same?"

He gave her a strange look. "Perhaps."

"Perhaps their romance has grown in the telling."

"They love each other. They always have. There's never been anyone else for either of them—ever."

Alyssa felt a moment of envy at his certainty. "I hope you find it—the once-in-a-lifetime love that you're looking for."

He shrugged. "I'm not looking for it. But if I find it, I'll recognise it and embrace it. And in the meantime I'm not settling for second best."

"Don't you get lonely?"

He shrugged again. "Not really. I date. I've got friends—"

"And family." Joshua had friends, he was highly respected, he ran a successful winery. Yet more than anything Alyssa coveted his family.

"Yes, my family is important to me."

"And your staff…" She waved a hand around the tasting shed.

He nodded, his eyes softening. "Saxon's Folly is more than a workplace, more than a winery. It's home."

"If you ever marry, your wife is going to have to love this place."

"It's in my blood," he said with a simple acceptance that she envied.

"What about Caitlyn?"

He blinked at the sudden question. "What about her?"

"Have you ever dated her?"

"Caitlyn?" He gave a surprised laugh. "What makes you think that?"

"It seemed like such an obvious partnership. The winemaker and the winery boss."

"I like Caitlyn. She's smart—a great winemaker. But she's always been one of the boys. There's no chemistry."

"One of the boys?" Caitlyn? Alyssa stared at him in astonishment. Was he blind to the other woman's tall, slim strength? Granted, she wore jeans and boots and men's shirts that gave her a tomboy look. But her light blue eyes, dusting of Celtic freckles and strawberry-blond hair had an undoubted charm even if her hair was always pulled back in a no-fuss ponytail and she wore no make up, but she hardly resembled a boy.

Men! Alyssa shook her head in disbelief, but she couldn't prevent the relief that flowed through her that he'd never been attracted to the other woman.

Joshua leaned toward her. "Here come your first customers. Are you ready?"

She looked up to see three women and two men in their late twenties approaching. Alyssa gave them what she hoped was a welcoming smile and waved them onto the barstools in front of the counter.

"What would you like to taste?" She lined up five tasting glasses. One of the women and the two men chose the Cabernet Merlot, the other two women pondered indecisively. Alyssa poured the red wine into the three tasting glasses and watched as they picked up and swirled it around.

"I'll try the Semillon," said one of the two who had been undecided.

"Sav Blanc for me, please," said the other.

"Black currants," said one of the men, sniffing at the dregs of the red in his glass. "It smells of black currants."

The others laughed. "I tasted red grapes," said the blonde who had tasted the red.

"You wouldn't be wrong to say black currants," Joshua's voice was low and serious.

"And I suppose the Sav tastes of grapefruit?" The woman with the Sauvignon Blanc gave him a flirtatious look from under her lashes.

Unaccountable annoyance rose within Alyssa. "The Saxon's Folly Sauvignon Blancs are known for their stone fruit flavours." She forced herself to smile blithely at the flirt.

"Stone fruit?" The woman gave her a blank look.

"Yes, peaches and nectarines." Alyssa poured a little more wine in her glass.

"Can you tell the difference between a Sauvignon Blanc and a Chardonnay," asked one of the men, giving her an interested look.

"Yes." Alyssa took out two clean glasses and placed them before him. She poured a little Chardonnay in the one and a sample of Sauvignon Blanc in the other. "You're looking for taste on the palate. The Chardonnay will have hints of oak—it's been barrel fermented—not in the bottle. It's also a little buttery, whereas the Sauvignon Blanc is fruitier. Have a taste of each."

"Ooh, can I try, too?" one of the women asked.

"Sure." Alyssa repeated the ritual for her.

"I taste a hint of peaches," said the woman.

Joshua had said she tasted of peaches when he'd kissed her up on the hill. A tremor ran through Alyssa. She flashed him a sideways look from under her lashes—and found him gazing at her, his gaze hot, his eyelids heavy.

A flare of excitement ignited deep in her belly.

"The stone fruit flavours are very specific to this region, if you travel down to Marlborough, you'll discover that the flavour's grassy, reminiscent of gooseberries." Joshua's voice washed over her talking about fruit and flavours and she listened to the mesmerising cadence of his voice, words like *peach* and *smooth* and *creamy* creating a sensuous flow that surrounded her.

"Can you taste the differences between the same wines?"

"You mean, from different producers?"

The tall man nodded.

"That's called horizontal tasting. So Saxon's Folly makes Sauvignon Blanc, and over the hill at his winery my brother makes Sauvignon Blanc, too. They're different. He's a fine winemaker…but so is Caitlyn Ross our winemaker—"

"A woman makes wine here?" One of the men sounded shocked.

"Good wines, too." Alyssa found herself bristling a little.

"Of course you'd say that, you work here."

"Actually I'm a journalist—"

"Ooh, you're doing a story? How exciting. Which newspaper?"

Alyssa told her the name of the magazine.

"I know you," said the tall man. "You're Alyssa Blake— you have a column in the Sunday papers, too. And I've seen you on television. So what do you think of the wines here?"

Alyssa gave him a smile, aware that Joshua was growing tense beside her, his hand tightening around the bottom of the wine bottle. Did he really believe that she would say something that might be detrimental to Saxon's Folly?

"You taste and tell me what you think," she responded, passing a glass to the man who had spoken. Out of the corner of her eye she noticed that Joshua's grip had relaxed a little, his knuckles were no longer white.

"Make sure you get some photos of him—" the flirt pointed at Joshua "—I might even buy a copy of the magazine." The woman batted her eyelashes in that way that Alyssa found intensely irritating. But she swallowed her annoyance and said nothing.

In the end the group walked away with a purchase of three cases of wine and Alyssa let out the breath she'd been holding.

"Hard work?" Joshua asked, a glimmer of laughter in his eyes.

"Let's just say it's not quite the easy sell I thought it would be." She looked up at him. "So you can tell the difference between the wines you brew and those that Heath makes, hmm?"

He nodded.

"And I suppose you can tell the difference between different Saxon's Folly vintages?"

"Piece of cake."

"And then you try and tell me that the samples you supplied for judging in the Golden Harvest Wine Awards taste the same as the same label available for sale in the supermarkets?"

Joshua froze. "Trying to ambush me?" he asked very softly.

Alyssa refused to be intimidated. Joshua made a big deal about his reputation, about how honourable he was. She was entitled to know if that was the truth. What she wasn't sure about yet was what she would do if she discovered it was all lies. She didn't want to hurt Kay and Phillip Saxon—or their children. Not now. Not while they were grieving. And she couldn't bear to find out that Joshua was dishonest.

It surprised her how much she needed to believe that he was as solid and real as the hills surrounding the vineyards he loved. She badly wanted to accept his word.

But she owed a duty to the public. The consumers who were possibly being scammed. She couldn't rely on her feelings, her desire to find the best in Joshua. Growing up, her father had drummed into her that people lied. All the time. Facts counted. She needed proof. Hard evidence.

It tore her apart to think of what she might discover....

"No," she said finally. "Just trying to get to the bottom of a disturbing rumour that the Chardonnay Saxon's Folly supplied for tasting in the recent competition is far superior to what's available at the retail outlets."

Seven

"So that's why you gate-crashed the ball."

Joshua had known all along Alyssa had an agenda. Bitter disappointment corroded the fondness and respect that had been developing against his will. He'd been right not to trust her.

He propped one elbow on the tasting counter and swivelled his body to face her. "And that's why you inveigled an invitation to stay at Saxon's Folly."

Her eyes flickered. "I told you before, your mother invited me."

"Right." Disbelief and sarcasm loaded his voice.

"Honestly, I didn't know about this until recently. I haven't agreed to do the story."

He should've known *Wine Watch* would be on to the story. "I'm supposed to believe that?"

"Yes."

Her amazing eyes widened ingenuously. But he wasn't about to be taken in by a pair of purple pansy eyes and an act of injured innocence. She'd known, all right. And he'd *almost* been suckered. And Alyssa Blake would not turn down the opportunity to do such a story.

Then the thought crossed his mind that Roland might have let something slip to her. Pillow talk after a hot session between the sheets.

Anger twisted his stomach into knots.

Pushing away from the tasting counter, he straightened to his intimidating height of six foot two inches.

Alyssa didn't flinch.

Roland had known about the dark cloud hanging over one of the premier Saxon's Folly wines. As soon as Joshua had learned there was a potential problem with the wine judging, he'd told Roland. He cast his mind back. The conversation had taken place a few days before the ball. He'd wanted to pull the wine from the competition. Roland had assured him there was nothing to worry about, that the sample provided for tasting was uniform and no danger of adverse publicity existed.

Would he have told his lover about the debacle? Joshua didn't want to believe that Roland had let something so confidential slip to a wine writer who'd already slated Saxon's Folly in the past. Joshua assessed her. But the wide eyes and patient smile revealed little.

Was it possible that Alyssa had found out from another source? The competition organisers? Highly unlikely. Wine-tasting competitions were run with rigorous secrecy.

Roland *must* have told her. He must have been taken in by Alyssa's inviting eyes and confiding manner. Damn! Annoyance at his brother's gullibility shook him. Being led around by the libido was the oldest trick in the book. Joshua could hardly believe Roland had fallen for it. But Roland had never been able to resist a pretty face.

Joshua scrutinised her. Shiny, dark red hair framed her face in a smooth sheet, the wide-spaced pansy eyes promised untold sensual delights. Yup, definitely a very pretty face. His gaze moved lower. Long legs went on forever in the new denims and the stretchy top, the colour of the lavender that grew outside the homestead, moulded the generous curve of her breasts.

No doubt about it. Roland would've have been utterly infatuated. Okay, so maybe he could understand why Roland had blabbed. Alyssa Blake was certainly the sexiest thing he'd seen for a long time. In Mata Hari mode she would be lethal.

He ignored the whisper in his head that suggested he might be every bit as susceptible as his brother had been; that Alyssa Blake had him tied up in knots. He narrowed his eyes. This crazy wanting had never happened before. Why now? Why *her?*

How was he supposed to deal with the fallout when she reduced him to this damn idiotic state of constant arousal? He fought to get his thoughts in order.

While she knew there was a problem with the judging, it didn't appear that she knew much more, otherwise she wouldn't be here, digging for a story.

The story she insisted she wasn't doing.

Maybe there was still time for damage control. He gave her a grim smile. "There will always be some variations between batches—it's only the small vineyards with small outputs that can almost guarantee that every bottle will taste the same. We bottle thousands of cases of Chardonnay. There's going to be a little variation—"

She gave a snort of disgust. "I'm not talking about a small amount. I'm talking about a huge difference—enough to make it taste like two completely different wines. Please don't take me for a total idiot."

Joshua held on to his temper with difficulty. "What you're suggesting is not possible. When we have a batch that comes out so much better, we bottle it as a reserve selection. Why would we pretend it's the same? Especially when we can command a higher price?"

"To garner awards? To deliberately entice the public to come out in droves and buy an award-winning wine when the one they get is vastly inferior to what they're expecting? Not that they'd ever find that out."

His brows drew together at the accusation. "We would *never* do that."

"Maybe I should ask Caitlyn that question, since she makes the wines." Alyssa started to turn away.

She was going to confront Caitlyn? After he'd told her not to question his staff? She was challenging him, walking away from him, after all but calling him a liar. He glared at her shapely back, irate that he noticed how her hips flared in the snug jeans. "It's not necessary. I am the boss. I speak for Saxon's Folly. We don't indulge in questionable practices designed to mislead the consumer. You can quote me on that in your damned article."

Looking past her he saw that a new group of tasters were heading in their direction. "We've got company. Better behave yourself," he said softly, and he knew by the sudden tension between her shoulder blades that she'd heard.

Arranging his features in a pleasant, welcoming smile, he added, "You leave tomorrow. My final word is that you're not to go to the winery…or try to interview my staff without me present."

She threw him a searing look over her shoulder. "I've no reason not to behave. I'm telling you the truth, Joshua. I've no intention of writing this story. I'm too close to…everything."

But instead of feeling relief at her revelation, Joshua felt annoyance because it underlined how much his brother had meant to her. *Too close to…everything.* His irritation was exacerbated as Alyssa flashed the wide smile that caused his body to snap to attention. Even more irritating was the fact that it wasn't directed at him, but at the approaching enthusiasts.

He couldn't trust her for a moment. She would do exactly what was best for Alyssa Blake, as always. He started to seethe.

Mata Hari indeed.

* * *

When Alyssa stirred on Monday morning, an appalling sense of dislocation rocked her at the thought of leaving Saxon's Folly later today.

The end had come before the beginning had started. She still had so much to learn about Roland. Grief eroded to a raw ache as she walked down to the stables for the last time with an unusually silent Joshua beside her.

Earlier, she'd considered calling off the ride, given Joshua's annoyance with her yesterday. But now as Alyssa watched Joshua saddle the two horses, she found she was looking forward to visiting a place that Roland had loved.

It would give her a chance to say goodbye. Closure. That's what she was looking for.

Then she could put Roland finally to rest. She wished that she could tell the Saxon siblings the truth. She'd come to like them all very much. She watched Joshua tighten the girth. With him the connection went deeper than fondness. The last thing she wanted was to leave him with the wrong impression of her relationship with Roland.

But she'd promised Kay....

In return for her silence she'd gotten a week to trace Roland's footsteps, learn about his life. And that week of time had a high price: her secrecy. She'd given her word and she could not go back on that. End of story.

Joshua led Breeze toward her, his expression unreadable. "Come, I'll give you a leg up."

She approached a little nervously. Breeze turned her head, pricked her ears and gave Alyssa an enquiring look.

"Bend your leg."

Alyssa obliged. The next moment Joshua hoisted her through the air. She landed in the English saddle and picked up the reins, while he adjusted the stirrups.

She stared down at his dark head. His hand brushed the inside of her jean-clad thigh, causing a frisson of heat. Her breath caught. She hated this tense awkwardness that yawned between them like a chasm and craved a return of the Joshua who had shown her around the vineyards. The Joshua with love for the land and passion in his eyes.

Even though she'd told David she couldn't do the article, Alyssa couldn't help wishing that Joshua would cooperate on the story. That way he'd have a chance to air his side of the situation to the public and she'd be able to do the article that David wanted so badly—and even clear up the damage she'd done to Joshua's reputation last time.

The end result would be win-win all round. Then she and Joshua might be able to resolve this friction between them. Become colleagues or even—

"How does that feel?"

At the question she abandoned her wishful thinking and stood up in the stirrups. Both legs felt even. She pulled a face. "Wobbly. Like I haven't been on a horse in a very long time."

Joshua's head tilted back and his black-as-midnight eyes clashed with hers. Her heart flopped over.

"Your stirrup leathers…are they even?"

"They'll do." Alyssa made a pretence of fiddling with the reins—anything to avoid looking at Joshua, not to feel that shameless heart-stopping surge of want that simply glancing at him aroused.

"Okay." With economy of movement, Joshua swung himself easily up onto the bay's back. Alyssa watched furtively through lowered lashes as he settled himself. He sat straight, totally at one with the horse beneath him; the broad shoulders tapering down beneath his blue-and-cream-striped shirt to where his faded jeans rode low on his hips. She didn't even see the command he gave to make the bay move. No doubt he'd been riding all his life.

As they rode out of the stable block, a black horse trotted poker-legged along the length of the fence, neck arched, his head held high. Beautiful but defiant.

"I'm glad you're not riding him." Alyssa tipped her head in the stallion's direction.

"I want to enjoy the ride." Joshua turned his head to look at the horse. "And I won't if I ride that animal. It takes hours to catch Ladykiller."

Alyssa gave the stallion a look of sympathy. But the horse belonged here. She didn't—and never would.

Joshua had made that very clear.

An hour later the rolling grasslands ended. The trail entered dense, overgrown bush and narrowed dramatically. They rode in single file with Joshua ahead.

Alyssa looked around with interest. Roland would've taken the same path and passed beneath the same trees. She called out, "So how much farther to go?"

Joshua turned in the saddle. "Not long now. We're nearly there."

Birds chirruped in the canopy overhead and bits of sunlight dappled the lush green ferns under the trees. Alyssa's heart lifted. She banked the scents and sounds to remember later, when she was back in the rat race of Auckland amidst the hurly-burly of deadlines and rush-hour traffic.

"Hold tight," Joshua said a few minutes later.

Alyssa's breath caught in her throat as she saw the incline that he planned to ride down.

She tugged on the reins to slow Breeze down. "I can't go down there!"

"Yes, you can. Believe in yourself. Lean back a little, hold the pommel of the saddle and try to relax. Come, follow me. You can do it."

Already he was descending. Alyssa could hear the scrabble of loose stones under his mount's hooves, could see his back swaying in time to the horse's stride. Rigid with apprehension, she let the reins slide through her fingers as Breeze extended her neck, lowered her head and pricked her ears forward. Alyssa grabbed at the pommel, and stared through the space between the mare's ears and hoped frantically for the best.

At the bottom of the incline she let out a whoop of triumph that caused Breeze's ears to flicker back. "I did it!"

She couldn't believe the sense of achievement she felt.

Joshua was waiting. He shot her the first grin he'd given her for what felt like a century. "Of course you did. Did you think I would've let you get hurt while you were in my care?"

As she heard the words, a penny dropped. Joshua was the boss. The final responsibility always stopped with him. Shielding a female worker from ugly gossip after she'd been harassed, making sure his mother wasn't upset while she mourned her dead son, protecting Amy from any sexual indiscretion that Roland might have committed. How many more burdens did he assume?

The boss. The guy who carried all the weight. Didn't he ever tire of it?

"Don't you ever want to share the load a little?"

"What load?" The grin disappeared and he stared at her blankly.

Alyssa wanted the grin back, wanted to see the flash of white teeth and the way his eyes lit up and crinkled at the corners. "The load of taking care of everyone around you. It must grow exhausting."

"Not really. I like to see people grow and achieve things that they doubted they could." He nodded at the incline. "Like you did there." He wheeled the big bay around and moved forward.

And that was the quality that made him such a great boss. She'd watched him at work in the winery. He had the ability to encourage people to try new things, to strive to do their best. Alyssa was thinking so hard about Joshua, she almost missed the first view of the waterfall as they rode into a sunlit clearing, and Joshua reined in ahead of her.

Her breath caught at the sight of the water tumbling down the sheer rock face, frothing into a lazy pool at the bottom.

Roland must have spent hours here. A perfect swimming hole for a hot summer's day.

Breeze stopped alongside Joshua's bay.

"I didn't bring togs to swim in," Alyssa said.

"The water is icy this time of the year. In a month or so it will be warmer. We can eat instead."

Hunger rumbled in her stomach. "I didn't even think of food."

"I brought some lunch," Joshua revealed, dismounting. "We can eat that beside the waterfall."

"You made food?"

"Not me, Ivy made it."

But he'd remembered to organise it. Alyssa had always considered herself organised, but Joshua's attention to detail was overwhelming.

He helped her off the horse, his hands firm at her waist. Alyssa suppressed the flare of awareness. Relief overtook her when Joshua moved away to tether the horses. She sat down on a soft mound of grass above the water's edge. From here the view of the waterfall was spectacular. It bubbled over a ledge of rock and plummeted over the drop into the dark green pool below, the sound oddly soothing. A sense of peace stole over her.

"It's beautiful. I can see why Roland loved it here."

Joshua flung himself down beside her and started to unzip the saddle pack he held. "It wasn't the beauty that Roland loved. It was the danger the place represented."

"Danger?" Alyssa stared at him. "Where?"

"See those rocks?" He pointed to boulders at the side of the ledge over which the waterfall flowed. "Roland liked nothing more than challenging a friend to dive from there."

Alyssa's heart sank like a stone as she took in the sheer height of the drop. "Was he insane?" The words burst from her.

"He loved the adrenaline rush. Roland never felt fear."

She had to ask. "Didn't anyone get hurt?"

Joshua nodded. "Roland had a friend who slipped and

broke a leg climbing up there—of course, the parents never knew the full story. Once, I cut my head on a rock in the pool when I hit the water headfirst."

Alyssa swallowed at the thought. He could've drowned! "You were equally reckless."

"I did it to stop Heath. Roland bet him that he couldn't, that he was too chicken to dive in. I took Heath's place. Although if I hadn't been hurt, Heath would probably still have dived in. He was as mad as a snake that I'd taken his turn. So my big gesture was probably for nothing," Joshua said wryly. "The joys of being sixteen—and impatient to be a man."

And the man had become every bit as responsible as the boy had striven to be. She eyed him furtively. Gorgeous, too. And loyal to the point of fault.

Alyssa remembered his mother saying she hadn't known how he'd been hurt. So he'd never dobbed his brother in. She didn't know if the loyalty was stupid or admirable.

"Here, have a bagel." He held out a paper bag.

"Thank you." It was perfect. Fresh and slightly chewy, filled with smoked salmon, avocado and cream cheese. Eating distracted Alyssa from what she'd been going to say next. But at least Joshua was talking to her again. She'd had enough of the silent treatment to last her a lifetime.

Next he produced a bottle of Pinot Gris and two glasses out of the pack. Once he'd filled the glasses, Alyssa took a sip. The slightly sweet, well-rounded sturdiness of the wine took her by surprise.

"Very nice," she said appreciatively, squinting at the label. "I didn't realise Saxon's Folly produced Pinot Gris."

"Not in large amounts," Joshua said. "You need to be on our loyal client mailing list to even get a chance of snapping it up. We hold the grapes on the vine until early May, so it's essentially a late-harvest wine." He swallowed a mouthful. "Mmm, the really special thing about this wine is that we sourced the vines from an ancient Alsace clone."

Alyssa dusted her fingers of the last of the crumbs from her bagel. "Alsace? In France?"

"Yes, imported into New Zealand in 1886."

"That *is* ancient."

Joshua topped up her glass. "And to complement fine wine…" His voice trailed away and he dug into the pack again. With a flourish he drew a punnet of strawberries and a container of chocolate dipping sauce.

"Oh my, this is decadent." There was something incredibly sexy about a man who provided food. A primitive leftover from ages past when the male had been the hunter. It was disgusting to be so impressed. There should be no need to feel so nurtured. She was a modern woman, totally able to take care of herself. Self-sufficient and sensible enough to be able to forage for herself.

Alyssa glanced around the clearing but couldn't see anything in the surrounding bush that would've appeased the appetite that the fresh air and ride had whetted. Not even the birds that called from the treetops.

Then there would be the little problem of catching them, cooking them. She slid a glance at the man beside her, his fingers long and tanned against the bright red berries. Okay, so he'd probably make a plan to find food in the bush. While she'd only poison them both.

City girl.

Fast lane….

Joshua's words came back to haunt her. So what if she was out of her comfort zone? This was Joshua's world. He'd been born and raised here.

"Try this." He held out a strawberry that had been lightly dipped in the chocolate.

She took it and bit into the ripe red fruit. Juice leaked over her fingers, her lips. She gave a little self-conscious laugh as she licked them. "Juicy, aren't they?"

He didn't reply.

She looked up into blazing black eyes.

"Joshua?" she whispered, her nipples hardening under the pink cotton T-shirt she wore, warmth flowing through her body to pool between her legs. The heat and desire and that other emotion...something terribly primal...in his eyes set her instantly alight.

"God, but you are the most provocative woman I have ever met."

She stretched her eyes wide. "What did I do?" But she already knew. The fire in his eyes was unmistakeable.

She'd turned him on.

"You bit into the berry," he said, his voice cracking.

The hoarse sound caused shivers to spread across her skin. Alyssa didn't know how this had happened. Didn't want to think too much about it. She only knew that she wanted more of the heat, the exquisite arousal that softened her body, the excitement that churned in her stomach.

She picked up a strawberry, swirled it through the chocolate sauce and offered it to him, her pulse racing. "Your turn to bite."

"Oh, yes," he drawled, his eyes dark and slumberous. "My turn."

Eight

The heat that scorched through him at Alyssa's offer turned Joshua's lower body to fire. Bending his head, he took a bite of the strawberry she held. His teeth sank into the soft flesh of the fruit and instantly his mouth was filled with an assortment of flavours.

The succulence of the strawberry.

The sweetness of the chocolate.

The complexity of the Pinot Gris.

There was another flavour, too. The unmistakable spice of desire. Slowly he chewed, swallowed, then raised his head.

A hectic flush staining her cheeks, Alyssa quickly popped the remaining half of the berry into her mouth. Their eyes held. She swallowed. Joshua groaned and leaned forward.

His mouth closed over hers. She tasted sweet. Of fruit and juice and wine. He moaned, licking the soft inner skin of her cheeks, sealing her lips tightly with his lest any sweetness escape.

His head spinning, he finally lifted his head. He cradled her chin between his cupped hands and stared into her glowing eyes. "Was that good?"

She nodded.

"Tell me you want more."

She hesitated. An unfamiliar emotion flickered in her eyes. "I want more."

Satisfaction settled in him. She'd come with him for this. And he wasn't objecting. Instantly Joshua wanted to take her mouth, slake his hunger for her. What was it about this woman? With one searing look, a couple of words and she made him throw all his customary caution to the wind. He'd had girlfriends…lovers…women that he'd easily kept at a distance while he waited for the right one. But no one like Alyssa. Never this hunger.

Why her? This woman could never be right for him.

His brother's lover….

Alyssa Blake, the woman who had once before humiliated him in print. Compromised his reputation and Saxon's Folly's profits. And would do so again in a flash. A woman who took what she wanted, to get what she wanted. To desire such a woman was *his* folly.

He forced himself to slow down, told himself he was in control of his senses, his tight-wound body. Sure, he was. He told himself he could control this reckless desire as easily as he controlled a busy and successful vineyard, told himself that he could take his pleasure and watch her walk away later today with no regrets.

He almost believed it.

"So you want more." He coupled the gentle taunt with a deliberate, measured smile and watched her breasts rise and fall as her breathing quickened. He picked up another strawberry. The strange colour of her eyes deepened. Clearly she'd expected him to kiss her, not feed her.

"Oh, no, my beauty," he whispered softly. "We're going to take this slowly."

A trace of fear flitted over her face. If he hadn't been watching her so closely, he wouldn't even have seen it. And that was what concerned him most about Alyssa Blake. She wasn't easy to read. He never knew what this woman was thinking. Hell, he still didn't even know what had been behind her gate-crashing of the masked ball.

Why had she come to Saxon's Folly?

To patch up a relationship gone wrong with Roland? And if so, then why the hell had she let *him* kiss her that night? If Heath hadn't interrupted them…she would have made love with him. In his bed.

For revenge? Because Roland hadn't done what she wanted? Except Joshua couldn't forget how those kisses had sizzled. How could she have wanted Roland back…yet have kissed *him* with such abandon?

Was it possible that she had come to the ball intending to seduce *him*, the CEO of Saxon's Folly Estate & Wines, hoping to get a scoop on the story she was after? The story that she now denied chasing.

Was that why she'd leapt at riding out here with him alone today? Had this been her intention all along? His head felt as if it was about to explode. His body, too, as her lips parted and he glimpsed the tip of a pink tongue. Without planning, his hand moved closer, the juice of the berry staining his fingertips. Joshua felt himself hardening as her lips closed over the fruit he held.

And why the hell was he hesitating? She was less than an arm's-length away. Her pink tongue a hair's breadth away from his fingers. If she wanted to seduce him…well, hell, he was more than willing. He craved her. Right now he didn't care if he would regret it later…after she was gone.

He wanted her…would have her.

Every sexy inch.

"Taste good?"

Even to his own ears his voice sounded hoarse.

She nodded and her tongue ran over his fingers, licking off the sticky strawberry juice.

It was enough.

Joshua took that as consent. He placed his hands on her waist, and hauled her toward him. She landed in his lap with a gasp of surprise. She filled his arms with soft, womanly warmth, her curves fitting against the hard angles of his body. Exotic perfume clung to her skin, her hair. He inhaled sharply. She smelled of sweet strawberries, jasmine…and desire.

This time his kiss was careful. Joshua was conscious of stepping into the unknown as his tongue probed her mouth, tasting the sweetness within. Of the shifting boundaries between them. Their relationship wouldn't—couldn't—be the same again.

The want that swirled in his lower abdomen was strong and hungry. Astonishingly so. Joshua suspected that he was going to be thinking about Alyssa Blake long after she'd returned to Auckland…that this interlude would change him, even if he never saw her again.

He told himself that her leaving was for the best.

But his body didn't agree.

She wriggled in his arms. Under his fingers, her top rode up. The smooth skin of her bare stomach was silken to his touch. The feminine feel of it tipped him over the edge. He pulled her closer, filling her mouth with the ferocious hunger that was building within him, threatening to explode, threatening to destroy everything he'd ever believed about women…about sex and desire…and love.

She didn't hesitate. She kissed him back with everything he desired, her purpose clearly the same as his. To make love…and the hell with tomorrow. Her tongue moved under his…giving as much as he took…as much as he wanted. With a hoarse groan, Joshua rolled, taking her with him, mouths locked, landing on his back in the cushioning grass. Pulling her above him, he shoved his hands under her top and his fingers ran riot over her back. Around them the air was redolent with the pungent scent of sweet, crushed grass. And Joshua felt his tightly leashed control start to slip.

In a staggering moment he realised that the forbidden attraction he'd been fighting had taken over. It was stronger, more powerful than anything he'd experienced. He surrendered to its force.

Even as the relentless hunger took him, he knew he had to have her. Just once. Before he let her leave Saxon's Folly.

Joshua's torso was solid beneath her. She felt safe…not exactly loved…but certainly cherished. It felt like coming home.

"This is in the way," Joshua murmured.

"This" turned out to be her T-shirt. Alyssa shifted, lifting herself so that he could push it up, then her breath caught as his hand slipped forward…further up…under her bra and touched her breast.

"Ah." She sighed and her head fell forward against his shoulder.

His other hand fiddled with her bra clasp. It gave. Then his hands were cupping her, shaping her, holding her apart from him. Eager to help, to prolong her pleasure, she braced herself on hands planted on the grass beside his shoulders.

Another gasp—sharper this time—escaped her as his head lifted and his mouth closed on one nipple then the other. Then his fingertips took over from his mouth…massaging…until an achy sweet sensation pierced her.

A hand moved between their bodies in restless little circles over her stomach. Down. Under the waistband of her jeans.

She was panting now. The sound loud in her ears. Alyssa shut her eyes. Patterns danced across her eyelids. He touched her where she was already wet with wanting. Blood rushed through her ears. She felt as if she might pass out.

Then he was rolling again, and she lay flat on her back,

while Joshua rose above her. Alyssa kept her eyes closed, focusing on the stroke of his hands as he ran them over the skin that his caresses had laid bare.

"You're hot and soft."

The throaty drawl was uttered against the bare skin of her belly.

His hand moved again. She heard the rasp of a zipper.

Alyssa's eyes shot open. Ohmigod. "What are we doing?"

His lips curved, sensual, satisfied. "Isn't this what you wanted?"

His words shocked her. *"What?"*

Maybe it was what she wanted. But she hadn't even admitted that to herself. How on earth did he know?

"That's why you came here with me…to be alone."

"You—" Words failed her. She pulled away from him, disappointment piercing her heart, and tugged her T-shirt down, uncaring that her bra was ruched up. Right now she wanted her breasts…her belly…covered.

"No need to be shy about it. We're consenting adults." The dark eyes simmered. "I have to admit it's a huge turn on to be seduced by a woman who knows what she wants."

"Knows what she wants…?" Alyssa stared at him. The smoked salmon…the strawberries…the Pinot Gris. He thought she wanted…this. He'd planned it down to the last detail.

Damn, but she'd been dumb.

She covered her face. How could he have misunderstood so badly? "I wanted to come here because Megan said that Roland had loved it here…that it had been one of his favourite places."

"Roland." His tone was peculiar, flat, dead.

After a long moment she pushed her hair back and looked up at him. "Yes, because of Roland."

He gave a laugh, but it held no amusement. "I thought you wanted something from me."

She blinked. "Why would wanting something from you involve coming here alone and—" not making love "—having sex?" What kind of woman did he think she was, for heaven's sake?

"Something you wanted enough to allow yourself to eat strawberries from my hand while your eyes promised me untold delights."

Alyssa felt the flush start on her chest, spread up her face. But she forced herself to hold his gaze.

"Something you wanted enough to forget your lover."

Her lover? Oh, yes, Roland.

She bit her lip at that. "And what was I supposed to want so much?"

"The big-break story. The insider's report on whether we lie to our consumers."

"Oh, for heaven's sake. I told you I'm not doing that story."

His intense, disquieting eyes stayed locked with hers. "So if you came on this ride today only because of Roland, why did you kiss me…respond to me…so convincingly?"

Alyssa gulped. How was she supposed to answer that? Tell him that he confused her? Bewildered her? Tied her up in knots? Made her feel emotions she'd never known?

No way was she handing him that much ammunition! He'd never believe her anyway. He'd think it was another seduction attempt. How utterly humiliating….

But his question hung in the air. Why had she kissed him…responded to him so wildly? Alyssa groped mentally for an acceptable explanation.

"Grief?" she offered at last.

"*Grief?*" He looked poleaxed.

Sorry, Roland. "Yes. Grief does strange things to people." She was babbling now. She wanted to run away. Hide. "Everyone reacts differently. Being here—" she waved a hand at the waterfall "—thinking and talking about Roland set me off. I'm leaving today. I'll never see you again. I didn't think you'd mind. I mean, guys don't take sex as seriously as women…" She stopped talking as anger ignited in his eyes.

"Didn't think I'd mind? I suppose I shouldn't care that it's just my bloody bad luck to be the butt of my brother's clandestine girlfriend's lustful grief attack."

Alyssa couldn't think of any suitable response to that.

It was just as well that she was leaving.

Thank goodness she hadn't agreed to do the story David had wanted her to do. If she stayed any longer, there was a very real danger that she was going to do something incredibly stupid…like fall in love with Joshua Saxon.

They headed home in silence. As the bush gave way to grassy fields, Alyssa scanned the surrounding countryside with nostalgic eyes. Even though she'd come with the express purpose of being closer to Roland, Alyssa knew she would never think of dense green bush and cascading water without remembering the tall, commanding man who rode beside her.

She cast him a sideways glance. A frown carved a deep furrow between his brows. She glanced quickly away before he could catch her looking at him, her silly heart in her eyes.

As they drew closer to the stable yard they heard a commotion.

"What the—" Joshua broke off as they were met by the sight of the black stallion racing up and down along his paddock fence, his tail held high like a banner and his nostrils flared so wide that the inner red tissue showed. In the adjacent paddock horses whinnied frantically, milling around in a tight bunch.

"What's upset them?" Joshua nudged his horse into a trot.

Alyssa followed more slowly.

The black horse, still galloping along the length of the fence, slammed to a halt at the gate and trumpeted with rage. It was then Alyssa saw the two youths in the paddock, half concealed behind the trunk of a gigantic oak.

"Hey," Joshua yelled.

The pair took one look at Joshua and ran across the field,

vanishing round the back of the stables. A moment later an engine roared and a motorbike came racing out from nowhere.

"Look out!"

But Joshua's warning came too late. The stallion came catapulting over the paddock fence, rushing headlong toward them. Breeze had gone rigid between her legs. Alyssa snatched at the mare's mane. At the last moment the black horse swerved around Breeze, so close that Alyssa could smell his sweat, and galloped past, his iron-clad hooves ringing on the ground.

Unsettled by the motorbike, the enraged and screaming stallion, the mare shied violently to the side.

Alyssa lurched in the saddle. For a moment she thought she might stay on, but then she felt herself tossed skyward. She hung suspended in the air for a moment, conscious of the plunging distressed horse below her. Then she was spinning toward the ground, sound and colour rushing past.

"Let go of the reins." It was a frantic yell.

Alyssa opened her hands. Breeze bolted free. The impact of the cobbles was bone-numbing. Alyssa sobbed with pain, which turned to fear as she discovered that she couldn't breath.

"Lie still."

Joshua's voice boomed above her. His black boots came into her line of vision and then he crouched down beside her. She caught a glimpse of dark, worried eyes.

She gasped, trying to speak.

"Hush, you're winded. Don't talk."

A moment later a sound escaped her throat. Agony.

"Does your head hurt?" His voice was urgent.

She shook her head again. "My back," she sobbed.

He went white, his lips pale. "Don't move. I'm going to call an ambulance."

There was the sound of light feet running on the cobbles. Caitlyn? Joshua turned his head and barked out a terse order.

Then a fresh stab of excruciating pain stopped her thinking. "My hand!"

"Breeze must have stepped on you." Joshua touched her fingers.

"Ouch!" She nearly blacked out.

He pulled his hand away. "The ambulance won't be long."

Alyssa was barely aware of the ride to the hospital as she shifted in and out of consciousness. But even as everything closed in and went dark, Alyssa knew that Joshua sat beside her, his eyes full of concern, never leaving her face.

After her examination in the emergency room had been completed, Joshua entered the curtained-off area where Alyssa lay.

"How are you feeling?" he asked.

Terrible. She hated the hospital. The sterile smell, the hushed sounds all brought back the nightmare of Roland's accident—of Joshua breaking the devastating news that her brother had died.

"Sore," she said finally, coming back from the hellhole to find his gaze fixed on her face.

"They'll operate on your hand soon. Is there anyone you want me to call?" Concern etched deep lines into his face. And there was something more. Something that made her heart tremble.

"To call?" she said stupidly, closing her eyes so that the gorgeous features with the misleading concern would go away. Joshua didn't give a damn for her. He thought she was the kind of woman who seduced men for career gain. Allowing herself to build hopes on his concern for her would bring nothing but heartache.

"Your family. Your friends. To let them know what has happened."

Her editor.

It reflected the barren state of her life that the only person who came to mind related to her work. Her boss…not family…not a friend. But David could wait until after the operation.

Thankfully the emergency-room doctor had confirmed that

there was no damage to her spine—only some bruising on her back, and damage to her fingers where the reins had wrenched the ligaments and the fracture of her thumb where Breeze must have trodden on her. It would need setting. And perhaps a pin, the doctor had said. Nothing life threatening.

No, there was no one who desperately needed to know. No one who would drop everything and rush to hold her mangled hand. A tear slid out the side of her closed eye.

Alyssa turned her head away, reluctant to let Joshua witness her bout of self-pity. The silence lengthened. He—her nemesis who was being so unexpectedly kind—was waiting for her reply. She moved her head from side to side against the regulation hospital pillow.

"No one?"

Was that disbelief she heard? Swallowing the lump in her throat, she opened her eyes. "My father lives in Australia with his new wife and her children," she murmured huskily, her throat raw from suppressed tears. She gave him a tremulous smile. "He's taking his retirement from the bench seriously."

"I'm sorry you're alone." Joshua sounded more subdued than she'd ever heard him, no sign of his usual take-charge arrogance remained.

Clearly he'd remembered that her mother was dead, that she was an only child.

"What about friends?" he asked. "Can I call anyone?"

"They have their own lives...families, children."

"They're all married?"

"Yes. All except Lanie, my best friend, but she recently moved to Christchurch."

Emotion flashed in Alyssa's eyes. An emotion that caused Joshua to blink. Pain? Vulnerability? Loneliness? He looked again. But her eyes were already closing.

"I'm tired," she whispered.

And Joshua wanted to kick himself for interrogating her when she least needed it.

"Rest," he said feeling utterly powerless to do anything about her misery. "It shouldn't be long until they operate."

In the end, Joshua waited until the operation was over and had been declared a success by the surgeon he'd arranged—the best in the region. Once Alyssa had been moved to the private ward he'd booked, Joshua sat beside her while she blinked sleepily after a hefty dose of painkillers.

The surgeon would be doing rounds before he went home, and Joshua had every intention of cornering him to discuss Alyssa's prognosis.

He looked down at her. She'd been a real trouper. Uncomplaining. Pleasant to the nurses. A dream patient.

On cue, almost as though she'd heard his thoughts, her eyelids fluttered.

"My boss is going to be mad. I'm going to need even more time off work." She gave him a sleepy look from under heavy eyelids and pushed the covers back with her uninjured hand, revealing a white hospital-issue flannel gown.

Instantly his body stirred. God, the woman was hurt… drugged…and one sleepy glance was all it took to electrify him. To bring back the memory of strawberries and soft skin and—

He pressed his mouth into a hard line.

"Have no fear, I won't be staying at Saxon's Folly," she muttered, misinterpreting his frustration.

"Yes, you will." It had been bothering him ever since the doctor had asked who would be looking after her. "You're staying. I'm the boss, remember? What I say goes."

"I thought you couldn't wait to be rid of me?"

"So did I," he growled.

But she didn't laugh as he'd half-intended. Instead her irises darkened her eyes to an unfathomable shade. "What of your concerns that I might stir up trouble with your mother… and Amy?"

"I'll confine you to your room—so seeing Amy won't be

a problem." Joshua smiled to make sure she knew he had no real intention of locking her away. "And for some strange reason your presence seems to be doing my mother good." He hadn't expected that. "Everything she says is prefaced by 'Alyssa thinks…' It's her latest craze."

Her expression softened. "I like your mother very much, too. I couldn't impose on her. She has enough on her plate emotionally without an invalid in the house."

"You don't have a choice." Joshua stood and stretched, his back aching from the hard hospital chair that he'd occupied for the past hour. "You're staying at Saxon's Folly."

"Because you feel that what happened was your fault?"

Trust Alyssa to see through his offer to the self-blame that lay beneath. "Yes." He raised an eyebrow and added with barbed humour, "And because I don't trust you not to rush away and get legal advice so that you can sue Saxon's Folly. Consider my invitation an attempt to save on legal costs."

That managed to raise a smile. "Okay, then I definitely have no choice. But don't accuse me of trying to seduce you."

"I wouldn't dream of it." He couldn't blame her for her reluctance to stay. He'd done all he could to drive her away, scared that she might hurt his family. And then there was his other unspoken fear.

The fear that stirred whenever she came too close.

The deep-seated fear that she could seduce him anytime she chose seemed unreasonably absurd when, eyelids drooping, she said softly, "Thanks, Joshua."

The fear melted away beneath her gratitude.

"My pleasure."

The hands of the clock on the wall moved forward, and Joshua sat quietly by Alyssa's side as her eyes remained firmly shut. Not even the bustle of activity when the night staff came on duty caused her to stir.

He stared into her pale face. She was beautiful in sleep, her features perfect. The straight nose, the curved lips, the ivory skin and dark auburn hair that spilled against her fine-grained skin. How could he have missed her perfection?

Awake, Alyssa was so animated—so opinionated—that all consideration of her beauty was driven from his mind. He was always aware of *her*…the spirit of her…the very essence that was Alyssa. She annoyed him. She frustrated the hell out of him. And, yes, he'd admit she intrigued him more than any woman in a long, long time.

The night of the masked ball his attention had been captured by her figure, her poise, her assurance…and the in-your-face challenge that she radiated. Once he'd held her in his arms…well, hell, his hormones had taken over.

And then at the hospital, when his only concern should've been for his brother, he'd discovered he'd been turned on by Alyssa Blake, his dead brother's forbidden lover.

The discovery had shaken him to the core.

Now he stared at her, remembered the flash of vulnerability when she'd spoke of her married friends with their families.

The loneliness in her eyes had called out to him.

Did she yearn for a family…children? Had she expected to find them with Roland? Or had his sometimes obtuse older brother caused the emptiness he'd glimpsed hidden inside her?

Then there was Amy, the woman who Roland had been supposed to marry before Christmas. Joshua had been eager for Alyssa to leave—before Amy found out Roland had been screwing around with another woman.

He felt torn between looking out for Amy, his mother's goddaughter who he'd looked out for all his life, and the responsibility he'd acquired to Alyssa. She was hurt, in hospital, with no one to call on to tell about her operation.

Tough, opinionated Alyssa Blake needed *him*.

Watching her, something heavy shifted deep inside his chest. Alyssa wouldn't be able to leave tomorrow. And even when she'd recovered enough to drive, how could he let her go back to Auckland, where clearly there was no one to take care of her?

Suddenly Joshua wished Roland had lived so that he could throttle his brother. How dare Roland have been so irresponsible? He'd always been a bit of a playboy…but to mess around with two women simultaneously was stupid. Hadn't he expected them to find out about each other? And now Joshua was stuck with the mess.

Joshua stared at Alyssa. The worst of the whole mess was that he was starting to suspect that if she crooked her little finger at him, he'd come running.

He wanted her for himself.

A memory from earlier in the day flashed into his mind. Of her head tilted back, her eyes shut and her glorious hair spilled over the grass beside the woodland pool. God. He'd nearly damn well had her. He'd touched her pale skin, kissed her soft, sensitive breasts. He'd taunted Alyssa, asking if she wanted more. The raw truth was he'd craved more. Much more.

If the knowledge that she'd gone with him only because she'd wanted to see Roland's favourite spot hadn't been flung over him like a bucket of icy water, he would've taken her.

He almost wished he had.

A soft groan of shock escaped him.

What kind of man lusted after his brother's lover…a brother who hadn't even been buried for a month?

Nine

Alyssa woke to find pale gray, early-morning light filtering in through the half-closed blinds. Outside the ward she could hear the clank of heavy trolleys, hear the attendants offering patients tea down the corridor.

She started to sit up. A movement in the corner of the still-dim room startled her.

Joshua unfolded himself from an armchair. "Let me help you."

"Thanks." She leant forward. He bent over her and immediately his masculine scent embraced her. Sun and earth and a hint of lemon and something a little spicy. He propped a pillow in behind her back.

She couldn't help thinking how unfair it was. She must look a mess, her hair rumpled, her eyes sleepy. Whereas the hollows beneath Joshua's eyes gave him a jaded appeal that simply made him more attractive. The events of the past week had added edges and angles to his handsome features. Shadows darkened his eyes to black pits and in the depths she could discern his turbulence.

"Don't tell me you stayed up all night?" she asked.

He nodded.

She clicked. "You should've gone home. That chair must've been terribly uncomfortable. Did you get any sleep?"

He came closer, till he stood beside the hospital bed. "Not much. There's a lot on my mind."

She could imagine. Joshua took his responsibilities seriously. And right now they must be piling up almost out of control. Saxon's Folly took up a huge chunk of his time. He had his parents' emotional well-being to look after…and Kay had told her that he was the executor of Roland's estate. And beyond that lurked the threat of scandal about the tastings in the wine competition. No wonder he looked drained. All those matters must weigh heavily on his mind.

His eyes scanned her face, inspecting every feature, until Alyssa started to feel self-conscious. "What is it? What are you thinking about?"

The dark eyes met hers squarely. "You told me once that you loved my brother a great deal."

He seemed to expect a reply. Alyssa swallowed hard, not knowing what to say. At last, she simply nodded.

"But you let me kiss you." He brushed her lips with his fingertips. "Here. And here." His fingers skimmed her neck, touching the base of her throat.

"Joshua!" Eyes stretched wide, she objected to his touch.

His hand moved to rest on the covers beside her. "I'd like to think that you would not have responded to me like that if you loved Roland."

"I loved him." It was a squeak of sound. Alyssa found that she couldn't hold his gaze. She glanced down. His hand lay on the crisp white bedcovers. She jumped as he lifted it and placed a finger under her chin.

Tilting her head, he looked down into her eyes and asked, "Did you ever sleep with Roland?"

Her pulse started to hammer. She swallowed nervously. "What kind of a question is that?"

"Answer me."

She shook her head.

Something gave in the bleak, black gaze. "Now we're making progress. I don't believe that you'd sleep with one man, and then respond to me like you did down at the water-fall so soon after his death. Not if you really loved him—not with your black-and-white views of the world. Not even because of grief."

Trapped, she stared back at him. Better she remain silent.

Five seconds dragged past. "What do you say about that?"

Alyssa thought of her promise to Kay. Not to tell. Ever.

This time when she shook her head, his mouth tightened. "You know what I think? I don't even think you wanted him to break off his engagement to Amy. I don't think you were waiting for him to come to you. Because after yesterday, I no longer believe that you loved him."

"I did love him." This time the silence stretched until Alyssa's nerves started to fray.

Joshua finally broke it. "I'll get to the bottom of this."

She believed him. His jaw was set. She had no doubt he was going to do his best. But she had no intention of breaking her word. "The answer is staring you in the face."

"What do you mean?"

She'd said too much. "I can't tell you!"

"Why not?"

Because she'd promised. And she never broke her promises. She shuddered and covered her face with her hands. "I just can't."

"Staring me in the face." He narrowed his gaze. "It's something to do with you."

She lay unmoving, refusing to look at him.

Taking great care not to hurt her hand, Joshua lifted her hands away from her face and gently set them down. "Help me here." His eyes held hers. Intent. Demanding answers she could never give.

"This isn't some game of charades, Joshua." She sighed. "I can't help you. I shouldn't even have said as much as I did."

"What are you so worried about?"

Again she shook her head. "No more. Don't ask me." She closed her eyes, refusing to answer. But when his hands landed on her stomach they shot open. "What are you doing?"

Joshua didn't respond. Instead he examined his hands moulding her belly. He couldn't bear thinking of her carrying Roland's child. After a pause, he said, "You can't be pregnant with Roland's child. Not if you never made love. So it's not that. But it must be physical."

He studied her, searching for something that was staring him in the face. Her colour was good. Her eyes didn't look dull and lifeless. "You're not suffering from any dread disease, are you? I helped complete your admission and surgery forms—there was nothing you felt a compelling need to share. So it can't be that. It's not linked to any medical condition you have that Roland might have been a match for…blood, bone marrow, kidneys."

He was fishing now. Alyssa pursed her lips in a straight line. She'd seen through his ploy. Joshua could see that she wasn't going to tell him a thing.

He stared at her, feature by feature. From this close, he could see the fiery lights in the dark red hair. The pansy eyes were more navy than purple right now. And even lying in a hospital bed the scent of jasmine and some spice—cinnamon perhaps?—clung to her. Joshua noticed something he'd never picked up on before. A feeling of disbelief swept him. "You know something…you share the same colouring as Roland. I never saw it before, because I wasn't looking for it."

She tried to laugh. "That's ridiculous."

"Good, you're talking." He was on the right track. He knew it. He frowned as the implications hit him. He touched her hair. It was soft, silky. "Your hair is red, not the bright shade of Roland's, but darker. Your eyes are such a dark blue that they appear purple in some lights. Roland's eyes weren't black—they were navy blue." He touched her cheek, the skin was smooth under his fingers. He heard her breath catch. Instantly his blood surged, and heat shot to his head. He fought to stay calm. He needed to. "Your skin isn't pale, nor does it bear freckles. Nor did Roland's, despite his red hair. Surprised?" He cocked a brow at her.

At that moment the tea trolley arrived. Relief swept Alyssa's face, and she accepted a cup of tea with a warm smile to the attendant.

Fingers drumming against the overbed table, Joshua waited impatiently for the attendant and the tea trolley to depart. Why had none of them noticed Alyssa's resemblance to Roland before? It explained her misery when he died…her insistence on staying for the funeral…and her endless questions about every aspect of Roland's life—even to the point that she wanted to visit the waterfall he'd enjoyed swimming at.

Once the attendant had left, a simmering silence remained. Joshua broke it. "I'm interested in why you feel you can't you tell me the truth, Alyssa."

She gave him a hesitant look from under her lashes. "I made a promise."

He pounced. "To whom?"

"It doesn't matter!"

"I think it does." His tipped his head to one side. "Cousins?" he mused. "Am I on the right track?"

"I'm not discussing this." She turned over in the bed and presented her back to him.

A startling thought struck Joshua. His heart started to pound. It couldn't be…or could it? Slowly he said, "When we were kids, Roland used to be teased that he was a foundling—the parents didn't know about it. The teasing stopped because we were three tough boys. Only fools took us on. I haven't thought about it for years. But now I'm starting to wonder—"

"Don't." She rolled back and gazed at him with a horrified expression. "Don't wonder. He was your brother."

Triumph surged through him. "But what was your relationship to him, Alyssa?"

"I can't tell you!"

"So there was a blood relationship."

She stared at him stonily. "God, you're sneaky."

"Brother and sister?"

It had to be that…there was nothing else it could be.

She shut her eyes. "Please go," she whispered.

"That would mean Roland was adopted." He paused, weighing it up. It was possible. He considered how he would feel if it were true. Nothing changed. Roland was still—would always be—his brother. But why had they never been told? "Not something that my mother and father were likely to miss. Did you promise my parents you wouldn't tell?"

The pansy eyes were full of guilt. "They didn't want you to know."

"I worked it out. I should have realised something was amiss about Roland. You were so desperate—"

The smile she gave him was twisted. "That's why you decided that I had to be Roland's mistress."

"You loved him."

"Never in that way."

"But it was the only explanation that made sense. The truth was too far out of left field for me to even suspect—until I took a damn hard look at you." He gave her a small smile. "You didn't break your promise, you never told me anything. But there are questions I need to ask my parents. I want to know if he's my half-brother—"

"He's not." She put her hands over her mouth. "Damn, I

shouldn't have said that. You must ask your parents. But please wait till after I'm gone."

He nodded. He would ask. Later. He wasn't allowing Alyssa to leave. Not yet. "I won't say a word. First you need to recover."

David Townsend, *Wine Watch*'s editor, took the news of Alyssa's continued absence from the office far better than she'd expected. But there was a price, David warned her. He'd be expecting a terrific exposé about the Golden Harvest Wine Award tastings to show for her absence from the office.

A hollow weight settled in the pit of Alyssa's stomach as she found herself telling David that she would do her best. She couldn't refuse him anymore. He'd let her extend her leave, now he hadn't complained about her accident leave. She had to pay the price—and he would expect her to pull out all the stops.

It was enough to make her feel queasy.

On Wednesday morning, packed, her head still ringing with the doctor's discharge instructions to start physical-therapy sessions as soon as possible, Alyssa glanced up as footsteps slowed outside the door of the private ward.

Joshua stood in the doorway. He wore a pair of chinos and a white button-down shirt. He appeared tall, dark and totally overwhelming.

"I've come to take you home," he said. With the truth about her relationship to Roland out in the open, the tenderness that shone from his eyes jerked at her heartstrings.

Home to Saxon's Folly.

A complex mix of emotions raged through her. Relief…guilt that she'd had no choice about the story…and beneath it all shimmered the confusing hot need that Joshua's proximity evoked. Alyssa knew she should flee back to Auckland at super-sonic speed. Before she reached the point of no return. Instead, she let him take the bag of toiletries and feminine fripperies she'd accumulated and followed him out to the Range Rover.

Back at Saxon's Folly a welcoming committee awaited her on the stone stairs in front of the homestead. Kay. Phillip. Megan. Caitlyn. And even Heath Saxon.

"Really, I'm fine," Alyssa protested as they ushered her into the living room where Ivy waited with a tea tray. "Oh, a cup of tea will be lovely."

"Shouldn't you go to bed?" Kay asked.

"After two nights in hospital, I'm tired of being in bed," Alyssa said with brutal honesty.

"You can rest here." Joshua patted the chaise lounge beside the window.

"I'll feel like a Victorian invalid," Alyssa objected.

Kay and Caitlyn started to laugh. Then Caitlyn said, "The Saxon's are determined to cosset you, I suggest you give in gracefully."

Alyssa shot the winemaker a sparkling look. "You're saying I should surrender?"

Caitlyn nodded emphatically. "Enjoy it while you can."

Alyssa settled onto the chaise lounge, then Joshua claimed the armchair beside her. Again the wariness resurfaced. She had to take care. It would be all too easy to be seduced by this softer Joshua…particularly when he was being thoughtful and caring. And there was the seductive charm of his wonderful family.

It was vital to remember that Joshua would never fall in love with her. His view of her as an ambitious hack writer, out to get a story at any cost, hadn't changed. He still blamed her for blackening his—and Saxon's Folly's—name.

It lay between them like an unscalable abyss. Not even the new tenderness he showed to her, or the knowledge that she wasn't Roland's lover would change that. No doubt about it, falling for Joshua would be crazy. A sure road to heartbreak.

Hurriedly, to get her mind off him, she said to the room at large, "I can't wait until all these dressings come off." She held up her left hand. "I'm supposed to start physical therapy in a day or so."

"Let me know when your appointments are, I'll take you," Joshua said, his eyes smiling down at her.

Alyssa couldn't look away. "No need for that."

Joshua glanced pointedly at her bandaged hand. "Your hatchback has a gear shift. How do you propose to drive?"

He had a point. "I'll call a cab."

"I could drive you, too," Megan volunteered.

"Thanks." Alyssa smiled at her in gratitude.

The warmth faded from his eyes. Alyssa felt the absence. "I don't want to be a burden," she said lamely.

"You're not a burden," said Joshua firmly. "The accident should never have happened."

His eyes held hers. Alyssa's breathing quickened and happiness rushed through her at his caring expression. The knowledge that she was playing with fire, risking the danger of being painfully burned sank in.

If she had any sense, she'd keep herself busy. The story for *Wine Watch* would be a start. But Joshua didn't know that she'd agreed to do it.

Her contentment faded a little. He would not be pleased when he discovered that. Better to let him think she was otherwise occupied. "Is there anything I can do? I'm bored out of my skull."

"You could help with some press releases I need written," Megan said.

Joshua shook his head. "Alyssa needs rest."

His refusal stung. Did it stem from concern for her? Or distrust? What did he believe she could do to harm Saxon's Folly? The reality sunk in. He was justified in distrusting her. She'd agreed to write the article David wanted.

By morning Alyssa was back on her feet, dressed and ready to accompany Joshua to work. Spending the day in the winery and driving around the vineyards would be far easier than being cooped up in the intimacy of the homestead with Joshua.

But Joshua had other ideas.

"You're staying home. You're hand needs to heal…and the bruises on your back, too."

"The pain is much better," Alyssa said. "If I spend another day lying on the chaise lounge, I'll go stir-crazy."

"Rest," he barked out.

She rolled her eyes to the ceiling. They were still arguing when Joshua's cell phone rang. After a few moments, he pocketed the phone. "That was Caitlyn. There's a problem with one of the stainless steel vats. I'll see you later."

Alyssa sank onto the chaise lounge, relieved at her unexpected reprieve. Joshua popped in intermittently through the day to make sure that she had everything she needed. Over the next week Alyssa felt like a total fraud as everyone took turns to sit with her and keep her amused.

Megan drove her into town for a check up, and took her to two physical-therapy sessions. While Kay had decided to create a Roland scrapbook out of photos and mementos and had asked for Alyssa's help. Although Alyssa suspected it was a ploy to keep her occupied, she was thrilled to when she saw how much joy the project gave Kay. It brought her even closer to Roland's mother.

But Alyssa found that she couldn't relax. She was worried about Joshua's reaction to the story she was already working on.

Since he'd discovered that Roland was her brother, the barriers between them had been collapsing. She didn't want to deceive him. She couldn't go on like this, she decided, as she put away the notes that she'd compiled. When he came home that night, she cornered him in the lobby and said abruptly, "I need to talk to you. Alone."

Joshua slung an arm around her shoulders and guided her through the French doors of the salon. Outside, in the rosy light of the evening sun, she trembled beneath his touch.

He released her and leaned against the railing, radiating a relaxation he didn't feel. "Okay, what's on your mind." Whatever it was, was clearly worrying her.

"I've told *Wine Watch* that I'll do an investigative piece on the tastings." Her face was tense as she waited for his response.

Joshua nodded slowly. So much for her claim that she had no intentions of doing the story. Disappointment edged through him, chilly and sharp. Alyssa would never change—the story would always come first.

"I tell you what, I'll cooperate and answer any questions you choose to pose about the competition tasting."

Alyssa pinned him with a sharp glance. "You'll answer all my questions? No holding back?"

He nodded. "But there's one condition: all your questions must be directed at me. No one else at Saxon's Folly is to be badgered."

"I have your word? You won't back out?"

He nodded again. "Why should I back out?"

"You might not like the angle I take."

"I doubt you'd write anything to sully Roland's memory."

She looked at him. The slanting light turned his handsome features into a mask of gold. Then she looked past him to where the Nikau palms whispered in the breeze. Her fears about Joshua's reaction when he found out she'd agreed to take the story, dissolved. He was going to cooperate. She let out a shaky breath and brought her attention back to him. "I've already sent in the tribute I wrote for Roland. This is an investigative piece. About the rumours that the samples provided for tasting in the Golden Harvest Wine Awards differ from what's available in the stores. My editor won't go for a romantic, rose-tinted article," she said warningly.

"You can't do that without compromising your brother, too." His jaw was thrust forward. "Isn't that a conflict of interest?"

Alyssa considered that. Anything negative she wrote about Joshua or Saxon's Folly, would rub off on Roland, her brother, too. Which was exactly why she'd felt her objectivity for this story was compromised from the outset. It was a pity that her promise to Kay hadn't allowed her to share that insight with

David. "I have no choice but to take that risk. I'm not known for being soft," she warned again. But despite her tough words, the delight was spreading. She could hardly believe that Joshua had conceded, that the solution had come so easily.

He narrowed his eyes. "If I didn't know better, I'd think you were trying to scare me off."

She threw him a smile that revealed some of her pleasure. "If there's one word I'd never use to describe you, Joshua, it would be *cowardly.*"

"Thanks." His jaw relaxed slightly. "I think. Do I want to know what words you will use to describe me?"

Gorgeous. Sexy. Endearingly protective.

But those gave away too much.

"Hmm, let me think." She tilted her head to one side, and assessed him. Finally she said, *"Suspicious…"*

His eyes sparked. "You bet! And I'm not going to let you out of my sight while you pursue that story. I intend to watch every move you make."

"Distrustful…"

"Hey, I'm letting you do the story…I'm even cooperating," he protested.

It didn't take Alyssa long to discover that Joshua meant what he'd said. He watched her like a hawk and clearly had no intention of letting her talk to anyone other than him on the estate.

She'd barely taken out her pocket Dictaphone in the vicinity of Caitlyn, when Joshua came bearing down on her, a frown blackening his expression, making him look like a gorgeous—but fearful—fallen angel.

"This is not what we agreed, Alyssa." His anger was molten.

Caitlyn gave her an apologetic smile and disappeared with a mutter about getting to work before the boss fired her.

Joshua didn't even grin.

And once Alyssa met his fulminating glare, trepidation filled her. "Hey, Caitlyn didn't refuse."

"She likes you. You took advantage of her good nature."

"She's a grown woman."

"But she's not nearly as wary of you as she should be. She thinks you're her friend. She sees the whiteness of your smile, but misses your hunger for a story."

Ouch. Alyssa's shoulders started to sag. Then she squared them, refusing to let him get to her. "I only want to find out the truth. Caitlyn has become a friend. I wouldn't take advantage of her by asking her questions that would be a problem."

"Ask me. That was our deal. I'm available now."

She gave him a speculative look. He'd calmed down a little. Alyssa let him lead her to the rough-hewn, heavy wooden table and benches that sat under a trio of silver birch trees on the southern side of the winery. Her Dictaphone hit the wooden tabletop with a thud.

A challenge, Joshua decided.

The impression was reinforced when Alyssa said, "You don't mind if I record, do you?" And her pansy eyes dared him to object.

"I don't mind."

"That way you can't accuse me of putting words in your mouth." Her grin was edged.

Joshua suppressed his retort and contented himself with raising an eyebrow. "Feel better?"

"My hand is not as sore as yesterday." She looked mollified.

Joshua didn't have the heart to point out that he'd been referring to her barbed comment—and whether that had made her feel better. He let her take his comment at face value.

"I'm glad to hear that." Joshua was relieved that she seemed to have bounced back to her confident self. He watched her fumble one-handed with the Dictaphone and switch it on.

"So Saxon's Folly would never deceive the public?"

Joshua picked his words carefully. "When you're producing the volume of wine that we do, it's virtually impossible to guarantee that each batch will be identical. This is wine we're talking about, not manufactured widgets. There isn't a mould to make it from. It's science mingled with art. A fluid process. The winemaker will strive to bring out the best in the harvest, to make it consistent with the character that the winery is renowned for."

Alyssa paused the recorder. "I need to talk to Caitlyn—otherwise I'm not going to get a full picture."

"No!"

His face was tight. His jaw hard. Alyssa could see she wasn't going to move him. This was the Joshua Saxon who'd gotten under her skin. Arrogant. Opinionated. Certain that he was right.

Always.

"How can it hurt?" she wheedled.

"Plenty." He laughed. It held no amusement.

Alyssa gave up with a sigh and asked a string of questions. The answers he gave were insightful. It was going to be a great article. Finally, the sun prickling on her back, she brought the interview back to the point that was central to her story. "I'm aware that there might be certain subtle differences between vintages…but that's not what we're talking about. Here the issue is deliberately misleading the public. What do you say about that?"

"Saxon's Folly would never do that."

Looking at Joshua, Alyssa felt her conviction waver. "So you would never try to win awards with a superior batch of wine and flood the stores with an inferior version?"

He shook his head. "Not deliberately. As I said before there might be variations between batches, but only a very experienced taster would be able to detect the minuscule differences."

"I'm not talking about subtle differences."

"I've tasted them—I assure you they're substantially the same. But I'm certain you won't accept my word." A muscle flexed in his jaw. "I bet you wouldn't be able to taste the difference." He warmed to his topic. "I challenge you to a blind tasting, so that you can taste for yourself what the judges get and what the public buys. Let's see if your palate can detect the difference you believe exists."

Alyssa didn't hesitate. "Fine! I'll take you up on that—as long as I get the same samples you sent the judges."

"Of course." He inclined his head. "You'll be eating your words. In print. For all the world to see."

The look on his face was implacable. For the first time, apprehension shuddered through Alyssa. What if there was no difference? David would be expecting a story with substance. Then she straightened her backbone. Whatever happened, she would tell the truth.

That night Alyssa came downstairs to find the grand salon full of people. She paused at the high double doors, instantly aware of Joshua standing by the large sash window talking earnestly to his father.

Then the crowd dissolved into familiar faces. Megan sitting with Kay, and a quiet Amy. Caitlyn and Heath were chatting to the only man in the room who Alyssa didn't recognise, while Ivy bustled around setting down platters with hors d'oeuvres on the side tables.

Alyssa noticed that the discussion between Joshua and Phillip had come to an abrupt end with her arrival. Her journalist instincts went on full alert.

"What can I get you to drink?" Joshua came toward her.

She gave him a careless smile, determined not to show her curiosity. "I'll have a tall glass of lime and soda please." And glided across to stand beside Caitlyn.

Heath gave her a welcoming smile. And Caitlyn said, "Alyssa, did you meet Barry Johnson at the winery this afternoon?"

The stranger grinned at her and answered for them both. "We didn't have that pleasure."

Quickly Alyssa said, "I had a rest this afternoon." And held up her bandaged hand.

"Barry's here to investigate some ludicrous claims that Saxon's Folly entered fraudulent samples in a wine-tasting competition," Megan said, joining them. "I've no doubt that you'll tell the organisers what a bunch of rubbish that is, Barry."

Barry's smile was noncommittal before he requested a recount of Alyssa's accident. The next few minutes were spent talking about the dangers of horse riding—with Megan laughingly labelling Barry's more outrageous recounts of his own youthful experiences as urban legends.

"Alyssa's fall was certainly not funny while it was happening," Joshua broke in from behind Alyssa. "I blame that stallion. He caused Breeze to bolt. He's been an accident waiting to happen for a long time. I don't know how many times I told Roland to get rid of him."

"What happened to me wasn't the horse's fault," Alyssa objected as she took the drink he held out. "The two guys upset him."

"Yes. And I'll deal with them as soon as they're caught."

Alyssa shivered at the slashing tightness of Joshua's mouth. She had no doubt he would. She almost found a little pity for them—despite the lingering ache in her hand.

"Is there a possibility that they came to taste the wines?" Alyssa asked, taking a sip before setting the drink down on a nearby table.

"No. There's closed-circuit surveillance in the tasting shed and we didn't catch any footage of them. The investigating officer suspects that they're young hoods, part of a gang that has been causing some problems recently. They're determined to apprehend them."

"Good," Megan sounded fierce. "As long as they don't take too long about it."

Alyssa caught Joshua's eye and both of them started to grin.

"What are you two laughing at?" Megan eyed them suspiciously.

"You sound so bloodthirsty."

Megan snorted. "They could've hurt Breeze…or that black devil horse."

"That black devil can look after himself. It's Alyssa who could've died." Joshua gave her a brooding look. "She didn't escape unscathed."

A surge of warmth swept through Alyssa. For a moment the outlandish thought crossed her mind that Joshua really cared.

"I'm feeling a lot better," she said softly.

"I'm glad." His voice was smooth and deep.

Out of the corner of her eye Alyssa caught Megan's start of surprise. She felt herself flush a little with embarrassment. She didn't need another witness to this insanity she felt about Joshua Saxon. It was an infantile infatuation. All about sex. About being too long without a man. It was totally crazy. And it had no hope of surviving. Heavens, he didn't even trust her to do a story.

Joshua lifted his Baccarat wineglass and took a sip of Saxon's Folly's Pinot Gris. His meal finished, he watched Alyssa flick back the fall of spectacular hair that glowed in the dim lighting. Instantly his senses were assaulted by the memory of the last time he'd tasted the full-bodied wine.

On Alyssa's lush lips, mingled with strawberries.

Damn!

"Joshua?" He jumped as a hand touched his shoulder. "Sorry, I startled you."

He moved his high-backed chair a little as Caitlyn slid into the unoccupied seat beside him.

"Barry was asking me questions earlier."

"About what?" Disquiet rocked Joshua. The hairs on the back of his neck started to rise.

"That this isn't the first time that Saxon's Folly has been

suspected of misrepresenting samples," Caitlyn murmured, keeping her voice low.

"That's bull."

"Is it?" Caitlyn's eyes were wide and worried. "What if Roland did submit a better batch?"

"He didn't." Joshua refused to believe that of his brother. In life, Roland might have been reckless…fiercely competitive. But he'd never been stupid.

And intentionally substituting better samples would've been stupid.

"It's not illegal to use a better batch of the same wine," Caitlyn said falteringly, as if already trying to create spin.

"But it's misleading. While we all know there may be some variation, it shouldn't be so great that the wine the public buy off the shelves is vastly inferior. That's tantamount to a breach of trust." Or fraud. Now he was starting to sound like Alyssa. But it was what he'd always believed.

"Roland did like to win." Caitlyn sounded subdued. "He got a kick out of collecting the gold medals for our wines. He loved admiring the display case in the tasting shed. He used to say, 'The end always justifies the means.'"

Joshua finished the Pinot Gris and set down the glass on the damask tablecloth. "That was a joke."

"You think so?"

Joshua didn't like the doubt on Caitlyn's face. "You think he did it."

She drew a deep breath. "I don't want to leap to incorrect conclusions, but I think it's possible. There were better batches."

"But we used those for the Special Reserve."

Caitlyn's eyes didn't meet his. "What if…" Her voice trailed away.

What if Roland had used those batches as samples? That's what she didn't want to say. Joshua hesitated. Caitlyn was an experienced winemaker. She knew the quality of every batch they produced. Then he conceded, "The reserve batches would've been substantially different. Substantially better."

This time she met his gaze, and he read the worry. "Exactly."

Double damn.

"I don't want to—"

"Think about it?" Her eyes were apologetic. "I think you have to."

"I was going to say, I don't want to believe it. He was my brother."

"You're too loyal, too protective." She paused. "You and Roland were fundamentally different. You didn't always react in the same way." There was sadness in her eyes. "You're a born defender. But you can't defend the indefensible."

"I know. But I want more proof. Roland is dead. I can't allow his memory to be muddied." He glanced over the subdued glitter of antique silverware to where his parents sat at the head of the table. "I can't let that happen to them."

"Well, you can't bear the blame yourself, so you may have no choice."

So that would mean that Alyssa had been right all along. Her cynicism about Saxon's Folly had not been displaced. She'd simply misidentified the culprit.

How would Alyssa feel when she found out the wrongdoer wasn't the Saxon she detested? That it was Roland, her brother? It would place her in the intolerable position of blowing the whistle on her own brother. Joshua knew he would do whatever it took to soften Alyssa's pain—even stop her from writing the article she so badly wanted to do.

Not for the first time, he wished that he'd never agreed to cooperate on this damned story.

On Sunday Joshua found Alyssa in the tasting shed. He stopped behind her as the group she'd been tending made their way to the cash register and he frowned as she unconsciously shielded her injured hand.

"What are you doing here?"

"Helping out. It's busy today."

"If your hand hurts, take a break."

She turned her head, her eyes startled. For an instant he caught a glimpse of emotion in her eyes that caused his chest to tighten and his blood to pound. Then it vanished and her eyes became shadowed.

Joshua opened his mouth to reveal there was a good chance that she'd been right all along, that the Saxon's Folly entries in the competition tasting had been compromised.

"It's been busy. I might take that break." She stood and flexed her hand.

As she turned away, a stream of tourists from one of the buses that stopped regularly at the estate entered the shed. The next few minutes were hectic, and Joshua stayed to help Kay and the two students who worked in the tasting shed on the weekends.

But it was a struggle to concentrate. He found his thoughts wandering to Alyssa. Finally he abandoned the tourists to his mother's care and stalked outside.

To the southern side of the winery, Alyssa was talking to Barry in a courtyard planted with olive trees. Joshua felt himself bristle with annoyance.

What was she after? And what had Barry told her? Tension coiled tight in his chest.

Alyssa was a journalist. Nothing would be off the record. The last thing he needed was a huge scandal that dropped the share price and lost the public's confidence in Saxon's Folly wines.

And then there was Roland's memory.

He didn't want any hint of scandal attached to that. He walked forward with a stiff gait.

"What are you two discussing so intently?"

Barry frowned. "We were talking about food if you must know. Mediterranean cuisine. The olives prompted it." He gestured to the trees. "Have no fear, I'm not discussing the progress of the investigation with a member of the press." He glanced at his watch. "Which reminds me, I wanted to talk with Caitlyn about something."

"Perhaps I can hel—"

"No, stay here in the sunshine with this lovely woman," Barry said with heavy gallantry. "Caitlyn has the records I want to see."

Joshua smiled at the older man, hoping that none of his apprehension showed…but knowing that Caitlyn would never reveal her reservations.

After Barry had left, the tension between him and Alyssa grew worse as the seconds stretched past. Finally Joshua flung himself down onto a stone bench and patted the seat beside him. "Sit. If you have any further questions, you can ask me now."

Alyssa continued to lean against the low white wall that bordered the courtyard, the sun striking her hair and turning her eyes to an impossible shade of violet. Again he felt the relentless twist of desire.

Then she said, "I've already asked everything I need to know from you."

"You have everything you want from me?" His stomach dropped as the colour of her eyes deepened. The desire was sharp now. Urgent. He rose to his feet and advanced on her. The wind lifted her hair, swirling it around her face. Almost against his will, he raised his hand, sliding his fingers under her windblown hair, cupping the smooth, warm skin of her nape. He moved his fingers, rubbing gently, caressing, and he heard her gasp, "I don't think so. I think there's more."

Their eyes tangled.

Several emotions flashed in the depths of hers. Hunger. Apprehension and something more.

Refusal, perhaps?

But she didn't voice the hesitation he glimpsed. So he stopped analysing, pulled her toward him and simply kissed her.

His lips moved gently against hers, parting them, tasting her sweetness, and he tangled his hands in her hair and held her where he could taste her best.

It was a kiss full of fire, brimming with all his frustration and desire. Her hands came up and pushed at his chest. Hard. Josh staggered back. They were both breathing heavily.

"No, Joshua."

Disbelief surged through him. What little air remained in his lungs rushed out. "You responded. Right now you want me."

Colour rose in her cheeks. "Do I?"

Annoyance flashed through him at her prevarication. "You want *this*. Your lips are so soft. You're as hungry as I am."

Her lashes fluttered down. "Maybe I am. But not now. Everything's too…" Alyssa's voice trailed away "…too much. I need to keep some distance—from you."

"With all that lies unfinished between us?" Joshua bit the curses that threatened back.

She met his eyes. "Let me finish this story. Help me with that."

The imploring look in her eyes told him this was important to her. How the hell was he supposed to battle that? Short answer was, he couldn't. He sighed inwardly. "I've already agreed to cooperate. So what comes next?" he asked flatly.

"You promised I could taste the wines." She slanted him a sideways look. "To see if I can taste the difference."

He wanted to taste her…not wines. But her mind was on the damned article. Her work came first. He had to respect that. It was part of the woman she was. And he'd already committed to cooperating. Joshua gathered his wits together.

As he held her unblinking gaze, he thought about Caitlyn's concerns that Roland might have entered fraudulent samples in the Golden Harvest Wine Awards, about Barry's task here at Saxon's Folly to get to the bottom of it all. He thought of his parents' frail state of mind. He thought of the raw grief he'd felt when his brother died. And, of course, he thought about Alyssa, the tumbling want that had consumed him since the night he'd met her.

Unstoppable.

Relentless.

Consuming.

Alyssa, who was the fuse to the devastating powder keg of desire that hovered between them. He narrowed his eyes, thinking furiously. The sooner her story was done, the sooner he could get back to the unfinished business between them. This time he wouldn't let her push him away, wouldn't allow her to use her job to put a distance between them—even if he had to use this formidable sizzle to seduce her. Alyssa would own up to the attraction that burned between them. He'd make sure of that.

"What are you thinking?" she asked, the first flare of alarm brightening her eyes.

He smiled slowly, deliberately. "You'll have your tasting. This evening."

Ten

Alyssa hadn't expected Joshua to arrange the tasting so fast. Nor had she expected him to set it up in the underground cellar beneath the main winery building. If she'd thought about it at all, she'd have imagined an informal meal at the homestead and a few samples afterward.

But here in the cellar they were alone, with no one to witness her findings. Was that deliberate?

She scanned her surroundings, taking in the ancient oak barrels that marched along one wall and the refractory table covered with a white cloth in the centre of the room. A row of glasses topped the table. At the far end, a leather chesterfield was grouped with two leather wing chairs. It all felt very masculine.

"The cellar was originally cast out of concrete and used as immense vats where the wine was made." Joshua moved to stand beside her. "It was hard work in those days. Before I was born my father had this fitted out as a place where he could retreat and taste the wines he'd created."

"Very masculine." Alyssa examined the rough concrete

roof and the racks filled with wines that lined the sides of the cellar. She was conscious of his size, the warmth radiating from him. She fought her response, fought to keep this about business…about the story, about tying up the loose ends that had to be tied.

"Why did your father need a refuge from your mother?"

Joshua started to frown. "Don't misunderstand me. My parents' marriage has always been very happy. I don't want you printing any rumours to the contrary."

Alyssa raised her brows. Then why had Phillip Saxon needed a place to which he could retreat? Why not retreat to the homestead and the comfort of his wife? But seeing the annoyance in Joshua's eyes, she let the subject drop.

"Sit down," he said, pulling out one of the bentwood chairs for her.

"Aren't you going to join me?" she asked, gazing up at him through half-lowered lashes as she lowered herself.

He leaned forward. "In a moment."

He was too close. Too overwhelming.

"Where do I start?" Hurriedly Alyssa turned her attention to the tulip-shaped tasting glasses on the table. "I don't see the wine."

"I'm not risking having you read the labels." Joshua flashed her a heart-stopping grin as he produced three bottles from a slender box.

"I wouldn't cheat."

"I want you to rely on taste and smell. Nothing else." Joshua picked something up. A white silky length of fabric. "I'm going to blindfold you."

A thrill of dark emotion assailed Alyssa. She fought not to let the illicit excitement show on her face.

"But I want to see the wine, the colour, the way the light moves within the liquid," she objected as her heartbeat drummed wildly in her chest. She braced her hands on the table in front of her, and was amazed to see that there was no tremor.

Joshua stood behind her. His body blocked out the light from the lamp. She sensed him coming closer. But still she started as she caught a glimpse of the white strip of silk that passed before her eyes. Then the world went blank.

The pressure of the blindfold against her eyes, the touch of his fingers against her nape, caused her breath to shorten to shallow gasps. White-hot heat rushed through her veins, setting her senses ablaze. She resisted the urge to clench her fingers around the edge of the table and fought to keep her breathing steady.

She was damned if she was going to give him any clue about what he was doing to her.

"Here…" He slid a glass into her right hand, his fingers brushing hers. "Taste this."

Alyssa swirled it around awkwardly with her right hand, raised the glass and inhaled. Then she took a sip. The wine filled her mouth. She swished it around experimentally.

Blindfolded it was impossible to spit it into the spittoon she'd seen. She swallowed and it slid down her throat like velvet.

"What's the verdict?"

"Nice," she croaked as his hands rested on her shoulders.

"Nice? That's all you can come up with? And you wield words for a living?"

Words. Work…keep it about work.

"It's definitely a Chardonnay. Richly fragrant, with toasty oak aromas. It has a ripeness." She struggled to find the words to describe the elusive flavour. She tried again. "Hints of butterscotch and honey."

There was a sharp silence.

Joshua didn't move. No rustle of his clothes. No clink of glass against the table.

"Let me try the next one," Alyssa said hurriedly, eager to shatter the unnerving, ringing silence.

"First you need to cleanse your palate."

He was very close now. She could sense him beside her, the power of his body, the subtle tang of expensive aftershave.

"I'm going to give you some mineral water."

A glass rested against her bottom lip. She took a quick sip, swirled the water around and gulped it down.

"Open your mouth, Alyssa."

Heat swarmed over her skin at his command. It sounded unbearably erotic and she could feel the colour rising over her throat, over her cheeks. How in heaven could this be work?

Slowly, hesitantly, she opened her mouth. He placed a piece of biscuit on her tongue, crumbly and savoury. She closed her mouth and chewed.

"Ready?"

Ready? For…?

Images assaulted her. Dancing with Joshua in the moonlight. The touch of his hands on her bare back. Joshua bending his head, his full sensuous lips against hers.

Then she came back to earth. She reminded herself she'd wanted distance between them. Joshua wasn't doing this deliberately. He was simply talking about the next tasting. Nothing more.

"I'm ready." Could he hear the huskiness in her voice? God, she hoped not.

This time his fingers closed around hers as she took the glass. She lifted it, the glass cool and smooth under her fingertips and his hands cupped hers.

"Relax, I'll make sure you don't spill wine over yourself."

Alyssa sipped blindly, all too aware of his fingers wrapped over hers, the warmth of his breath against the side of her face. The disorientating darkness of the blindfold confined her to a highly charged, supersensitive world she'd never entered before. A world where every sense was magnified and every sound amplified.

She swallowed too quickly, overwhelmed by sensation.

"What do you think of that sample?"

"I didn't taste it properly…I need another sip." Her voice was husky. Barely recognisable. She coughed to cover up the real cause. "It's a little dusty down here."

"Can't say that I've noticed." He released her hand. His jean-clad leg brushed against the back of her chair, and the fabric rustled. "I'll close the door, perhaps there's a draft."

The tension within her ratcheted up another notch. Great. Now the intimacy was even more enforced. Her pulse was slow and heavy, each beat measured. Her body had picked up on her thoughts and taken it to the next level.

As long as Joshua didn't notice.

She raised the glass and concentrated on the wine. It smelt rich, ripe with the fullness of oak. Next she tasted. This time she held the liquid in her mouth. It was smooth and mellow, showing all the best characteristics of a Chardonnay.

"So, what do you think?" Joshua's voice sounded loud from beside her. Alyssa started and swallowed. Too quickly. The wine went down the wrong way. She started to sputter.

Joshua thumped her on the back. "Are you all right?" His fingers went to the blindfold, pushing it back.

Through streaming eyes, she caught sight of his face, directly above hers. His eyes were velvety with the now-familiar concern.

"I'm fine," she murmured hoarsely.

The concern changed to something else…something darker. Intense and a little dangerous. Her heart plummeted then started to pound with unmistakable purpose.

Picking up a cracker off the plate, Alyssa tugged the blindfold back into place. She popped the biscuit into her mouth, doing her best to get her body's responses under control. "Give me the next glass."

There was a moment's silence. Then, he said, "You haven't told me what you thought of that wine."

"It's a Chardonnay."

"Same vintage or different?"

She hesitated. "It's definitely familiar. But the same as the first sample? I don't think so." She held her breath, but he didn't respond. "I'd guess it's an earlier vintage. It's even better than the last sample, I assume the time in the bottle might've added to it."

He remained silent.

"Am I right?"

"I'm not answering any questions until afterward."

"I'm sure I'm right." Alyssa started to relax. "Even though I'm not a trained judge."

"But sometimes the obvious is not the truth."

Was he talking about wine? Or the story she'd done a long time ago? Or was he talking about Roland being her brother, not her lover.

"Are you saying that I'm wrong?"

She could hear him moving glasses, the sound of wine splashing into a glass, then the thud as the bottle landed on the table.

"No, I'm not saying you're wrong."

He was talking about wine. Alyssa relaxed a little. "Unfair," she countered. "You're trying to confuse me."

The glass touched her hand. This time she made sure their fingers did not connect. "It's okay, I've got it. You can let go."

"Always so independent."

"Yes." But she thought about his pointed observation. When her mother had died and her father had remarried and left for another country, her response had been to cling to her independence. She only had herself to rely on.

For a while she'd hoped for an emotional connection with Roland. But even that tenuous bond had been ripped from her.

"At least I can look after myself." She lifted the wine and took a small sip and forced herself to concentrate. Lovely rich, ripe flavours. Cream and butterscotch. "This is wonderful. You should taste some."

"I will." His voice held an odd note.

She heard liquid swirling into a glass. Lifting the tulip-shaped tasting glass, she took a tiny mouthful.

"I'll taste it now, I think."

She felt an instant of heart-leaping shock as his mouth closed over hers.

And then she yielded.

His tongue sank in, searching out the flavours of the wine she'd consumed. It tasted. It explored. It devoured. Desire exploded within her. Alyssa met his hunger with her own.

When he finally lifted his head, she could barely think, much less talk.

"Velvet smooth and darker than midnight."

It took her a moment to realise that he must be talking about the essence of the wine that lingered on her tongue.

"Open your mouth."

She hesitated, then realised he intended to feed her another sliver of biscuit. Too late now to baulk. That would be too revealing. Her lips parted, her tongue slipped out and ran along her bottom lip.

She heard his breath catch, giving her an instant of warning. When his mouth claimed hers again, she was ready for him.

From behind the blindfold it was easy to pretend that these desires didn't belong to her—Alyssa Blake—that they belonged to the mindless, sightless tasting cipher he had created.

But she hardly cared. All she cared about was the feel of him. He lifted her, she grabbed for the table, and a moment later she landed across his lap as he slid beneath her.

His arm circled behind her back, pulling her close.

"What about the tasting?" she murmured, one last, desperate attempt at levity.

He moved. Then she felt smooth, cool glass against her kiss-swollen lips. "Taste then."

She sipped. Immediately his tongue swept her lips, parting them, plundering her mouth, stealing the wine.

God.

She wasn't sure whose prayer it was. All she knew was when his head lifted, she gasped for air…and fought for composure. No easy task half sitting, half lying in his lap, while he supported her.

"I think that's the same wine as the first you gave me. You must've mixed up the bottles."

He growled, a low, deep sound in the back of his throat. "I didn't. But I don't really care."

This time the kiss went deeper still. His hand cupped her breast and all thoughts of keeping a distance between them fled. Alyssa arched upward, every inch of her responsive to his touch.

Why him?

Why this out-of-control attraction to Joshua Saxon, of all people? Why couldn't it have happened with someone safe? Someone who respected and admired her?

His fingers fumbled with her blouse. The edges parted. Cool air blew across her skin. Alyssa bit her lip…waiting.

He didn't disappoint her. His hand closed over her breast, and sharp slivers of desire stabbed her, cutting deep.

She arched again, moaning. There was a moment of waiting. His fingers loosed the ties behind her head and the silk fell from her eyes. Alyssa blinked against the sudden light.

Then Joshua's head bent, and her heart twisted over.

It seemed like forever before his lips left her breast and his shoulders bunched under the cotton shirt he wore. Alyssa squeaked as he lifted her. The hardness of the table was a shock after the comfort of his lap. She felt stretched out, more exposed than when she'd been cradled in his arms.

Apprehension feathered down her spine. She tried for humour. "You never did tell me what you thought of the wine."

"I've forgotten the taste. I'll have to refresh my memory."

As his head came down toward her, she gave a little laugh and murmured, "I no longer taste of wine."

"No, you wouldn't," he agreed.

He picked up the nearly empty tasting glass, his eyes heavy with intent.

A thrill of desire ran through her. But instead of tossing the wine back, he leaned over her. The glass tipped, and her breath caught as the liquid spilled onto her skin where the blouse lay open. His head swooped, and she watched as he licked the liquid from the valley between her breasts. Her nipples stiffened into tight peaks, almost as dark as the rich wine. She shut her eyes with a groan.

A second later his mouth closed on the peak closest to him and her world rocked as a bolt of lust, unlike any she'd ever experienced blasted through her. Her eyes shot open. She watched wide-eyed as his mouth worked her flesh, sending wave after wave of pleasure through her.

What was he doing to her? She didn't recognise herself. She'd been kissed—loved—before. But no man had unleashed the raw, primal response he ripped from deep inside her.

Who the hell had she become?

Even now he was advancing further, expertly unfastening the last buttons of her blouse. His fingers were frantic now and his shirt was off, too. She stared at his naked torso gleaming under the electric lights, the muscles bunched, ready for action.

He couldn't possibly know how new this wild wanting was to her. Could he? She shuddered, uncomfortable with the idea that he might know exactly how far he'd trashed her boundaries.

He stripped his jeans off, revealing long muscled legs. Then he was leaning over her, and sliding the denim down her legs. Her panties followed.

Bare legs, brushed against bare legs. His body was heavy and warm against hers. Joshua's hand brushed her hair off her face, he looked down into her eyes and then his hips drove forward.

Alyssa closed her eyes as he filled her, stretching her, pleasuring her with slow, deliberate strokes. She bit her lips as the tension tightened within her, pulling tighter and tighter. Lights danced against her eyelids as the instant of ecstasy took her by surprise. Shivers streaked through her bloodstream, hot then cold, and Joshua made a wild, keening noise.

There was a moment of utter bliss, then the shudders came. Alyssa let them embrace her, and finally she dared to breathe. Opening her eyes, she looked into Joshua's hot, molten gaze. Incredibly, she knew he'd experienced the same wonder as she had.

Afterward, still dazed, Alyssa sat on the edge of the table and pulled her jeans on, then slid her arms into the sleeves of the blouse.

"Wait." Joshua held a white linen cloth in his hands. "There might be some residue from the wine." He licked the corner of the cloth and gently wiped the damp edge over the soft skin between her breasts. But when the cloth moved over her breasts she said, "I can do it."

He looked at her then. And he gave her a soft, sweet smile. "I know. But I wanted to do it for you."

And a sensation of falling into a deep void, of entering the wide unknown overwhelmed her.

Alyssa gulped, and didn't say another word as he fastened her bra and buttoned her blouse with fingers that were a lot steadier than hers.

It was only when he opened the heavy cellar door that she realised that anyone could have walked in on them. She shuddered again. The stunned sense of shock at the passion that Joshua had unleashed in her was starting to sink in. How could she have allowed that to happen? She wanted Joshua to take her seriously, respect her professionalism.

Stupid!

Alyssa slipped off the table and hurried past him.

"Thank you," he said from behind her. "You blew me away."

She turned her head, took in the slight flush high on his cheekbones. He wasn't unaffected by what had passed between them. In fact, he seemed to share her mood…shaken, uncertain.

"The final tasting I did was contaminated. I was distracted…" She flushed and he started toward her, stopping when she said, "You don't mind that I wasted your time?"

"Wasted my time?" His unaccustomed uncertainty fell away, his high colour had subsided, but his black eyes still smouldered. "What happened back there was no waste of time."

She halted at the bottom of the stone stairs as his words struck her. The sense of wonder that had encased her after their intimacy, the fragile joy, shattered.

What happened back there was no waste of time. His lovemaking had been no spur-of-the-moment impulse. She swung around. "Did you plan what just happened?" The urgent words escaped before she could temper them. For a brief moment he looked discomfited, then he smiled, and the confident Joshua Saxon was back.

"You did plan it!" It was there in the dark edge of guilt in his eyes. "You planned to seduce me," she accused. Joshua had used the relentless attraction that simmered between them for his own ends, to distract her from pursuing the story, to stop her getting to the bottom of the imminent wine-tasting scandal.

The smile that curved his lips held irresistible wickedness. "So what if I did? You responded. Hell, you enjoyed it."

She hadn't been able to help herself. But no way was she ever admitting that. Annoyed that she'd been so easy, so gullible, that she'd fallen into his arms so readily, she said, "You deliberately derailed the tasting."

All humour vanished from his face. Without a word he brushed past her.

"Joshua," she called. "Wait…"

But the only answer was the sound of his footsteps against the stone floor. Right now she felt dazed, so disoriented she could barely find her way back to the house, much less around the labyrinth of half-truths surrounding the scandal that threatened Saxon's Folly.

Alyssa pressed trembling hands against her mouth. Had Joshua been distracted, too? Could he be as confused as she was? Was he every bit as ruthless and calculating as she'd ever thought?

Or had she made a terrible mistake? Was he simply the sexiest man alive—the man her hormones recognised as different from anyone she'd ever met? The man who could be incredibly empathetic and caring and make her feel like the most special woman on earth. Had his lovemaking been intended to make her recognise the force of the power that lay between them?

Oh, God…please not that.

She wanted to bury her face in her hands as the revelation came to her.

The truth that she'd fallen hopelessly in love with Joshua Saxon.

Eleven

There was an unmistakable air of tension at dinner that evening. Kay had invited Heath over and by the time Alyssa came down, Heath and Phillip had already argued and a sense of gloom hung over the family.

Kay and Joshua sat at either side of Phillip with Megan opposite her father, flanked by Alyssa and Heath. Caitlyn had excused herself from dinner to show Barry around the nearby art-deco town of Napier.

But none of the family's frictions touched Alyssa. The devastating discovery she'd made earlier cocooned her from everything. *She loved Joshua Saxon.* And she'd probably mucked up any chance of telling him…horribly.

Alyssa sneaked Joshua a quick look. His face was set, until their gazes clashed. Sparks flew, and his eyes glowed like burning coals. He'd been right. They had unfinished business.

How was she ever going to resolve their differences? The distance that she'd begged for lay like a chasm between them now. Too far to bridge.

But it had always been too late for them. The secret of Roland's birth would always divide them… It was a truth Joshua could never acknowledge. For his parents' sake. Any relationship between her and Joshua had never stood a chance.

What was love without trust? She didn't trust his motives for making love to her—seducing her—during the tasting. So how could she ever tell him she loved him?

During the meal Heath kept her wineglass filled. By the time the main course of roast chicken was served, Alyssa felt more relaxed, and the warmth from the wine and food had spread through her body, although nothing could fill the hollowness inside her.

After Ivy had cleared the dishes away, Kay rose to her feet. "Phillip and I have something to tell you." Her voice faltered.

A grave-looking Phillip pushed back his chair and placed an arm around his wife's shoulders. "These last weeks have been incredibly draining for all of us. Kay and I have had the terrible task of burying a son…something no parent should ever have to do, while Megan, Heath and Joshua lost a brother."

Phillip's gaze caught Alyssa's for a moment and then slid away. The bubble that she'd been existing in for the last few hours burst. Alyssa clenched her fists against the edge of the table.

After a minute she glanced up. For a moment her eyes tangled with Joshua's. His gaze softened. He made an involuntary gesture of comfort toward her, then stopped. But she knew he'd glimpsed the emptiness…the hopelessness…in her eyes.

Before she could react, Phillip was speaking again.

"With Roland's death came a very tough time for Kay and I—" He broke off and glanced at his wife.

Kay put her hand on his arm. "What Phillip is trying to say is that we were faced by some decisions to make. And I fear that we made the wrong ones."

"What do you mean?" Heath was the first to speak, his earlier annoyance with his father gone. "What decisions?"

"Many years ago, I struggled to get pregnant—"

"I never knew that," Megan said.

"It was a painful time, a time I try not to dwell on," Kay murmured. "I became quite depressed—"

"After a lot of thought we decided to adopt a baby boy," Phillip finished gruffly.

"Roland," said Kay softly.

Alyssa's heart started to thunder. She couldn't believe what she was hearing. She glanced around the dinner table. Heath sat openmouthed with astonishment, even Megan had nothing to say. As for Joshua…he was staring at his parents…tension in every line of his body.

"But—" Heath was the first to rouse himself. "I'm not adopted am I? Hell, I look just like Dad, like Joshua…even Megan."

"Thanks," said Megan. "But I'm prettier."

"No, you're not adopted. None of you are." Kay's smile was tremulous. "It was a miracle. After adopting Roland I fell pregnant. It was as though those barren years had never been."

Finally, Joshua spoke. "But why did you never tell us?"

Phillip shrugged, looking trapped. "We intended to. But as the years passed, it became increasingly difficult. In the end, we never told Roland he was adopted."

"We were concerned that Roland might feel like an outsider." Kay's hand tightened on Phillip's arm until her knuckles turned white.

"So why tell us now?" This time it was Heath.

"Because—" Phillip stopped. "Your mother and I haven't handled this as well as we should have."

Kay's gaze flickered to Alyssa. Joshua's eyes followed. His gaze caressed her, she could feel the tenderness, the support.

"For a few months a young woman has been trying to contact Roland. At first she sent letters…and later…e-mails." Now Kay didn't look in Alyssa's direction.

"What did she want?" Megan asked apprehensively.

"Was she pregnant?" Heath interrupted. "Did she want money? Was she blackmailing Roland?"

"It's obvious what she wanted." Joshua's voice was loud in the sudden silence.

Kay made a sound that was halfway between a groan and a laugh. "She wasn't Roland's lover. She was his sister. His younger sister."

Pandemonium ensued. Everyone was talking at once. But Alyssa only had eyes for Joshua. Unsmiling, he was watching his mother. Alyssa couldn't see his face, had no idea what he was thinking. Had he set this up? Had he asked his parents to confess the truth?

Then he turned is head as if he'd felt her gaze on him, and mouthed, "Okay?"

She nodded, feeling comforted.

Kay sighed. "The only blackmailing she did was to tell me that if I didn't tell her all about the brother she'd been seeking for years…then she would tell you all that Roland was adopted."

"So you agreed to hcr blackmail," Heath said.

"Oh, poor girl. We want to meet her." That was Megan.

"You already have." Joshua's voice resounded around the room.

"What?" Megan turned to him.

"She's sitting right here."

The family grew utterly silent. All eyes fell on Alyssa.

Megan was the first to move. She pushed her chair back and came around to hug Alyssa. "Why didn't you tell us you were Roland's sister?"

"I couldn't." She looked over Megan's shoulder at Joshua. "None of you knew that Roland was adopted. I promised your parents I would never reveal that. I kept that promise." Joshua had guessed, she reassured herself, she hadn't told him.

At last Joshua said, "What I can't understand is why Roland never told us that he was adopted."

"He never knew, either," Phillip answered.

"But what about the e-mails and letters from Alyssa? Surely he confronted you and Mother with them?" Joshua's frown cut deep into his forehead.

"He did," Kay said very softly, lines of worry creasing her face. "We told him that Alice McKay must be crazy or a fraud. That of course he was our son. We convinced him not to respond, that it was an extortion ploy. He wanted to go to the police—we had to talk him out of that." Kay's shoulders rose and fell as a deathly silence fell over the room.

A sense of horror rocked Alyssa. Roland had thought she was a crazy, a stalker? Then reality settled back. But that meant that Roland had not rejected her....

She shook her head, trying to clear the confusion. "But you told me that he wanted nothing to do with me. That he chose his Saxon heritage over the opportunity to be reunited with me, his birth sister."

Kay's eyes met Alyssa's. "I'm very ashamed of what we did. Alyssa, I wish we could turn the clock back."

Alyssa bit her lip to stop herself from saying the bitter words that wanted to spill out. She found it impossible to hold Kay's gaze without letting her condemnation show. She'd liked Kay...laughed with her. Yet Kay and Phillip had betrayed her, lied to her brother and killed any chance of their fragmented little family ever finding each other.

"Mother!" Megan had let Alyssa go. "How could you and Father have done such a thing?"

"I thought if he found out he was adopted, he'd reject us." Kay's shoulders sagged. "You have to believe, if I'd known that Roland would die...that Alyssa would never get a chance to know her brother... That's why I called her when Roland was dying...to give her a chance to say goodbye. I couldn't keep Alyssa from him any longer."

Kay dropped her face against Phillip's chest.

Her husband's arms closed around her. "Kay has gotten to know Alyssa very well. She couldn't carry on the deception."

So Joshua hadn't spoken to his parents....

Alyssa didn't feel the relief she'd expected. Instead she felt more shattered than the three Saxon siblings looked. Megan was clearly more excited than upset, Heath stared at her with interest...and as for Joshua, well, he was impossible to read. All Alyssa could think about was that there was no longer any reason to stay at Saxon's Folly. As Kay left Phillip's side and went to hug each of her three children, Alyssa sneaked out of the dining room, seeking the solace of her bedroom to come to terms with what she had learned.

Joshua entered her bedroom while Alyssa stood staring out the window into the darkened night. She'd changed into her sweats and a T-shirt and was trying to summon up the energy needed to finish packing the bag that gaped open on her bed.

He didn't knock. But she heard the door squeak open, heard the soft fall of his footsteps as he came up behind her.

"Why are you leaving?"

She swung around at the sound of his deep voice. He looked unbearably dear and familiar. But his face was etched with lines that had not been there on the night they'd met. The night of the masked ball. The night they'd first kissed. The night Roland had crashed.

How could he ask that? Did he not know how that scene downstairs had devastated her? "I think we all need some time. I'll leave in the morning."

At some level she wanted...needed...him to persuade her to stay. Alyssa searched his eyes. There was concern. Even a little anger. But she couldn't find the emotion she was searching for. The emotion she wanted above all else. Right now she couldn't even spot desire.

Too much had happened.

She'd been insane to think that she and Joshua stood a chance together.

He nodded slowly. "Perhaps you're right. Come have a nightcap with me."

She paused. Was it possible to reach a truce? "A cup of tea would be nice."

But he didn't take her to the main kitchen, instead they made their way down the old servant's staircase to his suite. He settled her on the overstuffed sofa in the living room he'd shared with Roland and slipped into the state-of-the-art kitchen next door. He was back before she'd even had time to gather her thoughts, with a mug of coffee for himself and a cup of tea for her.

"My parents should never have lied to Roland. It was wrong of them."

Alyssa picked up the teacup. "I know. There were times I wished I'd never promised your mother that I'd keep it a secret."

He was angry. She could see it in his eyes. But it wasn't directed at her. "Of course you couldn't break your word. Your integrity and crusade for truth is part of what makes you special. Hell, you even felt the need to defend Tommy Smith because you believed he'd been unfairly dismissed."

"His version checked out." Alyssa said, as he settled beside her. "I even called you for a comment on it."

"And I never called you back. But I was critically busy. First with the harvest, then with a fire in the winery." He stroked her hair and drew a deep breath. "I'm so sorry that you were robbed of time with Roland. He would've loved you…your grit…your sharp tongue…your fierce loyalty."

The prick of tears caught her by surprise. "Thank you. You're a very kind man."

"Nothing kind about me." But he reached for her and took her in his arms. There was nothing sexual about the embrace. There was only comfort and understanding. How had she misjudged him so badly? A curious sense of belonging in the safety of his arms swept Alyssa.

Alyssa finished her tea and set the cup down. They sat in a companionable silence, his heartbeat slow and steady against her ear. She dozed a little, until she felt herself being hoisted up.

"Sleep," he murmured as she stirred and uttered a protest.

Seconds later a mattress gave beneath her. Then Joshua's arms surrounded her again. Alyssa let herself float into a dreamless sleep.

In the bright morning sunlight that slanted through his bedroom window Joshua looked down at the sleeping face of the woman in his arms. A surge of tenderness overwhelmed him. Her eyelids fluttered up and she blinked as the light registered. Then she turned her head and snuggled into his chest.

Heat flooded Joshua.

She'd lain in his arms, her bottom pressed up against his stomach all night. He'd barely slept. By the time dawn had broken, he'd been ready to quietly come apart.

But things were different. The basis of their relationship had shifted. Publicly. Irrevocably. Alyssa was almost family.

Everyone knew she was Roland's sister.

He couldn't have a reckless, no-strings-attached affair with her. He could never do casual with this woman. She might look tough and uncompromising…but he'd seen the vulnerability beneath. He owed her more protection—even from himself. With a sigh, he started to move away.

"Where are you going?" her voice was husky with sleep, sexy as sin to Joshua in his aroused state.

He asked the question he knew he shouldn't. "Do you want me to stay?"

"Please." She stretched a little, like a supple, slender cat.

His blood started to pound.

He pulled her toward him and she came without resistance, her eyes sleepy. She was beautiful to him with her clear skin and tangled hair, her body warm from a night under the covers beside him. And the bittersweet emotion that blossomed in his chest was wholly unfamiliar.

Her hip brushed his belly. He heard her breath catch as she felt his hardness. Her eyes met his, wide and startled, suddenly very much awake.

"*Joshua?* Now? Here?"

"Whatever you want."

She came to him, slipping off the T-shirt she'd slept in. He'd already removed the sweats the night before so she wouldn't cook in the night. Her breasts were full and beautiful. Then her panties were off. She lay back against the plump pillows and curved her lips in the most provocative smile he'd ever seen. And waited.

Joshua growled.

His hand smoothed over her belly, down between her legs. She was already moist.

"Open for me, babe."

She obeyed. He slipped one finger into the secret heat, then another. She groaned. "Joshua, you only touch me and I go up in flames."

Her words were enough to tip him over the edge. Pulling her over him, her breasts against his chest, he nuzzled his lips against her neck. Little kisses against soft skin. Then by some magic, he was inside her.

They moved slowly, in concert, until the pleasure that had started in his groin spread through to every part of his body. As the intensity grew, his thrusts sped up. He felt her internal muscles tightening…contracting around him. And then he was falling through space, Alyssa's heart thundering against his.

When they surfaced, a sense of power overwhelmed Joshua. He felt invincible. He gave her a brilliant smile.

"Wow."

She wrinkled her nose at him. "Just wow?"

"Just wow," he agreed. "Anything more could kill me."

Then her face grew serious, and he wasn't sure that he would like what was coming.

"Where do we go from here?"

He relaxed a little. He'd thought she might talk about leaving—and never coming back. He couldn't let her go. Even if she was Roland's sister.

"You said you wanted time to come to terms with last night. There must be a part of you that's furious."

She brushed her hair off her face. "No, I meant what happens to us?"

She wanted to know what his intentions were. Joshua drew a deep breath and felt he'd stepped off into uncharted territory. "A little later we'll tell my family that we have a relationship." He didn't think it would come as a surprise.

"But you live in Hawkes Bay and I work in Auckland. That's a little problematic."

That brought his mind back to the real problem: the damned story that she was doing. Sooner or later she would discover that it was highly likely that Roland had intentionally submitted samples from a superior batch of wine for the competition. It would kill her to have to do that story. Of course, there was a good possibility that she might decide that she had a conflict of interest and have her editor assign the story to another writer. But Joshua suspected once she knew the truth, she'd view it as a failure of her duty to the public not to report it.

Last night she'd looked shaken. It had hurt him to see her in that state. If she did the story, her pain would only increase. "Alyssa, drop the story."

She pulled away and sat up. *"What?"*

"Give it up. There'll be other stories."

"You can't ask that of me. Not when you say it's my defence of truth that you admire. I can't believe you're saying this." She scanned his eyes. "Or do you know? You know who submitted the samples. You know who committed the fraud. Was it Caitlyn?"

He shook his head. "This has nothing to do with Caitlyn."

"Who are you protecting this time? Was it Phillip? Your

mother? Last night proved they will do whatever they think necessary."

"They thought they were protecting Roland." Joshua felt compelled to defend his parents' inexcusable actions.

"They were mistaken. He should have been allowed to make up his own mind. He's an adult, not a child."

"I agree with you. But this story will hurt them, too. Surely you can see that?"

"Who are you protecting? Megan?" She paused, looking poleaxed. "Or was it you, after all?"

Her distrust tore him apart. He reminded himself that he was doing this for her. "I'm not answering, Alyssa." He paused. "Pursuing this story is going to hurt you."

"You're asking me to drop it, because of you?"

Joshua stiffened at her tone. Clearly she believed him involved. He wasn't prepared to muddy her vision of Roland. To let her suffer more hurt. But was he prepared to risk losing her over it? Finally, he said, "Yes, drop it for me."

She'd never looked more gallant...or more upset as she said, "I don't think I can do that. Not even for you. It's my career—what I do. And I do it well. But it's more than that. You're asking me to turn my back on everything I believe in, all the values I was raised to fight for. Truth. Justice. What I do is about keeping the industry clean and the players ethical. It's about doing the right thing."

And the betrayed expression in her eyes told him that she thought he was motivated by ruthless self-interest to protect himself and his family at all costs. Joshua knew he wouldn't be telling his family that he was romantically involved with Alyssa. His demand had killed any chance of that. And he was damned if he'd tell her the truth to save a relationship built on such shaky ground.

Twelve

An unwelcome suspicion crossed Alyssa's mind as she made her way to the winery an hour later to say her final farewells to the Saxons. If Joshua had made love to her in the winery cellar to stop her tasting and identifying the wines, was it also possible that he'd made love to her this morning with the sole purpose of getting her to drop the story?

She didn't like the idea one little bit. But she couldn't help remembering that after she'd spoken to Barry outside the winery, Joshua had asked if she had any questions, then kissed her. Had even that kiss that had seemed so sweet and tender been given to distract her?

Then she shook her head. No. It couldn't be true. She remembered his sensitivity…his vulnerability. She would never fall in love with a man who was so devious and manipulative.

But still the suspicion festered.

She needed time, she told herself. Time to put everything into perspective.

The first person she saw as she walked into the winery with

its immense stainless steel vats was Barry Johnson. She forced herself to smile in greeting.

"Well, I might was well give you a break," he said. "But you're not to run it in the next twenty-four hours. I know *Wine Watch* has a longer lead time, but you're not to run this in your newspaper column until I tell the competition organisers."

"You've come to a finding?" A tingle of fear vibrated down her spine. She couldn't help feeling a wave of pity for Joshua…the Saxons…at the thought of the coming bad PR. This would mean share-price drops all over again.

He nodded. "I've satisfied myself that there was no irregularity."

Alyssa gaped at him in surprise. Because of Joshua's behaviour, she'd been so sure Saxon's Folly had entered trumped-up samples. And if they hadn't, then why hadn't Joshua denied it when she'd demanded to know who he was protecting?

Joshua…

She groaned silently. How he must despise her. She'd all but accused him of being the culprit. She said goodbye to Barry and walked blindly on.

"Alyssa."

She swung around as Caitlyn appeared from behind the nearest vat, her faded jeans splattered with the residue of grape pulp. "I heard the news."

For a moment Alyssa didn't know what Caitlyn was talking about. So much had happened. Then she realised that Caitlyn meant about Roland being adopted and the news that she was his sister.

Caitlyn hugged her. "No wonder you seemed familiar. It's the red hair and your features at certain angles."

"I'm going back to Auckland," Alyssa told her.

"Today?"

Alyssa nodded.

"Oh, no. I suppose you need to get back to work?"

It seemed easiest to let Caitlyn believe that. Then Alyssa said, "I also heard the good news about the investigator's findings—you must be thrilled."

"I'll tell you, I had some worrying moments when Barry told me that it wasn't the first time that Saxon's Folly had been suspected of entering samples of better batches. So I searched through all my records of the batches and cross-checked which bottles had come from which barrels—everything is numbered and electronically tracked, you know." Caitlyn paused to draw a breath. "Then I triple-checked Roland's paperwork, to make sure he hadn't entered any of the batches that we'd earmarked for Special Reserve. Fortunately it was all clear."

But Alyssa was riveted on one fact. "Roland did the entries?"

"Well, yes, he was the marketing manager. He always did the competition entries and decided which contests to enter and which wines would do best. Didn't you know?"

Slowly Alyssa shook her head. "Did Joshua know all this?"

Caitlyn gave her a strange look. "Of course. I told him the other night at supper that I was very afraid of what Roland might have done. Roland liked to win. And he could be reckless." Then she put her hand over her mouth. "I'm sorry, I shouldn't have said that."

Alyssa's heart sank. "No, you should always tell it as it is."

That made Caitlyn look even more worried. "You won't write about that? It's speculative, off the record. We don't even know for sure if Roland did it in the past. Joshua drew bottles from the same batches that I was looking at, to taste himself. He didn't want mud to be slung at Roland. He's determined to protect his brother's good name."

"No, I won't use it in my story." She didn't tell Caitlyn that Joshua had demanded that she drop the story, that she'd refused. Then someone called Caitlyn from the other side of the winery. She gave Alyssa a final hug, told her to visit again soon and hurried off.

Alyssa stared blindly at the floor. All the time, she'd suspected Joshua was protecting someone.

It had been Roland.

Alyssa was touched by Joshua's loyalty to his brother, his determination to let Roland retain dignity in death. Had he been protecting his parents against more hurt, too?

Another possibility struck her. Was it possible that Joshua had been protecting her? What had he said? *Pursuing this story is going to hurt you.* She'd taken that as a challenge… even a threat…he'd said it out of concern. For her.

Then she remembered something. Caitlyn had said that Joshua had drawn bottles out of the same batches she'd crosschecked to taste. She started to run.

In the cellar under the winery the bottles still stood on the table, beside the empty glasses and the discarded blindfold.

Alyssa thought back, trying to remember. She'd been so distracted by what Joshua had been doing, his touch, his kisses that she could barely remember.

Concentrate. Two wines had tasted identical—or at least to her palate they had. She read the labels on the bottles. Two were recent vintages, one of which had been bought from a local outlet and still had the price on. The third was a vintage from three years ago and also bore a price sticker. She poured a little of each wine into three different glasses. Then she raised them and sniffed each one carefully. The one she'd thought was an older vintage was fuller, fruitier…it was a Chardonnay Special Reserve. But according to the markings on the bottle this was not what had been sent to the competition. It still had a price sticker from the store where it had been bought on it. The other two were identical to her fairly well-developed sense of smell. Of course, Barry would be an expert.

Joshua had not been trying to distract her.

He'd given her a sample from a bottle available from the shops, and a taste from a bottle that came from the same batch of wine that the competition sample had been sourced.

If she took the bottles to Caitlyn, she was certain it would all check out.

Joshua hadn't attempted to mislead her. Nor had he crowed when she'd announced that they were the same, vindicating Saxon's Folly.

He'd been too caught up in their lovemaking. She'd been at the forefront of his focus during the wine-tasting, he'd put her ahead of Saxon's Folly.

Alyssa knew that she owed Joshua a massive apology. But she was done with talking, this time she'd do it in print. A public apology. She owed him that. It was the only way she could begin to make up for her lack of trust.

Thirty minutes later Alyssa found Joshua in the vineyards behind the homestead. The leaves on the vines had started to unfurl in the warmth of the summer sunlight.

"I've come to say goodbye." She stopped in front of him, noticing how tall he was, how utterly gorgeous.

The sun gave his features a golden cast as he looked down at her, the expression on his face unreadable. "You've decided to leave then."

"Yes, I need to write my story. And I need time to come to terms with—" she fumbled for words, not wanting to accuse his parents of anything that she would later regret "—what happened."

He only nodded. Alyssa hoped he would understand, prayed she hadn't already lost him. There was so much she wanted to say, but she couldn't. She'd said hurtful, distrusting things and she needed to set that right. When she sent him the article, he would recognise that she was humbling herself with a public apology.

"I'll walk you to your car."

"Joshua, I probably should've trusted you—"

Hot emotion flared in his eyes. "Yes, you should've." He turned away.

So this was it. It was over. Her heart contracted in her chest, a sharp, painful sensation. Then she followed him. Her luggage was already in the trunk. Beside her car, they paused, and there was a moment's awkward silence.

Finally Alyssa plucked up enough courage to lean forward and kiss him on the cheek. "Goodbye, Joshua."

His eyes darkened but he didn't reach for her, didn't kiss her in the way that he had early that morning. Instead he opened the car door for her. Alyssa turned the key and the engine took the first time. She unwound her window.

As the car started to roll forward, she stuck her head through the window. "I'll send you the story as soon as it is done."

His mouth slanted and he shook his head. "That's not necessary. I'm sure I'll find out what you've written as soon as the magazine hits the newsstands."

"You need to trust me, too—trust cuts two ways." Then more softly, she said, "You also need to know that I love you."

Her last view of Joshua in her rearview mirror was of his shocked, incredulous expression.

The story was done.

Alyssa had sent it in to David two days ago. And she'd posted a copy to Joshua, telling him that she'd never before shown her copy to anyone prior to publication, but she was happy to do it with him. She trusted he was satisfied.

She hadn't heard anything from him. But then, she hadn't expected to.

What she and Joshua had briefly shared had been over before it had even really started. Alyssa knew that it would take her a long time to get over Joshua. She'd gone to Saxon's Folly to find her brother. She'd found so much more—a family of strangers who had become so important to her. But more important than anything was the love that she'd discovered there. The love for Joshua.

But she was proud of the article. It had been the most difficult piece she'd ever written. The story was fair. She celebrated Roland's life, the successes of Saxon's Folly…and underpinning it had been the pain of her hopeless love for Joshua.

It was done. She'd vindicated Saxon's Folly publically, quoting Barry liberally. In a couple of weeks *Wine Watch* would be out there on the newsstands—her apology to Joshua.

The doorbell rang.

With a puzzled frown Alyssa made her way to the door. Who could be calling on a Friday morning?

Joshua stood on the doorstep, his beloved features wearing an expression that made her heart leap. "Can I come in?"

"Of course." She scanned him hungrily. There were still shadows under his eyes, and the hint of sensuousness in the bottom lip still made her insides turn to liquid. He was dressed more formally than usual—a dark suit, with a pin-striped white shirt…but no tie. As always, he looked gorgeous. The attraction that he held for her remained unchanged. It always would. And so would her love for him.

He must've received the article.

Why hadn't he called first? What did he want from her? She stood aside to let him in, hoping, hardly daring to breathe.

Inside he looked around at the mix of creams and grays with splashes of lilac and blue, and the windows positioned to take advantage of the light. "This is nice."

"Yes, it's a lovely bright sun trap."

He sucked in a deep breath. "I came to give you this." He held out an envelope. Alyssa took it from him. The paper was heavy. One corner bore the crest of Saxon's Folly. Her gaze met his. "What is it?"

His mouth slanted. "An invitation."

Oh, how she'd missed the quirk of his mouth, his wry humour. "It's not dark blue, embossed with silver, so it can't be to the ball." She sought refuge in humour.

He started to smile. It crept up until his dark eyes gleamed with laughter. "No, it's not an invitation to the ball. That's past.

I'm afraid you remain a gate-crasher. But you're welcome to attend next year. If you choose."

Her heart sank a little. She'd had such high hopes when she'd first seen him on her doorstep. That he'd come to tell her he loved the story…that he'd recognised and accepted her apology…that he wanted her back.

Ridiculous.

She didn't deserve it.

She slit the envelope open with her finger to find the invitation he'd deemed important enough to deliver himself and drew out the card inside. On the outside was an image of the gracious homestead surrounded by the rolling green vineyards that she'd grown to love. She flipped the invitation open. The Saxon family welcomed her to attend a planting of a new cultivar in honour of Roland Saxon.

It was to take place the coming Monday.

"It's very short notice, I know," Joshua said quickly. "But we wanted to do it four weeks after his death. It's been a mad rush these past few days to get it all organised."

"I understand." She swallowed her disappointment and looked up. "I'll be there."

It would be painful to return to Saxon's Folly. It would be even harder to leave afterward. Leaving Joshua once had been a wrench, this time it would break her heart. But by her distrust she'd forfeited any chance with him. All her life she'd placed so much stock in values like truth and justice. She'd thought that they needed to be underpinned by hard evidence. But that hadn't allowed for emotion. And she hadn't known how to deal with the feelings he'd roused in her. She'd doubted him. Despite the signs that he was the most caring, responsible person she'd ever met. She'd failed to trust him. It would haunt her forever. Slowly she placed the card carefully back in the embossed envelope.

She gestured to the love seat under the window. "Would you like to sit down?"

"I can stay awhile." He moved to the sofa, shrugged off his jacket and dropped it over the back of the love seat.

Alyssa hovered uncertainly. "Can I get you something to drink?"

"No, come sit." He patted the empty space next to him.

Heart pounding, Alyssa made her way across the room and dropped onto the plump cushion beside him. Instantly his warm male scent surrounded her. She inhaled deeply. She'd missed that, too.

"Alyssa…" He paused. "I know now how badly you wanted to meet Roland…to get to know him. I'm sorry it never happened." He shook his head. "And I'm sorry for mistakenly believing he was your lover."

She turned to face him, propping her back against the padded arm of the loveseat. "I couldn't tell you in the beginning. I'd promised your mother—I always keep my promises."

"I know." His eyes met hers, their dark depths soft and tender. "It must've been very difficult for you."

Alyssa thought back to the confusion she'd experienced, the sense of being torn. "It was."

"My mother—and father—hope you'll forgive them. When you come next week, you'll find them very contrite."

"Of course I will." But Alyssa knew that it would take her some time to come to terms with what Kay and Phillip had done. But they'd tried to make amends. She had more than she might've had. "I will forever thank your mother for at least giving me the opportunity to say farewell to him."

Joshua was talking again, his black gaze intent. "I can never give your brother back. But I can share my family with you. If you want that. Anytime you want, my family would be proud to welcome you to Saxon's Folly."

His words were incredibly moving. Her throat tightened. How could she ever communicate how much his offer meant to her? She knew that she would take him up on it. Even though it meant that every time she visited her heart would be torn out by seeing him…being close to him…and then leaving again. "Thank you," she said huskily. "I'd like to share your family."

"But, I'm warning you, if you want a brother, you're going to have to make do with Heath."

Alyssa stared at him. Then her heartbeat rolled into a drumming that resounded in her ears.

"Because I want a wife. A lover."

"What are you saying?"

"That I love you, that I'm asking you to be my wife." His dark eyes were intent. "We can start a family of our own. Will you be part of my dream?"

Joy rushed through her. Tears of happiness blurred her vision. "Oh, Joshua, I'd *love* that."

He closed the space between them, scooping her up in his arms. "I hoped you'd say that."

It was warm in his arms. Like being cocooned in sunshine. A safe, familiar place that Alyssa knew would always be home. "I can't believe you want me…after I trusted you so little."

Joshua bent his head. "I don't only want you. I love you. More than you can ever know."

He brushed his lips across hers and instantly excitement tightened in her stomach. She sneaked her arms around the back of his neck, holding him tight, as though she would never let him go. His mouth was soft and tender on hers, telling her so much more than words about his feelings for her…about his relief at her reaction.

Alyssa wanted to save this magical moment in her memory forever.

When he finally lifted his head, it was to say, "But to be fair, the mistrust wasn't all on your side. I didn't trust you, either—I jumped to the wrong conclusion about your relationship with Roland. I'm sorry. It was only once I got to know you, once I knew what was developing between us, that I realised that my mistake couldn't be right."

She brushed a finger over his full bottom lip. "Thank you

for granting me that, for giving me credit. Because I would never have been able to tell you the truth."

"It was hard," he admitted. "Especially because I kept defaulting back to my dislike of Alyssa Blake, wine writer."

"I wish I'd never done that story in the past," she said, bitter regret filling her. "But at the time I believed I was doing the right thing, my research backed it up."

"I know. And my attitude at the time didn't help." His arms tightened around her. "But I couldn't tell you what Tommy had really done, it wasn't my story to tell. But I'll have the person tell you herself, then you'll understand. And how could I expect you to accept that? You had a job to do."

And by the sincerity in his eyes, Alyssa knew that he loved her…trusted her.

Alyssa smiled up at him. "You were so arrogant, but you had the sexiest voice I'd ever heard."

He looked discomforted. Then he growled, "It was dumb of me. You were part of the media. But I was—"

"Busy with the harvest."

He nodded. "And that takes precedence over everything else."

Once he mentioned the past story she'd done, Alyssa couldn't help herself. "So what did you think of my article?"

A blank look settled over the features she'd come to love. "What article?"

She pulled back in his arms. "You didn't receive it?"

He shook his head. "Not yet."

"Rural mail." She rolled her eyes. "I thought that's why you were here."

"Nope." He tilted her chin up. "I came because you told me you loved me. I would've been here sooner, but you wanted time."

"I needed to finish that story. I sent you a copy. Do you know what a concession that is?" She gave him a smile that held all her love. "I've never let anyone see an article before it was run. But this was different, I owed you an apology." But he hadn't waited to see the article, he hadn't needed her apology, he'd come anyway. He'd trusted her not to hurt him…or Saxon's Folly…in print. The last bit of restraint inside her melted away. "I love you, do you know that?"

Then without giving him time to answer, she wriggled out of his arms and returned with a sheaf of papers a minute later. "This is for you."

Joshua pulled her back onto his lap. Resting his chin on her shoulder, he scanned the pages swiftly. Then he planted a kiss on her cheek. "Apology accepted. Thank you, Alyssa. It captures the heart of Saxon's Folly. The sense of family we have, and how we try to put that joy into every bottle of wine we make."

Warmth filled her. The happiness spilled out of her and she couldn't seem to stop smiling. "I'm glad you like it. That means a lot to me. I only wrote about what I found at Saxon's Folly."

Josh met her eyes squarely, the glow subsided a little and her smile faded. A wave of apprehension swept her at what was coming. Then he said, "You're a city girl. Will you be happy living at Saxon's Folly?"

Was that what he was worried about? Relief shook her. "Joshua, I'd be happy living anywhere you are." She gave him a look filled with all the love she felt. "I love you. Where you are, my home is."

He gave an audible exhalation of relief and tightened his arms around her. "You are my heart, do you know that?"

She couldn't imagine Joshua being happy living anywhere else. She gave a laugh. "Were you really worried that I wouldn't want to live at Saxon's Folly?"

"Very much." The big body relaxed against hers. "We'll remodel the suite downstairs. Or, if you want, we can build a new home on the estate."

Alyssa inched up the sofa, snuggling closer to him. "You know I love your family but when we start that family of our own we may need a new house." Right now she didn't even want to think about a family. All she wanted to concentrate on was Joshua.

Starting now.

She stretched up and kissed him. The top button of his shirt was already undone, she searched for the second button and undid it. "Do you have anything planned for the rest of the day?" she asked throatily, pressing a kiss against the skin she'd just revealed.

"Right now I can think of nothing more important than staying here," he said.

"Good."

"Alyssa?"

She glanced away from the third button that she'd been loosening with single-minded determination and looked up at him. "Yes?"

"You haven't said you'll marry me." Joshua gave her a grin filled with teasing and love. "Promise you'll marry me? Make an honest man of me?"

"I promise." And Alyssa knew it was a promise she would never break, that their marriage vows would be a promise she would keep her whole life.

* * * * *

SPANIARD'S SEDUCTION

BY
TESSA RADLEY

It's people who make places great to work in.
To the team at Jay Inc…thanks for the wonderful years!

One

Rafaelo, Marques de Las Carreras, was seething with hot Spanish rage. And when Rafaelo seethed, wise people gave him a wide berth until he cooled down to his normal impeccable courtesy.

Rafaelo told himself he had reason to be furious. He'd flown from Spain via London to Los Angeles and on to his final destination of Auckland, New Zealand. A security furore in Heathrow had caused a six-hour delay, resulting in a missed transatlantic connection to the United States.

There had been no first-class seats available on the flight he'd finally caught and the carrier had been packed as full as a tin of *sardinas*. He'd been wedged between a sweating overweight car dealership owner and a fraught-looking woman with a screaming baby. It had not improved his mood.

By the time Rafaelo landed in Auckland eighteen hours later than scheduled, it was to discover that his monogrammed Louis

Vuitton luggage had vanished, and to top it all, the Porsche reserved for him had been hired out when he'd failed to turn up earlier.

Not even flashing traveller's checks, his platinum bank card or large-denomination American dollars could commandeer him a vehicle. Sorry, no cars available. There was an international sporting event on in the area, explained one car-hire company after another.

The Marques de Las Carreras wasn't accustomed to apologies, certainly not from an indifferent middle-aged woman filing her nails—who didn't respond to either his most charming smile or, when that failed to get results, to his dangerously lowered tone.

It was unheard of for him to be treated like a *peon*—usually his name was enough to secure him the best. The best seats at the bullfight, the best table in the restaurant, the best-looking woman in the room. And to come back to his present situation, the best car for hire.

He blinked, told himself this couldn't be happening. Finally he managed to rent a vehicle—if the battered and dented yellow-and-black apparition plastered with neon-coloured *Make Waves* and *Shoot the Tube* stickers could be called that—from an operator most appropriately named Wreck Rentals. It had cost him plenty.

Not only had he been royally ripped off, but he also hadn't slept in two days and a night. Nor had he showered. His clothes were creased. He was driving an abomination.

Twenty minutes later, teeth gritting as the thing—he couldn't truthfully label it a vehicle—shuddered, Rafaelo slowed at a large hand-carved sign welcoming visitors to Saxon's Folly Winery, home of the Saxon family.

The lane into which he turned was lined with established trees. Farther along the lane, a modern winery complex appeared. Through the trees Rafaelo glimpsed a large stately residence.

The car rolled to a stop.

He stopped breathing. The house was exactly as his mother

had described it. Tall. White. Lacy wrought iron trimmed the balconies. The elegant triple-storey Victorian homestead was drenched in history.

Cold purpose settled in the pit of his stomach.

Letting out the breath he'd been holding, he edged forward and parked the abomination in the shade of a giant oak. It was then that he discovered that the hand brake didn't hold. To Rafaelo's immense displeasure, he had to climb through a triple-strand wire fence to find a suitably large rock to place under the back tire, and by this stage his hands were dusty and his immaculate suit had a smudge of mud down the front.

"Madre de Dios," he cursed with quiet ferocity, then set off to find Phillip Saxon. And his destiny.

Caitlyn Ross noticed the stranger the moment he arrived at the memorial service being held for Roland Saxon in the winery's courtyard. Behind her the vineyards stretched to the hills in the distance, to the hills that formed The Divide. But for once she didn't spare a glance at the vines.

Her attention was riveted on the stranger. It wasn't his height, the dark, overlong hair or his black eyes that caught her attention. With Heath and Joshua Saxon in the vicinity, there was no shortage of tall, dark, black-eyed men.

Rather, it was the fire that lit those black eyes and made them snap with energy, the way he stood holding himself with stiff formality at the back of the crowd that had gathered to remember Roland Saxon.

She had no idea who he could be. Or what his association to the Saxons was. And that was unusual. Having worked here since she left university, Caitlyn was part of the inner circle of the family. But this man was definitely a stranger.

Beside her, someone sniffed and pulled out a handkerchief. Phillip Saxon had finished his speech.

Remembering the occasion, Caitlyn forced her attention away from the mystery man. Alyssa Blake was speaking now, a short, moving address. Roland had been her brother. No one had known that he'd been adopted by the Saxons as a baby until very recently. Caitlyn knew it had to be a huge adjustment for Heath, Joshua and Megan, the Saxon siblings, who had believed that Roland was bonded to them by blood.

Her gaze sneaked back to the stranger. Even sandwiched between Jim and Taine, two of her cellar hands, he stood apart. She watched as he scanned the gathering, those snapping eyes assessing…making a judgement…then moving on to the next person.

Who was he?

Yet another journalist come to dig up dirt on the family? They didn't need that. Not now.

She examined the tall, suit-clad body. Despite the dusty patches on his suit, he didn't look like a journalist. He couldn't be paparazzi because there was no giveaway bulge of an over-sized camera lens anywhere to be seen. She supposed he could be a school—or university—friend of Roland.

Caitlyn slipped through the throng, murmuring apologies as she went. It took her only a minute to skirt the edges of the gathering. She paused beside Jim, who made way for her with a sideways smile. Caitlyn nodded in acknowledgement and edged into the space created beside the stranger.

Yes, he was tall all right. At least three inches taller than her own five feet eleven inches.

Softly she murmured, "We haven't met."

He raked her with those hellfire eyes. A bolt of sensation shot through her. An awareness that she hadn't felt in a long, long time.

"I am Rafaelo Carreras." His voice was mesmerizing, the accent deliciously foreign. Within Caitlyn, in a deep-down sealed-off place, warmth uncurled. She tamped down the unwelcome sensation. No hint of New Zealand in that voice.

Perhaps not a school friend after all.

Curious, and wanting to hear him speak again, she asked, "Did you know Roland?"

It was possible. As marketing director of Saxon's Folly Estate & Wines, Roland had travelled all over the world.

"No."

One word, abruptly spoken. And clearly he wasn't volunteering any further information. Again the suspicion that he might be a news journalist, carrion descending to feast on the family's sorrow, stirred. The Saxons had been through enough. All her protective urges aroused, Caitlyn said in a low, fierce voice, "Then what are you doing here?"

He inspected her. His narrowed gaze started at her shoes—the serviceable black leather pumps that she'd had for ten years and only wore for wine shows. He considered her unstockinged legs, pale from a longer-than-normal winter spent under worn jeans. His gaze lingered on the hemline of her skirt, an unfashionable length this season. But then, she never wore anything other than jeans and trousers, so what did it matter? Then he studied the jacket that she wore. It had cost her a fortune and she'd only bought it because Megan, whose sense of style was fabulous, had insisted. The peach-coloured linen did wonderful things for her Celtic skin and ginger-blond hair—she knew that because Megan had told her—but it probably wasn't suitable for today's sombre occasion.

Finally he lifted his eyes to her face. As his gaze met hers, the impact jarred through her. There was nothing in the black depths to suggest that he'd liked anything he'd seen. To the contrary, she could find only a disdain that made her flinch.

"You are a member of the Saxon family?" He raised a haughty brow.

"No, but—"

"Then why I am here does not concern you."

Caitlyn blinked. She was not used to such blatant rudeness. How to deal with him? Her gaze flickered to Pita, the security guard who patrolled the winery every night. Since an incident three weeks ago when a pair of youths had caused mischief down at the stables, security at Saxon's Folly had been stepped up. Pita was big and burly. He would have plenty of men here to help evict this man if need be.

She eyed the dark-haired stranger covertly. It would take quite a few men to restrain him. Under the dark suit his body appeared lean and his shoulders broad. The man was built like a fighter— an impression strengthened by the harsh features, the ridged nose and fiery eyes. He wouldn't back away from a fight.

She held his gaze. "Well, I am concerned."

"Don't be."

His mouth clamped into a hard line causing apprehension to weigh heavily in Caitlyn's stomach. Another quick glance showed that Pita was still within earshot. She wavered. Should she summon him, have the stranger escorted away?

Did the Saxons need the commotion? She glanced around the gathering. Alyssa was speaking in a breaking voice about how she'd grown to know Roland through the memories of his mother and his siblings—Joshua, Heath and Megan. No, commotion was the last thing the Saxons needed right now.

What if this man turned out to be a valuable business connection? And she'd tried to have him thrown out? Caitlyn shuddered just thinking about it. No, she'd leave him alone. For now.

A rustle and the soft murmurs of the crowd caught her attention. Alyssa had finished speaking and was stepping down from the paved stage, wiping her eyes. Joshua Saxon moved forward and put his arm around her, his head close to Alyssa's as he led her away. Joshua and Alyssa were engaged now. Despite the upheavals in the past month, they had managed to find each other…and love.

A pang of some unfamiliar emotion shot through Caitlyn. Not jealousy—she'd never felt anything vaguely romantic toward Joshua—but something a little like envy.

She wanted to find love.

She was tired of being Caitlyn Ross, chief winemaker at Saxon's Folly, top graduate of her year…the smart student that all her fellow students considered one of the boys.

She wanted what other people had.

Love. Togetherness. A life.

But she knew that her chances of that were scant. Not that she was complaining. There was nothing wrong with her life. She loved Saxon's Folly. There had been a time when she'd hoped she and Heath Saxon might…

But there was little chance of that now. And to be truthful Heath had never seen her as anything other than Good Ol' Caitlyn. Damn, she was practically one of the boys.

Although nothing about the bold inspection she just received made her feel remotely like one of the boys. She resisted the temptation to slide her gaze sideways to the stranger beside her. His inspection had been heavy with male arrogance, but there was no doubt that he'd been assessing her as a woman.

Even if he had found her wanting.

It had been so long since she'd drawn any male attention— these days she took care to avoid it. At last, against her will, resenting the effect he had on her, she gave in to temptation and peered sideways, to see what those never-still eyes were looking at now, and her stomach plummeted into her practical black shoes.

He was gone.

Rafaelo had found his target.

Silently, unwaveringly, he made his way in the direction of the tall man with the distinguished wings of grey at his temples.

Phillip Saxon.

He stopped behind the older man and waited for what was clearly a memorial ceremony to end. He'd wanted to savour this meeting. He'd called Saxon, spoken to his PA, and without listening to her protests that Saxon wasn't seeing people right now, had advised that he would be arriving to meet with the older man. He hadn't revealed why he wanted to see Saxon—only that he was the owner of a Spanish vineyard of some reputation. But he hadn't planned for this meeting to take place in public.

A movement behind him caught his eye. Rafaelo frowned impatiently as he watched the crowd part for the tall, slim strawberry blonde who had waylaid him minutes before.

He tightened his lips as she came closer. She was not beautiful—she lacked the self-awareness that beautiful women possessed. But she had something…

Then he met her startlingly pale blue eyes, read the determination in them.

He glanced dismissively away. She couldn't stop what he'd come all the way to New Zealand to achieve. Nor would he allow himself to be distracted.

The crowd was shifting. A tall, black-haired man stood at the edge of the courtyard beside a vine and a rosebush that the raw earth beneath revealed had recently been planted.

"These have been planted in the memory of my brother, Roland. May he live in our hearts forever," the black-haired man said.

All around Rafaelo women were reaching for handkerchiefs. But he barely heard the gut-wrenching sobs of sorrow. He only heard the words *my brother, Roland.* So Roland Saxon was dead. That would make the speaker either Joshua or Heath Saxon. An unfamiliar heavy heat coalesced in his chest.

He turned to gaze at Phillip Saxon and instantly the emotion became identifiable. *Rage.* Saxon moved forward, away from him. The ceremony had ended.

Now.

Rafaelo tapped him on the shoulder. *"Disculpe."*

The older man spun round.

There was a long silence as Rafaelo stared into Phillip's face. He examined the narrow nose. The dark hair that sprung back from a high forehead. He stared into the dark eyes—so like his own—and watched them widen.

"No." The denial burst from Saxon.

Another beat of time passed. Rafaelo waited, letting the other man put it all together.

"It can't be." Saxon was shaking his head.

"Phillip?" The strawberry blonde stood there. "Is everything okay?"

Rafaelo resented his focus being taken from Saxon. But he did a double take at the unfriendly suspicion in the pale eyes that clashed with his. A frisson of a wholly unfamiliar sensation prickled the back of his neck. He did a startled double take.

Get rid of her. As a young man he'd survived countless bullfights by listening to his senses. He heeded the warning now.

"We would like some privacy, please," he demanded, giving her the freezing glare that he usually reserved for the paparazzi.

Phillip looked horrified at his statement.

"Do you want me to go?" Her words were directed at Saxon, but she never took her eyes off him.

"No—stay."

Rafaelo reassessed. She must be more important than he'd initially thought. *Estupido!* He could kick himself for dismissing her as a nonentity. Narrowing his eyes, he scrutinised her. He knew she wasn't Megan Saxon—he'd met Megan once, briefly, at a wine show in France several years before. This woman was too tall and her colouring was all wrong. And she'd denied being part of the family earlier.

So who the devil was she? He examined her from head to toe,

ignoring her indrawn breath. She lacked the polish of the circle the Saxons moved in, lacked the salon-set hair, the designer-label clothes. That meant she had to be an employee, he decided. A presumptuous one.

"You want her to stay? On your head may it rest," Rafaelo addressed Saxon. "I didn't think you'd want this conversation to be public knowledge. At least not until we've had an opportunity to negotiate."

Saxon understood. His spine straightened and relief flashed in his eyes, coupled with contempt.

He thought he could buy off Rafaelo.

"Caitlyn, perhaps you should leave us."

Caitlyn? That would be Caitlyn Ross. Rafaelo did a double take. She didn't look anything like what he'd anticipated of the acclaimed Saxon's Folly winemaker. He'd thought she'd be older for starters. More sophisticated. This woman looked to be in her midtwenties, too young to have accomplished everything that his research had told him she had.

Caitlyn was shaking her head. "No way am I leaving you alone with him. What he—" she jabbed a slender finger in Rafaelo's direction "—said sounded like a threat." The pale eyes duelled with his. "I'm staying right here."

Brave, too. Foolishly so. "You should stay out of things that do not concern you," he told her, lowering his voice.

"So now you're threatening *me*." Colour flooded her translucent skin.

"Advising, not threatening. There is a difference," Rafaelo pointed out with gentle irony. "This is family business…." He drew the phrase out mockingly. "It has nothing to do with you." Then he turned his narrow-eyed attention back to Phillip Saxon.

"The family's business has everything to do with me," she said hotly.

"Caitlyn is like family," Phillip spoke at the same time.

The look she gave Saxon was filled with gratitude—and annoyed Rafaelo immensely. He pushed his hands into the pockets of his suit pants and glared at both of them.

Saxon swallowed convulsively and Rafaelo watched mercilessly as the man sought the words that might make Rafaelo go away.

He wouldn't find them.

For the first time since he'd learned the truth, Rafaelo felt his heart lighten. He started to enjoy himself. Saxon was in a tight spot and he wouldn't get out. And this woman, who looked as innocuous as milk and honey, was proving to be a challenge that he had not foreseen.

"Caitlyn, dear, where did you arrange with the caterers for the canapés to be served?" Kay Saxon sounded harried as she joined them.

As Caitlyn opened her mouth to answer Saxon's wife, Rafaelo stepped forward. "Introduce us," he commanded.

Phillip Saxon blanched. He gave his wife an agonised look, and then his eyes darted back to Rafaelo.

"I… Kay, this is—" He broke off.

Rafaelo waited in stony silence.

"I'm sorry," Phillip said at last, "I do not know your name."

Rafaelo smiled. It was not a nice smile. He was too angry for that. "My name is Rafaelo Carreras."

The wife gave him a polite smile and held out her hand. "How do you do, Mr. Carreras."

So she thought him a business associate. She had absolutely no idea. Rafaelo's smile widened and his anger sharpened. "Ah, a handshake is so English. And I know we will be getting to know each other extremely well." He stepped forward and brushed her cheeks with his in the European way. Over her shoulder he saw the horror…the despair…in Phillip Saxon's eyes. He had the look of a man tied to the railway tracks in the face of the rush of an oncoming express—his tortured expression revealed that he knew the crash was inevitable, that he could do nothing except wait for the approaching disaster.

Good, the man was afraid. Phillip Saxon had sensed that he, Rafaelo, could destroy his privileged world, everything he held dear.

Then a movement forced his attention to Caitlyn. Her hand was outstretched. "If you're going to get to know the Saxons well, then we'd better introduce ourselves, too. I'm—"

He ignored the proffered hand, and her introduction trailed away into silence. Placing his hands on her shoulders, he leaned forward. She smelled of wildflowers, soft and subtle.

"Encantado de conocerte." Very happy to meet you. His lips brushed one cheek, he heard her gasp. His head lifted. Deliberately he kissed her other cheek, no social brush, but a careful placing of his mouth against the pale, silken milk-and-honey skin. He paused for a moment before whispering in her ear, "The pleasure is all mine, Miss Ross."

She pulled back, a startled expression on her face, a touch of fear in her eyes. "You know my name?"

She was too modest. Of course he knew her name. Rising star. Winner, two years ago, of a silver medal at the World Wine Challenge. And last year she and Saxon had secured a coveted gold medal. His mouth curved. "You'd be surprised by how much I know."

He heard Phillip's indrawn breath.

The fear subsided and her eyes sparkled with anger. "Perhaps you don't know as much as you think, Mr. Carreras. It's *Ms.* Ross."

"Ah," he said softly, eyes narrowing at her attempt to hold him at a distance with icy formality. "I should've known." And he watched the fresh annoyance flare in those pale, clear eyes.

He preferred her anger to her fear. For a split second he wondered what she was afraid of—because she couldn't know why he was here. Then Saxon shifted and he moved his attention back to the man he'd come across the world to find.

"Caitlyn, Kay, perhaps it is better that I speak to Mr. Carreras alone." Saxon sounded anxious.

A frown pleated Kay's forehead. "But why should that be necessary?"

"There may be things that your husband hasn't told you, Mrs. Saxon." The address held a certain irony that only Rafaelo was aware of.

She waved a dismissive hand. "My husband tells me everything."

"Perhaps not." Rafaelo's mouth slashed upward.

"You're impertinent."

It was not Kay Saxon who spoke. Rafaelo turned his attention on the blonde. If anyone was impertinent, it was her. He was the Marques de Las Carreras. All his life the family name had commanded respect. Until now…

"Be careful," he murmured.

"Or what?" Caitlyn challenged. "What are you threatening to do? This is Saxon property, there is security—" She gestured toward a burly man in a dark uniform.

"Caitlyn." Phillip put a hand on her arm.

But with her protective instincts roused, she would not be stopped. "Call Pita. He can't just walk into Saxon's Folly and threaten you, Phillip."

Rafaelo stared at her. "I am not threatening anyone. I will not be evicted. But I am certain that that he—" Rafaelo couldn't bring himself to address the man directly "—would prefer to talk alone."

Phillip released her. "Caitlyn, perhaps he is right."

"I would like to hear what this man has to say, what he thinks you might not have told me." Kay Saxon dug her Ferragamo-clad heels into the ground. "Caitlyn is right—he is impertinent."

Anger ignited deep in Rafaelo's heart. All the inconveniences of the past two days flamed high, and the pain and rage he'd been keeping under tight control for the past months burst into a blinding conflagration.

He raised an arched, black eyebrow. "It is impertinent to travel all the way to New Zealand to meet my father?"

Phillip dropped his head forward into his hands and uttered a hoarse groan.

"Your father?" Caitlyn looked bewildered. "What does that have to do with—"

Rafaelo glared at her. "It has nothing to do with you—it is a family matter. But trust me, Phillip Saxon is my father."

Two

Trust him?

Never! Caitlyn drew a shaking breath but kept quiet. Lashing out at the arrogant Spaniard wouldn't help the fact that she'd exposed Kay to a dreadful revelation.

If she hadn't pushed him, challenged him, the outcome might have been very different…

"What did you say your name was?" Kay was asking Rafaelo, her face suddenly pale.

"Rafaelo Carreras."

Slowly Kay started to shake her head. "I don't know anyone by that name."

"He's lying," Caitlyn said fiercely, determined not to let Kay be upset. She had enough to contend with already.

"Kay—"

"Wait." Kay warded off Phillip's attempt to talk to her. "Carreras, it's Spanish, isn't it?"

Caitlyn didn't like the sudden gleam in Kay's eyes. Nor, it appeared, did Phillip.

"Kay, love, let's go. There are people waiting to pay their respects." Phillip curled an arm around his wife's shoulders, the skin stretched thin across his cheekbones.

But Kay didn't budge.

Rafaelo placed his hands on his hips, and thrust his shoulders forward. He looked ready for battle. "Madam, my full name is Rafaelo Lopez y Carreras."

"Lopez? There was a girl…a young woman…" Kay's brow pleated as her voice trailed away. "I think her name was Maria Lopez. In fact, I'm sure of it. She was researching her family… I seem to remember that her father, or perhaps an uncle, had died in the Napier earthquake. Yes, that's right. It's coming back to me. Her name *was* Maria."

"My mother's name is Maria," Rafaelo said in a flat voice, his eyes shooting daggers at Phillip.

Eyes widening, Kay put her hand over her mouth and, shrugging out from under his arm, turned to her husband. "Tell me this isn't true."

Caitlyn's stomach dropped like a stone at the expression in Kay's eyes. She clenched her hands into fists. Surely, Kay couldn't believe what Rafaelo claimed was true?

Phillip took a large white handkerchief from his pocket and, without unfolding it, rubbed it across his brow.

"You are not going to deny it, are you?" Kay's face had drawn into tight lines. She turned her attention back to Rafaelo, studying him with critical eyes. "How old are you?"

"Thirty-five."

Kay was not telling Rafaelo to get lost.

"That's the same age as Roland." Kay paused and sucked in an audible breath. "When were you born?"

Rafaelo told her.

Hurt flickered across Kay's face. "That makes you Phillip's eldest son…even if Roland our—my—first child hadn't died."

There was a world of reproach in the look that Kay gave Phillip.

Hurriedly he reached for her. "Kay, I'm sorry. I never—" He broke off, shamefaced.

"Never wanted me to know?"

Phillip didn't answer and Kay tugged her hand free and walked away. After a horrible silence, Phillip took off after her.

Finding that her hands were shaking, Caitlyn balled them against her mouth. God. It had all happened so fast…

And it appeared that Rafaelo wasn't lying.

A sideways glance revealed that Rafaelo's face held no expression. No glee. No gloating. So why had he done it? Why had he come all the way across the world and dropped this devastating bombshell on the Saxons?

He met her questioning gaze with a decided lack of expression and said, "So I am not a liar."

Then Rafaelo was walking away from her, too, his back ramrod-straight, his black head held at a proud, arrogant tilt. Caitlyn stared after him, her mouth hanging open. Finally she came to her senses.

"What were you hoping to achieve by staging that little scene?" She hurled the words like pebbles at the space between his shoulders.

He stopped, then turned.

Caitlyn glanced around. A little way off a couple stared curiously in their direction. Farther away groups stood around talking. "It's too public here for the conversation I have in mind. Come with me."

He didn't look like the kind of man who followed orders. She half expected him not to follow as she crossed the lane that led past the winery to the house and wound her way along the shoulder of the hill, down the northern slope planted with

Cabernet Franc vines. For once Caitlyn didn't notice the pale green of the leaves, or how the land opened up to meadows where wildflowers had started to bloom in deep drifts along the fence line. She was too mad.

His fault.

Normally, she was even-tempered, easy to get along with—she never lost her temper and rarely even told off any of her cellar hands. But Rafaelo Carreras had managed to get under her skin with his intransigence, with his hard-ass, unbending attitude. She glanced back, he was following. Good.

She quickened her pace.

Caitlyn took him to the stable block. As they entered the yard in front of the L-shaped block, several horses stuck their heads over the half doors, ears pricked with interest. The familiar warm smell of horses and hay calmed her a little. At the end of the row, one stall was closed top and bottom and Caitlyn could hear the animal inside battering the door with his hooves as he demanded to be let out.

That would be Lady Killer. Apart from him, there should be no interruptions. Certainly, there would be no danger of being overheard by guests who'd come to attend Roland's memorial service.

She swung around and glared at Rafaelo. "Do you have any idea what you interrupted?"

"I called the winery. I made an appointment."

Caitlyn raised her eyebrows. "I don't think so. Not for today. Not when Kay and Phillip are unveiling a memorial plaque for their son."

"No, no. The appointment was for yesterday." His hands raked his hair. "But I experienced some delays."

She scanned his appearance. Not even the wrinkles and specks of dust could hide the fact that the suit was unlike anything she'd seen before. It fitted like it had been handmade—even if it was looking a little shabby right now. "The security scare in London?" She nodded at his startled look. "I heard about it on the news. I'm sorry, but Phillip and Kay haven't been taking appointments for the last few days."

He looked a little abashed. "The woman who answered the phone said something but I wasn't listening."

So he wasn't lying. The frustration in his eyes was too real.

"You must've spoken to Amy, the winery's PA. Roland was her fiancé." Poor, poor Amy. She would almost certainly not have remembered to tell Phillip about any appointment. She was perilously close to a breakdown. "So I'm sorry, but Phillip probably didn't get the message." But that still didn't excuse Rafaelo's harsh behaviour. "Once you realised that a memorial ceremony was taking place, couldn't you have left?"

"So the memorial service is for Roland? The eldest son?"

His face wore a strange expression. Caitlyn gave up trying to decipher what it meant. "Yes, Roland died in a car accident, several weeks ago." The night of the annual Saxon's Folly masked ball. "A terrible tragedy."

"My condolences." He bowed his head. Briefly. Politely. Then, like a dog with a bone, continued, "I have travelled many miles, I came with a purpose—I'd made an appointment. I wasn't to know Saxon knew nothing of it. Nor do I have any intention of turning tail and leaving without fulfilling that purpose."

"That's it? That's all you can say?" Caitlyn stared at him in disbelief. "After that confrontation you just forced?"

"I had no intention of forcing a confrontation—it was you who provoked that."

He gave her a frown filled with dislike. Caitlyn opened her mouth, then shut it again. Oh, why hadn't she stayed out of it?

Yet she knew that would've been impossible. She'd taken one look at the tall, dark foreigner, heard the sardonic edge to his voice as he harangued Phillip and she'd leapt into the fray to protect her employer. Hell, Phillip was more than an employer. He was her sounding board…her mentor…a dear friend.

"You must understand that the Saxons are like family to me." It was true. "I could no more leave you to bully Phillip than I could walk away from a delinquent drowning a kitten."

"I am not a bully," he growled, blood rushing under his olive skin. "I am not a delinquent. I do not drown kittens. I am a man of honour, something that your employer is not. I would never leave a young woman pregnant and alone."

Suddenly aware of his height and the strength of him as he loomed over her, Caitlyn felt a whisper of fear and took a step back.

He followed, relentlessly closing the space she'd claimed. "I wanted to face my cowardly father with the fact that he has a son he has never cared to acknowledge—and a woman who he had abandoned without giving her any emotional or financial support."

Another step and the whitewashed wall of the stables pressed against her back; Caitlyn could feel the roughness of the plaster through the linen jacket. She swallowed nervously. "Maybe he didn't know—"

"He knew!" Rafaelo loomed over her, dark and menacing, and planted a balled fist on either side of her head. "My mother wrote to him when she first learned she was pregnant."

"Perhaps—" Her voice cracked as he bent forward. Up close the snapping eyes were full of anger, his mouth drawn into a hard line that highlighted the small white scar below his bottom lip. No sign showed of the good humour that the laugh lines around his eyes suggested.

She didn't know this man at all.

He was a stranger.

What had possessed her to seek out privacy far from everyone else? Caitlyn swallowed again, horribly conscious of how isolated they were here in the empty stable yard.

Bravely she found her voice. "Perhaps the letter went astray."

"My mother wrote to him again, she was desperate. Is it likely that *two* letters went astray? New Zealand is, after all, hardly Mars."

The turmoil in his eyes twisted Caitlyn's insides into a knot and her anxiety about her own safety subsided. She fell silent. It *did* sound bad. But she couldn't believe Phillip would act so callously. Despite Rafaelo's accusations, she knew Phillip *was* a man of honour, a decent man, respected throughout the region for his business acumen and the fund-raising he did for charity.

She *had* to make Rafaelo understand that.

But before she could try to convince him, he pushed his hands away from the wall. The suffocating space between them widened, and Caitlyn sucked in a breath of relief.

"My mother even contacted him by telephone. Phillip Saxon made it clear that he wasn't interested in the child he had fathered, told my mother that he wouldn't be leaving his wife." There was a corrosive bitterness beneath that exotic accent.

Caitlyn glimpsed pain and suppressed rage in his expressive eyes. Unbidden, her hand came up, driven by an urge to rest it on his shoulder, to comfort him. Then the memory of his head bending over hers—of the suffocating closeness of a moment ago—returned and a sharp sliver of the poisonous fear pierced her. Hastily she dropped her hand to her side.

"There must have been some mistake," she whispered at last, thinking the response that he roused in her was definitely a mistake. She didn't want, or need, this.

"It was no mistake. Phillip Saxon abandoned her."

The edge in his voice took her mind off her body's incomprehensible reaction and made her think about what it must have been like for his mother to find herself alone and pregnant. Three decades ago it would have been worse; society had been much less accepting.

Yet Caitlyn couldn't help the wave of sympathy for Kay that

flooded her. Poor Kay! How humiliating this must be. How horrible to discover her husband's betrayal of their marriage vows at a time when she was struggling to come to terms with grief over the loss of her son.

In front of her Rafaelo shifted, his eyes unseeing, focused on an inner hell.

The last lingering vestige of apprehension left her. Caitlyn stepped away from the wall. "You're not the only one who has suffered." Surely Rafaelo would see that he had more in common with his father than he believed? "Phillip lost a son recently. Can't you find it in yourself to show him pity?"

"I'm well aware that I am not the only person to suffer bereavement." From this close her eyes were level with his mouth. His mouth…

Quickly she glanced up, only to find Rafaelo looking down his haughty nose at her. At once Caitlyn realised that he'd misunderstood her.

"I meant both of you are grieving. Perhaps you can offer comfort—"

"I have no intention of offering him anything," Rafaelo growled. "I owe him nothing. *Nada.*"

Caitlyn's cheeks grew hot at his stubborn intransigence. "He's your father, and he's just lost a son. Why don't y—"

The black eyebrows jerked together. Something violent flashed in the depths of his stormy eyes. "Phillip Saxon is *not* my real father. My father is dead. My father taught me to ride, to fish, to swim—and about wine. And that man is not Saxon."

"I'm sorry," she muttered in a subdued tone, not knowing what else to say.

He sighed then, a harsh, grating sound. "On his deathbed, the man who all my life I'd believed to be my father, informed me that he and my mother had lied to me, that I was not his son."

He'd felt betrayed. The sympathy Caitlyn felt for him grew.

It had been wrong of his mother to keep the truth from him. But what choice would Maria have had? She'd probably wanted to forget Phillip existed. Now Rafaelo had arrived at Saxon's Folly, betrayed, grieving…angry at the world.

It was an explosive situation. "Kay doesn't deserve—"

"I concede that my timing is unfortunate." The dark eyes lost a little of their angry fire. "But it was not my intention to deliberately set out to cause Kay Saxon pain."

"Only Phillip," she retorted, and watched his head jerk back. "You want to hurt him. *Why?* Because he rejected you when you were a child? Or because you're scared that he won't accept you now?"

A range of emotions flickered across his face, receding one by one, until only irritation remained. "I am not a child. I am a realist. I don't even know this man who fathered me—"

"But you want to get to know him?"

"No! I don't need to know him. I dislike him. I have no respect for hi—"

"So you want to wound him, don't you?" Caitlyn could feel herself getting hot and bothered as annoyance spread through her. "What do you plan to do to make up for the hurt he caused you?"

"It's not about me. I want the bastard to pay for what he did to my mother." The words burst from him in a torrent.

The silence that fell between them was deafening, broken only by the scrape of an iron shoe as a horse shifted.

Rafaelo looked astonished.

There was another emotion, too. Bewilderment? Confusion? Irritation? It passed too quickly for Caitlyn to read. Either way, it showed there was a chink in that impenetrable armour.

Before she could respond, her cell phone rang. "Where are you?" Megan demanded. "We need you."

Oh, damn. She was supposed to be helping with the reception.

"Be there shortly." Caitlyn hit the button to end the call.

Meeting his gaze, she said, "I have to go—and so should you. I think you've caused enough disruption today."

His eyes flashed. "I have every right—"

"Not today," Caitlyn said with certainty. "You need to calm down before you speak to your father." She tensed, waiting for him to rail at her for calling Phillip that. But to her surprise he didn't interrupt, so she continued, "Give the Saxons a chance to mourn, to remember Roland with dignity."

His eyes narrowed until all she could see were slits of onyx. "Tomorrow."

Caitlyn started to thank him. The compromise could not have been easy, but he steamrolled over her. "In the evening I am flying back to Spain. I do not have time to—how do you say?— twiddle my fingers."

"Twiddle your thumbs." She started to smile, refusing to let his disgruntlement spoil her pleasure in his concession. "It will be for only one night."

Rafaelo stared at her. Caitlyn shifted uncomfortably.

"You will have dinner with me tonight? At my hotel?"

Suddenly his eyes held a lazy warmth that turned Caitlyn's knees to liquid. The sensation was disturbing…and extremely unwelcome.

"No, I will not have dinner with you." She couldn't. Dared not. Not even to try and talk him out of the hatred he held toward the Saxons. "But may I suggest—"

"You are about to order me around again, *no?*"

She drew a deep breath. "No. Not order. Make a suggestion that will benefit both you and Phillip—and your relationship in the future."

"I have told you, I have no relationship with him." He was all disdain again, looking down that arrogant nose, the glimmer of interest that had warmed his eyes a moment ago well and truly doused.

The Spanish grandee, Caitlyn thought with a brief pang of regret at the loss of his more approachable manner. Then she said, "I think you do want a relationship with your father, otherwise why else did you come all this way?"

"Because—" He checked himself. "This is none of your concern."

Caitlyn suppressed the urge to roll her eyes skyward. "Oh, yes, because I'm not family, right?"

He stared at her unblinkingly, until an uncomfortable prickle started beneath the loose hair at her nape and shivered down her spine.

Hastily Caitlyn said, "I suggest that you spend the evening planning how best to cement the relationship with your father. I also think you should call tomorrow and let Phillip know that you're coming and give him some idea what you wish to see him about."

The edge of his lips curled up. The smile—if it could be called that—was full of male superiority and mockery. And it set her teeth on edge. It was a smile that made it clear that he would not take advice. Not from her. Not from anyone. Rafaelo Carreras was his own man and he would do what the hell he wanted.

Finally his lips moved. "It is not my way to let the opposition prepare."

Damn, but he was annoying with his formal diction, his immaculately tailored suit, and his give-not-one-inch manner…and that beautiful mouth that said such hateful, intransigent things.

"He's your father…not the opposition." Caitlyn heard her voice rising.

His face darkened and his lips parted.

She struggled for calm. "Okay, okay. You don't need to say it."

"Say what?"

"That he's not your father."

Rafaelo's mouth snapped shut, but his expression remained black as thunder. As she watched that very same mouth compressed into the hard line she was starting to recognise. Then he said, "Phillip Saxon has done nothing to earn the title of father. Right now he is my enemy."

Caitlyn tore her gaze from that riveting mouth and met the pair of black, smouldering eyes, where she read his implacable hatred for his father. And unexpectedly her heart ached for Rafaelo—and the Saxons.

After the disturbance he'd caused, Caitlyn was determined to escort Rafaelo politely off the estate herself even if the delay meant that she'd have to contend with Megan's wrath. She wanted no further chance encounters between Rafaelo and the Saxons. At least, not until this day was over.

But as she marched him back along the lane that led to the winery complex, Heath's voice broke in from behind them, "Caitlyn, do you know what happened to Mother? She's crying."

"Uh…" Caitlyn's heart sank and she suppressed the urge to utter a short, sharp curse. Making her way to the verge of the lane to get out of the path of an approaching car, she said, "Kay's crying?"

Kay hadn't cried since Roland had died. Her unnatural stoicism had caused the entire family much concern. But given today's emotionally charged occasion, it was hardly surprising that she'd broken down. Beside her Rafaelo paused, too. Caitlyn was aware of his body quivering with tension as he slowly turned to face Heath Saxon.

"I regret I said something that upset your mother." Rafaelo stood his ground, lean and dangerous as a jungle cat. "But that was never my intention."

Caitlyn looked from one man to the other—half brother to half brother. Now that she knew the truth she could see the similarities. Heath was younger, of course. But the dark eyes, the slope of their angular cheekbones, the determined set of the jaw branded them blood kin. Would Heath recognise it?

"What exactly did he say?"

Heath spoke directly to Caitlyn. He didn't even deign to look at the Spaniard. Misery sliced through Caitlyn as she recognised the icy set to Heath's features. She sensed the whole unfortunate situation was about to escalate to the next level.

And she had been the catalyst.

Before she could answer, Rafaelo cut in, "I am here, you may address me. I have a name. It is Rafaelo Carreras."

Heath gave him a brief, insultingly dismissive look. "Did you say something?"

Caitlyn tensed.

But Rafaelo didn't rise to the bait. "My name is Rafaelo Carreras—"

"I don't particularly care what your name is," Heath interrupted. "I want to know what you said to upset my mother."

Enough was enough. That had been more than rude; it had been downright incendiary. Caitlyn stepped between the two men.

"Heath—" She broke off and rested her hand on his arm, dearly familiar, and tried not to tremble.

It was painful to see Heath and Rafaelo bristling at each other like this. Profiles so similar, so classic, like two sides of an ancient coin.

"Heath, Caitlyn, Megan sent me to find you both. Aren't you coming to join our guests for coffee?" Joshua Saxon was crossing the cobbled lane toward them.

"First I want to hear what he—" Heath gestured to Rafaelo with a contemptuous flick of his head "—said to make Mother cry."

Joshua's eyebrows jerked up. "Mother is crying?"

"Yes, and he's responsible."

Caitlyn felt terrible. She'd caused this. If she'd left well enough alone, Rafaelo would have confronted Phillip alone— without her and Kay present—and there would've been a whole different outcome.

"Heath," she said. "It isn't his fault Kay is crying. It's m—"

"He might not have intended it." Heath shoved his shoulders forward. "But whatever he said still upset her." Heath ploughed forward, thrusting Caitlyn aside with one hand. She stumbled against the kerb stones. Heath made a grab for her, apologising profusely as she regained her footing.

Rafaelo moved like lightning, his jaw clenched tight. "Be careful," he snarled at Heath. To Caitlyn he said, "Are you okay?"

She gave him a small smile. "I'm fine. Just clumsy." The stumble had been worth it. It had checked Heath's aggressive rush at Rafaelo.

Except Rafaelo was staring at where Heath's hand rested on her arm. Discomforted, feeling as though she'd been caught doing something wrong, Caitlyn pulled free.

Heath raked his fingers through his hair. "You still haven't told me what you said to my mother." There was aggression in every line of Heath's lean, loose-limbed body. Caitlyn knew that stance. Even in university days, Heath-the-hellraiser had never backed away from a brawl, often throwing the first punch.

It would be terrible if he hit Rafaelo.

And for once, Caitlyn wasn't sure that Heath would win. Rafaelo looked tough and mean, his eyes narrowed, the small scar beneath his mouth pale against his dark skin. *A fighter.* An accomplished one, she suspected.

That thought was disturbingly disloyal.

Then Rafaelo's shoulders squared. "I came here today because six months ago I learned something has been kept secret from me all my life. I learned that the man I believed is my father never was, that a man who lives across the world is."

Caitlyn felt a little of the tension seep out of her. Rafaelo was making every attempt to stay calm and measured in the face of Heath's animosity. Perhaps the situation could still be saved.

"What does that have to do with—"

"You're Heath? Correct?" asked Rafaelo.

"Why are you asking?" demanded Heath.

Rafaelo shifted his attention to the taller of the two Saxons. "Then you must be Joshua."

Joshua nodded, his eyes hooded.

"I am Rafaelo—" he held up a peremptory hand as Heath started to interrupt "—and I am your half brother."

Heath sucked in his breath, an audible sound. "I don't think so. I think you're a scammer!"

"Heath!" Caitlyn's hands went to her mouth.

"This is not a scam." Rafaelo's hand dropped and curled into a fist at his side. "You think this is easy for me?"

"You expect us to believe that you found out six months ago? And it took you until now to act on this laughable claim?" Heath sneered. "Why wait so long?"

"I had responsibilities. I had a man to bury—the man I believed to be my father," Rafaelo said with what Caitlyn considered great restraint. "Afterward there was my mother to comfort and legalities to tend. I came as soon as my obligations allowed."

With Rafaelo standing to one side, his fisted hands the only evidence that he wasn't quite as relaxed as the curl of his lips would have them all believe, the air grew thick with menace. Caitlyn held her breath. Heath and Joshua stood shoulder to shoulder, brother beside brother, staring him down.

Caitlyn had seen that pose before. She shuddered. It wouldn't take much for the frozen tableau to ignite into a brawl.

Determined to prevent that at all costs, she stepped forward to stand beside Rafaelo and, without thinking, placed a hand on his arm. "Rafaelo is about to leave."

He turned his head. "I am?"

There was a sardonic light in his eyes.

She tightened her grip on his arm. With a sudden sense of

shock she felt the texture of the fine wool of his dark suit give under her fingertips, felt the hardness of flesh and muscle beneath. It scorched her.

"Yes, you are. I was walking you to your car," she said with quiet determination, even as her heart began to race, and the terrifying fear that she worked so hard to avoid bolted through her bloodstream.

"That's our Cait!" Heath said loudly. "Mate, you better do what she says if you know what's best for you."

Rafaelo went rigid under her hold. "I am not a milksop." He gave Heath an insulting head-to-toe-and-back-again look. "I do not let a woman placate the enemy on my behalf. I do what I want—not what a woman dictates." When his eyes met Caitlyn's appalled gaze, his features curdled with contempt. "So you fight his battles all the time?"

Instantly the thrill of apprehension that touching him roused and her irritation at his overt chauvinism were superseded by horrified concern. Not for him—if the Spanish grandee had his features rearranged by Heath it would serve him right. The concern was all reserved for Heath…for the Saxons. Kay would hate to learn that her sons had gotten into a brawl on this day because she'd cried.

Was Rafaelo stupid? Did he not realise what he was provoking? Or did he want a fight for reasons of incomprehensible masculine pride?

That notion caused her to worry even more. But there would be no fight. Not if she could help it.

"Sometimes the little woman knows best," Caitlyn cooed up at Rafaelo, fluttering her lashes, and moving squarely in front of him, daringly brushing his lapels free of imaginary fluff. Anything to stop Heath swinging the punch that she suspected was pending. But the tension in the lean body so close to hers, the sudden bulge in the chest muscles under her fingers, made her wish she hadn't been so reckless.

Heath watched and laughed uproariously. "Our kitten is now Cait-the-seductress. Priceless."

That hurt.

She blinked back the sudden prick of tears and, feeling totally ridiculous, she yanked her hands away from Rafaelo.

Furiously angry with Heath for highlighting how unwomanly she was, with Rafaelo for starting this whole debacle just by being there, and with Joshua for doing nothing to stop it, Caitlyn swung away, turning her back on all three of them.

"Fine," she said in a voice that indicated the situation was anything but okay. She pushed an annoying strand of hair out of her face, wishing it was back in its customary ponytail. And wishing that she could kick off the uncomfortable shoes and skirt and unfamiliar jacket. Above all, wishing she was a million miles from this maddening trio. "Do it your way. I'll just leave you all to bash each other's brains out. See if I care."

"Slowly, *querida*." Rafaelo caught her arm.

His hold was firm, possessive. His fingers were square and tanned against the apricot hue of her jacket. No rings. But the knuckles were ridged. Yes, a fighter.

Shockingly, her arm started to tingle alarmingly under the warmth of his touch. Caitlyn lifted her gaze and gave him a fulminating glare. There was speculation in his expression—and something else. He glanced at Heath and back to her. He released her arm, and his gaze became calculating.

And that was when she knew that he'd seen what no one else had. The miserable remains of her hopeless infatuation for Heath.

Horror swept her. He wouldn't say anything, would he?

Then she realised that of course he would. Why shouldn't he? The damn man didn't like her one little bit. She'd been a thorn in his side since the moment he'd arrived. Why shouldn't he humiliate her?

But instead of adding to her humiliation, she heard him say,

"Caitlyn will walk with me. I am leaving. But be warned, I will be back."

Relief flooded her as he wheeled away from Joshua and Heath. But Caitlyn wasn't sure whether it was because the fistfight had been forestalled…or because one of her heart's innermost secrets had been saved. Either way, she couldn't help feeling a surge of gratitude toward Rafaelo as she trotted off in his wake.

Three

A lanky youth with a baseball cap jammed down on his head was standing with his back to the door when Rafaelo walked into the reception area of the winery the next morning.

"Buenos días," he said, "I'm looking for Phillip Saxon."

The youth turned and Rafaelo found himself staring into a pair of very familiar pale blue eyes. No youth this. Those unique eyes could only belong to one person…

Caitlyn Ross.

He did a rapid inspection to see how he could have made such an unforgivable mistake. The jeans she wore were faded and baggy, stained with the juice of grapes. The oversized navy-and-white striped T-shirt bore a sports team's logo and swamped her slender body. The baseball cap pulled low over her forehead hid the fine, beautiful copper-blond hair. Every trace of the feminine creature he'd met yesterday had vanished.

Except for the eyes.

Those hadn't changed. They met his directly, challenging him, stirring a primal need. The slow pounding of his heart under the force of her gaze ensured that he paid careful attention to everything about her.

"Did you call to let Phillip know you were coming?"

The awakening attraction withered. "Are you always so—" he searched for the word he wanted "—bossy?"

Irritation flashed in her eyes. She edged toward a stone archway. "I'm not bossy. I just don't want you causing trouble with the Saxons."

¡Vale! Okay, she'd made her feelings clear enough. Rafaelo followed her through the arch into the winery. Immediately the familiar smell of French oak surrounded him. Two rows of vats lined the long, dimly lit room where they stood. Another step forward brought a newer fragrance. The feminine fragrance of wildflowers. Caitlyn's fragrance.

Subtle. Evocative. Unexpectedly fragile.

Rafaelo drew a deep breath. "So you've decided that I'm the big bad wolf coming to eat your lambs?"

She shook her head. "I'd hardly describe Phillip or his sons as lambs."

Tipping his head to one side, Rafaelo said, "Perhaps they are the wolves…and I am the lamb?"

"Cute!" She beamed at him. It broke up the serious intensity of her face and revealed a dimple on the left side of her mouth and gave her expression a mischievous cast. "Definitely not. You're a wolf—pretending to be in lamb's clothing."

Desire jolted through him. But he wanted to laugh, too. The dimness of the winery seemed to grow brighter. The unrelenting heaviness that had consumed Rafaelo ever since he'd first learned he wasn't fathered by the man he'd always called *Papa* but by some not-so-perfect stranger who'd never wanted anything to do with him—or his sweet mother—started to lift.

"I am a Lopez on my mother's side—so maybe I am part wolf. You'd better take care and treat me with *mucho* respect." He gave her a lazy grin, showing his teeth, his heart lightening still further as her smile broke into peals of unrestrained laughter.

"Lopez? Oh, of course, lupis. Yes, you'd have to be a wolf."

Her gaze dropped to his mouth, and the fresh wave of desire that crashed through him shook Rafaelo to the core.

"My, my, what sharp teeth you have," she mocked gently.

"Is that an invitation for the wolf to bite?" He leaned toward her, drawn by the irrepressible sparkle in her eyes. The scent of wildflowers intensified. He wanted to yank her into his arms. Kiss her until she was breathless. "To hunt?"

She flushed, a flood of scarlet across the pale skin and drew quickly away, her smile fading.

"No…no."

The sudden panicked look she gave him made Rafaelo frown.

Before he could ask her what he'd done to bring that blind fear to her eyes, she shuffled away. "Uh, I have to go. You'll find Phillip in his office. Go out that door, past the stainless steel vats. Turn right and head down the corridor to the office at the end."

And then she was hurrying away without offering to show him the way into his father's lair. Rafaelo stared after her tall, slim body with consternation. What had happened? One moment she'd been laughing, teasing him…there'd been a bubble of suppressed excitement surrounding them…and then she'd run.

What had scared her? Him? *Dios,* he didn't pose any danger—at least, not to her.

Still trapped in a tizzy over the amused interest she'd glimpsed in Rafaelo's eyes and the shameful surge of desire that had been so quickly followed by fear, Caitlyn crossed the forecourt outside the brick structure that housed two immense stainless steel vats.

As she approached the tasting shed, a streak of silver flashed past her peripheral vision.

Heath.

She paused. For so long she'd been attuned to his every move. A glimpse of his silver Lamborghini usually stirred secret yearnings. Impossible yearnings. But today she merely frowned. With Rafaelo here, Heath's presence would only lead to more tension.

Heath seldom appeared during working hours. It was no secret that he and Phillip had differences of opinion—differences that had been significant enough for Heath to walk out of his job as winemaker at Saxon's Folly three years ago.

She lifted a hand and waved.

Heath waved back. Slowly Caitlyn made her way over to where he'd pulled the car in beside Rafaelo's beaten-up rental. Heath was already clambering out of the low-slung car under the angled doors.

Propping her hip against the battered vehicle, she folded her arms and asked, "What are you doing here?"

"Dad called. He wants me here for a meeting."

"Phillip called you?" She raised her eyebrows in surprise. Phillip and his youngest son usually did little but argue—each convinced that their own opinion was the only one that could be right.

"Yep. Before you start thinking reconciliation, he called Joshua, too. So your job is safe, kitten," Heath teased, ruffling the top of her head.

She ducked her head away and pulled off the baseball cap. "I'm not worried about you wanting my job. You put me up for it, remember?"

He tugged her ponytail. "Course I remember, rat's tail."

Instead of the hopeless longing that usually filled her at his joking, brotherly manner, Caitlyn felt only annoyance. And irritation with herself for wasting so much time on a man who never looked past the fact that she'd been a first-year student when he'd been studying for his doctorate. Then she'd been one of the few girls in a department dominated by guys and had chosen to become one of them—rather than the trophy that they bickered over, a path that would have put her truly on the outside.

She couldn't help thinking of the way that Rafaelo had looked at her in the winery earlier. His scrutiny had made her wish she hadn't been wearing scuffed sneakers and stained jeans.

That was until they'd started the talk about wolves and hunting, before she'd chickened out and hightailed it away as fast as her legs could carry her. Predatory males scared her spitless.

She shoved Rafaelo out of her thoughts and concentrated on Heath. "So Joshua is coming, too?"

"Yeah, apparently there's someone that Dad wants us to meet."

Rafaelo.

It had to be.

Phillip couldn't know that Joshua and Heath had already met Rafaelo yesterday…and almost come to blows.

Or maybe he did. "Uh…Heath…did you say anything to your parents about meeting Rafaelo yesterday?"

"Rafaelo?" Heath's cell phone started to ring and he dug into the pocket of his jeans to retrieve it.

"The Spaniard," she clarified, as the ringing grew louder.

"I remember exactly who Rafaelo is. I can't see why I should be bothering to discuss his spurious claim with Father."

Caitlyn waited as Heath answered his call, resting the phone in the angle between his shoulder and jaw.

"I'm here, Dad." He winked at Caitlyn. "What's the hurry?" He listened for a moment and all humour left his face, he started to frown. "Be there in two minutes."

His expression filled Caitlyn with dread. "What's the matter?"

"Sounds like Dad's got a bit of a problem."

"Problem?"

"Six foot–plus of pure bastard by the sounds of it. But not for much longer."

Heath tore across the drive, Caitlyn hard on his heels.

She thought of Rafaelo, his reluctance to call Phillip by his given name…or to acknowledge him as "my father." She thought of the isolation he must be experiencing among the tight-knit Saxon clan. She thought of Rafaelo standing toe-to-toe with Heath yesterday. She thought of his fury about Phillip's treatment of his mother.

Her heart sank. A fight was brewing. "Wait, I'm coming, too."

Caitlyn rushed into Phillip's office hard on Heath's heels. The office—if it could be called that—had windows with old-fashioned wide wooden sills that overlooked the vineyards, an antique desk clear of everything except a blotter and a gold pen in a marble holder, and a conference table with four chairs arranged around it. Three of the chairs were currently occupied by Phillip, Joshua and Rafaelo. The tension in the room was palpable.

"So this is about him?" Heath gestured with a thumb toward Rafaelo and took the last seat.

"Yes," Phillip did not elaborate.

Caitlyn hovered, feeling a little out of place—she was after all not family—then Rafaelo rose to his feet.

"Caitlyn…" he gave her name an exotic resonance "…take my chair."

"No, no, I'm fine."

"I insist." He stepped away from the table and perched himself on the windowsill.

"Sit down, Caitlyn."

She gave Phillip a quick smile. "Thanks."

Phillip didn't smile back. There were shadows of strain around his eyes, and a grim set to his mouth. He looked like he hadn't slept a wink last night.

Once seated, Caitlyn—and the Saxons—had to look up to Rafaelo where he sat, turning their heads at an uncomfortable angle. With the light behind him, it was impossible to read his expression. She wondered if Rafaelo had been aware of these advantages when he chose the spot by the window that put him outside the family circle.

Except the family circle was incomplete. At least two members were missing. "Where's Megan?" she asked.

"On her way," replied Josh.

"And Mother?" This time it was Heath who asked the question that Caitlyn had dared not voice.

Phillip hesitated. "She's working on a press release with Alyssa. She thought it better that she wasn't here. Alyssa excused herself, she says she needs to get the release off."

"But Mother always attends any family meeting." The words burst from Heath.

"Not this one apparently." Phillip looked pained.

Megan came through the door like a whirlwind. "Sorry, I was with Mum and Alyssa." She sounded out of breath, as though she'd been running.

"Here, have my seat," Caitlyn leapt up, increasingly conscious that while she was part of the inner decision-making team of Saxon's Folly, Rafaelo was right, this was not her business. This was family stuff. As much as she viewed the Saxons as extended family, she probably shouldn't even be here.

"Sit," Megan insisted. "I'll pull up Dad's desk chair." Heath rose and helped her bring it over. They all shuffled around to make space for her.

"Now what's this about?" Megan demanded.

Caitlyn squinted toward Rafaelo, interested to see how he was going to bridge the gap with his father…his siblings…to start to build the relationship that, despite his denials, she was convinced he'd come across the world to build.

"I want my share of Saxon's Folly." Rafaelo spoke from the window.

Caitlyn stared at Rafaelo in disbelief.

"*Your* share?" Heath was on his feet.

"Sit down, Heath," Phillip ordered.

Heath sank back, dark colour rising beneath his tan. He gave Rafaelo an unfriendly glare.

"Yes, my share." Rafaelo's voice was very smooth, his Spanish accent very evident. But Caitlyn noticed that sparks leapt from his eyes. He wasn't as calm as he appeared. "The birthright I was robbed of when he—" Rafaelo pointed at Phillip "—refused to acknowledge my mother's pregnancy."

"We've only got your word that my father is yours." Heath was the first to retort.

Rafaelo looked at him as though he'd crawled out of a muddy pond. "Even your mother acknowledges that my mother once lived in the area. Even she recognised the probability that—"

"*Probability?*" Heath mocked.

Joshua looked from one to the other. "Heath—"

"What?" Heath swung round. "He's scamming us—"

Joshua rested a steadying arm on his brother's forearm. "I wouldn't be so sure. Looking at the two of you is like looking into a slightly warped mirror. The resemblance is there, even though it's a little off."

Heath did a double take, then his gaze narrowed. "You're saying he's Dad's son?"

"I am! He—" Rafaelo nodded in Phillip's direction "—can confirm it."

"Sit." Joshua tugged Heath's arm. Once Heath had settled down, he added, "It's a definite possibility. He looks like us. His heritage is stamped all over his features. Given that, I don't think there's any point going down the prove-your-paternity road now. Although I'm sure Father will have the necessary DNA tests done." Joshua cast his father a glance.

"So what does that mean?" Megan asked.

"It means we have a problem. Rafaelo feels entitled to a share in Saxon's Folly. How are we going to solve this?" Joshua directed the last at Rafaelo.

"I want what I am owed."

The dark fire in Rafaelo's eyes that had so appealed to Caitlyn had subsided, leaving an empty void of black. No emotion. No anger. No hatred. Nothing that she could understand.

"What about your mother's responsibility in all this? Even what—thirty-something years ago?—women knew the risks of unprotected sex. It was hardly the dark ages." Megan shrugged. "I feel sympathy for your mother's plight, but she was foolish enough to mess around with a married man."

"She didn't know he was married." Rafaelo didn't raise his voice, but suddenly there was a sense of danger, a very real threat in the room. "He lied to her."

All the Saxon siblings looked to their father.

"Is that true?" It was Megan who asked the damning question that was in everyone's eyes.

"I don't remember—"

"Don't compound your lie with another." There was contempt in Rafaelo's voice.

Phillip dropped his head in his hands. "Okay, it's true. But later she knew I was married…and she didn't break it off."

"She loved you." Rafaelo's tone was thick with contempt. "She thought you were going to leave your wife and marry her."

Phillip's head reared back. "I *never* promised her that."

The Spaniard shook his head in disgust. "Tell them how young she was."

Phillip shook his head. "I don't remember."

The look Rafaelo gave him was loaded with disbelief. "She was eighteen. *Eighteen.* Little more than a child. And you took advantage of her inexperience."

"What about Mother?" Megan nailed him. "Did she know of this affair?"

Phillip shook his head. "Not until yesterday. After Maria left she never returned."

"But she tried to contact you." Rafaelo's mouth curled. "She came to New Zealand to visit the grave of her great-uncle Fernando, a monk who'd come from a Spanish monastery to follow his faith in Hawkes Bay. He'd died tragically in the earthquake of nineteen thirty-one. My mother was given the journals that he'd kept by a local historical society. She made the mistake of showing them to her lover—" he glared at Phillip "—who stole the methods Fernando had perfected."

Journals? Caitlyn's stomach tightened.

Phillip bent his head and stared blankly at the table in front of him. Then he murmured, "I do not have any such journals in my possession."

Misgivings filled Caitlyn. She was acquainted with the journals that she suspected Rafaelo was ranting about. Three volumes. Bound in black leather. Penned in black ink in a stylish sloping hand. A learned man's handwriting. Probably a monk's writing. Possibly Rafaelo's great-great-uncle's handwriting.

She opened her mouth. Phillip lifted his head and caught her eye. She closed her mouth.

Right now those volumes lay in her possession. In her bedside drawer to be precise. Her stomach heaved. Why was Phillip obfuscating? Could it be true? Had Phillip Saxon stolen the works from a young, impressionable woman? Was it possible that Phillip had seduced Maria only for the diaries?

Caitlyn didn't want to think about it. It was too awful. But Phillip's life's passion had been his fascination with creating a fortified wine that would win international awards and respect— it was a vision he'd ignited in Caitlyn when she'd started working at Saxon's Folly as a raw student.

The sound of a snort of disgust roused her from her uneasy reflections.

"If this share that you claim belongs to you is based on the fortune we supposedly make from sherry, then you're sadly misinformed," Heath said. "With the increase in taxes on fortified wines, it's hardly a prize worth pursuing. My father and I have had differences of opinion over his stubborn persistence in continuing down this road before."

The sick feeling in Caitlyn's stomach intensified. Along with guilt. Because she'd shared Phillip's obsessive interest. They'd discussed…dreamed…of buying a tract of land in the Jerez region of Spain, of producing a blend that could be properly labelled and sold as sherry. It would be a winner.

"Or perhaps it's nothing more than an opportunistic get-rich-quick scheme?" Heath's voice was filled with derision.

The Spaniard drew himself up, his gaze turning to black ice. "I don't need a get-rich-quick scheme. I am the Marques de Las Carreras."

Megan gasped. "The Marques de Las Carreras? Then you spoke about *manzanilla* sherry at a show in Paris—"

Rafaelo switched his gaze to the youngest Saxon. "Yes, we met briefly."

"I congratulated you on the silver medals your estate attained for the world-renowned fresh, light *manzanilla* sherry you produce."

Rafaelo nodded. "Unfortunately not quite as magnificent as the Saxon's Folly *fino* product."

Joshua was frowning. "So if it's not a question of money, what do you really want?"

"I want him—" Rafaelo nodded his head toward Phillip without sparing him a glance "—to make good the wrong he did me—and my mother." He slid off the window seat and dusted off his hands. "I want a proportionate share of Saxon's Folly—and, as the eldest son, I would expect an additional portion. And I want Fernando's journals back."

Four

"Have you no pity?" Caitlyn caught up to Rafaelo as he strode out into the blinding sunlight. She shuddered at the memory of the uproar that had erupted after Rafaelo's demand. He'd simply looked down his nose and told the Saxons that his lawyers would be in touch. "The Saxons are grieving."

Rafaelo didn't answer as she bowled along beside him, her long legs easily keeping up with him.

"If it's revenge that you're after, you're making a massive mistake. The biggest loser will be you."

He stopped and swivelled around to face her.

"How can I lose?" Thankfully the black void had gone. The fire was back snapping in his eyes. "And what if I do want revenge? After what that bastard did to my mother, I'm entitled to it."

Caitlyn blinked at the virulence in his tone.

"It's not about whether you're entitled to the satisfaction it brings you, Rafaelo," she said finally. "It's about whether you can let it go."

"I'm not listening to this mumbo jumbo. I will have my revenge. I will get my share in Saxon's Folly—and then I will sell it."

"Sell it?"

"Yes, sell it."

Caitlyn stared at him aghast at the utter finality in his voice. This, then, was what he'd come for. And he'd ruthlessly honed in on the Achilles' heel of the Saxon family. "The Saxons have always kept control of the business. They've fought off attempts by conglomerates to buy them out. You *can't* do this."

He gave her an evil smile. "Just watch me."

His timing was perfect. There had never been a better time to destroy the Saxons. It would take time for the family to regroup after the shock of Roland's death. Time that they didn't have…if Rafaelo made good on his threat.

Couldn't he see what he was doing—what he was destroying? *He couldn't do this.* A sense of calm settled over her. Caitlyn squared her shoulders, her spine stiff and straight and stared him down. "I won't let you do this."

His gaze was implacable, revealing no emotion. "I never expected you to say anything else, *Ms.* Ross. You're on their side."

Rafaelo could see that Caitlyn Ross was fighting not to argue with him. Her shoulders rose and fell under the ridiculous oversized sports shirt that served only to emphasise her slender femininity. The slim column of her throat framed by the crisp white collar, her wrists so narrow under the banded cuffs.

He watched in silence as she released her breath in a shaky sigh. So she'd seen the wisdom of refraining from arguing—but the effort to remain mute was costing her dearly.

"Nothing to say?" he raised an eyebrow and suppressed a triumphant smile when she gave him a searing look.

"Plenty," she said from between tightly gritted teeth, "but I'm trying not to antagonise you."

Her honesty surprised a shout of laughter from him. "Why hold back? You've been forthright until now. Say what you think."

"But where has it gotten me?" she asked. "All I've done is make everything worse. Because of me Kay's hurting—"

"She would've found out." His mouth slanted. "The appearance of a bastard son is hard to hide."

"Thanks for that." But her expression remained tight.

Rafaelo wanted the sparkle back. "Come, heckle me, tell me what you were going to say."

"You think I'm too outspoken, don't you?"

"It's refreshing." He couldn't tell her that few people—much less women—argued with him these days. That would sound conceited. It was clear she already considered him an arrogant, entitled bastard.

"Tell me what you wanted to say. Would it have antagonised me? Or did you want something from me?" He added the last with a certain degree of wearied resignation.

Most women wanted something from him—marriage, his title, his wealth. A life of indolent luxury as Marquesa de Las Carreras. Even those who gave up on the wedding ring and settled for a skirmish in his bed, expected to be lavishly showered with jewels and clothes and to be royally entertained during their tenure as his mistress.

When had it all grown so tedious?

When had he given up hope of finding a woman who loved him for who he, Rafaelo, was?

"What do I want from you?" Her gaze locked with his, scorching him with the impact. "I want you to reconsider what you intend to do."

"You mean give up the share that's rightfully mine?" he objected, disconcerted by the glow of those peculiarly translucent eyes.

"No, no. I can understand you wanting a share in all this—" she waved a hand to encompass their surroundings "—in the wealth, the family, the land, the beauty that is Saxon's Folly. I don't expect you to forfeit that. And I'm sure you'll be able to work something out with the Saxons. But don't sell it. Stay. Get to know your family—"

"I'm a busy man—I don't have time to take off."

"What's a month? Or even a couple of weeks? You've got years ahead of you." She looked like she was about to stamp her foot. "Darn it, they're your flesh and blood, Rafaelo. Your family. And if you can't do that, can't forget about your thirst for revenge, then go catch that airplane this evening."

Was she daring him? He stared at Caitlyn. No, she couldn't be. She didn't understand who, what, he was. She didn't know about the huge estate, Torres Carreras, he owned in Spain. She didn't know about the power he commanded. She only saw him as a threat to her beloved Saxons. Nothing more.

He'd never met anyone like her.

She didn't seek engagement rings or glittering baubles. She wanted nothing monetary from him. He had a suspicion if he turned and vanished into the ether and never returned she would be relieved.

The realization came as a shock. It had been a very long time since he'd met someone who didn't demand something material from him. All she asked was that he befriend his father—his half siblings—or, if he couldn't do that, she expected him to leave.

What she wanted was selfless—for the Saxons.

But he couldn't oblige. But she needn't know that. Yet. "I'm no longer leaving this evening. I changed my flight booking."

But she wasn't fooled. Rafaelo read the disappointment that clouded her exquisite eyes. She knew that he was staying because he wanted his share of Saxon's Folly with a driving lust. Not because he needed it. But because of what it represented, the chance to set right the wrong that had been done to his mother…to Fernando's memory.

Rafaelo suspected she even understood that he wanted the satisfaction of watching Phillip's face when he broke the news that he'd sold his share to the first bidder. Caitlyn Ross saw what others didn't. She'd known he wanted revenge.

To his astonishment he found himself saying, "If I do as you want, if I extend my stay from a couple of days to a couple of weeks will you have dinner with me?"

A stillness came over her and a frostiness descended around her. "That's not fair!"

"Why not? If I stay, I'll be doing what you want—and I'll be doing something I don't want to do."

Her eyes went from cloudy to utterly opaque, blanking out all emotion. "It's not that I don't want to have dinner with you…. I don't date."

Rafaelo was puzzled by her response. Annoyed, too, his pride affronted. Women didn't turn him down when he invited them out. Usually they leapt all over him. *Yes, Rafaelo. Whatever you want, Rafaelo. Do you want it now or later, Rafaelo?* Instead Caitlyn was edging away. So what in the devil's name was this about?

"Don't date?" He looked her up and down. "But why not? You're an attractive, nubile young woman."

She coloured and looked away, then said softly, "I don't talk about it, either."

Her closed expression warned him to tread carefully. It had to be about her romantic mooning over his dumb-ass half brother. Rafaelo's annoyance grew. "Is it because of what you think you feel for Heath?"

The look she gave him was horrified. "What do you mean?"

Rafaelo waited.

At last she said, "It has nothing to do with Heath." She gave a broken little laugh. "How can it? Your brother doesn't even know I exist."

"Half brother," he corrected. "He's a fool. And so are you for pining over one man. *Madre de Dios*—" he raked a hand through his hair "—how long has this been going on?"

She spread her hands helplessly. "It's complicated. You don't—can't ever—understand."

"So I'm a simpleton?"

"No…no. Please, I'm not insulting your intelligence. It's my fault."

Mouth twisting with wry humour, he murmured, "Ah, this is one of those circumstances where a modern woman would say, 'It's not you, it's me,' hmm?" The consternation in her eyes made him regret the impulse to tease her. Almost. He made one of the lightning-fast decisions that he was famed for. "I'll stay. Two weeks. I'll extend my booking in town."

"No!" At his look of surprise she tempered her tone. "You can't possibly stay in a hotel. There are three guest cottages on the estate. I'm sure you can stay in one of them."

"All right."

Her face lit up, as if he'd promised her Christmas.

Rafaelo gazed into her pale eyes. They should have been cold and wintry. They ought to have frozen out this *loco* attraction. Instead they sparkled like clear, pure crystal, radiating enthusiasm and pleasure, drawing him deeper under her spell.

With a struggle he found his voice. "Don't read too much into all this."

"I understand," she said at last. "You're still going to sell your share in Saxon's Folly."

"And don't think you'll change my mind," he growled.

Several days later Caitlyn let out a tired sigh. The path that led over the gentle hill from the winery to the stables, where she lived in a loft apartment, seemed longer and bumpier than usual. Her hot, tired feet dragged.

In the distance the golden glow of the late-afternoon sunlight cast a creamy glaze over the whitewashed stables. To the left, a ray of sun glinted off the chrome trim of Joshua Saxon's Range Rover, where he inspected the vines. At the end of the block a copse of native trees marked the start of rolling grass meadows dotted with horses, some grazing, others slumbering, heads low, tails whisking to keep the flies at bay.

It had been hellish in the winery. Surrounded by oak casks, Caitlyn had spent the day racking wine, transferring it from one cask to another to remove the lees. She'd worked quickly to lessen the exposure to air. Her back ached and her feet were hot and sore in the scuffed sneakers. She longed for the sharp needles of a cool, refreshing shower…followed by a good book and her own company for a while.

Except today was Thursday. Family night. The night the Saxons all made a point of having dinner together—and included regulars as part of the extended family. Caitlyn was one of those regulars. Even Amy, Roland's grief-stricken fiancée, would be there. Since Kay had reluctantly agreed that Rafaelo could stay in one of the vineyard cottages, it was possible Rafaelo would have received an invitation to dinner, too.

If the Spaniard was there, the Saxons would need all the support they could muster, she couldn't abandon them. Caitlyn glanced down, caught sight of her jeans and wrinkled her nose. Kicking a stone out of her path, she decided that solitude and the best seller she was reading would have to wait. But a shower was a necessity—along with a clean change of jeans—before she'd be respectable enough to grace anyone's dinner table.

The sound of whistling gave her pause. Her head came up. She searched and located Rafaelo lounging on a tussock just inside a paddock near the stable block, his back propped up against the fence post, his harsh profile softened by lips pursed to whistle. Caitlyn couldn't help noticing that his overlong hair gleamed blue-black like Tui feathers in the sun. She slowed, her heartbeat accelerating with the discomforting awareness that the sight of Rafaelo brought.

She looked away.

Lady Killer was standing a distance away, ears flickering back and forth, the muscles in his haunches bunched and his tail tucked between his legs, every line of his body screaming his protest at the human invading his space.

"Come, sit." Voice low, Rafaelo patted the mound of grass beside him.

Her pulse went wild. She could no longer pretend she hadn't spotted him and sneak past. "I thought you were sleeping."

He cracked one eye open. "That's what I wanted the stallion to think."

"He hates people, that horse." Caitlyn drew nearer and folded her arms across the top railing of the fence, propping her chin on her forearm. At the sound of her voice, the stallion's ears flattened against his skull.

Rafaelo continued to whistle, a slow mesmerizing sound. Lady Killer stood, stiff-legged, not grazing, his tension showing his fury and his resentment.

Eyes half-closed, the Spaniard murmured, "Sit down. You're threatening him by standing there."

"Me? Threatening *him?*" Caitlyn gave a snort of disbelieving laughter and glanced nervously to the patch of grass Rafaelo was patting.

Taking in Rafaelo's long, relaxed body reclining on the invitingly green grass, his lazy gaze focused on the horse, she decided that the man was no threat to her. Bent double, she stepped through between the railings and lowered her tired, aching body beside Rafaelo.

He didn't react. A fantail twittered and fluttered crazily in a nearby bush. Gradually the tension leached from Caitlyn's muscles. It was heaven to rest back on her elbows and inhale the fresh scent of crushed grass.

Rafaelo didn't even open his eyes to spare her a glance. Caitlyn snatched up the opportunity to examine him. The hawkish profile, the sensually pursed lips, the olive skin stretched tight across his cheekbones, the small jagged scar beneath his mouth. He was too male to ever be called beautiful.

Then it came to her. The perfect word to describe him.

Macho.

"He's not as tough as he'd have everyone believe." At his words, she turned her attention back to the horse.

"Ha! Don't believe that. There's a reason he's called Lady Killer—and it's not because of his flirty ways with the mares," she muttered darkly.

"He's not a killer. He's an Andalusian," Rafaelo continued. "In my country we value such horses. We care for them and train them. We do not leave them to become wild and wary like this stallion."

"He hasn't been abandoned," she protested. "Roland bought him about four months before his death. He had plans to turn him into a dressage horse. But the horse is difficult. And with all the work at the winery, Roland didn't have enough time to put into him. Then he died."

"Someone needs to take the horse in hand."

"No one has the time."

"Or the interest." Rafaelo's voice was flat. "I have two weeks. I will speak to my father. Someone needs to give that animal time."

Caitlyn glanced at him in shock. He was no longer pretending sleep; all his attention was fixed on the stallion. Caitlyn had been furious with him for pursuing his plan for revenge, to wrest a piece of Saxon's Folly away from the Saxons. But perhaps it had cooled his anger. It was certainly the first time she'd heard him refer to Phillip as "my father." She suspected Phillip would be relieved to have Rafaelo's time occupied, preventing him from skulking around the winery, poking around the fortified wines that they produced. But contrarily she said, "It will be a waste of time. No one can catch that horse, he leads them a fine dance. Jim simply opens his door in the morning and shoos him into the paddock, leaving him a hay net for the day. In the evening, we open his stable door and he comes in for his evening meal."

The eyes that connected with hers were frighteningly direct. "Who is Jim?"

"One of the cellar hands. He helps Megan feed the horses and muck out the stalls in the morning. Although some students from the local polytechnic who do their practical coursework here also help. And so do I when Megan's overseas at a wine show."

"You can ride?"

"Yep, I usually exercise Breeze when Megan's away." She pointed to a pretty chestnut mare in the next field. Under his intent gaze the tingling returned, and she moved restlessly. "What can you do with the stallion in two weeks?"

He shrugged. "Teach him to trust me."

"No chance. That horse doesn't trust anyone."

"He already knows I won't hurt him."

"Hurt him?" She gave a disbelieving laugh. "If anyone is going to do hurting, it's that mad creature."

"He's not mad, he's scared."

She stared at him. "Scared? How do you work that out?"

He didn't turn his head. His profile was harsh and jagged against the verdant grass and the foliage of the surrounding trees. "The first time I raised my arm, he squealed and kicked and tried to bite me. Now, when I raise it, he flinches and puts his ears flat. Someone has hit this horse around the head." There was cold fury in Rafaelo's voice.

"It wasn't any of the Saxons." Caitlyn sprang to their defence. "He was already difficult when Roland bought him."

"Stop worrying. I don't suspect your precious Saxons. But it angers me that a good animal has been ruined by someone's uncontrollable anger."

Caitlyn fell silent. She perused him, a new respect filling her. His strength and power was clearly visible in his long, whipcord body and inflexible will, yet he was gentle, too. She didn't want to examine why that moved her so profoundly.

"Does anyone groom the stallion?" he asked.

Caitlyn focused on the horse with relief. "Not since he trapped Jim between those powerful hindquarters and the wall and aimed a vicious kick at his head. Jim was lucky to clamber up the wall out of the way."

Rafaelo fell silent.

The fantail was still twittering and over near the stables Caitlyn saw that a pair of swallows had appeared in the evening sky—the first she'd seen this season.

Rafaelo spoke suddenly, "I'll make you a deal. Dinner in town says that within a week I'll have that horse caught, groomed and eating out my hand."

"Loser pays?" Caitlyn started to laugh. There was no chance that Rafaelo was even going to get near the horse. "You better bring your wallet."

"I don't intend to lose." He threw her a narrow-eyed look that stirred the flutter of butterflies in her stomach and caused her laughter to die. Then he smiled, a wide white grin that sparkled with victory, causing adrenaline to jolt through her.

"I'll do that," he said softly, "we've got a date."

Too late she saw the trap. Caitlyn stared at him. Win or lose, she was committed to an evening out with him.

Great going for a woman who didn't date.

Five

An hour later, scrubbed and clean, Caitlyn pushed back the heavy drapes and stepped through the French doors into the formal salon of the Saxon homestead. She stopped at the sight of Phillip and Rafaelo eyeing each other across the wide expanse of a magnificent Persian rug like a pair of wary wolves.

Both men turned to her, relief in two sets of dark eyes. The tension eased a little when Caitlyn started prattling about Lady Killer. A first. Normally the mere mention of the stallion's name was enough to cause dissent, but for once Phillip appeared to welcome the topic and soon the men were debating whether the stallion could be turned into a dressage horse.

Caitlyn fell silent, watching Rafaelo warily. She hadn't forgotten how easily he had lulled her into a sense of false security earlier. Her wariness increased when she caught Rafaelo's hooded eyes scanning the room as he examined the paintings, the furniture, the jewelled hues of the acres of Persian carpet underfoot that contrasted with the polished kauri floorboards.

Was he calculating the value of what his share in the immense historic Victorian homestead might be worth?

"Just be careful," Phillip was saying, "that bloody horse caused an accident last month. Alyssa was badly hurt."

"Do I hear my name?" Alyssa picked that moment to enter the salon, Joshua at her side. Sleek and sophisticated, she was wearing a burnt amber dress that suited her dramatic beauty and dark red hair.

By comparison Caitlyn felt underdressed in denims faded almost to white and not even her newest sneakers and the black tank top she wore eased the sensation. Then she shrugged the discomfort away. Joshua was wearing jeans, too. There was no expectation to dress for dinner at Saxon's Folly. There never had been. The Saxons might be wealthy, but they weren't pretentious.

"We're talking about your fall," Caitlyn said, remembering that awful moment when Alyssa had lain on the cobbles in the stable yard, so still and so pale, Joshua kneeling beside her, his eyes wide with panic.

For one horrible moment Caitlyn had thought Alyssa was dead—and so had a devastated Joshua. The memory still made Caitlyn's skin crawl.

"My hand hardly hurts anymore." Alyssa held up her hand, showing off a narrow bandage. "The physiotherapist says I'm well on the mend, I just need to keep doing my exercises."

"I should've shot that stallion." Joshua put an arm around Alyssa and pulled her close.

"It wasn't his fault," Alyssa protested, huddled against his chest.

"Alyssa was riding the stallion?" Rafaelo looked surprised.

"No, no," said Caitlyn. "She was riding Breeze. Two kids were lurking behind the trees in the paddock. Lady Killer—"

"I do not like that name," Rafaelo interjected. "It makes the horse sound like a murderer."

"He damn nearly killed Alyssa."

"Nonsense, Josh, I'm fine," said Alyssa.

Joshua brushed his cheek against Alyssa's hair, his expression bemused. Alyssa smiled up at him, love in her eyes, the rest of the company forgotten. Caitlyn couldn't stop the melting sensation that filled her at the sight of them together. This was the kind of love that she'd once dreamed of finding…one day.

Little chance of that now…

Finally, Joshua said, "He's a Devil Horse."

"Then call him Diablo, it's better than Lady Killer," Rafaelo suggested. He inclined his head to Alyssa. "I apologise for interrupting your account."

Caitlyn took over the story as Joshua placed a kiss on Alyssa's temple. "When Joshua and Alyssa arrived back from their ride, Lady Killer…Diablo," she amended at Rafaelo's hard stare, "was in a right royal lather with those hoodlums in his paddock. They made a dash for it. At the roar of the motorbike, Breeze bolted."

"Alyssa fell badly and needed treatment for her hand," Phillip added. "I'll accept that particular incident might not have been the stallion's fault, but what he did to Jim—trapping him in the corner of the stable—was downright mean. If anything like that happens again, I'm going to have him destroyed."

"Let me see what I can do with the horse first," Rafaelo cut in.

"Take care." Phillip appraised Rafaelo's height, his broad shoulders. "If you can master him, as far as I'm concerned you can have him."

Rafaelo looked startled. Then his features hardened into a determined mask. He started to say something, but paused as Kay entered the salon, Megan close behind her. With a frown Caitlyn noticed that Kay was wearing a dressy skirt. When had the dress code for these Thursday-night family dinners changed? The crease between her brows smoothed when she saw that Megan still wore work clothes.

"Dinner will be another fifteen minutes," Kay announced.

"Looks like we're all here." Kay scanned the gathering. She barely glanced at Phillip and her expression clouded over as her gaze rested briefly on Rafaelo. Caitlyn sensed the older woman's pain at being faced with such incontrovertible evidence of her husband's infidelity. The lines around the older woman's eyes had deepened since Rafaelo's arrival—and the revelation of Phillip's betrayal.

"Amy's not here," said Caitlyn, more to distract Kay's attention from Rafaelo than for any other reason.

"No, she didn't feel up to it." Shadows shifted in Kay's eyes. "It's been quite a week."

That was an understatement. Kay must be thinking of Roland's memorial service…of her dead son.

"Heath hasn't arrived yet. He's late. Again." Phillip's tone was riddled with censure.

Kay looked even more upset.

In an effort to head off an argument between Phillip and Kay, Caitlyn said, "If his day was as crazy as mine, he probably finished work not long ago." Her swift defence of Heath earned her a narrow-eyed stare from Rafaelo that caused her stomach to dip and roll.

"He's late. Stop making excuses for him, Caitlyn." Phillip's bushy eyebrows lowered. "Now, why don't we sit down in comfort while we wait for my tardy son to arrive." He gestured to the pair of sofas that faced each other. "Can I get anyone a pre-dinner drink?"

Joshua collapsed into an armchair and Alyssa perched on the arm, while Megan settled herself in a navy brocade armchair that had always been Roland's spot. A pang of sadness shook Caitlyn. Roland was sorely missed. Joshua must've had the same thought because his hand slid over Alyssa's in a way that could only be described as comforting.

Caitlyn made for one of the sofas.

"Would you like a glass of sauvignon blanc or sherry?" Phillip asked Caitlyn.

"Sherry, please."

Rafaelo sank down beside her on the sofa. Caitlyn stilled, instantly aware of his overwhelming, breathtaking masculinity. Then she turned to him and said in a cheerfully polite voice, "You must taste *Flores Fino*. It's a Saxon's Folly favourite."

"I'll try the white wine." Rafaelo's lips were tight. "So, you call it sherry here, do you?"

Uh-oh. Detecting tension, she picked her words carefully. "Habit. The label doesn't refer to sherry—it describes it only as *Flores Fino*. But in the style what we produce is Spanish *fino,* based on—"

"Based on?"

Based on his great-uncle's process.

She shook her head and took a quick sip from the glass that Phillip handed her. Despite the sweetness of the amber liquid, her mouth tasted bitter. Rafaelo had come not only to seek vengeance on his mother's behalf but also because he believed that Phillip had stolen his great-great-uncle Fernando's journals. Yet after that dreadful confrontation in Phillip's office, Phillip had pulled her aside to explain that he'd bought the journals from Maria before swearing Caitlyn to silence. He didn't want Rafaelo getting his hands on the journals—or the magic methods they recorded.

To her relief Rafaelo didn't demand an answer. Instead he asked, "That is *Flores Fino,* yes?"

Her heart thudding with anxiety, she ran her tongue over dry lips, her mind blank. Finally she nodded.

"The first time I tasted *Flores Fino*—" Rafaelo nodded toward her glass "—I was, how do you say, blown away? It was what I had been trying to achieve for years. As a child my mother told me tales of the sherry my great-great-uncle had made. She tried to remember what she'd read in the journals." He gave Phillip a dark look. "She'd jotted down some short notes in her diary, the notes of a history student, not a winemaker. But, helped by my fa—by the Marques—they gave me a start."

Caitlyn swallowed, distressed by the longing in his eyes.

"I wanted to produce a *fino* sherry like that. A sherry that would've made my great-great-uncle proud." An air of poignant longing clung to him. Then he shook himself and it vanished. "Instead I tasted that in France. Everyone was excited by the outstanding quality. It was like tasting the nectar of the gods. Perfection." Rafaelo gave her a sidelong glance that made her heart sink still farther. "I noted the makers. Ross and Saxon. And admired—yearned for—their talent."

Caitlyn suspected she knew where this would end. "Rafaelo—"

"But it wasn't God-given talent, was it?" There was a rawness to his harsh tone. "I cannot tell you what I felt when my father—the Marques—revealed that my real father was Phillip Saxon." His eyes were flat and empty, all the energy and spark gone. "It was as if the missing piece to the puzzle had been dropped into my lap. I hardly needed to hear the story that my mother wished to tell. Because I knew."

Caitlyn waited, dry-mouthed.

"I knew instantly that the nectar I had tasted was too similar to the notes my mother had given me. I knew…" His voice trailed away as Phillip came closer. Looking from Caitlyn to Phillip, he asked with a hard edge, "So who is the expert then?"

In the manner of a true academic Caitlyn had been fascinated by the leather-bound volumes. She'd fished the dusty journals off the bookshelves and had read them, cover to cover. It had fired her up. She had seen the possibilities.

"I've always made sherry," Phillip said, trying to look modest, and Caitlyn's shoulders sagged. "Caitlyn worked with me when she first came, but once Heath left she had so much else to do."

For a moment annoyance at the dismissal of her role in establishing Saxon's Folly as a top producer of fortified wines overcame her relief. Then she caught sight of the fury in Rafaelo's face and she wanted to cry. Rafaelo believed Phillip's skill came from Fernando's journals—the very journals he believed Phillip had stolen from his mother. Phillip's attitude would do nothing to dampen Rafaelo's desire for revenge. Did Phillip not realise that far from establishing himself as a figure of admiration in Rafaelo's eyes, he was simply alienating, enraging, his firstborn son more?

Finally she compromised. Let Phillip have his pride, but she had to take responsibility, too. "Phillip has always been my mentor—it was something we were both fascinated by. But it's true that since Heath bought Amy's father's estate on the other side of The Divide and ceased to be Saxon's Folly's winemaker, I've had less time for sherry."

"Heath should never have left," Phillip muttered.

Across from them, Joshua started to frown.

"Too many things we couldn't agree on, Dad," Heath said quietly from the doorway. "And I will have sherry, thanks."

"You're late," Phillip said gruffly.

"Mother told me that Amy wasn't coming this evening. I stopped in on my way here to see if she was okay."

"It would've done her good to get out for the evening." Kay shook her head sadly. "She hasn't been at work the whole week."

"She looked so pale and unhappy the last three weeks, I think it's better that she's taken some time off." Megan looked troubled. "I don't think she ever grieved properly after Roland's death. She was so busy trying to cheer us up…and pick up the slack at the winery."

Heath came closer. "I tried to talk her into coming tonight—she didn't want to. Hell, I can't even get through to her right now." Frustration simmered in Heath's eyes. "Everything I suggest, she resists."

"Should I talk to her?" Joshua looked around at the others, his gaze alighting longest on Alyssa. "Will that help?"

Heath hesitated. "Maybe."

"Both of you need to back off and give her time. She's lost the man she loves." Alyssa turned her hand and threaded her fingers through Joshua's and squeezed. "In her shoes I'd be heartbroken."

"That she is." Heath collapsed on the sofa facing them, and Caitlyn decided that he looked even more weary than she felt. It was a terrible time for Heath, Megan and Joshua. Their brother's death, the shocking discovery of Rafaelo's existence and learning of their father's betrayal of their mother all meant that everyone's nerves were stretched to the breaking point.

Caitlyn wished that the clock could be turned back and everything made right.

Ivy arrived bearing a tray and offered around dainty glasses filled with amber-coloured sherry and glasses of pale gold sauvignon blanc.

Rafaelo bent forward to set down his glass of wine as Ivy departed.

"Wait." Caitlyn touched his arm. "Don't put it there."

He stared down at her hand on his arm, then lifted his gaze to meet hers. The impact was like a burst of static. From his raised eyebrow, Caitlyn knew he'd felt it, too.

His skin felt hot under her touch. Caitlyn started to snatch her hand away. Then stopped. No, darn it. She was a respected award-winning winemaker. What was she doing jumping away from a man's bare skin like some terrified little virgin?

So she left her hand on his arm and returned his stare. The contact was electrifying. Under her fingertips she felt the muscles contract. His eyes grew blacker than midnight.

All of the sudden Caitlyn had a sense of getting in deeper than she'd ever been before. For a cowardly moment she half wished she had withdrawn her hand, when she'd had the chance, but now that moment had passed.

Irrevocably.

He smiled, and said so softly that only she could hear, "I'm getting used to your telling me what to do."

She blushed. "Sorry, I didn't mean to. That table has been in Kay's family for centuries. I wanted to set down a coaster—" Caitlyn reached for a hand-painted box and extracted a pile of glass coasters, setting them out on the low table that separated the two long sofas. "I don't want it to be marked from the glasses."

"I'm surprised Kay places the table where it could risk getting damaged."

"She likes to surround herself with possessions with meaning. I don't think she'd mind it being marked—she'd see that as part of the beauty."

"But you're protecting her from heartache?"

"Yes. The Saxon family has been very good to me. It's my turn to protect them. Wouldn't you—if you were in the same position?"

Their eyes held for a long moment and a beat of perfect understanding arched between them.

Phillip's voice broke in, "What do you think of the sherry, Heath?"

Heath lifted the sherry glass and sipped. "Very good."

"It's more than good. It's a winner," said Phillip argumentatively. But Heath didn't respond. "Sure you don't want a taste, Rafaelo?"

"Quite sure." Rafaelo's tone was measured and frighteningly formal, his curved lips compressed into that hard line that caused Caitlyn to shiver.

She gave Phillip a quick look. He was so caught up in his battle with Heath that he didn't seem to sense that he was antagonizing Rafaelo. Couldn't he fathom that the sherry was a volatile topic tied up with Rafaelo's complicated relationship with his family? The mother, her great-uncle and the father to whom Rafaelo believed he owed his loyalty. She wished Phillip would shut up.

Heath stretched out his legs—jean-clad Caitlyn noticed with relief—and addressed Rafaelo, "That's where my path diverges from my father's. I'm not a trophy hunter, I simply make solid no-fuss wines to drink with meals."

"Don't pay attention to him." Joshua tipped his head sideways against the back of the armchair. "The wines he produces are superb—far from no-fuss."

"You should taste them, Rafaelo, they're fabulous." Caitlyn ran interference again, watching the byplay between the Saxon males and trying to fathom the underlying currents.

"Thank you for that endorsement, kitten," Heath said.

"Kitten?" Rafaelo's lip curled in disgust. *"Kitten?"*

"My nickname," said Caitlyn, very quickly. She flashed Heath a half smile, wishing that the undercurrents would evaporate.

Even Joshua's eyes narrowed, revealing his awareness of the rising tension in the room despite his outwardly relaxed appearance. On the other side of the room, Kay was chewing her lip, her eyes flitting from her husband to the Spanish interloper to her younger son—clearly Kay was worried, too.

And beside her Rafaelo felt like a powder keg about to explode.

In the golden glow of the tall candles, Rafaelo studied the straw-coloured wine in the Baccarat glass, then he glanced over the top to where Caitlyn sat beside him, her meal finished, too.

Kitten!

Rafaelo suppressed a snort. Heath had it wrong. This woman was no kitten. His half brother didn't know her. He drew comfort from that thought. She turned her head. Her eyes, the colour of pale, unearthly crystal, so clear, so pure, connected with his. Desire jolted through him.

She reminded him of a wolf. Fiercely protective. Her eyes glowing, all-seeing, uncanny in the candlelight.

"What do you think?"

He stared at her. What did he think? *Madre de Dios,* he couldn't think. Not while her eyes transfixed him, entrapped him in their clear depths.

"Would you prefer red?"

She was talking about the wine, he realised belatedly, jerking himself back to reality, to the glass in front of him, to the dining room in the Saxon homestead, and to the conversation dominated by weather and Brix.

A conversation that he would normally command. But not tonight. Tonight turbulence raged within him. He sensed resentment from his half siblings. Not that he blamed them. Anger lingered against Phillip—his dishonourable father—who blatantly offered around sherry, boasted about the awards he'd garnered, from a process he had stolen from a vulnerable, loving woman. Some of his dark emotion spilled onto Caitlyn; her name had been listed alongside Phillip Saxon's as winemaker.

He pushed himself to his feet. "Excuse me, please." Rafaelo stalked to the tall doors that led outside. For the first time in years he craved a cigarette. But he'd given them up a decade ago. He felt her presence before she stepped outside.

"I needed a breath of fresh air," he felt compelled to explain.

Then Caitlyn smiled and the blackness eased inside him. Rafaelo told himself that he was being too harsh. She'd been an employee, acting under instructions… Phillip Saxon's instructions. And the desire for her that had been tamped down ignited again.

"So how did you come to work for Saxon's Folly?" he asked Caitlyn to get his head out of that dark black pit it was stuck in.

"Heath tutored me during my first year at university—we became friends. He organised a vacation job for me at Saxon's

Folly. After I finished studying, the family offered me a full-time position as a cellar hand." And she'd always wondered what had motivated that offer.

Rafaelo tilted his head sideways studying her. "What made Heath single you out?"

"He's a kind man. I think he felt sorry for me." Caitlyn laughed without humour.

Sorry for her? What was wrong with the man? Rafaelo wondered. "But why?"

She hesitated. "I was a swot."

"A swot?" Rafaelo asked, puzzled by the word.

"I studied too much. I came out of university with a first class honours degree, a willingness to learn and not much else. I always had my nose in a book."

"Ah." Had she seized the opportunity to work at Saxon's Folly because of Heath Saxon? Such a smart woman, so besotted over such a dumb ass.

Through the glass doors, Rafaelo cast his clueless half brother a damning look. Didn't he see under the worn jeans and sneakers to the woman she was?

"Heath was already winemaker here," Caitlyn was saying. "He'd taken over from Phillip, who had worked at a killing pace for the past ten years and wanted to start slowing down. Joshua studied locally and ran the vineyards, while Roland looked after the marketing side."

"That was around the time he—" Rafaelo couldn't bring himself to use Saxon's name "—decided to give his sons shares equal to those that his wife held in Saxon's Folly, while retaining the largest share himself." Only to the legitimate sons, of course.

Caitlyn's eyes widened in surprise.

"I made it my business to find out such things," he said in reply to her unanswered question.

"He gave Megan a share equal to her brothers'."

"Only later, once she'd finished her studies."

"She was younger." Caitlyn came instantly to Phillip Saxon's defence.

"So why did Heath leave Saxon's Folly?" That was one question Rafaelo wanted answered.

Caitlyn lifted her shoulders in a small movement and let them drop. "Heath and Phillip had had a bitter fallout. I was assistant winemaker by that time. Heath suggested that Phillip and Kay offer me the top job, winemaker at Saxon's Folly."

He read the pride in her eyes, the disbelief that still lingered. "Didn't you think you could do it?"

"It had been my secret dream, so deeply buried that I never saw any chance of it coming true."

"Especially not with a Saxon already in the winemaker role," he said drily. "You needed Heath to move on."

"I never wanted that!" Her eyes sparked with anger. "That's a horrid thing to imply. Heath's always been fantastic to me. Supportive, encouraging. I…" Her voice trailed away.

Rafaelo didn't need her help to join the dots.

Caitlyn shook her head. "Oh, what's the use of trying to explain? You'll never understand."

He understood. More than she thought. She fancied herself in love with Heath Saxon.

Caitlyn saw his mouth tighten. She wished he could get over this stupid antagonism that he and Heath shared.

How could she explain what it had meant to her to be promoted to chief winemaker? That had been Mount Olympus back then. Attaining such lofty heights had seemed more farfetched than the hope of catching Heath's attention—a dream which she was starting to realise had been nothing more than the crush of a bookish late developer. She turned away from Rafaelo, unwilling to think about what had prompted such a groundshifting revelation, and made for the tall glass doors.

"I'm going back inside." After a long moment, she heard him follow and tried to tell herself that she didn't care what he did—as long as he didn't harm the Saxons.

Later, after murmuring farewells to Phillip and Kay, Caitlyn glanced to where Rafaelo stood listening to Alyssa and Joshua argue about whether Saxon's Folly should be sponsoring a newly created food and wine TV show. Since their conversation, Rafaelo hadn't said much. Hell, he'd even declined dessert—no one ever refused a helping of Ivy's pavlova.

But then she'd been silent, too, caught up in the discovery that she wasn't in love with Heath Saxon—that it had been nothing more than a very convenient crush that had prevented the need for a boyfriend when she hadn't wanted one. And later…

Well, later it had meant there'd been no pressure on her to come to terms with what had happened.

Her breath hissed out. A whole new world opened ahead of her. One filled with men and passion and all the things she'd spent five years avoiding. She glanced toward Rafaelo.

In one of those freakish tricks of timing, Alyssa and Joshua stopped arguing and looked toward the French doors. Rafaelo's gaze followed. Caitlyn was caught staring. She gave them a little wave and mouthed, "Good night."

Rafaelo came toward her. "I'll walk you home."

"That's not necessary." Caitlyn gave a breathy little laugh. "Goodness, I've walked home often enough. This isn't the city. This is Saxon's Folly, I'm hardly in any danger of getting mugged. If I'd thought that, I'd have called Pita, the guard, to walk me home."

"I thought you might like the company," Rafaelo murmured. "I'm on foot, too. The stables are on my way home."

Coming up behind him, Alyssa said, "Caitlyn's right. Saxon's Folly is as far removed from the city as you can get—ask me, I'm the original fast-lane gal, aren't I?" And she gave Joshua a loving smile that had him hurrying to her side, his dark eyes melting.

For a raw instant Caitlyn felt a tearing of envy. *She* wanted to be loved like that. For a fraction of time she let her gaze rest on Heath, then she swung her attention back to Rafaelo.

His eyes were piercing. Caitlyn felt as if he could see all the way to her soul, to the need that lay there, beneath the frozen wastes.

"Thank you." Her voice sounded strangled. "I'd like you to walk me home."

Rafaelo glanced at Heath and back to her. "Would you?"

Six

Patches of moonlight danced on the pathway as they walked into the copse of tall, whispering trees. The bright light from the homestead receded behind them.

"What did you mean by that crack?"

Caitlyn sounded mad. Rafaelo glanced sideways. Her stride was long, her shoulders thrown back in challenge. No hint of Heath's kitten remained.

Rafaelo didn't pretend to misunderstand. "Heath has been your tutor, your friend, he arranged a job for you. You're in lo—"

She covered her ears with her hands. "Don't say it, please."

He shot her a frustrated glare. "¡Vale! I won't. But don't lie to yourself. Instead ask yourself why you're wasting your life? You're young, smart, beautiful. Why long for Heath Saxon? He calls you *kitten,* for heaven's sake." Rafaelo snorted in disgust. "The man doesn't even know your true nature. Find yourself someone else, someone who appreciates you for the woman you are."

Her hands dropped away from her ears back to her side. She didn't want to hear what he'd had to say. The silence told him how much she resented his interference.

No matter. He didn't need to say more. It might be harsh, but it was true.

They walked around a bend, and the trees thinned. Ahead the well-lit stables came into view.

At last Caitlyn spoke. "Is this some sort of crafty attempt to persuade me to desert the Saxons? Some divide-and-rule to get the revenge you crave?"

"Caitlyn—"

"It won't work. Heath has been a good friend. I'll always be grateful to him—he's done so much for me, he even gave me my dream job."

"So in exchange you presented him your heart." Jealousy uncurled within Rafaelo. "What else did you give him? You were young, impressionable, he was older, more experienced... did you feel obliged to give him your virginity in exchange for his tutoring?"

She stopped in her tracks.

"Rafaelo!"

The scandalised shock in her voice was too real to be feigned. A silver moonbeam slanted across her face as she looked up at him. "You make it sound so commercial...like a cold, bloodless transaction. It wasn't like that!"

"So he *did* take your virginity."

She gave a sharp sigh of frustration. "He was my tutor—not my boyfriend. And why suspect Heath? There were a gazillion other guys who were only too keen to initiate first-year students to the joys of sex."

"That's all?" Relief swelled through Rafaelo like a tidal wave, he ignored the fact that Caitlyn had found some other student to love. All that concerned him was Heath Saxon, the man who was in his face every way he turned, the man who was his half brother. "You never slept with him?"

"We became friends. That's all! Heath's never known how I feel about him, so I'd appreciate it if you keep it to yourself."

"You've never touched him like you touched my arm earlier?"

"No!"

"Never felt that bolt of awareness surge between you?"

"Never." Despite the cover of darkness, she averted her face. "You shouldn't be asking me these questions—my love life has got nothing to do with you."

He stopped dead. Grasping her chin, he demanded, "Look at me."

To his immense frustration the dappled moonlight was too dim to reveal her thoughts.

"How can you say it's none of my business? Didn't you feel the charge between us when you touched me earlier? Can't you feel this…*thing* between us?"

"No." She shook her head in fierce denial and her fine silky hair whipped against his arm. "There's nothing between us."

"Don't lie," he said quietly, furious that she could deny this…this…force that seared him.

"Let me go."

Silence.

"Please…" Caitlyn shut her eyes. It was hopeless. Rafaelo wouldn't listen. Her only hope lay in the fact that someone might hear her scream. It was late…dark…the Saxons were all up at the homestead.

"Caitlyn?"

She opened her mouth but couldn't utter a word.

"Caitlyn, look at me, *querida*."

Her eyes snapped open. Rafaelo stood in front of her, still big, still strong. He'd stepped away. He'd released her chin. Now he was frowning down at her. And he didn't look pleased.

"Caitlyn?"

He sounded worried.

"Are you okay?" He didn't take his eyes off her. "Do you want me to call someone? Megan? Or Kay?"

He wanted to call someone? Why?

"Come, let me take you home, you look like you're about to pass out."

She didn't move.

"I'll call the homestead—get Kay or Megan to help you." There was a note of sharp concern in his voice. He already had his cell phone in his hand, the other hand cupped her elbow. No fear flared. She felt only numbness.

She let him lead her to the foot of the black wrought-iron stairwell that led up against the exterior wall to her loft apartment. Heard him hit the buttons on his phone.

"I'm okay," she said. He wasn't going to hurt her.

He glanced at her and stuck the phone in his shirt pocket and hastily pressed her shoulders down, until she sank on the stairs. "You're as white as a ghost. Put your head between your knees."

She obeyed, heard him settle beside her. The panic had begun to recede.

"Do you need something?"

"No, I'll be fine."

His gaze was searching. "Has this happened before?"

Oh, yes. But she had no intention of talking about it.

She rose unsteadily to her feet. "I'd better go upstairs and make myself something to drink. Warm milk will help."

He didn't look convinced. "Can I take you to the doctor?"

"I don't need a doctor." She simply needed to be alone. To have a warm bath and get into bed. Then she'd sleep. She turned away and started to climb the stairs.

"I'll see you in."

Instantly the tension was back. "No... I'll be fine. Really." She drew a deep breath when he started to argue and hurriedly inserted the key in the door.

A last backward glance showed her that the black eyes were sombre as he stood tall and proud and allowed her to close the door in his face.

"So what do you want me to do?"

Caitlyn's impatient retort to Jim made her realise that she was being unreasonable. She took a deep breath, thought about the problem that Jim had come to her with and suggested a solution. Then she went and made herself a cup of tea and took it out into the courtyard to the south of the winery.

The morning had passed in a rush. For once the winery wasn't holding its usual fascination, the blend of art and science not captivating her as it normally did.

It was all Rafaelo's fault.

Embarrassment rolling like nausea in her stomach had woken her several times during the night. She took a sip of tea. He must think she was a nut. No, he thought she suffered from some medical incapacity.

Most likely insanity.

Setting down the mug on the bench beside her, she groaned in humiliation and buried her head in her hands. How was she ever going to face him again?

He'd wanted to kiss her last night.

But he hadn't. Because fear had closed in on her, taking over her, until she'd run to her sanctuary, victim to the terror that crawled through her. Silly, scared little kitten.

Kitten. The joking, childish nickname was suddenly a symptom of all that was wrong.

Was it any wonder that Heath had never viewed her as a woman? Rafaelo had been brutally honest last night, telling her that she was wasting her time on Heath.

Deep down she knew he was right. She needed a life. Yes, she needed a wake-up call. Not because she was sleeping—but because she was frozen. A solid block of ice that only looked like a woman. If she hadn't felt a tinge of bitterness at the waste, she might have found it funny.

But did that mean letting Rafaelo kiss her would be right? He was the cause of this restlessness, the dissatisfaction, the strange discomfort that lay in the base of her stomach, warming her, making her itch. And nothing about that was remotely humorous.

Rafaelo wouldn't hurt her…

Then caution kicked in. How could she know that? She barely knew the man. All she'd seen was the macho exterior, the snapping eyes that hinted at passion and dark depths of emotion beneath the handsome veneer. How could she be sure that he was safe?

Better to keep her distance.

He'd be leaving soon. She only had to keep a lid on her suddenly awakening libido for a week and a half, then he'd be gone. She could do that. But in the meantime he'd be spending all his time messing with a dangerous stallion. The horse had already proved he hated humans. What if Rafaelo got hurt?

It didn't bear thinking about.

The hour before lunchtime crawled. Despite resolving to keep far away from Rafaelo an unexpected worry for the damn man ate at her.

Finally at her lunch break Caitlyn couldn't bear the rising anxiety anymore. Telling herself she intended to make herself lunch…read her book a little to settle her restlessness…she made her way to her loft above the stables.

But the instant she reached the trees that lined the paddocks her palms started to grow moist, and Caitlyn knew she was deceiving herself.

She wanted to see that Rafaelo was okay. Except there was no sign of Rafaelo. Concerned, her steps quickened.

Surprise made her pause. Rafaelo lay on the ground. Asleep. His face shaded by a wide-brimmed hat, only the sensual curve of his mouth visible. The stallion stood beside him, front legs splayed, neck extended, deeply suspicious as he sniffed the unmoving Spaniard.

Jeans hugged Rafaelo's long legs. The khaki cotton shirt was open at his throat, revealing a wedge of smooth, tanned skin and the glisten of gold where a modest medallion lay. Her mouth went dry.

This was the man she'd been fretting about all morning?

So much for his bet that he'd have the darn horse caught and groomed by Thursday evening. To think she'd been fretting about his well-being for the past hour…how misguided could she have been!

She huffed her way into her cottage and fixed herself a BLT sandwich and wolfed it down. She was about to leave when manners got the better of her and she quickly made a sandwich for Rafaelo.

She extracted a can of soda from the fridge and placed the wrapped sandwich and drink in a cooler box. Pausing at the door, she grabbed a peach from the fruit bowl and stuffed it in the cooler, too.

The stallion was cropping the grass beside Rafaelo's ear when she reached the paddock. Despite Diablo's snorts of displeasure at her presence, Rafaelo didn't stir as she set the cooler down beside the fence post. Caitlyn waited two full minutes before it became clear that Rafaelo was not going to wake. She used the time to examine his long lean body with a frank curiosity that she would never have dared exhibit were he awake.

Finally she made her way back to the winery and tried steadfastly not to think about the virile Spaniard.

Caitlyn hurried through her afternoon tasks. She tried to tell herself that her impatience stemmed from her eagerness to see what progress he'd made with the stallion. At five o'clock she made her way to the stable block.

The first person she spotted in the yard in front of the stables was Rafaelo. Tall and powerful, the Spaniard stood in front of Diablo's stable, the bucket that usually contained Diablo's evening meal at his feet. A small amount of Diablo's dinner formed a heap on the palm that he offered to the stallion.

Diablo was having none of it.

The stallion's neck snaked from side to side and every now and then he bared his teeth threateningly at Rafaelo.

Kay, Megan and Jim were perched on the white railing opposite the stable as quiet as mice. No heads poked out of the neighbouring stalls; the rest of the horses must be eating. Caitlyn settled beside Megan.

Without gazing away from the spectacle before them, Megan said in a tone of reluctant admiration, "It's quite a battle of wills. I think he's going to be riding that horse before the end of the week."

Caitlyn shook her head. "It took Roland nearly a month to get Diablo used to him—and he had help. Jim and your dad had to hold him so that Roland could mount."

"Well, Rafaelo is the most patient man I've ever seen. He's going to wear down that horse—and without the need for extra hands." Megan turned her head. "Why are you calling the horse Diablo?"

"That's what Rafaelo calls him."

"Oh." Megan scanned her until Caitlyn felt uncomfortable and started to fidget. Finally, Megan said, "That aqua T-shirt does great things for your eyes."

"Thanks." Caitlyn's cheeks warmed. Megan had been the one who had picked it out for her.

Megan tipped her head sideways. "But there are splashes of grape must on the shirt—and on your jeans, too."

Before Caitlyn could respond, Jim said, "We were racking this afternoon. Hard, thirsty work."

"I think it's time to go shopping again." Megan had a determined gleam in her eyes.

Caitlyn detested shopping. She never knew what to choose. She was a tall, lanky beanpole and so flat-chested that she felt horribly self-conscious when the sales ladies sized her up. She was always relieved when Megan came because Megan knew exactly what worked for her—and what she would actually wear.

"Caitlyn looks fine as she is," Jim said. "Why does she need fancy clothes to work in?"

Jim was right. She had two dressy outfits in her cupboard for wine shows, the rest of her clothes where jeans and tops—most of them stained and faded. If she bought more, they'd simply end up stained and bleach-faded, too.

Megan gave Jim the evil eye. "What do you know about what clothes women need anyway?"

Jim blushed and started to stammer an apology.

Caitlyn took pity on him. "I don't need clothes."

"Let me decide that!" Megan turned her attention back to Rafaelo. "You have to feel for him. It must've been a shock to discover the old Marques wasn't his father."

"And my shock?" Kay's voice was thin. "I thought Phillip and I had something special." She broke off.

After a brittle silence, Megan said with forced cheer, "You know, he's not a bad-looking guy, my newly found brother. What do you say, Caitlyn?"

After a concerned glance at Kay, Caitlyn looked. From behind, Rafaelo's shoulders were broad, his hips and thighs lean. A horseman's build. Why hadn't she noticed that before?

"So, Caitlyn, what do you think?" Megan teased.

"What do you want me to say? That he has a very cute butt? Tight and trim in those jeans."

Jim sputtered and leapt to his feet, his face crimson. "I'm out of here." He matched his actions to his words.

Kay rose, too. "I think I'm too old for this conversation. I'd better go supervise dinner."

Megan waved off her mother. "You're excused." But her forehead creased as her mother departed. With a deep breath, she turned to Caitlyn. "C'mon, admit that he's cute."

"What about all the texting you're doing, Megan?" Caitlyn gave as good as she got, sensing Megan needed the distraction. "Is the new man a long-distance lover? Spill! Have you finally found the man of your dreams?"

"Perhaps." Megan's smile glittered. "But talking might jinx it. And stop trying to change the subject, we were talking about you. So you think Rafaelo is sexy, do you?"

Caitlyn groaned as she looked past Megan straight into a pair of amused onyx eyes. She wished with fervent longing that the concreted walkway would open up and swallow her.

"I'm flattered," Rafaelo said throatily.

"Oops." Megan gave a little laugh. "Caitlyn's indulging in girl-talk."

She was indulging in girl-talk? Caitlyn wanted to kill her bubbly friend. She couldn't for the life of her think of anything to say to Rafaelo. Her face must be on fire. What comment would salvage a situation like this?

Rafaelo saved her from a response. "Thank you for the lunch. I will give you back your cooler tomorrow."

She found herself flushing more under Megan's interested stare. The other woman mouthed, "You made him lunch?" and raised an eyebrow.

Her gaze sliding away from Megan, she said to Rafaelo, "How did you know it was me? You were sleeping."

"That's what Diablo was supposed to think." His slow smile didn't help an iota. Instead it made her remember with cheek-reddening embarrassment how she'd leaned on the fence and stared at him like some wide-eyed sex-crazed teenager.

Did he know? She rather suspected he did. With a touch of desperation, she gestured to the bucket he held. "Shouldn't you give that to Diablo?"

He shook his head. "He has a hay net for tonight—and there's plenty of grass in the paddock."

"Just none of his favourite dinner." Caitlyn felt a stab of sympathy for the stallion. It looked like Megan was right; Diablo wouldn't have a chance. "How much did the stallion take from you?"

"Two handfuls." He smiled. "But tomorrow we'll go a little further. Slowly. Step by step."

"Megan thinks you're patient. I think you're ruthless."

"He won't starve," said Rafaelo dismissively.

"I certainly hope not! Do you use the same methods with women?"

Megan gave a shriek of laughter. "Caitlyn! What a thing to ask. I've got a call to make. And I want to catch up with Mum. Talk to you tomorrow." And she flitted away leaving Caitlyn alone with Rafaelo and the provocative question that she wished she hadn't asked hanging between them.

"It depends," he drawled.

"On what?"

"It depends on the woman, her experience. If she's sophisticated, she'll have different…demands, and wouldn't require as much patience. And she'll be hungrier." His heavy-lidded gaze made Caitlyn acutely aware of tingles racing through her body. "But if she has less experience…" his voice dropped "…then she will need much gentler handling."

"Gentler handling?" Outraged and on fire with the provocative images that popped into her mind, she objected, "You can't treat a woman like you would a horse."

"A woman is nothing like a horse," he replied. "I would woo a woman with patience and care… With kisses and conversation."

"And why are you telling me this?"

His lips curved up into a sensual smile that made her shudder. "Because you are interested."

She opened and closed her mouth. Finally a strangled sound emerged. "I hope you're not basing this on what you over-heard—"

"On what? That you think I'm sexy?"

"I never said that!" She was flushing now, her pulse erratic.

His smile widened. "But you do want me to kiss you."

The sheer arrogance of the statement caused her breath to escape in a hiss. "Are you always so vain?"

"Not vain." He came closer. "I simply understand women."

Caitlyn tried to laugh, but instead of the cutting sound of disdain she'd intended, all that emerged was an airless squeak. "You really think I want you to kiss me?"

His hands came down on her shoulders. "I really do," he murmured, his smiling mouth making her pulse stop.

Caitlyn's heartbeat went into overdrive as her body connected with his. She skittered back, putting space between them until the fence rail pressed up against her bottom, preventing her from backing away. She was trapped. There was no escape. All at once her sassy confidence evaporated. This was no longer a game of flirtation. This was the real deal. The breathlessness turned to apprehension.

Rafaelo lowered his head to hers and wild unreasoning fear fluttered inside her. She was alone with him in the empty yard. Everyone else had gone…and the terror was back.

<u>Seven</u>

Caitlyn tensed, expecting an assault.

But when the kiss came it was surprisingly gentle. There was no invasion, no bruising pressure to force her lips apart. Rafaelo's lips brushed hers, hesitated then brushed again.

At first she was frighteningly conscious only of how muscular he was, how big and strong. How little chance of escape—of help—there was in the deserted stable yard.

But then the warmth of his hard body seeped through the T-shirt to her body. He was warm, his flesh firm, and he smelt delicious—all male beneath the rich notes of cedar of the after-shave he wore.

She was astonished to discover that she wanted this…wanted to hold him…to kiss him. Rafaelo hadn't yet wrapped his arms around her, so the claustrophobic fear of constraint hadn't over-taken her. He touched her only with his lips. Lips that moved lightly against hers, softly, increasingly tempting.

The delicate, almost chaste kisses didn't hurt her, didn't bruise her lips nor did he make any attempt to thrust his tongue into her mouth, ram it down her throat in a disgusting parody of sex.

Inch by inch her fear started to recede.

His lips played with hers, then parted, his breath warm against her mouth. A tiny shard of anxiety splintered through her. Then he whispered Spanish words against her mouth.

A wild wave of heat flooded her, washing the anxiety away. The foreign words sounded so intimate, the movement of his mouth against her lips was endlessly tantalising. There was absolutely nothing to fear. She relaxed against him. Her arms slid up around Rafaelo's neck, and she stepped closer.

He didn't make a grab for her with rough, brutal hands. Nor did he grind his hips against her with threatening sexual purpose, his body suddenly hard and invasive. Instead he simply continued to murmur those husky, excitingly foreign words and kiss her with exquisite care.

Illumination started slowly… This wasn't about punishment. Knowledge followed in a rush—it was all about pleasure.

Only then did Caitlyn relax her full weight against the wall of his chest and start to kiss him back, their lips playing in a way that left her inexplicably aching for more.

As his fingers stroked along the sensitive skin of her inner arm her flesh rippled in reaction. Then his thumb played under the edge of the sleeve of her T-shirt before stroking down her arm again.

In the wake of his touch her skin prickled, itching for the caress to be repeated. She pressed closer. This time his fingers stroked all the way up her arm, until his hands cupped her shoulders and drew her against him.

No half expected flare of fear followed as the ridges and planes of his body fitted against hers.

Instead need rolled through her, softening her body, leaving her breathless. His hands stroked down her back in long, sure sweeps, his touch firm, confident, causing little bursts of pleasure to ignite along her nerve endings. Finally his hands came to rest at her waist.

Her lips parting, Caitlyn waited.

Again he surprised her. After a heartbeat of time, instead of devouring her mouth, the tip of his tongue slid across her bottom lip in a teasing caress that was gone before she'd realised what he was doing, leaving her craving more.

Then the taunting tip returned, outlining her upper lip, drawing patterns that brought her breath back in a rush. Hesitantly her tongue emerged to taste his. He stilled. With the barest whisper of a sigh, his tongue stroked hers.

He tasted of wood and warmth and man. Heat ignited within Caitlyn. Her nipples tightened. For the first time in years she yearned for the heady recklessness that a mouth-to-mouth kiss brought. She unwound into his body, half dreading, half revelling in the anticipated response.

Rafaelo's lean body tightened, tension singing through him, until she felt the tremors take him as he fought the urges that must be thundering through him.

She curled her hands into the thick black hair that brushed his collar, bringing his head closer, compelling him to taste her...now. Under her fingers the tendons in his neck bowed as he resisted.

His leashed restraint cost him. Against her breasts his heart raced, and she could hear the rasp of his breathing.

"*Dios.*" He lifted his head.

In a rush she became aware of her surroundings. Drawing in a deep breath, she struggled for composure and glanced around. The stable yard was thankfully still empty. Except for Breeze who watched them with curious velvet eyes over a half stable door. Caitlyn could hear the rest of the horses munching their dinner and a hoof scraped on the ground. Reluctantly she brought her attention back to the man who stood in front of her.

His eyes were on fire, his shoulders heaved as he fought to hold his breathing even. "See?" His voice was husky with the effort it took. "I will always be gentle."

Caitlyn scanned his face, her eyes appreciatively skimming the coiled muscles in his tall frame, all showing unmistakable signs of a man under tight control, the awesome patience frayed.

The skin across his cheekbones grew even tauter under her regard. "I would never—never—rush or push you into anything you didn't want."

Her gaze snapped back to his. Oh, dear heaven. Did he—could he—possibly suspect?

The kiss stayed with her all day Saturday.

So pure, so passionate. That night Caitlyn's restlessness grew as she relived it in slow-motion frames that left her melting, aching. Until flashes of other dreams—older dreams—tore into the exquisite memory, tainting Rafaelo's kiss, and wakening her to a breathless fear.

Rafaelo was not like that.

So what did he want? Why had he kissed her? Would it make a difference to how he kissed her if she told him everything? And what would be the point? She stared into the oppressing darkness.

Rafaelo, Marques de Las Carreras, wasn't staying—he'd made his intentions clear all along. Get his share of Saxon's Folly, sell it, destroy the Saxons and leave.

There was no possibility of a relationship developing between them. So what was she doing building wild hopes…impossible dreams…by fantasising about that kiss?

It was stupid!

Rafaelo and her… Why it was like fire and ice. They'd never exist together.

* * *

The impossibility of anything growing between Caitlyn and Rafaelo was underscored the next day.

Caitlyn and Megan returned from an early Sunday-morning ride, both of them breathless from the gallop they'd had along the fences at the top of the hill above the vineyards.

Despite the fact that it was barely eight o'clock, Rafaelo was already in the stable yard. He was not alone. A thickset, grey-haired man in a dark suit stood beside him.

"What's John Bartlett doing here?" Megan said as they approached, the sound of their horses' hooves crunching on the pathway.

And what was the valuator doing together with Rafaelo? The sinking sensation in Caitlyn's stomach warned her that this meeting could not bode well.

A smile lit Rafaelo's face at the sight of her as she and Megan rode into the yard.

"Hello, John. What brings you to Saxon's Folly so early?" asked Megan.

"I'm doing a valuation. I understand Mr. Carreras is a recent addition to the family."

Megan reined Breeze in. "Does my father know about this?"

But Caitlyn didn't hear the reply as she fixed Rafaelo with an accusatory stare. Instantly the warmth in the dark eyes evaporated. A cold edge of disappointment pierced her.

She'd hoped…

She'd hoped for so much. Too much. That Rafaelo would put his desire for revenge behind him once he came to know the Saxons. She'd hoped that Rafaelo could let the bitterness of the past go, that he would forgive Phillip and give up his mad notion of claiming his share of Saxon's Folly to sell it off. Clearly that wasn't going to happen.

Dismounting, Caitlyn led the mare she'd ridden into a stable and tugged the girth loose with unnecessary vigour. Rafaelo's behaviour had just brought home how much she'd been banking on him coming to terms with the Saxons. And how important the accord—and attraction—that had been growing between them had become to her.

She dumped the saddle on the stable door, taking care not to glance in Rafaelo's direction, and went to unbridle the horse.

By the time Caitlyn regained her composure sufficiently to come out of the stable, Phillip had arrived and was talking to John Bartlett while Rafaelo stood silently to one side.

Caitlyn hesitated. Then she strode forward. The Saxons were like family to her. Saxon's Folly provided more than her livelihood, it gave her a sense of community. She couldn't walk away.

Not even if it cost the fragile trust that had been budding between her and Rafaelo.

Deliberately she positioned herself beside Megan and Phillip and met Rafaelo's brooding gaze.

Nothing. She couldn't read a thing.

A sense of loss filled her.

Rafaelo looked dismissively away from her and said to the men, "I'd like to get started—the sooner we get this settled the better."

"Do Mother and Joshua know about this?" Megan still sat atop Breeze, looking stunned. "Because I didn't. Does this mean that Rafaelo really has a claim on Saxon's Folly?"

"Your mother knows why John is here." Phillip sounded weary. "Nothing has been finalised. So there is no need for you or Heath or Joshua to speculate about anything. You need to trust me on that, Megan. Rafaelo, myself, your mother and our lawyers have a meeting tomorrow morning." Phillip shot Rafaelo a hooded glance. "Rafaelo and I have a lot of talking to do."

Caitlyn's gaze clashed with the Spaniard's. Rafaelo had gone back to being one hundred percent the Spanish grandee. It was there in the implacable set to his jaw, the rigid straightness of his back and the tightness of the lips that had been so gentle against hers a couple of nights ago. How she wished he could forgive and forget.

But Rafaelo had always wanted his share in Saxon's Folly. For vengeance. From the expression on his face, there could be no other compromise. And Caitlyn knew she had little chance of stopping the inevitable.

On Monday morning, Rafaelo strode out of Phillip Saxon's office well satisfied with the way the meeting had gone. Both Rafaelo and his lawyer had decisively convinced Phillip that Rafaelo was not going away—until he gained his birthright.

Phillip had never supported Rafaelo's mother, and now he would pay, Rafaelo vowed. In blood, or rather its equivalent— in Saxon's Folly soil. The two lawyers had left ten minutes ago, Phillip's attorney promising to draft an agreement that would start the negotiation of the finer points. Rafaelo had spent the past ten minutes asking Phillip pertinent questions about the vineyard's finances. It was doing very well, and with his input it could do even better. It would be a solid investment, even though he'd always intended to sell his share....

Rafaelo didn't need to look at the man walking beside him to know that Phillip Saxon was less pleased about the outcome, or his life in general. Kay had not attended the meeting—Phillip had said that she was too busy. Rafaelo suspected she was angry and upset. But knowing that Phillip's marriage was in a state of turmoil didn't give him the satisfaction he'd expected.

Outside the winery, Caitlyn was busy hosing down the concrete under the immense stainless-steel vats. For a brief moment the tantalising memory of the kiss they'd shared on Friday evening flashed through Rafaelo's mind. But the accusation and disappointment in her eyes yesterday when she'd realised that he'd met with John Bartlett to get a valuation of Saxon's Folly overtook the softer memory.

Rafaelo paused.

"You haven't seen the whole operation yet, have you?" Phillip asked him, no doubt trying to get on his right side, before calling out to Caitlyn. "Caitlyn, will you show Rafaelo around the winery? He hasn't seen how we do things here."

"Of course I will. Where would you like to start?" Caitlyn asked as Phillip retreated. She didn't meet his eyes—and Rafaelo found that he didn't care for that at all. He'd grown used to her candour, her humour. And he'd been certain she liked him. For himself.

He shrugged. "I don't care. Just don't show me the solera where the sherry is produced."

"I won't," she assured him. In an artificially bright voice that grated, she said, "Let's start with where the destemming is done. And this is where we pour off those first premium juices." A steam of facts followed, and Rafaelo stopped studying her averted features and started to pay attention.

But he noticed that Caitlyn forgot her discomfort once she became engrossed in communicating her passion for Saxon's Folly. Her eyes sparkled as she told him her preference for French oak barrels—despite the cost—her hands gesturing to emphasise her point. Every passing moment made it clearer that if he took his birthright and sold it to cause Phillip pain, Caitlyn would suffer, too. Rafaelo frowned, uncomfortable with the discovery. He followed as she showed him where the racking was done, and led him through the winemaker's cellar where a bottle of every vintage was stored. Finally, she took him into the tasting shed. The large space was empty. The only sign of its function was the blackboard listing the wines on special, the rows of glasses on wooden counters along one side of the room and the wooden racks against the back wall filled with Saxon's Folly wines waiting to be chosen by customers.

"This is where we do the cellar door sales."

"There's no one here," said Rafaelo. "Not even staff."

"We don't open until eleven. Kay runs the cellar door sales with help from students from the local polytechnic. If it gets too busy we all chip in. It can be quite lively some weekends."

Rafaelo looked around. "Is there a restaurant, too?"

"Not yet. We have a picnic area overlooking the vineyards that's very popular. Megan has been saying we should open a café-style restaurant with a French chef and fine wine."

"That's not a bad idea."

"Roland was always dead set against it. And since his death I haven't heard Megan mention it."

"Perhaps she feels it would be disloyal," Rafaelo said, trying to imagine what he would feel in Megan's place. "Death can do that. I loved my father—adoptive father, whatever you want to call him. But we disagreed about plenty. Yet, since his death, I find myself doing things his way. Partly because I regret arguing with him about every trifle in the past, partly because it brings him back."

Caitlyn nodded. "I can understand that. We want to remember people for the good they did—the impression they made. Regret is so irreversible." She cast him a sideways glance. "You should reconsider what you are doing to Saxon's Folly—to the Saxons. They don't deserve it."

"Phillip Saxon does."

Caitlyn went silent for a moment. Then she said, "But Kay doesn't. And neither do Joshua, Heath or Megan. They're all hurting enough right now. What they need is support and sympathy—not conflict and more upheaval." She paused as Kay Saxon entered the tasting shed.

The older woman hesitated when she spotted him standing beside Caitlyn. Only for a split second, but it was enough for Rafaelo to know that Kay wished that he was anywhere but at Saxon's Folly.

He straightened his spine. The empathy that Caitlyn had

stirred in him for his father's wife should not deprive him of the right to be here. The past was not his fault. He had a stake in his future—a stake in Saxon's Folly that he intended to claim. The sooner Kay grew accustomed to the idea, the better.

But he could make it easier for her. So he smiled at her, his most charming smile. "The estate is wonderful. Caitlyn's been showing me around. It's impressive, you must love living here."

Kay's animosity receded, leaving her shame-faced. She looked away. "I always did. Saxon's Folly has the ability to wrap itself around your heart." Her voice softened.

Rafaelo felt a startling sense of connection with this cool, elegant woman who his father had married. He loved the estate where he'd grown up, too. The chalky earth was a part of him, the sap of the vines that grew overlooking the Atlantic ran in his blood.

"Saxon's Folly welcomed me, too," Caitlyn said beside him.

For an instant Rafaelo wondered if that was why she'd grown so fixated on Heath. Had she been more in love with Saxon's Folly than with the man?

Saxon's Folly was important to her. But it was important to him, too. Already his first goal was within reach: a share of Saxon's Folly. Now he needed to find out what had happened to the journals Phillip had stolen from his mother.

On Wednesday evening Caitlyn leaned against the sun-warmed stable wall and watched in disbelief as Rafaelo slipped a halter over Diablo's head and buckled it. For a moment the stallion resisted and sat back on his hocks, and Caitlyn thought he was about to erupt into a fury. Then Rafaelo walked away, unrolling the lead rope in his hand, leaving the horse nothing to pull against.

Caitlyn held her breath as the stallion's ears flickered uncertainly for a moment, then he gave a snort and the bunched muscles in his hindquarters eased. After a moment the horse started after Rafaelo. As the stallion pricked his ears, stretching his neck forward, and sniffed at Rafaelo's back, she shook her head in wonder.

Rafaelo had enchanted the damn horse.

She'd never thought it possible. And he'd done it in a day less than the terms of their bet. The certainty that he'd used some kind of horse magic solidified as Rafaelo led Diablo into his stable and, whistling tunelessly, started to brush him with long, slow strokes.

Caitlyn leaned on the door and shook her head. "I never thought I'd see this sight."

"He's a teddy bear."

"Not quite."

"Yes, he is." Rafaelo proffered the brush. "I bet you he'll let you brush him, too."

Another bet. She gave him an ironic look. "I don't think so. If you lose, I'll be flat on the straw with my head kicked in— makes me the loser, too. And it's not outside the realm of possibility. That's what he tried to do to Jim."

He'd already won the last damned bet they'd had. That she now owed him a dinner. In a fine restaurant.

A date.

She hadn't thought *that* would be possible either. Not before meeting Rafaelo.

"He won't hurt you." Rafaelo was already unbolting the door, ushering her in. "Come, let him see you, let him smell you."

His arm resting lightly on her lower back, he led her across the clean fragrant straw to the stallion's head.

"Put your hand on his muzzle."

She obeyed. It was soft as velvet. A moment later Rafaelo's hand closed over hers. "Now stroke your hand up his face, all the way to the soft bit beside his ears."

Caitlyn eyed the huge horse warily. "I thought you said he'd been hit around the head. Will he let me touch him?"

"Of course. As long as you're gentle."

Her hand moved up Diablo's nose, Rafaelo's hand over hers. Then Diablo dropped his head with a huge sigh and his eyes closed.

Caitlyn stared at the stallion's lowered head.

"He wants you to rub the base of his ears."

Diablo butted his nose against her, then lipped the T-shirt she was wearing. The disbelief intensified.

"Okay." She swallowed. "You're sure you're not a wizard?"

She felt a rumble of laughter behind her. Rafaelo moved closer, and suddenly she was aware of his bulk behind her, the powerful stallion in front of her. Yet she felt in no way threatened—not by the horse or by the man.

Brushing the horse was easy after that. There was a lazy rhythm to it and the stallion's muscles rippled under the fine ebony coat.

"I told you he'd let you brush him," Rafaelo said into her ear. "He's loving it. See how his eyes are half-closed? That's an expression of bliss."

"I can see that." Caitlyn gave a little laugh. "The terror of Saxon's Folly reduced to a teddy bear. Who'd have believed it? But I can't blame him. He's being pampered."

She started as Rafaelo's hands came down on her shoulders from behind.

"You'd like that? To be pampered?"

She gave a breathless half laugh. "Any woman would."

"You are not any woman."

Before she could ask him what he meant by that, his hands started to move, the flat palms gliding down either side of her spine.

Her breath caught. And her body tensed. Then his hands started on the return journey, his fingers kneading the muscles tightly knotted from the day's hard labour—winemaking might be art, but it could be damn hard work.

"Is that pleasant?" he asked, his accent dark and sultry.

She couldn't lie. "Yes, it is."

But it was disturbing, too—in a definitely pleasurable way. Yet beneath the frisson of delight, discomfort lurked. She stopped brushing. All of a sudden the confined space in the stable became claustrophobic.

Diablo's eyes drifted open and he nudged her, reminding her that she should be brushing him. Caitlyn drew a deep breath and forced herself to calm down.

Nothing ominous was happening. Rafaelo was still rubbing his hands up and down her back. He thought she was enjoying herself—and she was. His hands weren't staying, or doing anything inappropriate. He probably intended the back massage to relax her tense muscles.

She wanted to cry. If only she could shake the ridiculous fear that tormented her. If only that terrible night with Tommy hadn't left her stunted...

A searing, healing anger blossomed inside her. She was not going to cry. Tommy Smith was not going to paralyse the woman in her for another day. She was not going to let the past destroy whatever was happening between her and Rafaelo.

She stared at her hands automatically moving the brush over the stallion's coat. She concentrated on the rhythm of Rafaelo's hands rubbing her back, her shoulders, her nape. She forced herself to focus on the response that his hands—hands that had never hurt her—aroused in her. She forced herself to recognise that the sensations that shivered through her were linked to pleasure...not pain.

Rafaelo was not Tommy.

This was not Tommy grabbing her, tearing at her clothes. This was Rafaelo, so strong, so confident. A man who did not need to resort to force to have women falling at his feet. A shuddering sigh escaped her. His warm touch made her tingle, releasing the tension that had been building up for far too long.

The powerful, masculine hands stilled. "Are you okay?"

"I'm fine." Caitlyn started to smile. "In fact, I'm better than I've been in a very long time."

Her heart light, she turned to face him. "Thank you, that was amazing."

"You had some fearsome knots there."

"More than knots." But she didn't expand. Instead she leaned forward and placed a soft kiss on his cheek. "You're a very nice man, Rafaelo."

"Nice?" He laughed.

"Yes, nice. You're not going to ruin the Saxons, are you?"

His mouth slanted. "Why should you think that I've given up on the goal that brought me halfway across the world?"

Caitlyn paused. "You were very nice to Kay the other day." And you've been so patient, so gentle, with me.

But she left the last unsaid.

"I'm not as nice as you think." His smile held a hint of self-mockery.

"Why do you say that?"

"Diablo ate from my hand, I caught him and groomed him. Tomorrow is Thursday. And I'm not going to let you escape our bet."

Caitlyn couldn't argue with that. To be truthful she was no longer certain she even wanted to. "I'll make that reservation."

"Somewhere elegant." His eyes smouldered with some emotion she did not recognise. "I want to show you off."

Eight

"That's the one," Megan told her the next afternoon. They'd been shopping for just the right dress for hours now. Caitlyn had almost given up hope that she'd find something appropriate— something worthy of Rafaelo's desire to "show her off."

"Do you think so?" Caitlyn spun in front of the mirror. The dress fitted like it had been made for her. Flapper style, a long tube of beaded silver fabric that made her eyes sparkle. And it was comfortable. She hadn't expected that. Not from a dress. And especially not from a designer dress. When Megan had said "dress" she'd been dreading satin and taffeta, bows and ruffles.

This dress was almost plain in its sleeveless straight cut, with its scooped neckline. The glamour came from the fabric, the colour, the beads.

"There are shoes that match." Celeste, the designer, placed a pair of fabric-covered ballet-style slippers with a low heel in front of her.

More relief. She wouldn't be breaking her neck. "At least I know I'll be able to walk in those."

"And you've got to take this bag." Megan held out a tiny square that was so stylish that Caitlyn didn't dare look at the price tag.

"Done!" Caitlyn drew a deep breath and hoped she wasn't going to bitterly regret this primping.

But Megan didn't stop there. She dragged Caitlyn off to a fashionable boutique and Caitlyn found herself with two pairs of new jeans—one white and one French navy—a silk scarf top, an Indian cotton printed top in shades of melon and lime greens with white and a couple of Lycra tank tops in shades she'd never worn.

"None of these are for use in the winery while working with grape must, understand?" Megan gave her a mock frown.

"I understand," Caitlyn said meekly, her fingers lingering on the silk of the halter-necked scarf top. She bit her lip as she looked at the neckline. "I'll need to get a bra to wear under that."

"You don't need a bra under that," Megan said dismissively. "It's loose and—" She broke off.

"And I'm as flat as a board." Caitlyn knew she didn't have curves, but there was no way in hell she wasn't wearing a bra. No way would she ever again give a man an excuse to say she was asking for it. "I want a bra."

But the specialist store where Megan took her to purchase a bra was far removed from what Caitlyn had intended.

Instead of the functional—and highly invisible—underwear she'd been seeking, she was confronted by a confusing array of colours and styles. Underwear as outerwear. Pale ice-cream shades. Vivid, floral patterns. Stripes. Swirls. Dots. Black. White. Bright pink. Lace.

All of it brief and skimpy.

"Here." Megan stuffed some bits into her hand. "Have a look at these."

"These" caused Caitlyn to blanch. "Isn't there something more, um—" she cast a desperate glance around "—less revealing?" Her gaze alit on a wall of sleek underwear. "That looks more like me."

"Oh, Caitlyn! That's sports underwear. Heavy-duty gear—for marathons and the like."

"Perfect! Sounds like me. Practical." She retrieved a bra with a racing back off the wall.

"You're not wearing *that*—" Megan fixed a gimlet gaze on the beige piece of fabric in her hands "—under the silk top. Try this."

The feel of the garment Megan handed her was seductively soft. The apricot colour was feminine. Pretty. Not garish. Not tarty. Tasteful.

"Perhaps…" But she could feel herself weakening. A moment later she was in a changing cubicle stripping off her T-shirt and beige bra. By contrast the new bra felt luxurious. It was probably wildly expensive. Caitlyn glanced at the price tag and shut her eyes as she put her hands behind her and hooked up the back.

It pushed up her breasts, giving her a shape she'd never noticed having. Against the apricot satin her skin looked pale and creamy.

Feminine, she decided turning a little to the side and doing a double take as she saw the pert tilt that the bra had lent to her breasts. She cupped her breasts, the satin soft and sleek under her fingers, fascinated by the shape. For a brief flash she imagined Rafaelo's hands there in place of her own…

Her nipples pebbled under the fabric. A hot, unfamiliar sweetness pierced her.

"Caitlyn, try these." Megan's voice broke over her like a bucket of cold water.

Caitlyn ripped her hands away from her chest and felt herself flushing with guilt.

A hand appeared over the top of the changing-room door. "They're the matching panties."

She swallowed convulsively. "I don't need panties." Her voice sounded a little squeaky.

"Of course you need panties."

Caitlyn had a brief vision of the drawer back in her loft apartment stacked with beige underwear and her gaze slid guiltily back to the mirror…to the sight of her body clad in nothing but faded jeans and that exquisite bit of apricot satin that made her skin look like a pale baroque pearl.

She felt more feminine than she'd ever felt in her life. She even looked…well…sexy.

Not in a tarty way. In a natural, very classy kind of way.

Sexy.

It was a word she'd never thought of in relation to herself. Megan was stylishly sexy. Joshua's fiancée, Alyssa, was overtly sexy in a to-die-for way. She'd seen how men looked at both women—with appreciation, with narrow-eyed awareness. No one looked at her in that way.

No one except Rafaelo.

She swallowed at the unsettling memory of his dark intense gaze fixed on her. While the flashes of his uniquely exotic scent, the touch of his fingers, his lips seducing hers, all sent shivers of delight pulsing through her.

But for so long she'd gone out of her way to do whatever she could to avoid stares of masculine hunger that she'd reacted to him like a demented, hormonal adolescent who blew hot one minute and froze the next. He must think her a lunatic.

But she was no longer a teenager—which would justify some craziness—she was a twenty-eight-year-old. A woman. Caitlyn shucked off her jeans and pulled on the panties. Then she straightened to her full height and turned to face the mirror.

She looked so…naked.

Her colour high, she glanced away from the exposed plains of her pale belly, her long legs, and shivered. Then inexorably her eyes were drawn back to her reflection.

A woman's body.

The panties were cut high, higher than her own that she still wore beneath. They dipped down across her waist, below her belly button, lower than anything she'd ever worn, revealing miles of pale, tender flesh.

She shuddered. Gooseflesh rippled across her skin, caused by the odd mix of discomfort…and some secretly exciting emotion that she was too scared to name.

"Try these." Another handful of fabric appeared over the door. "For under the dress you'll be wearing to dinner."

This time the garments were silk. A silver grey that reminded Caitlyn of the moonbeams that had lit the path the night Rafaelo had walked her home. The first time he'd so nearly kissed her…before she'd panicked and ran.

Her breath caught in her throat. "Megan, I don't need —"

"Just try them." There was a hint of impatience in Megan's voice. Then it softened. "Indulge me. I don't get you to the shops nearly as often as I'd like."

It was only underwear, Caitlyn told herself. Why the hell was she getting into such a state over a few pieces of silk and lace?

Her matter-of-fact facade held for as long as it took to don the new set. She stared at her reflection. The fabric was so delicate, so fine, that her areolae were visible beneath the bra cups. Even as she watched her breasts peaked again and the centres grew tight and seemed to darken to the hue of damask rose. Beneath the panties the tawny triangle of hair created a darker shadow.

"I can't wear this set," she said hoarsely. Hell, even if Rafaelo never saw how subtly revealing the underwear beneath her flapper frock was, she'd know. She wouldn't be able to meet his eyes the whole evening without blushing. She'd be tongue-tied. Gauche and naive—a world apart from the cosmopolitan Spaniard.

Caitlyn gave a soft groan of mortification. Then she pulled herself together. "But I'll take the apricot set." She stripped off the exquisite silver-grey lingerie and tried not to regret that she didn't have the guts to wear them.

To forestall Megan from pressuring her any further, Caitlyn changed back into her serviceable cotton, emerged from the change room and said, "Maybe I should take another set in the same style as the apricot set." Moments later she'd picked out a pretty lilac set that Megan said did wonderful things for her skin.

With a last wistful glance at the silver-grey silk, Caitlyn collected the bits of lavender and apricot lingerie that she had chosen and made her way to the till.

For one crazy moment she wished she could tell Rafaelo— or even show him—the huge step she'd taken into the unknown today.

"You look lovely, *querida*." Coming from Rafaelo, the compliment sounded very different from how it had sounded spoken by Megan only an hour ago when the other woman had helped her get ready and presented her with the exquisite set of silver-grey lingerie. "Just for you," Megan had said when Caitlyn had tried to protest. Now the rough timbre of Rafaelo's voice ignited a heat deep within her.

"You look pretty good yourself."

It was an understatement. Rafaelo looked magnificent. It wasn't only the well-cut suit—Caitlyn didn't know enough about men's fashion to hazard a guess at the name of the designer, but it looked expensive. Nor was it the bright white shirt that set off his Mediterranean complexion. It was so much more than that.

The dark eyes that glinted with appreciation. The mouth that curved into a smile. The features that looked so hard until one saw the lines of humour around his eyes.

He was special. One of a kind. Caitlyn drew a deep breath. Where the hell had that thought come from?

Hastily she said, "I hope you enjoy the place I chose."

"I'm sure I will."

Ten minutes later Rafaelo pulled the BMW Z4 he'd collected from the car-rental company yesterday into a packed outdoor city car park. Alighting from the car that was a far cry from the battered wreck, he came around and held her door open.

Caitlyn emerged, straightening, and with a slight sense of shock Rafaelo looked into her eyes. He was reminded afresh that she was almost as tall as him. He wasn't used to that from the women he escorted.

"You smell nice," she said a trifle breathlessly as he lent forward to close the car door.

He laughed in surprise at the compliment and breathed in the essence of her. *Wildflowers.* "So do you."

"I'm not wearing perfume," she said sounding chagrined.

"I know. But I can smell the shampoo you used, the lavender of your soap."

She gave an embarrassed laugh. "I should have remembered. You're a winemaker after all." She stepped away from the car. "I don't normally wear perfume because it interferes with my sense of smell. And tonight I forgot."

"You don't need perfume. Your skin smells sweet and clean like the wind over a meadow of wildflowers."

He heard her breath catch as he gazed into her eyes—gleaming silver in the yellow glow of Napier's art deco streetlights.

A soft "thank you" then she was striding away, her legs long and slender and her body infinitely seductive in the silver slip of a dress that she wore.

Slowly, with a sense of foreboding, Rafaelo followed her.

* * *

All That Jazz was a shock. Instead of the upmarket café she'd expected, Caitlyn found herself in a dim cavern with smoke swirling around a small dance floor under muted lighting. While on the stage, a band of jazz musicians readied themselves to play.

Table twelve turned out to be in an alcove on a mezzanine level, giving a sense of privacy, a dangerous intimacy that shrieked seduction.

She picked up the cloth napkin, unfolded it and placed it across her lap. Her hands were trembling slightly as she stretched and took a piece of bread from the complimentary platter. The pâté knife clattered as her hands shook. Nerves. Caitlyn concentrated fiercely on spreading tapenade onto the morsel.

"Relax." Rafaelo's voice was low. "No need to be nervous."

"I'm not nervous," she said in a tight little voice. But she lied. Her insides were a bundle of writhing nerves. Caitlyn felt woefully out of her depth in these surroundings. The smart supper club. The exquisite beaded dress she wore. The man who sat across from her, his eyes hooded, unreadable.

"You have no reason to be—" Rafaelo paused and she got the impression he was choosing his words with care "—worried." He gestured around them. "We're in a public place—your choice, your territory."

She opened her mouth to correct him, to tell him he was far more at ease here in these sexy sophisticated surroundings than she. Then, remembering she was supposed to have chosen a restaurant she liked, she shut it abruptly. Well, the only advantage she possessed was—rather ironically—the fact that she'd lost the bet, so she'd be paying for dinner. She could terminate the evening at any time she chose.

There was no need to feel so shaky. She had control of the situation. Caitlyn threw him a quick look. He sat sprawled across the chair, looking relaxed and far more in command of the situation than she felt. A shivery kind of need arced through her at the sight of his hard line of his smooth-shaven jaw and the intent, snapping eyes that pinned her to her seat.

Then she forced herself to get a grip. Rafaelo was right, they were in a public place. Nothing could happen here.

Nine

"So do you come here often?" A provocative half smile curved Rafaelo's lips.

He knew! Or did he? Could he possibly suspect she'd never set a sneaker-clad foot in this venue before? The slow beat of the jazz music started up, incredibly sultry in the dim surroundings. After a moment's hesitation Caitlyn turned her hands up in supplication. "I've never been here in my life. Megan recommended it."

His smile widened, wicked with a touch of the devil. "I'm glad."

"Why?" Instantly she became defensive.

He covered her hand with his. "We'll discover it together."

Together. That silenced her. An experience that would bind them closer, increasing the intimacy she'd been trying to avoid. She stared at their joined hands, his so much more tanned than hers, the contrast marked even in this muted light. His knuckles were scarred and battered. A fighter's hands.

Caitlyn searched for a distraction.

She wrinkled her nose as she caught sight of her nails. Short, unpolished. Working hands. She curled her fingers under her palms, hiding them. No doubt the women Rafaelo dated would have beautifully manicured hands. She could imagine those pampered hands, resting on his arm, touching him. Caitlyn didn't like the sharp emotion that writhed inside her.

"Your skin is like silk," he murmured and his rugged hand stroked hers where it lay clenched on the white damask cloth.

Her pulse throbbed where her wrist lay on the table's edge. Panic began to rise within her. With great care Rafaelo lifted her hand and brushed his lips across the back.

Caitlyn froze as sensation shot through her, piercing, shockingly erotic. But before she could jerk her hand away, he'd released it. The waitress arrived with a short menu and an even shorter list of Saturday-evening specials—and after ascertaining her dislikes, Rafaelo ordered.

He handed her the wine list. "You choose."

Stuttering, her composure in pieces, Caitlyn ordered a fine red that had garnered much praise. The waitress returned after a few minutes with the wine, poured it, before disappearing again and leaving them alone.

Silence separated them.

On the stage a woman in a black-and-silver spangled dress started to sing, a throaty ballad about lonely yesterdays. Taking a sip of her wine, Caitlyn was overwhelmingly conscious of the man opposite her.

Curiosity stirred. She didn't know much about him. Only that he'd come proclaiming that he intended to hurt the family she loved. Yet, instead of cruelty, he'd revealed flashes of kindness and humour—to Diablo, to Kay and to herself—that had soothed the edges off her fears. Within her the unrelenting pressure began to ease; sensations she hadn't experienced for years were returning to life. All because of Rafaelo.

Somehow he'd taken her fear of his sheer masculine presence and managed to make her feel beautiful…sexy…qualities she'd never been aware of possessing leaving her disarmed and tongue-tied. Making a concerted effort to push the shyness aside, she set her wineglass down, flipped back her loose hair and met Rafaelo's liquid gaze. "Tell me about your home in Spain."

"Torres Carreras?" His face took on a faraway expression. "The building stands on a chalky slope overlooking the Atlantic and gets its name from two towers that were rumoured to have been built by the Moors." There was a mesmerising smoothness in his voice. "I always miss it when I am away. It is hard to believe that when I return this time, Papa will not be there to welcome me home."

"Your father, the Marques, died there?"

He nodded. "In the bed where he was born. It was in that room that I learned he'd adopted me, that Phillip Saxon was my biological father—" he glanced at her "—making me a bastard."

She flinched. "The first time we met you said Phillip was your father. I called you a liar. I owe you an apology for calling you that." Caitlyn deeply regretted the outburst. It would've hurt him. "I didn't even know you. But I couldn't believe Phillip could do such a thing to Kay."

"You were protecting the Saxons." The hard line of his mouth softened. "Your loyalty was commendable. I admire you for it."

Her breath escaped on a whisper of a sigh. He'd forgiven her more easily than she deserved. "They gave me more than a job. They gave me a home." And after Tommy's attack the Saxons had given her a sanctuary.

"That's another thing we have in common, then." Rafaelo's fingers touched her wrist, fleetingly, then lifted away to where his wineglass stood. But the brief gesture was enough to send her pulse crazy. "My stepfather gave me a home. I never realised his generosity," he continued, examining the dark red wine. "I took

Torres Carreras for granted. He made very generous provisions for my mother—and left the house and land and the rest of his estate to me."

Pretending that her awareness of him hadn't gone into overdrive, Caitlyn said, "You never suspected you were adopted?"

He took a sip of wine, set the glass down and shook his head. "Not until he told me. He thought I deserved to know the truth. And to have the opportunity to meet my own father—get to know him—before he, too, died." Rafaelo's mouth turned down. "I don't know how he could believe I would want to get to know a man who had betrayed my mother so brutally."

His unforgiving words steadied her, halting the dizzying high that filled her. "Weren't you curious about Phillip… Whether or not you had brothers or sisters?"

"Not about—" he hesitated "—Phillip, but I did wonder about brothers and sisters."

He was interrupted by the arrival of their food. Caitlyn was barely conscious of eating her meal. The crisp duck was sweet and succulent. But Caitlyn barely tasted it. She was too consumed by curiosity.

"What did your mother think about the Marques's insistence on telling you the truth?"

"She was worried I might blame her." He shook his head. "But once she'd told me about her visit to New Zealand to learn about her great-uncle, about the journals she'd discovered, I knew I had to come. One day this week I intend to retrace Fernando's steps." He cocked his head. "You may come with me if you wish."

"I'd like that." Then Caitlyn wondered if the acceptance had been wise. A whole day spent in Rafaelo's company might be more than she could survive.

The music had grown louder. The singer's voice was husky and ragged, and the sophisticated notes of the saxophone seeped into Caitlyn's soul with a poignancy that hurt.

"My mother was given the set of journals that Fernando had written by a local historical-society member… I want to find out more about those and what happened to them after they were stolen."

Caitlyn tensed. She thought of the three leather-bound journals that lay in her bedside drawer and her breath caught. *Tell him.* Yet Phillip had ordered her to keep silent; he owned them.

"My mother was delighted to have the journals, a link to her past. She hated the fact that they'd been stolen from her."

She opened her mouth to tell Rafaelo that his mother had sold that link to the past to buy a passage home. Then she closed it again. How could she contradict what his mother must've wanted him to believe? It was not for her to open more wounds. "How did your mother meet Phillip?"

Rafaelo's eyes grew hard. "The chairman of the society suggested to my mother that she contact Phillip—the Saxon family had acquired the monastery where the monks originally lived and turned it into a homestead. He thought Phillip Saxon might be able to tell my mother more about the monks who had prayed and planted vines there." His sensuous lips pursed. "He arranged to meet my mother in the town. She was bowled over from their first encounter. Naturally Saxon never told her he was married. She was eighteen…a long way from home. He hid his marital status from her. He seduced her."

"Rafaelo, did she ever tell you that he used force?" Playing with the stem of her glass, to avoid his gaze, she shifted uncomfortably in her seat. "Is that why you hate him so much?"

"No." He sounded shocked. "It wasn't rape. But he was older. Wiser. He should've known better. *Dios.* He even took her to Saxon's Folly, showed her around, raising her hopes that the attraction between them was serious, that he meant to marry her. He never breathed a word about a wife—or the child he was considering adopting."

Caitlyn thought of what Kay had told them. About her desperate desire for a baby. About how Phillip had felt neglected when she'd become lost in her world with their newly adopted baby. Her pity for Maria, Kay and Phillip grew. But it would be tactless to voice it.

Instead lifting her head she said, "Your stepfather sounds like an amazing man—to bring up another man's child as his own."

"He was." The smile that lit Rafaelo's face was full of fondness. "My mother loved him. I am certain of it. Phillip was a youthful aberration—lust."

Caitlyn nodded, noticing that he was no longer casting all the blame on Phillip. But she had no intention of entering a discussion about lust. Not with Rafaelo.

"What does your mother do now?"

"She's involved in the business—in Spain sherry is big business. It would impress her that you are a winemaker. She would like you."

Caitlyn smiled, knowing he was paying her the highest compliment he could. "I'm sure I'd like her, too."

"You should come and visit."

"Maybe, one day." She considered him, then opened up. "I've always been intrigued by the Jerez region—and the notion of producing real, authentic sherry."

She'd fantasised about going to Spain, had spoken to Phillip of taking a year off to study the methods. But after Heath had bought Chosen Valley Estate, Saxon's Folly had consumed every waking moment of her time.

Now she waited, with bated breath, for Rafaelo's volatile reaction to the sherry word. For a moment he didn't speak, and the music from the band filled the silence between them. Then he surprised her by changing the subject, and asking, "And your parents, are they winemakers, too?"

"Nothing so grand." For the first time she was glad that

Rafaelo, Marques de Las Carreras, wasn't some blue-blooded marques—even though he did bear a title. Caitlyn raised her chin. In a rush she said, "My mother was a milkmaid, my father a cattle herdsman. They had five children. I was the middle child."

He looked at her contemplatively, no hint of shock marring his handsome features. "As an only child of a very rich man, I had everything I desired. I'd imagine your upbringing was very different."

"Yes." It came out a whisper. She remembered the sleepless nights as a child when she'd vowed to herself that she would never fall into the poverty trap that snared her parents. "I was lucky—I loved school. And I realised good grades were my ticket out. Not lotto. Nor the betting on the dog racing that my father sank his weekly wages into every Friday night."

"That was wise for one so young."

"My oldest brother escaped the cycle, too. He's a property de-veloper." Rhys was ruthless. "Between the two of us we bought my parents a smallholding. They're content." And she no longer had to worry about them.

"What about your other siblings?" Rafaelo asked.

"James is a labourer. Shannon and Rhiannon work on a sheep farm down south. Rhiannon is beautiful—she's the youngest, she's so tall, she could've been a supermodel." Caitlyn lifted her glass, the smooth wine slid down her throat, wine that neither Shannon nor Rhiannon would ever recognise. Would her naive, simple young sister have survived the cutthroat world of mod-elling? Perhaps not.

"Honest work. You must be proud of them."

"Of course." She blinked. Why was she telling him all this stuff? She never talked about her childhood. Too depressing. Some people even looked at her strangely—behaved a little dis-tantly—after finding out her parents had been lowly wage-earning farm workers.

Yet Rafaelo's eyes didn't go blank, nor did his lips curl in disgust. Instead he looked interested, concerned, his gaze intense as it centred on her. "It must have taken a lot for you to get where you are today, Caitlyn."

"Hard work—and lots of determination. I spent most of my teen years with my nose stuck in school books." Later at university she'd stayed in while her mates dated and partied. She'd needed top marks to secure the scholarships that had kept her at university.

"And sacrifices, I'd imagine."

She nodded.

Rafaelo could have been reading her mind. She thought of the dates she'd missed out on. It hadn't mattered back then, she'd had her priorities—and a fat crush on Heath Saxon.

But it mattered now. Tonight she wished she had some woman-of-the-world experience to deal with a man like Rafaelo. She glanced away from him to the bandstand. The singer had moved into a lively piece and the dance floor seethed with movement.

He followed her gaze. "Would you like to dance?"

Flushing, she hesitated a beat too long. "Thank you."

Rafaelo was on his feet, helping her up, leading her down the stairs to where couples crowded onto the small dance space. Then she was in his arms, barely a respectable distance between them, blood rushing in her ears and her heart hammering in her chest.

"I have to tell you that I admire you."

There was no hint of guile in his eyes. Only admiration…and something that made adrenaline burst through her with sharp stabbing force. Unaccountably she felt herself flushing more deeply.

"I've embarrassed you," he said.

"I colour easily. It's this Celtic colouring. The one thing I got from my father."

"What about your height?"

"Both my parents are tall—and my mother is every bit as skinny as I am."

He dropped the hand that he held and rested both his hands on her hips. "Not skinny—slender."

His hand moved over the curve of her bottom and her breath died in her throat. She'd been so lost in their conversation, she'd forgotten what she was wearing. Caitlyn had a vision of the slips of mist-coloured silk beneath his hand and quivered.

Damn. She had to get a grip over her reactions. Rafaelo didn't have X-ray fingers. He'd never know what she wore beneath her finery. But sooner or later her edginess would give her away. Hell, he might even think she fancied him…that she was trying to encourage him.

That thought caused her to wiggle uncomfortably—and become even more aware of the wretched panties she was trying so hard to ignore.

Instantly his hands lifted from her bottom and came to rest very properly around her waist. But her breathing didn't return to normal.

"Relax, *querida*."

But his deep voice, the soft words breathed into the curl of her ear had the opposite effect. Every muscle in her wayward body tightened. She tried to pull away, his hold eased, but the push of the dancers around them left her with nowhere to go.

But his gentle hold, the beat of the moody music, the singer's husky voice and the dark anonymity of the smoky club all conspired against her.

She was safe here.

Nothing could happen.

She relaxed her hands against his shoulders, and let her hips move in time to the music. Without crowding her, Rafaelo moved with her, their rhythm in tune. When had she last danced like this? Hell, when had she ever danced like this?

Lost in the unfamiliar world, she allowed herself to be caught up in the next song when it came, her body fluidly following where Rafaelo led. The floor grew more packed, the smoke machine pumped out more smoke. She edged closer to him, linking her fingers around the back of his neck, her fingertips catching in the long hair that brushed his collar.

His hair felt smooth...thicker than hers...different from anything she'd ever touched. Her fingers seemed to assume a life of their own, playing with his hair, stroking the heat of his nape.

"Caitlyn." He dipped his head, his breath hot in her ear.

Shivers of pleasure shot through her at the startling, unfamiliar sensation, and her entire body convulsed against his.

He bent his head. When his lips brushed the ridge of her naked shoulder she gave a start of surprise, her skin prickling under the flirty touch. "What are you doing?"

"Kissing you."

He spoke against her skin. His mouth opened at the side of her neck, under the secret veil of her long loose hair, and her whole body reacted.

"Rafaelo!"

He raised his head. "Too fast?"

Unable to speak, she stared at him, blinded by the violent arousal that leapt through her, unlike anything she'd ever experienced before.

"Too fast," he murmured.

Too fast? Hell! Heart hammering against her ribs, she tore out of his arms, not daring to look at the wicked mouth that had just done such seemingly innocuous, utterly erotic things to her.

"Let's sit out the next one," she suggested, staring ahead, breathless with tumult.

Back at the table she made a frantic effort to pull what was left of her composure together. When the waitress returned, Caitlyn refused dessert and coffee and asked for the bill, desperate to leave, before she disgraced herself by begging Rafaelo to dance with her and dissolved in his arms.

Out of her peripheral vision she saw Rafaelo raise his

eyebrows, but she didn't care. *She* was in control, *she* was buying dinner. If she wanted to call the evening to an end, then that was her prerogative. He didn't need to scan her with those sharp eyes—or shoot his brows to the ceiling in that superior, masculine way.

But she had no intention of meeting those perceptive eyes. Not after what had just happened on the dance floor. She'd never felt anything like that in her life, she hadn't even known such wild pleasure existed.

She was torn between fear—of the feelings he aroused in her—and a more basic apprehension that she might never feel this way again. She was tempted to snatch at what he offered.

However reckless.

Slow down, she warned herself. There was no point losing her head over this sophisticated Spaniard. No matter how compelling he was. In a few days he'd be leaving. Forever. She'd do well to remember that.

When the bill arrived in a leather folder, the waitress handed it to Rafaelo with a flirtatious smile. Caitlyn reached out to intercept it saying, "I'll take that."

But Rafaelo already had the folder in his hands and when Caitlyn grabbed the other end he didn't relinquish his hold. For several seconds they tussled, until Caitlyn snapped, "I'm supposed to pay—I lost our bet."

"I won a date."

"I don't date."

The waitresses glanced from one to the other goggle-eyed. And Caitlyn felt her colour rise. Now even the waitress was regarding her like a freak—and probably wondering what on earth a man like Rafaelo was doing with a beanpole who didn't date.

Every nerve felt on edge. She swallowed her humiliation. "Give it to me." Then tacked on a belated, "Please."

He shook his head slowly. "You paid your dues by coming on a date you didn't want."

Even less did she want to be in his debt. She cast an agonised look at the interested waitress. But she wasn't admitting that in front of a third party, so she pressed her lips into a tight line. Once Rafaelo had signed the chit and the waitress had departed, Caitlyn said, "I'd like to leave."

That was an understatement.

She *had* to leave.

The glance that Rafaelo sent her was measuring, and she knew he'd picked the coolness in her voice. But she couldn't help it. The relaxation had gone and her tension had returned a hundredfold worse than before. Then she hadn't known what she knew now. She'd been innocent. So certain she was paying, so certain she was in control.

On that dance floor she'd lost any control she had. By paying he'd taken her security. Now she was struggling out of her depth. No longer certain that she could call the shots, or had the power to end the evening.

She wanted to go home. She didn't want to risk any further unpredictable changes to the evening's schedule.

Caitlyn gathered her micro bag and was on her feet before he could draw out her chair. She exited the restaurant with Rafaelo right behind her. Caitlyn paused for a moment and drew in a breath of salty sea air filling her lungs before exhaling sharply.

"What's the matter?"

"Nothing." How could she tell him about the tightness of her skin? The frightening awareness of him that increased exponentially every time he came close? How much it terrified her?

"Do you want to walk?"

Maybe a walk would help the restlessness. Maybe a walk would prove what had happened back on that dance floor was…was a figment of her fevered imagination. She nodded jerkily, then wished she'd refused when they reached the foreshore and found it deserted. The huge golden globe of the moon hung over the sea, and the thunder of the sea crashed in the night. A moist sea breeze caressed her arms, heightening her senses.

"Do you want my jacket?"

She was too hot, her skin felt too tight. "It's warm enough out here by the sea," she said, softening her rejection.

"It's windy."

"I'm okay." She couldn't accept his jacket, couldn't bear to be enfolded in his scent, to feel frissons of the emotions he'd awoken trembling through her. Swinging away from the sound of the surf, Caitlyn walked toward the nearest source of light, an immense art deco fountain.

"Look." She spoke as though it had always been her intention to show him the fountain. "It's lit up every night."

They stood and watched as the fountain changed colours. The stillness gave her an opportunity to regroup as they watched the greens and reds melt into one another.

"It's magical, don't you think?"

"Magical," Rafaelo agreed. But he was looking at her.

What was left of her control shredded. Helplessly Caitlyn started to tremble.

By the time Rafaelo nosed the car into the stable yard Caitlyn was a mass of shivering expectation. Did she dare allow him to kiss her? To make a little love to her? A faint doubt flared. Could she really trust him to stop if she got cold feet?

Fleetingly she considered that he would be leaving any day. *So what?* With a burst of apprehension mixed with awe she remembered the intensity of the sensations that had shaken her on the dance floor.

Could she cope with that?

Yes. She'd had enough of being a scared little mouse. She had to try start living again sometime… So why not tonight?

"We didn't have coffee at the restaurant. Come upstairs, I'll make you a cup." Her voice was high, squeaky with the enormity of what she was contemplating.

"Thanks." He gave her a slow smile that made her heart twist in her chest. "I don't think so, I should go."

Suddenly she didn't want him to go. It became vital for him to stay. Before she chickened out and never screwed up the courage to try this again. "A nightcap?"

He gave her a long, level stare. "One nightcap." His mouth twisted into a mocking line. "A sherry, perhaps."

"I don't have any." And it was a relief. She had no intention of becoming embroiled in this futile rivalry between Phillip and Rafaelo. She headed for the stairs. Over her shoulder, she offered, "I can offer you a glass of ice wine instead."

His feet sounded loud on the steel stairs behind her. "I've read about that."

Caitlyn unlocked the door and stepped inside. "Wait until you taste it."

"This is nice." Rafaelo stood in her sitting room and looked around the whitewashed walls, the wooden floor covered with scatter rugs and the exposed dark-stained ceiling beams with approval.

"It's home." Caitlyn dropped her tiny bag on the wooden chest that served as a coffee table and made for the fridge in the kitchenette, returning with a bottle of Canadian ice wine and two slender glasses. "I have great views over the vineyards in the daytime."

She poured a little wine into each glass and placed them on the chest. Gesturing to the love seat, she said, "Have a seat."

Standing, Rafaelo dwarfed the room. Caitlyn was relieved when he dropped down onto the love seat. She handed him a glass and watched him take a sip. "Deliciously sweet. Rich."

She laughed at his descriptive shorthand. "It's utterly luscious, isn't it?"

"Luscious…" He gave her a look that caused her laughter to dry up. "But not cloyingly sweet. There's no aftertaste."

Caitlyn relaxed once she realised he was talking of the wine. Plonking herself on a padded footstool, she said, "At Saxon's Folly we use chardonnay—and a small amount of pinot gris. It's freeze concentrated and while we attain a lovely fruity richness that comes from the slow, temperature-controlled fermentation, we haven't gotten near the perfection that the Canadians have achieved."

"It's not cold enough in winter here for the ripest grapes to freeze on the vines?"

Caitlyn shook her head. "Not in Hawkes Bay—down in South Island that works. It always amazes me how resilient grapes can be." For a brief moment the notion returned that she'd been every bit as frozen as those iced-up grapes. But she was finally starting to thaw.

Because of Rafaelo.

But there would be no sweetness, only bitterness. The image of the journals flashed into her mind and a hollowness rested in the pit of her stomach. Rafaelo had been so patient, so gentle with her, and she had not been very forthcoming with him.

It was time to tip the balance a little in his favour. She couldn't tell him about the journals—those belonged to Phillip, it was up to him to reveal their existence to his son—but she could share a secret side of herself.

Plucking up her courage, she said, "I told you that Heath put a good word in for me and got me a job at Saxon's Folly while I was still a student?" Rafaelo nodded, his eyes reserved. "At that stage he'd finished studying and was working at the winery. And I told you Phillip offered me job after graduation…" Her voice trailed away.

"But?" Rafaelo knew there had to be a but—it was in her tone, in the shadows in her usually crystal clear eyes.

"Something happened."

Rafaelo saw that she was struggling with whatever she wanted to tell him. He forced himself to be patient.

"There was a cellar hand who worked here." All vitality leached out her face.

Since meeting her, he'd thought Heath was the reason she froze him out. But for the first time he concluded that there was something more. Tensing, he sat up. The movement brought him closer to her. Had this man broken her heart? "*Querida,* you don't have to tell me about old flames—"

"He's *not* an old flame." She sucked in a deep, shuddering breath. "Tommy was young, good-looking—a little arrogant. He'd swagger around—most of the girls thought he was gorgeous."

Rafaelo frowned, puzzled at the distaste in her voice. This didn't sound like love. "You didn't think he was gorgeous?" He posed it as a question.

"No. Because I—" She gave him a hopeless look.

"Because you fancied Heath." A statement, flatter this time.

"Yes." She looked away. "Even though I knew there was no chance that he would ever look at me."

"Why?" His harsh question brought her startled gaze back to his face. "Why shouldn't he ever look at you?"

"Well, that's not hard." She spread her fingers. "One, I was too tall, too gangly—nothing like the petite, curvy dark-haired type of girl he always dated." She marked off another finger. "Two, my background, the chasm between us was too big to bridge."

"Because you're a labourer's daughter?" His eyes drilled into her.

"Yes, the Saxons are like local aristocracy."

"You're telling me Heath Saxon is a snob?" Rafaelo gave a snort of disgust. "That you'd fall for a man like that?"

"Perhaps I was more conscious of the differences than Heath was," she conceded.

"You were tempted to date this other man to get over Heath?"

"No! I was too involved in my work. I was painfully conscious that I had to do my best. I wanted a full-time position here as a cellar hand after I graduated from university."

Because it would keep her close to Heath Saxon? Rafaelo thrust the unwelcome thought aside.

"Even if I didn't get a job offer, I wanted a reference from Phillip Saxon."

She'd been building a career. It made sense, given what she'd revealed about her upbringing. "And?" he prompted.

"I was working late one evening. I was alone—except for Tommy. It was a hot evening. I was wearing denim cutoffs and a tank top. It was bright sunshine-yellow." Her voice cracked. "How clearly I remember that."

Rafaelo had a sudden, shattering premonition of where this was going. He reached for her hands. They were icy-cold under the touch of his fingers. "He tried—"

"To kiss me," she cut across him. "I didn't really like it. But I'd never had a boyfriend. I was twenty-three years old and my whole life had been about studying. I was curious. The next time someone talked about guys I didn't want to sit there flushing. I thought to myself that it wouldn't do any harm to let him kiss me."

"But it didn't stop there, did it?"

"No." She gave him a hunted look, her fingers biting into his. "He tried to…touch me…grab me. His hands were all over my tank top. They were grubby. It was disgusting! I wanted him to stop. He wouldn't. I struggled. He started to swear at me, made me feel dirty. The things he said." She let go of his hands and put her hands over her face, her long, elegant fingers shaking.

"Caitlyn—" Rafaelo tried to break through her distress "—he's not here now. He said those things because he was trying to bully you, intimidate you into doing what he wanted. Let them go. Don't let him keep that hold over you."

"I know that." Her fingers parted, the crystal eyes that stared through the cracks between her fingers were murky with pain. "But it wasn't just what he said. It was what he did."

Horror shook Rafaelo. "He *attacked* you?"

"Yes." It was a tiny mewing sound.

"He raped you?"

"No." She lifted her head. "Not that. He ripped my top off, tearing it. I wasn't wearing a bra. He grabbed me." Her breath came in labouring gasps. "He hurt me, hit me…tried to rip my shorts off. I started screaming." She stopped, hunching forward, her shoulders shaking.

"You don't have to tell me this."

After a moment she continued tonelessly, "I was lucky. Joshua had forgotten his house keys in the winery. He caught Tommy. He fired him on the spot. I didn't want him to tell anyone what had happened. I was too humiliated."

"So Tommy got away." Rafaelo kept his voice level by tremendous strength of will. He wanted to touch her, tell her that she was okay. But her expression warned him that now wasn't the time to reach for her.

"No, Joshua convinced me to lay charges. He was convicted— jailed for assault."

"Good!" Rafaelo tried to temper the fierce anger that surged through him. It was just as well Tommy was incarcerated, otherwise Rafaelo would have felt compelled to seek him out and teach him a lesson he would never forget.

"Despite the doctor's evidence listing my welts and bruises, in court Tommy said that I was asking for it. That I wanted it. That I led him on. *Consent,* his lawyer called it."

"He lied." Not wanting to scare her with his anger, Rafaelo deliberately kept his voice empty of the red-hot rage that burned in him against the unknown Tommy and his scumbag defence lawyer.

"And now I worry—"

"About what?"

"That a decent guy might think—"

"Might think it was your fault?" Rafaelo stared at her in disbelief, shaken by what this man…this animal had done to her.

Ten

"*Never.*" Rafaelo's eyes burned with outrage, and a muscle worked overtime in his jaw. "Any man who thinks what happened to you was your fault is not decent."

Perched on the footstool, Caitlyn stared at him through beaten eyes, her shoulders sagging at what she'd revealed. "Rationally I know all that. But sometimes I still feel…" She hesitated, not sure what he would think if she told him about the invasive demons that lived in her head.

"Guilty?"

She nodded miserably.

"Caitlyn, *querida,* you have nothing to feel guilty about." He opened his arms, and his eyes called to her to cross the small space that separated them.

She hurled herself into his arms, landing half sprawled across his chest, half on the sofa beside him. "I even feel guilty about feeling guilty," she said against the comforting wall of his chest.

"And sometimes I think that the only reason I got a full-time job here is because the Saxons feel responsible for what happened to me."

"Don't think that!" His lips brushed her ear. "They were fortunate to secure you. With your results you could have walked into a winery anywhere in the world and have been offered a position."

"Thank you," she whispered.

Above her head, he murmured, "I'm going to tighten my arms around you. I want to hold you, is that okay?"

"Yes, of course it is."

Then his arms closed around her and she felt safe. Wonderfully, heart-wrenchingly safe. She could stay here forever.

"I'm going to kiss you now."

For a moment she froze up. Then she thought about his patience, about the wonderful evening they'd shared, about how he'd stopped the moment he'd realised he was going too fast…and nodded her consent.

As his finger slid beneath her chin, she closed her eyes and lifted her face.

"*Querida,* open your eyes. I want you to see who is kissing you." His voice was so gentle that a lump formed in her throat.

Her lashes fluttered up. "Okay."

Rafaelo's head came down, his lips hovered a tiny bit above her. "Why don't you kiss me?" His eyes were warm and there was laughter in his voice. Just like that she relaxed.

It was going to be okay.

She stretched forward and placed her lips against his. He kissed her back.

The shock of it jolted her. It was unbearably sweet. He tasted of ice wine. When he lifted his head, she silently wished that he hadn't stopped. He must have seen something of her yearning in her face because he gave a little groan and lowered his head.

His lips were hungrier than before. For once the fear that had imprisoned her for so long didn't ignite and consume her. Instead curiosity stirred…and her own hunger. Tipping her head back she let her lips part.

Instantly his breath escaped in a rush and he took the kiss deeper. Briefly. Then his mouth moved to her cheeks, kissing her. Softly. Tenderly. Slowly.

Trusting him, Caitlyn moved closer, sliding her hands over his chest. Under her palms his heart gave great thumping jolts, at odds with the gentle, patient kisses he was pressing against her face.

For the first time she realised what this was costing him. He was an experienced man of the world. No doubt the women he consorted with knew the score. And yet, here he was, taking his time, content to go at her pace.

The sudden burst of affection she felt for him took Caitlyn by surprise. Not only was he awaking sensations long dormant—she *liked* him, too.

His fingers traced the scooped neckline of her dress, tickling a little. She wriggled. He moved his fingers onto the fabric. Then she stopped breathing as his hand slipped down…over the curves below. And paused. He cupped her breast and she waited, her heart thundering so loudly she was sure he must hear it.

His tongue touched her lip and she gasped. She could feel her senses sharpening, every nerve ending prickling. Every place his body touched hers—his lips, his tongue, the hand cupping her breast, the solid chest that she leaned against—all conspired to build the ache within her.

She buried against him.

"Slowly, *querida,* slowly."

After being frozen in ice for so long the return of emotion was agonizing. She felt raw and terribly uncertain, anxious, trying to second-guess what Rafaelo was thinking.

"Are you okay?" His voice was husky.

"Fine." She wished he'd stop talking and kiss her again.

His hand moved. "Still okay?"

"Yes."

"Not too fast?"

She shook her head frantically.

His thumb moved against the crest of her breast and a stab of pleasure pierced her.

The dress had ridden up. His other hand touched her leg where the dress ended. She watched his tanned hand moving against her pale bare skin, watched as it disappeared under the hemline and she began to shake.

"Anytime you say, we stop," he murmured. "You're calling the shots."

Earlier she'd thought by choosing the restaurant, paying for the meal she'd be in command of the situation. She'd been so wrong. She had no control. Her body didn't obey her anymore. It had gained a life of its own. Wild sensations tumbled through her reducing her to jelly.

His mouth was back on hers, sealing it closed. Now he was kissing her deeply, filling her, his tongue tasting her with slow, sensuous licks. His fingers inched along the soft skin of her inner thighs…higher…higher…. She gasped.

His hand stroked back toward her knee, the hand on her breast stilled, his head lifted. "I think that's enough."

No. But she didn't utter it aloud. She couldn't. She couldn't speak.

He pulled her into his arms. "Ah, *querida*."

Hell, but she was a wimp. Why was he even still here? Any other man would have fled by now, heading for greener pastures, leaving the loony alone.

"I'm s-s-sorry," she stuttered.

His head reared up. "Sorry? Caitlyn, you have nothing to

apologise for. It is I who should apologise for taking things too far, too fast."

Too far, too fast?

Caitlyn gave a laugh that came out sounding like a sob. He'd done little more than kiss her… All very innocent between grown adults. "I'm fine. Truly."

He hugged her closer. "I won't do anything that brings you discomfort."

"I know."

That brought his head up. "You do?"

"Yes." She paused. "I trust you."

Something flared in his dark eyes—relief?—before he closed them. "I swear to you that I will never hurt you. I will never do anything you don't want to do. We will proceed at your pace. Okay?"

"Okay," she whispered. He'd convinced himself that he was taking it too fast. It was up to her to convince him otherwise.

Lying in bed, staring through the dark, Caitlyn could not believe that after their evening together Rafaelo had simply given her a chaste kiss on the cheek goodnight.

After five years in deep freeze her body had thawed out with a vengeance. She hadn't wanted Rafaelo to stop.

She would not have stopped him.

Yet he'd left.

And he'd left her wanting. Burning for him. A state that she'd never expected to find herself in.

Not in a million years. Caitlyn rolled over, restlessly pulling the covers with her and the cotton sheets were cool and smooth against her hot, aching skin. The heat that ripped her apart was a world away from the adulation she'd felt for Heath. The response Rafaelo roused in her was intense, physical, consuming.

And damn it, she liked the man, too.

For an instant she wished that he hadn't flown from across two oceans…that he wouldn't be leaving once he'd gotten what he came for.

What he came for…

His share in Saxon's Folly.

The high that she was on came to a shattering end. Suddenly she felt chilled. Dread filled her. She stared into the darkness that had turned hostile.

Rafaelo would never be able to reconcile with his father. There was too much bad feeling between them. And she was trapped in the middle: between the Saxons whom she adored— and the man she was growing to love.

Rafaelo frowned as he searched the figures working in the winery for a glimpse of strawberry-blond hair. Caitlyn was nowhere to be seen. Apart from a few fleeting encounters on Monday, he'd barely seen her since their date on Saturday night. He suspected she was avoiding him.

He eventually found her in the tasting shed helping Kay shine glasses. He paused in the vast doorway. The moment she caught sight of him a startled expression crossed her face…and something else. Something that made heat shoot to his belly.

"I'm going to spend a week with my brother in Australia. I leave tomorrow," he overheard Kay say to Caitlyn.

"Kay—" Caitlyn gestured to him.

Kay turned and caught sight of him. There was an awful silence.

"You're taking a vacation?" he asked.

"Yes," Kay said with a sigh, picking up a tasting glass and giving it a rub with a soft white cloth. Setting down the shiny vessel, she added with a hint of defiance, "Alone. Phillip won't be accompanying me. But I may stay longer."

"I'm sorry," he murmured, the words totally inadequate, but he could think of no others that would ease her pain.

Kay met his gaze. "It's not your fault."

That's what he'd told himself, too. But coming from Kay Saxon, he felt guilt eating into him.

"I should not have come."

"Of course you should have." She tossed down the white cloth. "Otherwise Joshua, Heath and Megan would never have known you exist."

"But if I had stayed away, you would not have discovered—" He broke off, not wanting to admit his father's adultery aloud.

"The truth." Kay came around the counter and patted his shoulder. "Truth is a strange thing, Rafaelo. Tamper with it and it rebounds on you. Not long ago, Phillip and I told a lie. A lie that hurt Alyssa very much. Because of a promise I'd extracted from Alyssa she couldn't tell Joshua the truth, so he believed the worst of her."

Caitlyn shifted from foot to foot, the movement drawing his gaze. Her light eyes had turned curiously opaque.

"It nearly tore them apart," Kay continued, and the brief thought that Caitlyn might be feeling guilty about some transgression faded as he focused on Kay again. "We had to confess that we had lied—to our children—and, in a different, more painful respect, to Alyssa. I have to live with it every day of my life that Phillip and I cost Alyssa the chance to develop a relationship with her brother." She drew a shuddering breath and lifted the hand from his shoulder. "I can't do that to you—or my children. You deserve to know each other."

"That's exceptionally generous," he said, not daring to admit that he'd had no interest in getting to know his siblings. He'd already been a knife's edge away from a fistfight with Heath. The place where Kay's hand had rested on his shoulder felt hollow. Rafaelo suspected he would feel marked by her generosity for a long time to come.

"It's not easy for me," she said frankly. "But it's important for you—and my children."

What she said humbled him. She could think of him in the same breath as her children, even though his existence must irk her all the time. While he'd come to spit in his father's face, claim his share of Saxon's folly and sell it. Nothing more. For the first time, he considered the wisdom of the course of revenge he'd embarked upon. Perhaps there was something in Caitlyn's advice that he needed to come to terms with the past—and forgive Phillip Saxon.

Kay was talking again. "Phillip lied to me—and to your mother. He's escaped the consequences of his behaviour for years. Your coming has made me realise that there are cracks deep within our marriage, cracks I'd pretended didn't exist—because it was easier."

"What do you mean?" Caitlyn spoke at last.

Emotion clouded Kay's eyes. "After Phillip and I married, we should have been so happy. We were young, in love, and we had a dream—to create fabulous, world-renowned wines in this corner of Hawkes Bay where we would bring up our children. But I struggled to get pregnant. Phillip went on to create the wines alone while I stewed in my unhappiness.

"My inability to conceive put pressure on our marriage. Finally, Phillip suggested we adopt a baby. At first I refused, but slowly, perhaps too slowly—" she gave Rafaelo a meaningful stare "—I came around. From the day Roland first lay in my arms, he was mine. It didn't matter that I hadn't given birth to him."

She stared into space. "Phillip said once that I had time for nothing but the baby, that I shut him out. I told him that he was being silly, that he had the vineyard. Then all of a sudden a miracle happened. I was pregnant, and I gave birth to Joshua. And then there were two babies to care for."

Her eyes were vulnerable. "Perhaps I did neglect Phillip. But I find I can't accept—"

Rafaelo had stiffened. "Me?"

Kay shook her head. "You're not the problem. It's Phillip's infidelity I can't forgive."

Caitlyn stared at Kay, shocked. "Don't do anything hasty."

"I need a little time to decide what I'm going to do." Kay gave a winsome smile. "I won't be hasty. I'll think very carefully before I start divorce proceedings."

"Oh, Kay, I can't tell you how sad this is." Caitlyn hugged Kay. "Don't stay too long in Australia."

And Rafaelo found himself murmuring the words his mother always used, words she had uttered before he left Spain. *"Vaya con Dios."* Go with God.

Kay nodded, her eyes sad. "Thank you, both." Then, forcing a smile, she said, "Now, Rafaelo, I'm sure you didn't come to the tasting shed to hear about my problems. How can we help?"

He glanced at Caitlyn and said, "Tomorrow I will be going to explore Napier and follow in Fernando's footsteps. I thought Caitlyn might like to come."

Uncertainty misted Caitlyn's eyes. "I have work to do."

Was she worried he might try to kiss her again? After her experiences at Tommy's hands he could sympathise if she had reservations. He produced his most charming smile. "I could use a guide."

Kay intervened. "I told you that you're working too hard, dear. Why, last night you worked through the night on racking wine—and with Taine sick, today's going to be equally hectic."

"It's only because the wine can't be exposed to oxygen," Caitlyn said swiftly. "Once the racking is finished, it will be better."

"All the more reason for you to take tomorrow off," said Kay with a smile.

"If I take any time off, I should use it to catch up on sleep," objected Caitlyn.

She wasn't making it easy for him, Rafaelo decided.

"You can sleep anytime. But it's not every day that you can accompany such a fascinating visitor." Kay gave him a little wink.

Rafaelo was tempted to sweep his father's wife off her feet and kiss her soundly. He'd hated Phillip for betraying his mother. Now he disliked his father for betraying this classy woman. How could one man screw up the life of two women? He gave her a broad smile in return, sensing a truce had been forged between them—no, more than a truce. A bond.

"Okay, I'll come." Caitlyn's words brought his focus back to her.

She wore her hair in a braid today, the fine mass drawn off her face to reveal elegant cheekbones and exposing her clear eyes to his gaze. Her lashes looked a little darker than normal, emphasising the stunning uniqueness of her eyes. Her mouth—usually bare of lipstick—wore a slight pale pink gloss.

Rafaelo wanted nothing more than to kiss it rosy.

But he'd promised himself that she was out of bounds. With time she might grow to love a man. But that man would not be him. It would take a lot of time—and time was one luxury he did not have. Soon he would be gone.

Emptiness filled him at the thought. He shook it off.

It would pass. Everything passed. Just as the seasons completed their cycle and the grapes flowered and were harvested, so, too, this emptiness would pass.

"Good, I'll meet you at the stable yard at ten o'clock tomorrow morning," he said, and silently renewed his resolve not to do anything that might cause her to fall apart. "And, as you're understaffed, I'm at your disposal today."

Wednesday morning dawned fresh and summery. The hot sun reflected brightly off the sea as Rafaelo and Caitlyn headed for town, the road clear of traffic ahead.

The first place Rafaelo took Caitlyn to was the historic building that stood off the foreshore where Fernando Lopez and a number of other monks had boarded on first arriving in New Zealand.

Standing outside the wooden building that had survived the

earthquake, Rafaelo stared up at the facade. "Fernando arrived after the first World War—part of a wave of immigrants who settled in New Zealand hoping for a better life. Europe was in shambles." His mouth lifted into a self-deprecating grin that made her heart leap. "You see, I did not come from a privileged background."

Caitlyn grew pensive. "You know, there's a grim irony in the fact that he came to New Zealand for a better life and died in an earthquake—while you, his great-great-nephew, were raised in Spain and became a marques in the country he had abandoned."

He shrugged. "My mother had a stroke of luck. Not many noblemen would marry their housekeeper on discovering she was pregnant."

As they walked back to the car, Caitlyn said, "He must have loved her very much for her pregnancy not to worry him."

"He never told her of his love—not for a very long time." Rafaelo paused, holding the passenger door open for her.

Their eyes held for a long, simmering instant. She was aware that Rafaelo was every bit as special as the Marques—and aware, too, that too soon he would be gone. A moment later he slid in beside her.

"He knew she'd only married him to give her baby a name. He knew she hoped Phillip Saxon would come for her." Rafaelo's mouth curled. "But of course that never happened. It was only when she gave up hope, that my father—the Marques—finally told her that he loved her."

"So when he proposed she didn't know why he wanted to marry her?"

Rafaelo shook his head. "He told her only that he needed an heir. That he was too old to find a wife. He convinced her that she was doing him a favour." Rafaelo's eyes had softened and his smile told Caitlyn how much the old man had meant to him.

"How romantic."

"My mother grew to love him. He was a true gentleman—a man of honour."

Caitlyn hesitated as the car fired up, then she drew a deep breath. "And he taught you to be a man of honour, too?"

Rafaelo inclined his head.

"Would he be proud of what you intend to do? Taking a share of a family estate and auctioning it off to a stranger?"

Rafaelo pulled out into the traffic and made his way down the Marine Parade lined with Norfolk pines. "I am not doing it for myself. I am doing it for my mother. For reparation for the humiliation she suffered at Phillip's hands." His profile was uncompromising.

"Would she want you to do that?"

He didn't answer. Silence fell between them.

Caitlyn busied herself directing Rafaelo to the site where the monks had built a smaller, modest monastery before they'd erected the magnificent building at Saxon's Folly. It had been turned into a community hall.

Rafaelo pulled over and parked in the shade of a tall hedge. Before he could open his door, Caitlyn turned to face him. "I don't believe the Marques would condone what you are doing. He told you who your father was to give you the opportunity to get to know him. He loved you, Rafaelo. He wanted to give you the chance to find your blood father…your brothers and sister. Who knows…maybe he even felt guilty for not doing it sooner and denying you the right to love your father…your birth family…for most of your life."

Rafaelo looked staggered. "No one could have been a better father."

"Perhaps he thought he was old—that he didn't run around enough with you, that he'd cheated you of growing up with your siblings."

"He couldn't think that." But Rafaelo was frowning. "No one could have hoped for a better father. You are wrong."

"Maybe." She'd said more than enough. Caitlyn opened the car door. Once out in the fresh air, she glanced curiously toward the overgrown meadows behind the building. "That must be where they planted the Cabernet Franc vines they brought with them from Spain." Descendants of those vines grew at Saxon's Folly.

"In the beginning they made red wine—for the sacrament." Rafaelo sounded preoccupied.

Unwisely Caitlyn said, "It was only later when they built Saxon's Folly that they started making fortified wines with some commercial success. Everyone knows that," she said hastily when he gave her a curious look.

"Fernando and another monk had served together in a monastery in Spain. They had experimented with making sherry years before and had learned ancient secrets passed from generation to generation of monks. They worked on perfecting what they had learned. That was the knowledge that Phillip stole from my mother."

One look at his face warned Caitlyn that now would not be a good time to defend Phillip or to question that the journals had ever been stolen. It was Phillip's word against his mother's. Instead she said, "Let's see if there's anyone here to show us around."

An hour later they drove back to Napier. They bought fish and chips and found a picnic table on the promenade overlooking the sea.

Unwrapping the food attracted raucous seagulls. Caitlyn laughed as Rafaelo leapt up waving his arms to shoo them away.

"All that land over there—" Caitlyn gestured with a sweep of her hand as he resumed his seat "—was originally all marsh. After the earthquake of nineteen thirty-one the land plates rose about two metres and the marsh drained away." She helped herself to another chip. "Not much of the city centre was left standing. When the city was rebuilt it was done in the art deco style. The most current ideas of the day were incorporated." Caitlyn nodded to a nearby building where a statue of a naked woman danced.

"Women were experiencing greater freedom and emancipation so the motif of the free new woman can be seen in plenty of places around the city." Then her cheeks reddened as she realised how pert the woman's nude breasts were, how natural her naked sensuality looked. Bowing her head, Caitlyn wished she'd kept her mouth shut and made a pretence of picking at the last of the chips. If only she could be so relaxed and at ease with her body…

"What are you thinking about?"

Caitlyn jerked her mind back to the present.

"He should've been shot," said Rafaelo grimly, guessing at her thoughts.

"He's in jail." Caitlyn didn't want to think about Tommy Smith. Not while she was savouring the last of her time with Rafaelo. "But it doesn't help to know that someday he will be back on the streets."

Rafaelo placed his hand on her thigh and Caitlyn twitched. "One day you will meet a man who will help you through this. He will be a very lucky man."

"You really think so?"

Her tone held a poignant note of hope that caused a crease to appear between his eyes.

With a nod, he said simply, "I do. I wish I could be that man."

By the time Rafaelo dropped her off, Caitlyn was pleasantly tired. To her disappointment Rafaelo made no move to kiss her.

In fact, as she undressed and thought about the day, she realised he'd barely touched her—he'd made no moves at all. They'd talked. She'd discovered he had a keen interest in history and a firm commitment to family. Yet not once had he even flirted with her. Not even when she'd pointed out the flagrantly naked statue. Did he regret kissing her the other day? Had he decided she was not worth the aggravation of pursuing?

Because he was leaving?

Her heart plummeted. What had he said? She tried to recall his exact words. He'd said that any man would be lucky to have her. For a moment she grew optimistic.

Then a let-down feeling overtook her as she clambered into bed. Even if Rafaelo stayed, how could he want her while she was hiding one of the things he most wanted? Fernando's journals…

She slid into a restless sleep.

Eleven

Caitlyn came awake at the first shrill wail of the smoke alarm. Growing up on a farm meant that a healthy respect for fire was bred into her.

She sniffed. The faintest hint of acrid smoke hung in the air. Another sniff in case she was imagining it, then in one smooth movement she was out of bed. She felt for her sneakers without putting on the light. Her all-weather jacket hung on the back of her bedroom door and she pulled it over her flannel pyjamas. Before she left the bedroom, she crossed to the bedside table and quickly extracted the soft bag holding the three journals.

Out in the sitting room, the smoke alarms were deafening. She scooped her handbag off the coffee table, thankful that she was a creature of habit, and stuffed the pouch containing the journals inside. Grabbing the handset of her cordless phone, she wrenched open the door.

Stepping out onto the dark stairwell, Caitlyn paused as she caught the unearthly glow of fire.

The horses.

Already she could hear the crashing in the stables below. In minutes everything would be ablaze. Pita's shift would be finished. But where was the night guard?

Feeling for the buttons of the handset, she hit the speed dial for the homestead. Megan answered sounding half asleep.

"Megan, the stables are on fire. Check that the fire station has dispatched a truck." The smoke alarm was wired through to a call centre that should already have alerted the fire station.

Caitlyn killed the call and hurried down the last few steps. Rounding the corner, she grabbed a fire extinguisher off the wall. The flickering glow was coming from the end where the hay bales were stored. She ran down past the row of horses whickering uneasily.

One look at the flames that leapt from the bales and Caitlyn abandoned any idea of putting the blaze out with the fire extinguisher she held.

She had to get the horses out.

Caitlyn U-turned. At the first stable she reached for the halter that hung from a hook beside the door and opened the door. Breeze whinnied, a tremor of fear in the sound. Clicking reassuringly, Caitlyn secured the halter and led the mare out.

Pushing open the gate set in the fence opposite the stables, she led the mare through and loosened the halter to set her free.

Six horses to go.

A glance at the shed revealed that the flames were leaping high, fed by the dry bales.

She started to run.

Where was the damned guard? If the fire engine had been dispatched as soon as the alarm went off, it would take at least thirteen minutes to get here. A lot of burning could happen in the meantime.

She opened the second stable door.

Magic Man, Kay's dressage horse, was drenched in sweat. Caitlyn wasted valuable minutes trying to corner the frightened animal.

By the time she got the horse out, the flames had devoured the wooden beams of the hay shed and were roaring furiously.

Where was Megan? Why wasn't she—and Kay and Phillip— here yet? No, Kay was gone…to Australia. Caitlyn gave a sob of despair.

She was never going to be able to get all the horses out by herself. And once the roof caught fire…

She shuddered.

Which horse next? How could she choose which animals should live and which should die?

The crashing from the stable at the far end forced her to act. *Diablo.* Halter in hand, she ran to the stallion's stable and opened the top door. His head came bursting over the half door. She realised what the fool horse intended to do a split second before his head went up and his hooves flashed past her.

"Caitlyn, get out of the way." The shout came from behind her.

"No," she screamed, waving her arms wildly in the stallion's face to deter him from jumping the stable door and hurting himself. "Get back."

Eyes rolling white, Diablo pulled back.

Beside her Rafaelo was unbolting the door. Wrenching it open, he yelled, "Out of the way."

Caitlyn leapt sideways as a ton of enraged black horse flesh bolted past.

"There's no time to lead them out," Rafaelo shouted as Caitlyn charged toward the next stable. "Just unbolt the doors."

She glanced up. The roof above Breeze's stable was on fire. Then thankfully Megan and Phillip were there, too.

They worked swiftly, a team, opening doors getting every

horse out and when the fire engine howled through the night, Caitlyn sighed in relief.

An hour later the fire had been brought under control. The guard's unconscious body had been found beside the path behind the stables. An ambulance arrived, and the police had been summoned.

The stables were extensively damaged. Caitlyn's apartment had not caught fire but the water damage from the hoses was substantial.

"You won't be sleeping there tonight," Megan said. "You'll have to come back to the house."

"No, I can't." Caitlyn didn't want to add more strain to the situation.

"Where are you going to stay?" Megan demanded.

Caitlyn barely heard. She felt cold and suddenly shaky, despite the fact that her skin was tight and dry from the blasting heat of the fire.

"She can stay with me. The cottage has three bedrooms." The rough edge of Rafaelo's voice cut through the floating sensation.

Then she heard someone saying faintly, "I feel ill."

Hands closed around her arm—Rafaelo's hands—she recognised the strength of his hold. "You've had a scare, *querida*. You gave me quite a scare! Let's get a paramedic to check you out— I want to make sure there's no permanent damage."

A motherly female paramedic checked her out. "No burns, you were lucky. You'll be all right. A hot drink and a night's sleep and you'll feel a lot stronger in the morning."

When a pair of arms came around her, Caitlyn relaxed into Rafaelo's hold. He lifted her off the ground, whispering to her so softly that she couldn't hear a word. At once she felt safe…and secure. It was incongruous given his muscled frame and dark bullfighter looks. But she knew the gentleness—at least toward her—was real.

* * *

Rafaelo half led, half carried her to Vintner's Cottage where he was staying. Cottage was a misnomer for the three-bedroom stone house with a wide balcony on three sides. Caitlyn had been there before. As he made her comfortable on a sofa in the living room, she looked around.

Rafaelo had put his individual stamp on the place.

His leather jacket was draped over the arm of the sofa and the newspaper he'd been reading lay folded on the coffee table. The fragrance of his cologne hung in the air mingling the essence of leather, cedar wood, moss and man. Even as she inhaled the now-familiar scent, desire uncoiled within her.

She gave him a furtive look. His eyes were shuttered against her stare, but the muscle in his jaw was working. He was upset. Quickly she asked, "Which room should I use tonight?"

"I'm using that one." He pointed to the master bedroom that Caitlyn knew had a view over the vineyards to the rolling emerald hills beyond that made up The Divide.

"I need a shower." Caitlyn wasn't sure how to handle this silent, uncommunicative Rafaelo. She rose to her feet. Instantly he was at her side. "I'm fine."

He fell back. She chose the nearest bedroom and dropped her handbag—her only baggage—on the double bed before shrugging off her jacket.

Weariness swamped her and her shoulders sagged. Contrarily she wished she were back in the living room with him. Too tired even to cry she sat on the edge of the bed, her hands hanging between her knees. Her fingers were covered in dirt. Stable grime. Smudges of soot. She must smell of smoke and horse.

She definitely needed a shower. Stumbling to her feet, Caitlyn made her way to the en suite, stripped off the grimy pyjamas, turned on the faucet and stepped into the shower.

It was blissful. Minutes later, clean, warm and feeling much stronger, she wrapped herself in one of the luxurious soft bath sheets and made her way back to the bedroom. It struck her that she had a problem. She had no clothes except for the smoke-soaked pyjamas she'd dumped on the ground.

Retrieving her own clothes was not an option. The fire chief had warned that her apartment was not safe—it needed to be structurally checked before she returned. Even if her clothes survived they would be sodden.

She thought with regret of the new garments she'd purchased with Megan. They might have to be replaced. But in the meantime what was she to wear?

The towel wrapped tightly around her, Caitlyn strolled into the lounge determined to project a quiet confidence she didn't feel.

Before she could say anything, Rafaelo looked up and smiled.

When he smiled like that, she forgot about her fears, she forgot about his sheer physical power, his threatening solidness. She saw only the warm eyes, the caring man who tugged at her heartstrings.

"You look like a—" he hesitated "—a waif."

With his accent for a heart-stopping moment Caitlyn thought he'd said *wife*. She stared at him with wide eyes. Emotion twisted her heart.

Waif. He thought she looked like a waif—vulnerable… forlorn…*pitiable*.

The last thing she needed was his pity. "It's this bath sheet— it's drowning me. I need some clothes."

"You can borrow my bathrobe if you want." Not waiting for an answer, he was already moving to his room.

Caitlyn waited. He returned holding a navy robe with a mono-grammed crest. "Tomorrow we'll go to town and get you some clothes, *querida*."

"Or I could borrow some from Megan in the morning," she said. Retreating to her room for a second time, Caitlyn closed the door and dropped the bathsheet. The robe was a little big, but it would have to do. She was conscious of her naked skin beneath fabric that was imbued with his scent. It was intimate. More intimate than anything she'd ever experienced being surrounded by him, so close to her skin.

Caitlyn marched back into the sitting room to find that he was reading the paper again.

"Thank you," she said formally. "For helping with the horses, for the robe, for giving me a bed for the night."

He looked up. Instantly she reassessed. The melting heat in his onyx eyes was not that of a disinterested man. He wanted her. But he was capable of restraining himself.

And Caitlyn was no longer sure she required him to be quite so upstanding.

"Come, sit down. I poured you a glass of wine." Rafaelo indicated the chair next to the sofa on which he sat. "I've a platter of tapas in the fridge. Once we've eaten a little you can go to bed and have a good night's sleep."

Instead of taking the chair, she settled down on the sofa beside him. He turned his head, surprise in his eyes.

She felt a sweep of satisfaction. It was good to know that Rafaelo couldn't predict everything she did.

She took a sip of wine. Sauvignon blanc. Cool and citrusy with a hint of green gooseberries. *Gooseberries?*

Caitlyn held the glass up and squinted into the light. "This isn't one of ours."

"Should it be?"

"No." She flushed. "You have every right to drink what you like." Another sip. "Heath will be pleased that you're buying his wine—I'm sure he'd give you a case if he knew you were interested."

Chagrin flashed in his eyes. Caitlyn grinned inwardly. It was good to catch him off balance for a change.

"I wouldn't ask—I simply wanted to check out the competition."

"Competition?" She stared at him. "Heath isn't competition. He's your brother."

"Half brother," he growled. "With none of the closeness from growing up together that the word *brother* suggests. We are strangers to each other."

"But it needn't remain that way. Don't you see? This is what your father—the Marques—wanted. He wanted you to have the chance to get to know your family."

"I have a family. I don't need—"

"You have a mother. That's all." She glared at him in frustration. "Here's the chance to have so much more. Brothers. A sister. Even a birth father."

"Phillip only supplied the seed for my existence."

Caitlyn shook her head. But at least he wasn't rejecting the brothers and sister quite to the same extent as Phillip. Perhaps there was still a chance. But she'd flogged this horse to death, now was not the time to say more.

"Nothing to say?"

She remained silent.

"Sulking?"

That got to her. "I never sulk. All I can say is that I grew up in a large family and I wouldn't give up any of my brothers and sisters. Sure, we've squabbled over the years, but I love them. Think about that, Rafaelo, before you wrest a share in Saxon's Folly and auction it off. Think about the love that you might be shutting out your life."

"Quiet! I don't need a lecture. The only kind of love I care about is this kind." Before she could object he'd swept her onto his lap and he was kissing her.

She knew that he'd intended to shut her up. She was furious with him for choosing this tactic...and with herself for caring. But she loved him and she loved the Saxons. It was a hopeless situation. Yet she couldn't stop what she felt. The emotional connection had grown stronger with every passing day. She loved him.

So she kissed Rafaelo back with all the pent-up longing that had been building up for days. He tensed as her fingers locked behind his neck and pulled his head down to her. Then he exhaled and she knew she'd won.

She was not going to make this easy for him. She was not going to let him do what he'd come to do and walk away unscathed…and forget all about her.

He'd learn to care. *He had to*. Because she already cared far too much.

The robe parted. She heard his shocked exhalation as it gaped open, baring her body for his inspection. For one wild moment his eyes took in the full creamy mounds, the stiff dusky-pink tips, then he swore and flung himself away from her.

"Forgive me, Caitlyn, I never intended for this to happen."

Twelve

"Don't go."

Rafaelo halted. Caitlyn was staring at him with an expression that on another woman's face he might have described as hunger.

But never on Caitlyn's.

She'd fought a fire. Her home was water-logged. Her personal belongings drenched by the fire hoses. Her most treasured possessions possibly destroyed. She must be feeling desperately vulnerable, seeking reassurance.

To imagine she wanted him would be crazy—a sign that he'd lost his reason. Although he nearly had when he'd seen the fire at the stables. The idea of anything happening to Caitlyn—

He refused to think about it.

"Do you want a cup of tea?" That might soothe her and help her sleep. He needed a stiff drink.

"I still have some more wine." She raised her glass and he watched with a frown as she took another sip. The eyes that peered over the glass at him were bright and defiant. "I don't want you to stop."

Maybe she was tipsy. He could understand her not wanting him to leave…but to want him to keep kissing her? That had to be the wine talking.

"*Querida,* if I kiss you again, I might never be able to stop." Under the circumstances Rafaelo was proud of the patient tone he managed.

"You'd stop if I asked."

He would? There was such blind trust in her statement that Rafaelo's chest tightened. He quaked at the thought of drawing back once he'd tasted her…

Her trust was important. Taking a deep breath, he said. "Yes, I would."

She patted the cushion beside her. "Then come here."

He sank down beside her, his gut churning with a mix of desire and concern and a feeling that he was taking the most dangerous risk of his life.

As he lowered his head she said, "I want more than kisses, Rafaelo."

"What?" Shocked by her primal throaty tone, his every sense on red alert, he reared back.

"I want everything…everything I've been missing for my whole adult life."

"Caitlyn." He sucked in a shuddering breath. "Let's take it slowly, there's no hurry."

"No! I don't want to wait any longer. You'll be leaving soon. I could've died tonight. I didn't. I'm fine. But it could have happened. Tomorrow I could be killed in a car accident—like Roland Saxon was. I've spent years trapped in the past. I don't want to live like that anymore. I want to be free."

Mierda. He tried to clear his head. He didn't need to be reminded that he might have lost her. He'd been trying not to

think about that. Nor did he want to think about why a world
without Caitlyn would be as empty as a world without joy. "What
you're feeling is a normal reaction to a traumatic event. You'll
feel different in the morning, believe me."

"I won't. I want you."

She'd hate him tomorrow if he did what she asked. And she'd
detest him when he left for Spain without her. Though the
thought of that was becoming harder and harder to accept. He
couldn't make love to her; he had to protect her from herself.
"You don't want me. All you want—" He stopped midsentence.
She'd pushed the robe off her arms and now reclined naked in
front of him.

He blinked furiously.

"Do you believe me now?"

"Caitlyn!" Her skin looked as soft and luscious as a ripe peach
and her hair spilled over delicate pale shoulders presenting a
vision so excitingly sensual that he swallowed hard and closed
his eyes to shut out the blatant temptation she offered.

"Don't you want me?"

His eyes snapped open. "Not want you? Don't be an idiot."
He took in the uncertainty in her eyes, the hectic flush that lay
across her cheeks. She was embarrassed. Uncomfortable. She
imagined he was rejecting her because he didn't desire her.
Idiota. "Of course I want you. But I am trying very hard to be
noble—to do something that's in your best interests."

"*My* best interests?"

Her disbelief stung. "Look—" he pointed to his groin and said
brutally "—does that look like I don't want you?"

She glanced to where his black pants revealed the thick ridge
of his erection. Her breath snagged with an audible gasp. Instantly Rafaelo felt his flesh surge as she lifted wide eyes to his.
Yet instead of apprehension, the eyes that met his glowed with
anticipation.

"Caitlyn," he said hoarsely, "you are making this very difficult."

"I want to make it impossible." She leaned over him, her long silky hair brushing his face. No hint of smoke lingered. She smelled of fresh shampoo and wildflowers.

So tempting.

Too damned tempting.

"I want it to be you." Her eyes, so clear and bright with emotion, blinded him. "I know that you will be gentle…and patient."

Madre de Dios. He shook his head—a last-ditch effort to deter her. "You can't know that."

"I do know," she insisted. "You were patient with Diablo—"

He swore softly, in Spanish. "Diablo is a horse. That is no recommendation." Then he suppressed the insane urge to laugh. Never had a woman asked him to make love to her on the basis of his skill with a horse. Usually it was because of his family name, his connections, his wealth. His eligibility.

Only Caitlyn didn't care about the things that every other woman wanted. Only Caitlyn touched his heart with her candour, her honesty. When…how…had she become his whole world?

She was speaking, he jerked his attention back to her. "The day you convinced me to stroke Diablo, with your hand over mine, you said someone had hit him around the head. You crooned to him so gently. It reminded me of something. The way you comforted me when I was afraid. I trust you, Rafaelo. I know you would never hurt me."

Why the devil was he arguing? He wanted her with a hunger that was foreign to him. "If you're determined to do this, then I suggest we retreat to the bedroom."

Apprehension clouded her eyes. Then she said, "Okay."

He'd fully expected her to chicken out—to tell him that she'd made a mistake—when he rose to his feet and made for his bedroom. But she was incredibly brave. Foolishly so. She followed him, catching his fingers and threading them between hers. He could hear her shaky breathing, and her fingers trembled under his. In the master bedroom, he sat down on the king-sized bed so as not to loom over her.

She hovered in front of him, his robe gaping open in the front. For a moment he thought she might have had second thoughts and he groaned inwardly. He forced himself to keep his gaze on her face, not to peek at the bare skin that he craved another glimpse of. She was so lovely, so incredibly gallant.

Suddenly he didn't want her to be sensible, to back out.

Surrendering her fingers, he put his wrists together and stretched them toward her. "Tie my hands if it makes you feel easier."

Shock glinted in her eyes. *"Tie your hands?"*

"You might feel safer."

He watched as her throat bobbed. But something gleamed in her eyes. Curiosity? Excitement?

"Look in the cupboard—there are ties and belts that you could use." He gave her a ghost of a smile, even though he'd never felt less like laughing in his life. *Dios,* he hoped she was going to change her mind. This couldn't be easy for her. He wouldn't blame her if she decided to cut and run.

"But you'd still have your feet free," she pointed out.

"Tie those, too—if you want."

She stared at him, clearly shocked. "You'd surrender that much control?"

"Lovemaking isn't about control. It's about pleasure." He gave her an oh-so-slow smile, doing his best to banish her fears.

"You… You are incredible, Rafaelo."

"No, *querida,* you are."

"Why didn't I meet you before…?"

The despair in her eyes tore at his heart. *"Querida,* I can't erase what happened in the past. But I can show you that not all men get their kicks out of fear and pain. I can promise you a night of pleasure…and passion."

She stared at him, and he could see that she was incredibly tempted. "Nothing bad really happened. I wasn't raped. I was attacked…and touched." She shuddered.

He didn't reach for her, but intense emotion burned in his chest. "Don't *ever* let me get my hands on him."

She gave a half sob, half laugh. "Joshua dealt with him. I don't know what he said to…him…before he fired him."

"Come here."

She perched on the bed beside him, a little stiff. Gently Rafaelo wrapped an arm around her, and tucked her under his shoulder. He rested his head against her hair, willing her to understand that he would never harm her.

"I don't need your hands tied," she said. "I don't fear them, I know that they will give me pleasure—not pain." She raised her head and smiled at him. It was like seeing the rainbow come out after the storm. "One day we can play those games, for fun. Tonight I want you to touch me—"

Rafaelo growled, his restraint breaking. "Oh, *querida,* I will certainly touch you…and taste you…and adore every inch of you."

Her heart leapt. And for once the fear remained absent.

Shrugging off his shirt, Rafaelo lay back on the bed. "Come here," he murmured huskily, pulling her on top of him.

At first the position felt precarious, being perched on top of him, but then as the heat of his torso penetrated the thin robe she wore, Caitlyn began to feel the hot stirring of desire. Bending her head, her hair spilling around his face, she placed her mouth against his, and his lips parted.

He tasted wonderfully familiar. The feelings that his kiss aroused started gently, seeping through Caitlyn in sensuous layers until her skin was warm and tingles started to whisper down her spine.

When his hands slipped under the robe, the warmth ignited into a hot glow. Caitlyn shivered with wakening desire as the robe slid down over her shoulders, his fingers smoothing over her skin…around her ribcage…across the sensitive skin of her neck.

She groaned against his mouth as he touched her and arched upward when his fingers found her nipples. Heat sliced through her, and her eyes closed.

Caitlyn's whole being was focused on his touch, on the delicious feelings he aroused within her. His fingers moved, caressing, playing with the pebbles of flesh. At last his hands moved away, and she moaned in disappointment as he braced them against her and moved her away from his torso.

Opening her eyes, she looked into molten dark ones.

Then he pulled her down. At the very last instant she realised what he was going to do. A wild moan broke from her as his mouth closed on the tip of her breast. A streak of fiery heat tore through her and gathered low in her belly and she shuddered, focusing fiercely on the unexpected dark delight that splintered through her.

Caitlyn didn't even notice when he finally stripped off the robe. It was no big deal to be naked against him, not when his mouth had tasted her, brought her so much pleasure.

His hands stroked her all over. Long, sweeping movements that left heat and fire in their wake. Caitlyn's whole body burned. When his hand slipped between her thighs, the temperature went up another notch, and her pulse hammered in her throat.

His fingers moved deftly and her breath caught at the sensation that ripped through her. "Oh, Rafaelo."

The smile he gave her was slow and knowing. "Take your time. Enjoy."

Her hips lifted higher as his fingers edged deeper. Her breath ragged, her pulse wild. "Stop," she demanded. "Or there'll be nothing left."

"Then we can start again." The promise in the eyes below hers made heat rush through her.

"It's hardly fair, you're wearing too many clothes," she

murmured when she realised she wore not a stitch, while he still wore pants.

"Are you sure?" He gazed up at her through heavy-lidded eyes.

A surge of emotion shook her. She loved him so much. "Very sure."

"You don't want to stop?"

She groaned. "No! It's not too far…nor too fast."

"Just making sure." He was smiling up at her, his full, passionate lips curving with amusement, the small white scar below giving him a wicked look that made her go weak with desire.

"Are you laughing at me?" she asked softly.

"I wouldn't dare," he said with a grin.

Caitlyn shifted. There was the sound of a zip rasping. His smile vanished. She moved, just enough to make him groan, then she pushed the black pants and his underwear away.

"Good," she purred. "I'm very pleased to hear that."

There was shock in his eyes—and something else. "Caitlyn—"

"Don't say a word." Legs either side of his hips, she shifted again. "Not a word."

The hard length of his erection surged against her softness. But he remained silent, except for the whisper of a groan as she tantalised him, riding him delicately.

By the time he slid into her, Caitlyn was moaning. There was a moment of resistance, Rafaelo gasped, stilled, then his arms pulled her close.

"That was not funny," he muttered. "But I am inordinately pleased."

And as his hands stroked her back in long deliberate sweeps, his hardness claimed her until Caitlyn felt herself shimmering, hanging on a thread, until she started to tremble. The thread snapped and she fell into an abyss of pleasure.

And Rafaelo's body shivered against hers as the pleasure shook them both.

* * *

"Will you marry me?"

Rolling away from the heat of Rafaelo's body, Caitlyn pulled the robe off the bottom of the bed and tucked it firmly under her arms. Decently covered, she felt safe enough to sit up. *"What?"*

"Will you marry me?" he repeated.

He lay on his back, staring up at the ceiling, his hands fisted by his sides.

This was so tempting…she *did* want to marry him.

But it wasn't sensible.

"It's not practical for me to marry you," she explained. "If I married you I would need to leave my work—which I love—and all the people who are very close to me."

A strange expression shadowed the face that had become so precious to her. "They're not even your family."

"The Saxons are as close as my family." Caitlyn watched as his brows lowered ominously.

"But you would be with me," he objected with a hint of his old arrogance. "I would be your family."

If he loved her that would be enough. But he didn't…

And even if he had loved her, once he discovered that she'd had the journals he'd sought all along, that she'd been a vital part of the success of Saxon's Folly's sherry-style fortified wines, that would all go up in smoke. She sighed. Better she end this discussion before it all became too painful.

Caitlyn shook her head. "No, Rafaelo, there's no point in this discussion." She slid her legs off the bed and got to her feet, clutching the robe around her.

"Where are you going?"

"I'll be back in a moment." She went to the bedroom where she'd showered and retrieved her handbag. For a long moment she hesitated. Then she spun around and made her way back to his bedroom, still clad in the soft robe.

She extracted the pouch out of her bag and threw it on the bed. "This is what you want."

He made no move to touch it. "What is it?"

"Open it."

Not taking his eyes off her, he sat up and reached for it. Caitlyn stood beside the bed and did her best not to stare. He made no effort to hide his very blatant, very male nudity. The journals fell onto the bedcover beside him. His gaze dropped and his expression changed. He knew what he was looking at. "Why do you have these?"

She didn't answer.

He flipped the cover open. "They're written in Spanish." He looked up, surprise in his eyes. "My mother never mentioned that. You speak Spanish..." His voice trailed away.

She nodded.

"It wasn't Phillip...it was you."

Caitlyn knew she'd never forget the expression in his eyes for as long as she lived.

"It was you who read them, you who studied Fernando's methods and applied them."

"Yes." She didn't lie. Nor did she apologise. It was way too late for that.

He pushed himself up and sat on the edge of the bed, raking his fingers through his hair. Stretching, he reached for his pants where they lay in a heap on the floor and pulled them on, before rising to his feet. Caitlyn felt the distance between them widening.

"Why didn't you tell me?" he asked, his eyes drilling into hers.

"At first I didn't realise how important it was to you. By the time I did, I knew you hated the Saxons—hated Phillip. That more than anything in the world you wanted to hurt him. I couldn't let that happen."

He stood in middle of the room, facing her. No hint of the lover remained. "He still stole them from my mother."

She could no longer let Phillip bear the full weight of his blame. "He didn't steal them—he bought them from your mother."

He lifted his head, giving her that Spanish grandee glare. It was as intimidating as ever. Then he said, "That's not true!"

She gave him a sad smile. "Are you saying that I'm lying?"

For a timeless moment the memory of their first meeting lay between them.

"No, I'm not calling you a liar," he said, his voice ragged. "There must be some other explanation. You must have been told a lie."

"There isn't another explanation, Rafaelo." Caitlyn's heart ached for him. She wanted to go to him, put her arms around him, tell him she loved him. But she couldn't. "Your mother sold them to Phillip. They sat in Phillip's office for nearly three decades. It wasn't until I read them that he realised exactly what was in them. He had some vague idea—Maria had shared some snippets. And he'd had a Spanish interpreter look at them, but she wasn't a winemaker and couldn't understand the nuances."

"You always said that you were fascinated by sherry."

Caitlyn didn't make excuses for herself. "And this was my way to make my mark in the industry. The girl from nowhere…to the chief winemaker of one of the most prestigious estates in Hawkes Bay." With every word the distance between them yawned wider.

To his credit, his expression didn't change. No sneer marred his near-perfect features. "I can understand that you were ambitious. The journals would have been a godsend to you, to help you establish the reputation you craved."

It sounded so cold, so ugly.

Caitlyn glanced away. "I'm sorry."

"The day I said that I wanted my share…that I intended to auction it…"

"Yes."

"Why didn't you speak up then?"

"I started to. But Phillip gave me a look that warned me to stay silent. Later he told me that he'd bought them from your mother. That telling you I had them would only lead to more problems. He feared you might not believe him—and lay charges of theft causing more scandal when Kay was already fragile. Or you might be angry that your mother had sold them." She drew a shuddering breath. "I didn't know what to do. I was torn apart."

There was a hint of softening in his gaze. Small, but it was there. "You've been caught between the devil and the dark blue sea."

"An impossible place." She hunched her shoulders. "But you wanted vengeance, to hurt the Saxons by claiming a share of Saxon's Folly and selling it—that made it easier to view you as the villain of the piece." Until he'd shown her the patient, gentle side of himself. Then she'd been lost.

Rafaelo sighed, a harsh sound. He raked a careless hand through the long black hair that she knew felt like rough silk. "So what happens now?"

There was a long silence. Caitlyn tensed. She couldn't bear to think about it. Their lovemaking had brought such exquisite joy. But now that feeling of oneness was gone, leaving her feeling drained. And empty. "I don't know. I suppose you go home."

He gave her a long, unreadable look. At last, his jaw set, he said, "I still want to marry you."

Hope flickered inside her. Could he possibly feel for her what she felt for him? "Why?"

After a long silence, during which Caitlyn's heart sank to her toes, she knew she had been right to refuse his chivalrous offer—however much she'd wanted to accept, he finally said, "I'm not sure where this desire comes from. I did not come to New Zealand to seek a wife."

She drew herself up to her full height, making every inch count. "No, you came seeking vengeance…and the journals."

His fingers attacked his hair again, pushing it back off his face.

"Maybe. That's why you won't marry me. Because by marrying me you think you would be betraying your beloved Saxon family."

Caitlyn took a risk. "I don't believe you would harm any of them." She stared at him boldly, holding her breath. "Given the care you took of Diablo, your gentleness with me, I don't think you could ever take something that means the world to the Saxons and auction it off to the highest bidder for cold hard cash."

His jaw clenched more tightly. "I could."

"But you won't. You wouldn't hurt Kay—or Megan or Joshua or Heath—because of Phillip's sins."

He gave her a calculating look. "Not if you marry me."

"Oh, no." Caitlyn shook her head so hard that her hair whipped around her face. "You're not blackmailing me. You don't even possess that share yet. And even if you did, I don't come with that kind of price on my head. There's only one reason I'd marry a man."

"What's that?"

"Love," she said quietly. "Not obligation, not barter for my virginity, not blackmail. Only love."

He frowned at her for a long moment. Then he turned away. "Then you are correct. There is no point discussing this further."

There had been frustration…and anger…in that look. But the rigid line of the naked back he presented to her, made it clear that there was no future for them.

Caitlyn couldn't help thinking that he must hate her. Especially when she saw he'd taken the journals with him.

Thirteen

Caitlyn's eyes were scratchy and bone-dry from lack of sleep. Last night, despite her exhaustion, she'd hightailed it from the Vintner's Cottage clad only in Rafaelo's robe. She'd been welcomed at the main house without any questions.

This morning she'd borrowed a T-shirt and a pair of too-short tracksuit bottoms belonging to Megan to wear to work—while Phillip insisted she take the day off—and give herself a chance to recover.

After lunch, Megan whipped her into Napier to buy some jeans and shirts, underwear and shoes. Caitlyn was grimly amused by the thought that after years of no shopping, suddenly it seemed she was doing little else. But when they arrived back at Saxon's Folly, her amusement dried up.

Rafaelo paced the forecourt waiting for her.

"I came by to see how you are." His eyes searched her, his inspection telling her more than words that he'd been worried. He must care. A melting sensation filled her, which she immediately suppressed.

He didn't love her, she told herself fiercely.

But before they could have the discussion he clearly wanted, a police car cruised slowly down the lane. Two police officers wearing stiff uniforms and sombre expressions stepped out and slammed the doors in unison.

"Caitlyn Ross?" asked the taller of the two.

She nodded.

"Is there somewhere we can talk?"

She took them to the winery, into the small cubicle packed with books and magazines and racks of wine that served as her office. It was with little surprise that she realised Rafaelo had come, too. He stood just inside the door, tall, dark, his eyes very fierce and his stance protective.

"We'd like to talk to Ms. Ross alone." The older cop was solid, with grey hair and a worn expression where life had lined his face with harsh experience.

"I don't think so." Rafaelo looked formidable. "Unless you'd rather make an appointment to meet her with her attorney present?"

"Ms. Ross doesn't need an attorney right now. We simply want a statement." The taller, younger cop's tone grew conciliatory as he eyed Rafaelo up and down.

Rafaelo stayed.

"Do you have any enemies, Ms. Ross?" The older of the two asked her after she and the cops had taken the only three chairs. Rafaelo loomed in the doorway, like a dark angel.

Distracted, Caitlyn shook her head. "Why?"

The older policeman spoke, "There are signs that last night's fire was no accident."

"You're saying it was deliberate?" She searched the front of his uniform for a tag. "But why, Constable West?"

"It's sergeant." He waved away her apology. "That's what we'd like to find out. You live above the stables, correct?"

She nodded again.

A horrible thought struck her. "What about the guard? Does this mean that it wasn't a piece of timber that struck him? That he was deliberately injured?"

"We can't say yet, ma'am. There's a lot of work to be done."

"Do you have any suspects yet?" Rafaelo asked. The older cop gave him a measuring glance, but neither answered him.

"What about ex-boyfriends who you parted with badly?" asked the younger cop.

"No one springs to mind."

"Anyone who rides a black motorcycle?"

She started to shake her head, then stopped. A black motorcycle…

Could there be a connection?

"There was a black motorcycle in the paddock several weeks ago. It scared the stallion, causing Alyssa to fall off the horse she was riding."

Neither cop looked surprised. Another note was made. Caitlyn had a feeling she wasn't telling them anything they didn't already know.

"Tell them about Tommy."

"Tommy Smith?"

Her heart started to thud at the cop's sudden expression of interest. Her gaze slid to Rafaelo. "But he's in jail."

"Tell them."

She did, hating every moment. But it was strangely cathartic. She hardly ever talked about Tommy's attack on her, she realised.

The grey-haired cop took copious notes. When he'd finished, he asked Caitlyn a few more questions, then they packed up their notepads and left.

Caitlyn turned to Rafaelo. "If the fire was started deliberately, I certainly hope they catch whoever did it."

Rafaelo drew her close. "When I think what might have happened…" A shudder shook his big frame.

Rafaelo walked into the homestead that evening, Caitlyn by his side, with the deliberate tread of a man with a mission.

Time was growing short. He didn't have much more time in New Zealand, Torres Carreras was waiting, and he'd stayed longer than he'd intended. But he had a lot to accomplish in the short time he had left. His hand tightened around Caitlyn's waist and he led her to where Phillip stood in a group with his sons— his legitimate sons.

For the first time Rafaelo felt no resentment. After setting the parcel he carried under his arm on a conveniently located side table, he nodded to Joshua and Heath. Both men stepped forward, their faces alight with welcome.

"Caitlyn, I've got a glass of pinot gris for you. What would you like, Rafaelo?" Joshua asked.

Rafaelo blinked.

The feeling of having walked into another world—a world filled with warmth and approval and acceptance—grew as Heath chatted to him about harvests, about rain, with no hint of animosity. But when Phillip turned to smile at him, Rafaelo knew something was wrong.

"What's happened?" he asked, suspiciously.

"We want to thank you for what you did."

"What I did?"

"For rescuing Caitlyn." Megan hugged him. "She's part of our family."

Rafaelo tried to relax.

"I can never thank you enough," said Phillip.

Rafaelo looked around the circle. All of them were smiling. They loved Caitlyn. She belonged here. How could he ever uproot her from the people who were her family, the place that was her home? He glanced at her. She was smiling, too, the translucent eyes smoky with an emotion that made his throat close.

She was smiling at him.

Finally he said, "She was doing fine by herself, she would've been all right."

"I couldn't stop wishing the cavalry would arrive," she said, contradicting him, her eyes still filled with that softness that he decided must be gratitude.

Ivy, the housekeeper, called them to the dining room and the meal passed in noisy conversation. Amy Wright arrived a little late. Rafaelo had seen her in the winery, her head bent over the computer, but he'd never really spoken to her. She was small and fine-boned with a dark bob and stricken eyes. Tonight she greeted him with a smile before Megan bore down on her.

Looking up he saw that Caitlyn was still smiling at him. He gave her a searing look that warned her that if she continued there would be consequences.

The smile turned wicked.

Rafaelo knew it was going to be a long dinner.

After dessert had been served they adjourned to the seating area in the salon. Phillip served chilled *Flores Finos* in small glasses. Rafaelo couldn't bring himself to refuse. He sat beside Caitlyn on one of the sofas and the award-winning fortified wine lingered on his tongue, the taste unique.

Phillip clapped his hands and everyone fell silent. "I have a gift I'd like to present to Rafaelo."

Rafaelo rose to his feet and picked up the parcel he'd set down on one of the side tables when he'd come in. "I have something for you, too. This is not a gift—it belongs to you." He'd read the diaries last night, savouring his great-great-uncle's words. It had given him great pleasure. "I understand from my mother that you bought them from her."

"Your mother?" The whisper came from Caitlyn.

He glanced at her and nodded. "I called her this evening, just before dinner. I wanted to let her know that I had a few matters to tie up here before I could come home. I asked her. She told me that she needed the money. You told me the truth." He tried to convey his appreciation to Caitlyn. But it was impossible for her to know what it meant to him. He turned back to Phillip. "The journals are yours."

"No." Phillip Saxon shook his head. "Fernando was your blood relative. The secrets in there belong to you. Those are yours to keep, my son."

My son. The words caused a floodgate to open in Rafaelo's chest. He felt relief, wonder…and deep down in the farthest reaches of his heart the first stirrings of affection for the man who stood in front of him, his blood father.

"Thank you." Rafaelo hesitated. "This is difficult for me, and I fear I am not yet ready…but I would like in time to call you 'father' if I may?"

The sheen of tears filled Phillip's eyes. He stepped forward and hugged Rafaelo.

For a moment Rafaelo froze, then he clasped Phillip's upper arms. Over Phillip's shoulder Rafaelo read the relief that spread across Caitlyn's face. It made him feel humble. This was her doing. She had brought him to a point where he could accept Phillip as his father.

Stepping back, Rafaelo said huskily, "You could not have given me a gift with more meaning."

Phillip looked a little embarrassed. "It was a little different from what I'd planned."

Rafaelo sank back down on the sofa beside Caitlyn and

reached for her hand. Heath, Megan and Joshua all looked expectant.

"What are you giving Rafaelo?" asked Alyssa, leaning over Joshua's shoulder.

"Hush," said Megan. "It's a surprise."

Even Amy looked interested.

Phillip waited. Once everyone had fallen silent, he said with great ceremony, "As a thank-you for rescuing Caitlyn and all the Saxon horses I'd like to give you that Devil Horse."

Rafaelo felt overwhelmed. "Thank you. I will value him every day."

"It's your job to get him to Spain," Phillip said gruffly, as Rafaelo clasped his arm.

"But that's not what we—"

"Hush, Megan, you'll give it away."

Phillip gave a slow smile. "My children are impatient. Come," he summoned them all around him. They crowded around the sofa where Rafaelo and Caitlyn sat. Joshua stood at his right shoulder, Megan on his left and Heath a little out of the fold at the back. Rafaelo was painfully aware of Kay's absence. Meeting Phillip's eyes, he read pain and regret. Phillip was missing his wife. Rafaelo's hand tightened around Caitlyn's.

"We have talked. We have reached an agreement—all of us, even Heath." Phillip paused, then added, "Even Kay. Rafaelo, I would like to give you a share equal to my other children in Saxon's Folly."

Rafaelo went rigid.

Caitlyn grew still beside him.

No words would come. Rafaelo cleared his throat, the emotion of the moment surrounding him. He rose to his feet and stepped forward.

"Kay agreed to this?"

Phillip nodded. "I spoke to her about it—she feels you are entitled to your share of Saxon's Folly."

Rafaelo could see that the conversation had not been easy. Phillip had a lot to make up for. But perhaps by calling Kay, Phillip had taken the first step.

"I can never tell you how much this means to me." Rafaelo met Joshua's gaze, then Heath's. Black eyes. So like his.

Megan wasn't as restrained. She flung her arms around him. "It's great having another brother, especially such a cute one."

He laughed. He was aware of Caitlyn grinning from the comfort of the sofa—laughing at him, damn it. But he knew that she trusted him. Trusted him not to sell the stake he'd just been given. As he'd threatened to do what seemed like a lifetime ago.

Phillip cleared his throat. "Rafaelo, son, I owe you an apology. I've already apologised to Maria."

"Thank you." His mother had told him—and that meant the world to him.

Now he waited.

"I'm sorry that I never took responsibility for you, for thinking that paying Maria a good sum for the journals absolved me of my paternal responsibilities." Phillip sighed. "Hell, I didn't even know she was pregnant when I made that offer, but I justified it in my mind. I did try to trace her later to offer her a lump sum for your upbringing. But she had vanished."

His mother had become Marquesa de Las Carreras. She hadn't needed Phillip's money, she never had. She'd wanted his love. But that had been impossible.

He glanced at Caitlyn. He'd come here talking grandly of honour. But she'd made him a better man. If it hadn't been for her, he doubted he would ever have realised the significance of his journey to Hawkes Bay. For the first time he acknowledged that he'd travelled across the world in the unspoken hope that his father would apologise for the decades of neglect.

What he hadn't expected was to be able to forgive him, to forge a bond that would last with his blood father, his brothers…and his father's wife. He suspected this was what his papa's final legacy to him had been: a family.

"Thank you for the offer. I appreciate it more than I can ever say but—"

He glanced again at Caitlyn. She still smiled. He knew without doubt that the desire for vengeance had gone forever…replaced by desire of another kind.

For them love was possible.

He took a deep breath. "But I can't accept it."

There was dead silence. Phillip's face fell, Megan's mouth dropped open and even Joshua looked disconcerted.

"But my lawyer—"

"My lawyer has instructions to contact him to say that the negotiations are over. I no longer hunger for a share in Saxon's Folly or for revenge." Rafaelo started to smile. "But there is something else I would like to take back with me. Something infinitely more valuable than a share in Saxon's Folly."

"What could be more valuable?" Typically, it was Megan who asked.

"Your winemaker."

Megan laughed. "You're that keen on our sherry?"

Caitlyn looked apprehensive. She shook her head at him. But Rafaelo was not about to stop. He'd screwed this up before, he wasn't going to screw it up again.

He bent down on one knee in front of Caitlyn, he picked up her hand and was aware that the salon had gone utterly still. "Will you do me the honour of marrying me?"

Her mouth barely moved, but he saw the word shaped on her lips. *Why?*

"Not because you are beautiful and sexy." Behind him he heard Megan whoop. "Not because I enjoy listening to everything you say." Alyssa started to laugh. "Not because I'm trying to get an inside track on the best *finos* sherry in the world." This time Phillip growled and Heath laughed beside him. "Not because I want you more than any woman I have ever met."

"Rafaelo!" Caitlyn flushed scarlet. But her eyes glowed. "Be sensible."

"I'm not interested in sensible. I know that I am asking you to take a big step, to come with me back to Spain. The only reason I can justify asking you to marry me is because I love you."

He fell silent. And waited. The rest of the room faded away. He was aware of only Caitlyn's clear crystal eyes and the tenderness in his heart.

"You love me?" There was amazement…and something more.

She had told him she would only marry for love. He would honour that.

"I do." It was in the nature of a vow. And he knew he would never let her forget it.

"Then the answer must be yes."

This time it was Rafaelo who whooped. He straightened to his full height, swung her up into his arms, twirled her around and brought his lips down on hers.

When they came up for air, he was as breathless as she.

"I think we need a little air," Caitlyn managed, pulling him toward the French doors. "We'll be back in a while," she threw over her shoulder, as she led him out into the starry night.

Outside she turned into his arms. "I love you, too."

"I suspected," he said with a touch of the arrogance that was ingrained.

"You did, did you?"

"Of course. Otherwise you would never have let me kiss you…touch you. You loved me."

* * *

Back at the Vintner's Cottage, it was late. Caitlyn lay sprawled across Rafaelo's chest, her face flushed with kisses. Happiness warmed her like summer sunshine.

"Thank you for giving me so many priceless treasures," he murmured, lifting his head from where he'd been nibbling at her neck.

She lifted her eyelids, and gave him a lazy stare. "Which treasures are you thinking about?"

"A new family—complete with brothers and sisters. Your love." He kissed the tip of her nose. "Yourself."

She made a moaning sound of utter delight.

"Are you sure you can bring yourself to leave Saxon's Folly?" he asked softly, a tinge of concern shadowing the joy in his eyes.

"My home is where you are, Rafaelo," she said. "And if that means living in the midst of the Jerez triangle, overlooking the Atlantic and producing *finos* sherry, then that sounds pretty damn wonderful."

"I was thinking about that," said Rafaelo. "We can visit Saxon's Folly often. And there's no reason why Saxon's Folly can't import sherry from Torres Carreras—and sell real, honest sherry."

"That's a wonderful idea. We can discuss it with Megan and Phillip tomorrow." Caitlyn drew back to stare into his eyes. "I can't wait to see Torres Carreras, to meet your mother."

"You'll love it there. My mother can't wait to meet you either. I spent most of my time on the phone to her earlier telling her how fabulous you are, how much I hoped you would agree to marry me."

"You weren't sure?"

He looked sheepish. "No. In one corner of my heart I didn't know whether you would be able to bring yourself to leave the Saxons—and Saxon's Folly."

"I feel bad about leaving them without a winemaker. But

Heath lives just over The Divide and he's more than capable of bringing in two harvests a year."

A thoughtful expression crossed his face. "I might have a word with him."

She laughed. "I can't believe you two are talking."

"I think we've sorted out our differences," he said with a touch of smugness.

"You know, I think I've been very silly."

"Why?"

"I rather suspect that thinking I was in love with Heath was a big smokescreen so that I didn't need to worry about guys. About dating anyone."

"Nothing silly about that. Sounds smart to me."

She drew a line along his lower lip. "I will tell you I never experienced anything like this dizzying desire for Heath even though I told myself I was in love with him for years."

"And that is why the man is still alive."

"Rafaelo! You're a brute."

"You're mine," he said, pulling her close, plastering her up against him and claiming her with a kiss so passionate that her legs gave out.

Or had she merely been in love with the idea of being in love? Trapped in her studies, had Heath been nothing more than a safe guy to fancy? And after the horrific incident with Tommy, she'd had no desire for romance and her crush on Heath had simply become a habit—a knee-jerk reaction.

It didn't matter anymore.

Rafaelo was the real deal.

She reached up and pressed a kiss on his lips. He tasted delicious. Then planted another kiss on the scar below his lip. "Hmm. I've been wanting to do that for a long time. Tell me how you got that."

His lips twitched. "I fell off my bicycle when I was five years old. One of the handlebars pierced my flesh."

"Ouch." Caitlyn pulled a face. "And there I thought it was from bullfighting. Or street fighting." She clicked her tongue.

"Oh, I have those scars, too." His eyes glittered with wickedness. "Do you want to see them?"

"You're having me on," she said uncertainly.

He gave her an indecipherable look. "Wanna bet?"

"No! Bad idea," she said firmly. "I have no intention of losing to you ever again."

And she kissed him again.

A fair time later, Caitlyn raised her head. "Do you really have scars?"

He nodded. "At least one really impressive one where a bull gored me when I was young and foolish."

Horror shook her. Then curiosity set in. "Can I see it? Touch it?"

He groaned something that sounded like "witch." And it was a long time before either of them spoke or laughed—or took on a bet.

* * * * *

PREGNANCY PROPOSAL

BY
TESSA RADLEY

To all my readers—this story is for each one of you. Every time I receive a note telling me how much you've enjoyed one of my books, you make my day!

One

Heath Saxon's footsteps echoed against the polished stone floor as he walked through the deserted reception area of Saxon's Folly Estate and Wines. He had expected more fanfare over his return as winemaker to the illustrious Saxon's Folly winery, located in the Hawkes Bay on the east coast of New Zealand. An olive branch from his father on his first morning would have been welcome. A fatted calf even better. After all, it wasn't every day that the family bad boy came back.

So maybe he hadn't come a long way in miles—he lived over in the next valley and most Thursday nights came for dinner—but the emotional gap he'd covered by returning spanned more than physical distance. Ever since that final, fierce altercation with his father he'd stayed well away from the winery itself where he'd once toiled long hours creating fine wines using a blend of science and art. Business and family just didn't mix.

Now he stared around the winery. The oak vats smelled

exactly as he remembered from when he'd been chief wine-maker here.

"Heath…"

Every muscle tightened at the sound of the soft voice behind him. *Amy.* He turned and his eyes drank in the sight of her.

A tentative smile played on her pearly-pink lips. Her bobbed dark-chocolate hair was smoothly tucked behind her ears, gold studs glinting in her lobes. Subtle makeup, only enough to hide the dark circles beneath her golden eyes, nothing more. If it hadn't been for those molten eyes, she would've looked like a schoolgirl. Not frumpy, but almost too neat to be true in the white shirt with a rounded collar and the navy skirt.

Innocent.

Or maybe not. Inside he sighed silently. He'd planned to avoid Amy today. All week. Forever, if he could. He started to move away. "Yes, Amy?"

The smile faded. "Taine just called in sick. He says it's a only a sore throat and he should be back at work tomorrow."

Taine was one of the Saxon's Folly cellar hands. "That's fine."

"He says to give him a call and he'll give you an update on what he was supposed to do today."

"I'll call him back."

Amy hovered. "Thanks, Heath."

"My pleasure." He bit off dark thoughts about what really was his pleasure. Amy's mouth swollen with his kisses…Amy lying on his bed…Amy saying—

Hell, why was he torturing himself like this?

He need look no further than her pursed pale-pink mouth to know that none of that was going to happen.

"Heath?"

"Yes?" He'd tried to control his frustration but Amy's amber-gold eyes darkened at his tone. "Sorry, I was thinking about finding Jim—" the other cellar hand "—to let him know Taine wouldn't be in."

"I simply wanted to be the first to say welcome back." Pursing her mouth into a tight bud, she tipped her nose in the air and turned on her heel and stalked away.

Heath was left watching her trim bottom in the demure navy skirt, her straight back retreat. He restrained the fierce urge to swear.

First day back and he'd managed to offend Amy Wright.

Just great.

So what else was new? He should be used to it by now. Ever since he'd waded in and bought the bankrupt Chosen Valley vineyard from Ralph Wright, Amy's father, he'd been separated from her and his family by more than just the range of hills between the two wineries that was appropriately named The Divide.

His heroic gesture had offended even Amy, who hadn't recognized it for what it was—an attempt to rescue her and her father from a crippling cycle of debt. As for his own father, Phillip Saxon had seen it as an attempt to go into direct competition with Saxon's Folly. Heath shook his head. Perhaps his armour was so tarnished no one could recognize his good intentions any more. So he'd retreated into grim silence, and the gap between him and his family—and him and Amy— had widened.

And now he was back at Saxon's Folly. Because Saxon's Folly needed a chief winemaker. Caitlyn Ross, the previous winemaker, had left to get married—to start a new life in Spain with Rafaelo, the half brother Heath had slowly grown to like and respect over the past few weeks.

Of course his father hadn't asked him to return. The old man was too full of stiff-necked pride for that. It had been Caitlyn who'd begged him to come back so that she could leave Saxon's Folly with a clear conscience.

It felt strange to be back. Heath's gaze narrowed as Amy disappeared through the arch that led into the reception area.

Heath suspected that once again his soft heart was going to cost him. Dearly.

For Amy the morning passed in a rush. The phone hadn't stopped ringing and everyone demanded her attention. With Saxon's Folly Summer Festival—a Christmas Eve celebration of the ripening grapes—now a little over three weeks away, a final panic had settled in.

"Amy could you order more candles for the carols ceremony?"

"Amy, would you mind getting these brochures printed?"

"Don't forget to hire three marquees for the festival, Amy."

"Omigod, Amy! Kelly Christie just called to say that she'd like to cover the festival for the Christmas Day edition of her midday TV show."

Most of the organizing was already done—with some things, like booking the jazz bands, done a year in advance—but last-minute crazy details like Kelly Christie kept cropping up. It hadn't been this bad last year. Amy wasn't stupid; she was the reason why there had been a constant stream of people arriving at her desk with requests. It had been going on—albeit on a slightly less insane scale—for weeks. No, make that months. Two months to be precise.

The Saxons were worried about her. She wished she could tell them that she was fine but they didn't ask. Their concern just lay in their eyes, in the way they hovered around her, coming with requests in person rather than phoning or e-mailing what they wanted through to her.

The only one who didn't have a million questions to ask or a zillion mundane tasks to keep her busy today was Heath Saxon.

Black sheep. Hothead. Bad boy.

She shut her eyes. She should've been grateful that he'd

kept his distance on his first day back, she should be saying thanks to—

"Amy, do you know where Alyssa is?"

Eyes snapping open, she found Megan, the youngest Saxon, in front of her.

Megan was staring at her in a way that made Amy's heart sink.

"Are you all right, sweetie?"

"I'm fine," Amy reassured her. For the past two months everyone had been handling her with kid gloves. It was time for the PA of Saxon's Folly to get back to normal. "Sorry, you caught me daydreaming. I think Alyssa went into town with your brother."

"With Joshua?"

Naturally Alyssa had gone with Joshua, her fiancé. Who else could she have gone with? Heath, of course, he was back at Saxon's Folly. But then Amy got a good look at Megan's face. She looked sad. Megan must be thinking about Roland. Amy swallowed and glanced away before the tears came.

There was a silence.

"Sweetie, don't be so hard on yourself. Give yourself a break." The gentleness in Megan's voice made Amy's throat grow thick.

She bit back the sob that threatened. "Really, I'm fine!"

But Megan's concerned eyes told her she didn't believe it.

"Okay, I'm just feeling a little emotional today." Amy dragged in a shaky breath. She pushed the strand of hair that had fallen over her forehead back behind her ears. "An Auckland florist called. Roland ordered a bouquet for me… they wanted to know what colours I was choosing for the wedding, so they could select suitable ribbons for the bouquet."

"Oh, my God." Megan covered her mouth. "Sweetie, I'm so sorry." She came forward in a rush.

Bracing her hands on the counter separating them, Amy shrank away. If Megan hugged her she was going to cry. She knew it. She shook her head frantically. "It's okay, really it is."

"No, it's not okay. Roland—"

"—is dead." She didn't want more pity. "And there won't be a wedding." Megan must be hurting too. Roland had been her adopted brother, though no one had known he was adopted until a little over a month ago.

"Amy, I'm so sorry." Megan covered Amy's hands where they lay on top of the reception counter.

Amy fisted her fingers. "Me too. He wasn't supposed to die."

"No, you were supposed to get married…live happily ever after. That's all you—everyone—ever wanted."

Amy's mouth trembled. "I think I was fourteen when I decided I was going to marry Roland Saxon. I told him when I turned sixteen but he said I was too young for him. So I proposed at my seventeenth birthday dinner." After he'd kissed her outside in the romance of the dark summer's night…kisses meant true love and marriage, didn't they?

How young she'd been. How very idealistic.

Megan's cell phone rang.

"You'd better get that," Amy said, sliding a hand out from under Megan's to rip a tissue from the box on her desk and determinedly wipe her eyes. The outside line rang, so she picked it up and said in a bright voice, "Saxon's Folly Estate and Wines," and then started to note down a booking for a tour group that wanted to do a wine tasting.

Megan's call ended. Clearly she wanted to talk. But Amy didn't. She gave Megan a quick smile, before huddling down behind the counter and starting to describe the various packages available for tour groups. When the call ended she looked up.

To her relief Megan had gone.

"I'm worried about Amy."

Heath stilled in the act of counting wine bottles shelved in order of vintage in the wine-master's cellar. A bottle of every wine the winery had produced since it was started by Spanish monks almost a century ago was stored there. At the sound of Megan's voice he stared fixedly at the cursive gold print on the label of the bottle in front of him.

Finally Heath turned his head and met his sister's direct gaze. "We're all concerned."

"Roland's death has been hard on all of us." Megan gave a sniff, belying her composure.

"At least we've got each other to share the grief with," Heath said. "You, me and Joshua have always been close."

"Exactly! But Amy's so alone, it breaks my heart. She pretends she's fine. But she's so fragile," said Megan, coming in and closing the door behind her. "I'm sure she's lost more weight."

Heath shrugged helplessly. "Dad suggested she take time off. Joshua suggested it. I suggested it. She took two weeks and came back looking worse than she had before. I don't know what to do next."

Megan leant against the antique desk where every chief winemaker at Saxon's Folly had worked, and said, "The wedding would have taken place in two weeks. She must be thinking about it all the time."

"Probably." Heath could feel himself growing tense. He'd spent so long refusing to think of Amy's forthcoming marriage to his brother that he hated being reminded of the occasion. Though he was certain Amy had thought of little but the frothy romantic event. Beneath that goody-two-shoes exterior lurked the heart of a romantic.

"She needs to be kept busy."

"*Why?*" He stared at his sister. In his opinion, Amy needed a break, a rest, time to reflect. Time to grieve.

"So that she doesn't get a chance to think about Roland's death." His younger sister loved organizing other people. "I'm going to get her even more involved in helping with the festival." Megan gave a shudder. "She was in the car with him—the memories must give her nightmares."

Heath closed his mind against the night his brother had died. He didn't want to remember…

Instead, he pondered his sister's suggestion. The annual Saxon's Folly Summer Festival took place the day before Christmas, a busy time of year. And it took a lot of work to make it happen. In the past Roland and Megan had done most of the organizing. Roland had been marketing manager and had worked closely with Megan, whose main role was PR. Since Roland's death Megan had been assuming more of the marketing role—and she'd drawn in Alyssa Blake, Joshua's fiancée, to do some of the overflow PR work. For all he knew, Amy might enjoy being more involved, too.

"That's not a bad idea," he said finally, "but the festival isn't going to replace her wedding."

Megan rocked back on her hands against the desk and rolled her eyes to the ceiling. "I know that, Heath."

"She has to face the fact that Roland is gone." Heath turned back to the wall and pulled a random bottle out of its pigeonhole.

"She knows he's gone." His sister sounded impatient. "That's why she's so lost."

Heath wasn't so sure. Amy had retreated into a place where no one could reach her. She'd frozen everyone out. He was almost certain it was her way of escaping reality.

Of hiding from the truth…

He stared unseeingly at the bottle in his hands. When she came out from that place, there was going to be a lot of pain: she was going to have to accept that Roland was gone. Forever. And at some point Amy was going to have to realise that she was still young, that her life wasn't over. That she still had a chance to live…and love.

"Maybe you can talk to her, Heath." Megan's voice held the forceful determination that he knew all too well.

No. He didn't want to talk to Amy—and he doubted she'd listen. He'd done enough harm already.

He slotted the bottle of wine back into its pigeonhole and walked over to the desk Megan leaned against, dropping down into the antique leather chair behind it and propping his elbows on the blotter.

"No." His answer was very final.

Megan swivelled around and eyed him curiously. "Did you two have a fight?"

"A fight?" He frowned at his sister. "What do you take me for? I couldn't do that to Amy. Not at this time."

"I thought it might be your idea of shock therapy."

"Shock therapy?" *God.* Heath raked his hands through his hair. "No way." Maybe he'd had some misguided intentions. But not shock therapy. Nothing that deliberate—or cold-blooded.

"Okay, I got it wrong." Megan picked up the exclusive catalogue of wines that they mailed to Saxon's Folly's top customers and flipped idly through it, her bangs falling forward over her eyes. "I noticed you've been avoiding her for the past couple of weeks and wondered. I thought you two were friends."

Heath was relived to be out of his sister's sharp eyesight. Since Roland's funeral Amy had rebuffed every attempt he'd made to offer comfort. Finally, he'd given up and taken to avoiding her.

"Not really." Not since she'd turned sixteen. What he felt for Amy wasn't friendship; it was a whole lot more dangerous.

"But surely after what you did for her—"

"What did I do for her?" he said too quickly.

The catalogue landed on the desk with a thud. "You bought the vineyard after Ralph ran it into the ground."

"I didn't do that for Amy." Heath folded his arms across his chest. "Whatever gave you that idea? I did it for myself. Once it became clear that Saxon's Folly wasn't big enough for me and Dad I had two choices—go work for someone else, or set up my own show."

"But why Chosen Valley? Surely you realised that buying a vineyard that close would get into Dad's face?"

"It was a good choice." He didn't elaborate further. He didn't need to—he'd been proved right.

"You didn't have to pay what you did—"

"It was a fair market price."

"But you could've—"

"Give it a rest, Megan."

"And you arranged a job for Amy here at Saxon's Folly."

He shrugged. "So what? I arranged for Dad to employ Caitlyn, too." He grinned at his sister, intent on distracting her, and took refuge in humour that he didn't feel. "Maybe I have frustrated latent urges to be a hotshot corporate recruiter."

Megan burst out laughing. "You? A hotshot recruiter? Never. You're a softie. Your only latent urges are to help people. You arranged that job for Amy because you felt sorry for her, because after being brought up as Daddy's princess she didn't have a whole lot of marketable skills and you—"

Relieved that Megan thought his latent urges had been motivated by altruism rather than something far more basic, Heath growled, "Back off!"

His sister gave him a triumphant look. "I will for now."

But once she'd gone, Heath brooded. If Megan had noticed that he was avoiding Amy, others would, too, and the last thing he needed was questions. The sooner he made his peace with Amy the better.

Amy saw him coming.

She ducked her head down and busied herself with entering a column of sales figures into the computer. When Heath finally stopped in front of the counter she gave a fake little start and her hands fluttered to her breast. "Oh, Heath, you surprised me."

She got the feeling that her deception hadn't worked. Colour rose to her cheeks. Amy never lied. Discomforted at being caught in the act, her hands stilled on her shirtfront, a barrier from behind which she could watch Heath.

He was tall, his hair so dark in comparison to Roland's bright-red mane. Heath's eyes were black. Brooding. Unreadable. The darkness underlined by the black T-shirts and black jeans he normally wore.

Black Saxon.

As a youngster he'd gotten into a lot of fights and gained a terrible reputation. She could remember a period when Heath had always seemed to have his eyes blackened, which was when the Black Saxon nickname had stuck. But he'd always been kind to her.

He'd been a rebel. He'd fought with his father, resisting his authority. His parents had been only too pleased to pack him off to university. She'd heard tales of hazings and wild parties, but when he'd returned he'd changed. Matured. For a while she'd considered him one of her best friends.

But somewhere along the line it had changed. He'd withdrawn. The silences between them had become uncomfortable. And when her father had almost lost the winery, Heath had charged in and bought it—no doubt for a song. Though he'd felt guilty enough to arrange a job for her at the winery. It had suited her…and brought her closer to Roland.

After the night Roland died, she and Heath no longer seemed to know what to say to each other.

She didn't even know what he thought about the discovery that Roland was adopted…or how he felt about the arrival of his half brother last month. Or what he thought about Caitlyn leaving.

But then she'd been so caught up in her own woes she

hadn't asked. Her self-absorption made her shudder with embarrassment. She needed to remedy that. "Do you think Caitlyn will be happy with Rafaelo?"

He gave her a strange look. "Why shouldn't she be?"

"I thought—" Amy broke off, flushing.

He came closer. "You thought what?"

"Uh…I thought that you and Caitlyn had something going."

He threw his head back and laughed out loud. "Me and Caitlyn?"

Despite the flash of white teeth from this close, Amy could see his black-devil's eyes weren't laughing. "I thought…"

"You thought what?" There was a fixed intensity in his eyes, an intensity that made her want to shudder in discomfort again.

"She came back from university with you." Amy glanced away from that penetrating gaze and fiddled with the computer keys, opening a file, feeling foolish.

She wasn't clever—not like Caitlyn Ross whom everybody knew was supersmart. Caitlyn had gone to university on a science scholarship. By contrast, Amy had tried hard at school, done exactly as she was told, but though she'd usually gotten a prize at the end of the year it was always for effort or citizenship rather than academic brilliance. *Teacher's pet.* The unkind taunt of her schoolmates came back in an unwelcome blast.

She felt, rather than saw, Heath shrug. "I tutored Caitlyn. It was no secret that she was going to go places. So I told Dad about her, and for once Dad actually listened to what I had to say." A bitter slant distorted his sculpted mouth. "He offered her a vacation job. She was so good there was no way he was going to let her go."

"Did it hurt that your father became her mentor? That she took your job as chief winemaker?" Amy had wondered about that when he bought Chosen Valley.

"Nah, when I resigned I suggested Dad promote her."

"So he took your advice again." Maybe Heath didn't see how much stock Phillip Saxon placed in him. It wouldn't hurt to point it out. It was awful that there was such a rift between the two Saxon men.

"He would've been stupid not to have."

Amy gave him a quick upward glance. "Maybe it was because you've always held her in such high regard that I thought you'd end up married."

Heath's shoulders rose under the close-fitting black T-shirt, then dropped nonchalantly.

He certainly didn't look heartbroken. A frown wrinkled Amy's forehead. She'd been so certain that Caitlyn had wanted Heath. She'd caught Caitlyn watching him in the past, a soft, yearning look on her face. All that had changed with the Spaniard's arrival. Rafaelo had swept her off her feet. Emotion clogged up her throat. "Oh, well, I hope Caitlyn and Rafaelo will be happy together. Have they set a wedding date yet?"

Heath gave her a sharp glance. "Next year, I believe."

A wedding…

Amy bit her lip and looked down at the keyboard. Her lip began to hurt. She bit harder.

"Amy?"

She didn't look up. She hit the keyboard with a series of random taps. A tear splashed onto the spacebar.

"*Amy!*"

She bent her head lower. Heath mustn't see her crying. Not him, of all people.

Too late. He'd come around the counter. He was standing beside her; she could hear his breathing, loud in the private space behind the counter. Amy's shoulders started to shake. Inside she felt hot and tight as if she were going to burst. As if she could no longer hold it all in—all the grief and emotion she'd been pressing down, terrified it might explode out.

"Hush."

Heath's hands came down on her shoulders. She stiffened. But the thickness in her throat grew more painful. She swallowed. That hurt. She could barely breathe.

He pulled. The typist's chair spun round. She caught one glimpse of his face, saw the torment in his dark eyes, and hurriedly shut her own eyes as tightly as she could. But still the tears leaked out, burning down her cheeks.

There was a rustle of fabric, as if he was crouching down. But she didn't dare open her eyes. Then Heath's hands tightened on her shoulders, pulling her from the chair. She gasped as she slid. Suddenly he was no longer behind her, and she landed in a sprawl across his thighs where he knelt beside the chair, the slim-fitting navy skirt riding up to expose bare pale thigh.

She tried desperately to tug it down.

The linen resisted. A moment later Heath's arms closed around her, drawing her tightly against his chest. He smelt warm and male, of sun and dust and a hint of lemon. She made a little choking sound and buried her face against his shirtfront.

"I know you loved him for so long. I know there's a huge hole in your life now."

The choke became a sob.

Her throat was hot. Her insides twisted. She wanted to order Heath to be quiet, to release her, to go away, but she couldn't find the strength.

Tears rushed down her cheeks.

"Cry all you want, Amy. Let it all out."

She couldn't bear for him to see her like this, in such a state. He was so contained, so controlled. He was no longer the impulsive bad boy; he'd grown up. Whereas she'd regressed. She'd gone from being the good girl who did everything right every time to someone she didn't know. Someone who felt like she'd lost total control of herself, her life.

Darn it, she didn't even know why she was crying. The tears

had come out of nowhere. For a moment she allowed her body to sag and great gasps of pain escaped her. Heath didn't move, didn't speak. He just kept her close in the circle of his arms. Embarrassed, Amy gave a gulp and summoned all her strength.

She pulled away from him. A horrified glance revealed that there were unsightly damp patches over the front of Heath's immaculate black T-shirt where she'd blubbered like a baby.

Kneeling on the carpet, she reached for a tissue from the box on the desk. No way was she dabbing at the sodden patches on his shirt with a tissue. She wasn't going near him. Sniffling, she retreated further and said, "I'm so sorry. I don't know what's wrong with me. I can't seem to stop crying."

He reached for her. "You've had a terrible time and I haven't helped—"

She fought her way out his arms and leapt to her feet, cannoning into the chair and causing it to shoot sideways. All at once the room started to tip sideways, before righting and tipping back the other way.

This must be what an earthquake felt like. Her vision turned spotty. "Heath, I don't feel well."

Her legs crumpled beneath her. She glimpsed a foggy Heath lurching toward her.

Everything went dark.

Two

To Amy's dismay, Heath high-handedly packed her into his flashy silver Lamborghini, drove her to his home—*her* birthplace, the home where *she'd* grown up—and summoned a doctor.

He'd hurried her past his concerned housekeeper, through the entrance hall and up the staircase to the guest bedroom on the first floor. When she'd last seen this room it had been a faded sky-blue, in desperate need of refurbishment. Heath had done that. The dove's-egg blue and ivory striped wallpaper was fresh and elegant, the padded bedcover pristine, and two paintings in hues of blues and greens hung over the queen-sized bed. Once he was satisfied that she was comfortable, Heath crossed to the window, pushed the heavy ivory drapes fully open and released the sash window to let in fresh, country air.

She waited for him to turn, then lifted her chin, saying brightly, "I'm fine now. I don't need a doctor." Amy knew she must sound like a chirpy little sparrow. But there was nothing wrong with her. She knew it. Now if only she could make Heath understand that too. Except he wasn't listening.

He was grey under his tan. His lips were set in a tight line and his eyes held a determined look that warned her that she wasn't going to change his mind.

"I called Dr. Shortt during your faint. He should be here soon."

"Dr. Shortt? But I haven't seen him for years. Not since I last had chicken pox." That had been the tenth anniversary of her mother's death and her father had been in a state. Amy had been fifteen, too old to be contracting chicken pox and definitely too old to be receiving house calls—in her teenaged opinion.

"Who is your doctor now? I'll call them if you don't want Dr. Shortt—though he's dropped everything to come see you."

"I haven't been to the doctor in years. I'm as healthy as a horse." Amy was still arguing five minutes later when Dr. Shortt entered the room, a worn black bag clutched under his arm. Except for a few extra pounds around his middle and a little more grey hair above his ears, the doctor hadn't changed from the last time she'd seen him.

"Amy, my girl, what have we done to ourselves?"

And he still spoke to her as if she were a child. Amy glared at Heath, unfairly blaming him for the indignity. He didn't react. Which irritated her even more.

Dr. Shortt glanced at Heath. "Sorry I didn't make your brother's memorial service last month. An emergency. A near drowning." Heath nodded at the explanation, and Dr. Shortt turned his attention back to Amy, his eyes softening with the concern that she'd gotten too used to seeing in the past two months. "It would have been a difficult time for you, my dear."

At least she'd graduated to *my dear.* Then she regretted her lack of grace. "It has." Unexpected tears welled up. Frustrated, she brushed the back of her hand across her face.

"Come, let me see what's happening." Dr. Shortt looked across to where Heath stood silently by the window. "We'll be downstairs soon."

"Heath can go back to work." Amy was annoyed to hear a wobble in her voice.

Her words had the unwelcome effect of focusing that black gaze upon her. "I'm staying."

"Not in here, you're not." There was no way she was tolerating his presence while the doctor examined her.

After a moment's hesitation Heath moved to the door. "I'll wait outside."

Amy fell back against the pillows when the door closed behind him and let out a sigh of relief.

Dr. Shortt peered at her from under those bushy brows, his eyes bright and observant. "So tell me how you've been."

"Tearful." Amy gave the doctor a tremulous smile as she stated the obvious. "But that's to be expected with Roland's death, isn't it? Everyone tells me that I coped so well after it happened, and the reality is kicking in now."

The doctor humphed and produced a tympanic thermometer. "Are you sleeping?"

Sitting up and tilting her head sideways, she brushed her hair away from her ear so he could take her temperature. "I didn't the first week after Roland died. But for the last month I seem to be tired all the time." That had surprised Amy because she'd always had a lot of energy.

Another humph. He glanced at the thermometer, scrawled something on his notepad and put it away. "Young Saxon tells me that you fainted?"

Young Saxon. Heath would love that…not. But the appellation made Amy smile. "I stood up too quickly. The blood rushed to my head."

This time there was no humph as he took a cuff from his bag and soon the room was filled with the sound of pumping, until he paused to read her blood pressure. "Hmm. A little on the low side."

The first wave of fear swept her. "Is there something wrong with me?" She'd paid very little attention to herself for the last two months. Her whole life had taken on a roller-coaster quality. She no longer knew where she was going, what would happen the next day. And for a while she'd hardly cared.

"Let me examine you."

The next fifteen minutes seemed to take forever. Dr. Shortt even made her go to the adjoining bathroom and produce a specimen. A few minutes later he examined an indicator stick, looked up at her, and announced, "You're pregnant, Amy."

Horror surged through her. "I can't—" She swallowed. It *was* possible. "Are you certain?"

He didn't take umbrage at her doubt. Instead, he smiled and said, "The tearfulness, tiredness, feeling faint…they're all symptoms. Even the slightly lowered blood pressure."

"Oh, dear God." Amy covered her face. "What am I going to do?"

He asked when she'd started her last period. Amy stared at him blankly. "I had a light one and missed the next. Because of stress, I thought."

He nodded. "You need to make an appointment to have an ultrasound scan. That will give us a better idea how far along you are."

Amy dropped her hands from her face and began to chew her lip. Then she said, "I know exactly how far along I am."

The doctor nodded. "That's good. But we can confirm your suspicions. Of course, you'll also need to tell the fath—" Dr. Shortt's voice broke off and Amy knew the full enormity of the situation had finally struck him. "I'm so sorry, my dear. Did you and Roland plan to have children?"

"One day. After we were married." Not now. She'd never envisioned being a single mother. It wasn't the way Amy Wright did things. Babies were meant to come into married unions. *Ms. Wright.* How wrong was that? She wanted to weep all over again. How had she managed to screw up her life this badly?

And what was she doing using vulgar terms like *screw up?* Amy's lip started to feel tender where she'd gnawed on it.

"Your father might be able to help."

Aghast, she stared at Dr. Shortt. "My father? He's barely got enough to subsist on—there's no provision for raising a child." Despite the liquidators' gloomy forecast that her father would be broke, by some stroke of luck he'd managed to get enough out of the sale of the vineyard to buy a very modest home in nearby Hastings. "He survives day to day only by being extremely frugal."

A card was pressed into her hand. "Make an appointment to see a counsellor—it may give you some options. But, my dear, if it's any comfort to you, after so many years as a doctor I still view the conception of a baby as a miracle."

A miracle. Amy pushed the card into her pocket, her mind blank with shock. How was she going to break the news to Kay and Phillip Saxon that she, the fiancée who never took a wrong step, was about to produce their first grandchild—an illegitimate baby—outside the bonds of marriage? And even if Kay and Phillip accepted it, how could she ever forgive herself?

Heath was pacing the corridor by the time Amy and the doctor emerged from the blue guest room. He paused in midstep, his heart drumming against his ribs as he took in Amy's deathly pale face.

"What's wrong?" he asked urgently.

"I'll leave Amy to tell you." There was an incomprehensible twinkle of delight in the doctor's eyes that should've reassured Heath but didn't.

One stride took him to Amy's side. "What is it?" When she glanced away, his concern increased tenfold. "Tell me!"

"I'll see myself out, shall I?" Dr. Shortt was already halfway down the stairs before Heath belatedly remembered the tea he'd asked his housekeeper to prepare. Too late to invite the doctor for a cup now. "Thank you for coming, Doctor," he called after the departing figure.

Heath heard the front door thud close. Wrapping an arm around Amy's stiff shoulders, he said, "Let's go down to the living room. Josie has made a tray of tea. We'll get you a cup, and then you can tell me what the matter is."

For a moment he thought she was going to refuse. Then she moved, her feet dragging against the pale, thick woollen carpet.

Downstairs, once he'd settled Amy into the most comfortable armchair, Heath poured her a cup of tea and, setting it on the small table beside her, said with an insouciance he didn't feel, "Dr. Shortt didn't look too concerned."

"No, he considers it a miracle." Amy's tone was wooden, her body stiffly upright in the chair.

The unfamiliar glint in her amber eyes caused his stomach to tighten. "What miracle, Amy?" He could think of no one who needed a miracle more.

"I'm pregnant, Heath."

For an instant a bolt of pure, blinding joy shot through Heath. He took a stumbling, half step toward her. "Pregnant? You're sure?"

"Yes," she snapped. "Three months' pregnant. Some miracle. I don't want to be pregnant."

Her words sank in. *Three months' pregnant.* And then her next statement hit him. The bottom dropped out of his stomach...out of his world. "You mean you're going to abort Roland's baby?"

Her eyes widened. If she'd been pale before, now she was whiter than the snow that fell on Mt. Ruapehu. "How dare you? How *dare* you believe that of me?"

Too late Heath remembered that Amy had firm, highly romantic views of family. No babies out of wedlock. White, splashy weddings with pageboys in attendance and rings on velvet cushions. Abortion wouldn't even feature. "I'm sorry," he said humbly.

She gave him a heated look. "Good."

"You're angry with me."

"Yes. No. I don't know." She bent her head and sniffed.

Oh, hell, she was about to cry again. Heath moved to kneel beside her chair.

"No," she squawked, cringing up against the padded armrest. "Stay away from me."

That annoyed Heath. Amy must know he'd never hurt her. Couldn't she understand that he only wanted to help? He rocked back on his heels to give her a little space and met her turbulent gaze squarely, "I can understand why you're angry with me."

"Can you?" She turned her head away and pursed the pink rosebud mouth that had been the subject of his most secret fantasies.

"Yes! Amy—"

"I don't want to talk about it." Folding her arms across her chest, she shrank further into herself.

Dammit, he wanted to see her eyes. He wanted to know what she was thinking. But he didn't dare touch her. Not while she was in this state. "Amy, we have to talk. We can't let this—"

"No." She was on her feet, her hands warding him off even though he hadn't moved an inch. "Take me back to work, to Saxon's Folly."

He narrowed his gaze, taking in the stiff, resentful line of her mouth, the rebellious glitter in her golden eyes. "You're not going back to work. I won't allow it."

The glitter intensified. "I am. You can't stop me."

"Of course I can," he stated through clenched teeth.

A flush of scarlet seared her cheeks. His chest contracted as her eyes grew dull and he read the despair that lay within.

"You'd keep me here by force?"

The insulting implication rocked him. Heath swallowed, his mouth suddenly dry. "For God's sake, Amy, you know I'd never do that. I only meant that I wouldn't drive you back to work right now—not when you've just recovered from a faint."

Her mouth firmed. "Fine. Then I'll walk back."

"No, you won't!" Heath exploded. God, she could be irritating. Under that good-as-gold exterior lay the most stubborn little madam he'd ever met. Lowering his voice, he continued, "I don't care if it makes you angrier with me, but I'm not taking you back to work today. You fainted. You should rest. Now drink your tea while I have Josie prepare the spare room for you. You can stay the night."

The high colour leached out of her cheeks. "That is absolutely not happening!" This time Amy bolted for the front door at a run, her navy skirt tight around her legs. "I'm going back to work. I'm pregnant—not sick."

Heath caught her as she struggled with the lock on the front door and glared at her, frustration broiling inside him. Why couldn't she see that he was only trying to do what was best for her? Putting a hand out, he stopped her struggles. "So now you're an expert. What do you know about being pregnant?"

She turned her head, and he found himself gazing down into eyes as desperate as those of a trapped animal. The vulnerability he saw there shook him to the soul.

"Don't worry about me." Her shoulders sagged beneath the white shirt. "This is my problem, not yours. I'll do what Dr. Shortt said. I'll have a scan, then I'll go to an antenatal clinic… I'll find out what I need to know…I'll take vitamins. Darn it, Heath, I'm not even feeling dizzy any more."

It was true that she hadn't fainted again, and she'd promised to visit the doctor. And she was right, it wasn't his problem that she was pregnant with his brother's baby. If he told himself that often enough he might even be able to butt out.

Heath unlatched the door and stepped away, giving her the space she clearly wanted. "I'm pleased to hear you've decided to be sensible."

"And I'm pleased that you've realised I'm not staying here." Amy couldn't prevent her voice from rising as she parroted his patronizing statement back at him. *Decided to be sensible? Hah.* Her chest rose and fell as she breathed deeply and counted silently to ten. She needed to get out of here. Now. Before she fell to pieces completely. "If you won't take me back to work, then take me home."

"This was your home for many years. Why don't you pretend—"

"No." A fresh surge of panic shook her. Pretence wouldn't help…she'd tried that and it hadn't worked. It had simply gotten her deeper into the mire. And staying here would finish it off.

Amy glanced back to the sitting room, taking in the leather furniture, the bold original acrylic painting on the wall above, trying to find something final—and cutting—to say. "I don't think of this as my home any more."

If her voice hadn't wavered, it might've rung true. After all, Chosen Valley was Heath's home now, even though she'd been born and raised here. He'd taken it over, redecorated the shabby rooms. The place should have lost all familiarity. Yet it still felt warm and welcoming.

Like home…

Perhaps because the antique rocking horse she'd loved as a little girl still stood in the corner of the living room—it had been too big to take with her to the cottage she'd rented. For some reason Heath had hung on to it—probably because of its value.

For a brief instant she imagined her child riding the rocking horse. She touched her stomach and instantly the pickle of the position she found herself in came back to her. *It was not possible.* The child would not grow up at Chosen Valley.

She couldn't bear to think about any of it right now.

"Amy—"

She fixed her gaze back on Heath. "I don't want you to tell anyone that I'm pregnant."

Heath's breath caught. "Why the hell not?"

"Don't swear," she told him. "Your mother wouldn't like it." Then she realised how utterly ridiculous—how prissy—that sounded. His mother would hardly like the fact that she was pregnant, either. She shuddered with humiliation. But the only way his mother would find out was if Heath told her. Narrowing her gaze on him, she said, "I don't want you telling anyone because I'm not ready to deal with it." She couldn't bear to think of the well-meaning questions she would face, the curiosity in everyone's eyes.

"Amy—" his face softened "—whatever you believe, it's not that bad. Dr. Shortt is right: it truly *is* a miracle."

She shook her head back in rejection. "No, it's not. It's awful. It's the last thing on earth I need. Promise not to tell anyone?"

A furrow appeared between his arched brows. "You're being unreasonable. My parents will be thrilled to hear that you're pregnant with Roland's baby."

She glared at him. He couldn't possibly understand the confusion, the despair, the shame that churned inside her. No one could. "I'm *not* being unreasonable. Roland is dead. It's *my* body. My choice. *My* baby." Oh dear. She hadn't wanted to think of the life within her as belonging to her. Upset by the direction her thoughts had taken, her breathing grew ragged. "Please, Heath, just promise me."

He threw his hands into the air. "Okay, okay, if it upsets you that much I promise I won't tell."

He didn't like it; she could tell from the troubled look in his eyes. Feeling wrung out, but desperate to get out of his house, away from him, Amy said, "Please take me to my home."

Three

*A*bortion.

That word again. Speechless, Amy stared at the woman who'd voiced it. Carol Carter, the counsellor, was a plump middle-aged woman with dark, short hair and kind eyes that looked like they had seen too much. She'd told Carol as soon as she'd walked in that she felt confused and guilty about being pregnant out of wedlock, that it went against her core beliefs. The ease with which the counsellor suggested a solution horrified Amy.

For a moment Amy wished that she had someone beside her. Roland. Or even outspoken Megan. She needed a hand to hold, to keep her grounded.

Roland was gone. She'd never touch him again. Megan had flown out this morning to go to Australia for two days, leaving Amy five pages of notes for the summer festival.

Finally she found her voice. "I can't do that!"

"You need to consider what you're going to do." Carol's

soft voice was at odds with the harsh reality of what she was saying. "You don't have a lot of time."

"Isn't it too late for a…termination?" Amy asked. If it was too late they wouldn't need to discuss this any further.

Carol glanced down at the sheet in front of her that Amy had gotten from Dr. Shortt after her scan the previous afternoon. "There shouldn't be any risk to you if the procedure is done in the next month."

Risk to her. That made Amy feel incredibly selfish. What about the…she searched for a word, baby was too emotive…the life inside her? "No, I can't do it." She couldn't live with herself if she did that. She was healthy, physically and mentally; there was no compelling medical reason for such an extreme step.

"The fetus is nearing the end of the first trimester."

The fetus. Yes, she had to think of it as *the fetus* not *my baby*.

"Or you could consider going to term and giving the baby up for adoption." Now Carol peered over the top of her glasses, making Amy feel like a schoolkid again. "It's worth considering very seriously. You'd be giving a very special gift to a couple who want a baby."

That made her feel even worse. *She* didn't want to be pregnant. But somewhere out there another woman was desperately yearning for a baby.

The ever-lurking tears were back. *What was wrong with her?*

"Think about it," said Carol. "Given your situation and how you feel about being a single mother, it might be better for the child. Let me know what you decide."

Better for the child.

Stunned, Amy stared at the counsellor. Could she give the baby up? Even if it was in the baby's best interests? Finding out that she was pregnant had been awful. She'd resisted the idea that a baby was growing inside her, been angry, resentful. But now she was starting to accept it. She wasn't sure any longer that she could give it up for adoption. Oh, she was so confused.

When she got out of the claustrophobic white room, Heath was waiting.

Shock ripped through her. Her heart stopped for a moment at the sight of him, tall and dark, dressed all in black—the extravagant Rolex on his wrist providing the only relief—and taking up more space than he should in the reception room. "What are you doing here?"

"I saw the appointment booked into your computer. I thought you might want support." His jaw was set; he didn't look very comforting at all.

He'd stood at her desk…touched her things…checked her whereabouts on the electronic diary? Amy wrapped her arms around her stomach. "You've been spying on me."

He came closer, lifting a hand. For a moment she thought he was going to reach for her. Then his arm dropped awkwardly to his side. "Not spying—I was concerned when you didn't come to work this morning. Dad told me you'd be in late because of a doctor's appointment, but I knew you'd been to the doctor yesterday. I was worried when I heard there was another appointment."

That made her feel like a wicked, bad-tempered witch. "I'm sorry." She thought of the hand she'd craved to hold. But she didn't want Heath's hand, she wanted—

She bit her lip. "I didn't want anyone to know I was going to see a counsellor. I don't want people to think I'm losing it."

"Oh, Amy." He looked like he wanted to say more. But then he slung an arm around her shoulder and drew her close.

Instantly she grew tense.

He sighed, and his arm fell away. "Come, I'll take you back to work."

Heath was trying to take over again. "You can't give me a ride. My car is parked around the back," she objected quickly.

He nodded. "I saw it when I walked past. But you don't

look like you're in any state to drive. I'll arrange for one of the winery staff to pick it up later."

Maybe she wasn't. The compulsion to argue with him vanished. The counselling session had drained her. "You're probably right," she conceded. "I'd be better off catching a ride with you."

"Aren't I always right?" His mouth curved upward.

Amy realised that he was trying to make her laugh. But she didn't feel like she was ever going to be cheerful again. The heavy weight of the decision she had to make pressed down on her. A decision that involved not only her, but the life growing inside her as well.

But Heath didn't take her straight back to Saxon's Folly. Instead he walked her through the heart of the town to a narrow restored art deco building that housed a coffee shop, a couple of blocks from the clinic. When Amy realised his intention, her shoulders tensed and for a moment Heath thought she was going to dig her toes in and refuse to enter the crowded, popular establishment. Then she crossed the threshold and he dismissed his concern. But once seated opposite her at a table that overlooked the street, he met eyes that sparked with annoyance, and realised that Amy was even madder than he'd thought.

Belligerently, she said, "I'll have tea. Green tea. Weak."

Heath frowned. For the first time he became aware of the chattering around them and the overpowering fragrance of the specially blended coffee. "It's very crowded in here. Would you rather go somewhere else?"

"I don't want to go anywhere with you. I thought you were taking me back to Saxon's Folly."

"I want to talk to you first."

The look she gave him was intended to sting. "Did it ever cross your mind that I might not want to talk to you?"

He'd known that. But hearing her put it into words still caused an ache inside him. After the night Roland died, Amy had withdrawn. Despite all his efforts, she'd made it quite clear that she didn't want him around her.

Narrowing his eyes, he said, "That's not negotiable. We're going to talk." And he watched her bristle. Hell, it was a lot better than being treated like he didn't exist.

"About what?"

"The baby."

"Oh." She fell silent.

Heath waited, sure she would tell him it had nothing to do with him. But she remained quiet, and he took the opportunity to examine her. The pallor of yesterday was gone. She looked well, her skin glowing with a pearly sheen and her dark hair glossy. His throat closed. Amy had never looked more beautiful—or been more unattainable.

"Why are you looking me like that?"

"Like what?" he asked, buying time.

"Like I'm a bug under a microscope."

That surprised a laugh from him. "Never a bug." He hesitated, forcing himself to keep smiling at her. "I was just thinking how well you look."

She flushed.

Heath changed the subject to a safer topic. "Is the smell of the coffee in here making you feel nauseous?"

"I haven't noticed anything turning my stomach—or any cravings either." A ghost of a twinkle lit her eyes. "So you needn't feel guilty about that."

Heath gave a sigh of relief. "Thank you. At least I know that by bringing you here I haven't made you feel ill. I'm glad you're not suffering from morning sickness…or uncomfortable cravings." He smiled at her, determined that she shouldn't realise how looking at her always tugged at his heart. "Of course, that's probably partly why you never realised you were pregnant."

"I feel like such a ninny!" She yanked a toothpick out of a white porcelain holder and ripped the protective shield off. "How could I not have noticed?"

Resting his elbows on the table, Heath leaned forward. "Hardly surprising. You've had a lot on your mind."

A waitress bustled up and handed them menus and, notebook open, prepared to take their order. Heath raised an eyebrow at Amy, "Only green tea? Sure you don't want lemon cheesecake or a slice of pecan pie?"

She rolled her eyes and shook her head, so he ordered. But the waitress's arrival had broken the moment of easy camaraderie. While they waited, Heath leaned back and watched as Amy fiddled restlessly with the wooden toothpick. She'd always been such a little thing. Finely boned. Pretty. As a child she'd attended years of ballet lessons and it showed in the way that she held herself, the graceful way she moved barely seeming to touch the ground.

Her fingers were dainty, the tips painted a soft shell-pink. Today she wore a pale pink shirt that reflected the matching hue that dusted her cheeks. An antique gold locket that always caused a little ache in his chest dangled from a gold chain just past the first button of her shirt—firmly buttoned down, of course. Her neat, bobbed hair had been pushed behind her ears and in the lobes she wore the pair of simple gold studs. From the top of her well-brushed head to her varnished toenails, Amy was a lady—the most feminine, delicate woman he'd ever met.

And if Roland hadn't died, in two weeks' time, Amy would have become Mrs. Roland Saxon.

She glanced up. Expertly, Heath wiped his face clean of all expression. He'd had a lot of practice hiding his emotions over the years.

"I forgot to tell you that your mother called yesterday morning—before I fainted," said Amy.

"Oh?" His mother had recently discovered that early in

their marriage her husband, Heath's father, had had an affair that had resulted in a child—Rafaelo, Heath's half brother. Shaken by her husband's treachery she'd left just over a week ago to stay with her brother in Australia. No one knew when she planned to returned. Heath was sorry he'd missed her. "Where was I?"

Amy shook her head. "She didn't ask for any of you. She wanted to speak to Phillip but I couldn't find him. She said she'd ring back—and asked me not to tell him."

"But you did?"

"I couldn't—I promised I wouldn't." She gave him a careful look. "I don't break promises."

And nor did he. "I won't tell Dad, either."

The waitress came back and set two steaming cups down—Amy's tea and his espresso—along with two glasses of water, and then she hurried away.

Uncertainty flashed across Amy's face. "I thought someone should know Kay had called."

"Thank you. It's been a difficult time for Mum." That was an understatement. The past couple of months had been ghastly for all of them. Roland's death in a car accident on the night of the masked ball. Rafaelo's arrival and the shocking announcement that he was Phillip's illegitimate son. He'd lost a brother…discovered a new brother. But Amy had lost the love of her life.

His eyes rested on her, and immediately she looked down at the toothpick between her fingers. "I don't know how she can bear knowing that your father betrayed her," Amy murmured.

"It's been very hard on her." Heath had seen the sadness in his mother's eyes. Rafaelo's arrival had turned her whole world upside down.

"What a terrible thing for her to discover." There was a strange note in Amy's voice; the toothpick between her fingers snapped and the splinters of wood fell from her fingers.

Heath's gaze sharpened. "Amy—" He broke off. Had Amy discovered what he'd always feared? That Roland liked to flirt—and sometimes more—with other women? Lord, he hoped not. And how could he even ask? What if he was wrong?

"Yes?" She was staring at him expectantly. There was no murky confusion in her eyes.

Amy didn't know.

He'd nearly made a terrible gaffe. Cautiously, he reached out and placed a hand over hers. "I want you to know that I don't break promises either. I told you I wouldn't tell anyone about your baby, and I won't."

Her fingers went rigid under his. "Don't call it that."

Amy's lips had barely moved. Surrounded by the anonymity of the chattering hordes, Heath had to crane forward to hear what she was saying. "What?"

"'Your baby.'" Her voice was unsteady. "Don't call it that."

Heath frowned, staring hard at her, trying to fathom what was going on in that beautiful head. "Why on earth not? It *is* your baby."

"But I don't want to think of it like that." Tears filled her eyes, sparkling like the early-morning dewdrops that collected on the vines. "Not yet. Not until I decide what I'm going to do. I don't want to grow attached to it. I don't want to love it."

Heath blinked. He hadn't fully contemplated what she must be going through. Amy had always been protective of younger kids, almost maternal. Having to make this sort of decision about her baby would be a calamity for her. He groped for something to say, but no words seemed adequately comforting…or helpful. So he tightened his fingers around hers instead.

"The counsellor suggested I consider an abortion," she said in a rush, and her throat moved visibly as she gulped.

Amy was much more upset than he'd realised. Heath wished he hadn't brought her here to this very public conversation spot, but he wasn't about to suggest that they leave. He wanted to hear what she had to say, and if they left he might not get her to open up again, might never discover her thoughts, her fears.

"What did you decide?" With his hand clamped over hers, he waited tensely for her answer. She'd been angry when he'd confronted her with the same question. Was it possible she'd changed her mind? Despite his envy of her relationship with Roland, he found he couldn't bear the thought of the last link with his brother being severed.

She shook her head and her fingers contracted under his. "I told her the same as I told you. I can't do it."

Deep inside Heath something gave, a tightness he hadn't even been aware existed. His hand gripped hers; he never wanted to let go.

Amy drew a deep breath, her fingers curling into his. "Because of my situation, she suggested I consider giving it—" Heath blinked at the emotionless pronoun but she ploughed on "—up for adoption."

He lowered his voice. "Are you considering that?"

"I don't know. I'm confused."

Her velvety eyes were naked, so vulnerable that a queer pain lodged under his breastbone. Heath wished he could absorb her agony, give her the answers she needed.

He slid his free hand under their joined fingers, cradling her hand between both of his. "You don't need to do that if you don't want to. There will be lots of people to love the baby, Amy, lots of people to help you. You won't be alone." It was a vow. He would do everything he could to make her life easier, to help her raise his brother's child.

She moved convulsively, pulling her hands free of his and spread her fingers helplessly. "What am I going to do, Heath? Under normal circumstances I'd never consider giving up my baby. But I'm not married."

"That doesn't matter—"

"It does to me," she said with a quiet dignity that made him fall silent. "And I keep remembering that Roland was adopted. Look how much joy he brought your parents. Imagine if they'd had no other children, Roland would have been their only chance. This—" her hands dropped to pat her stomach "—might do the same for another couple."

An overwhelming sense of loss shook Heath. If things had been different…if he'd been luckier…Amy's baby might have been his. Heath knew that his mother would be delighted to have a tiny piece of Roland. But he wasn't prepared to use that to blackmail Amy. She had to be content with what she decided—regardless of what everyone in his family would want. And he would support her in her decision. For him, Amy would always come first.

"Whatever you do, Amy, it must be what's right for you."

"Right for me? I've already messed that up but good. I never intended to bring a child into the world without a husband…without a father. That's my moral code. I don't know that I can bear the sideways looks, the gossip." She covered her face with cupped hands. "I suppose that makes me sound so shallow, so goody-two-shoes."

"No, it doesn't." Everyone who knew Amy knew she'd spent her life trying to do the right thing. Social conventions and good manners were important to her. She was the five-year-old who took flowers to her teacher on the first day of spring, the eight-year-old who'd never missed a day of Sunday school. At twelve she'd organized a car wash so that a classmate could dance at a competition abroad. At sixteen she'd been managing her father's house. And even now she still found time to volunteer for a string of charitable trusts.

Amy wasn't like Heath. He didn't give a rat's ass what people thought of him, but that mattered to Amy. Being bedded, unwedded and pregnant would not have been part of her life plan.

"You have to do what makes you happy. You're the one who will have to live with the decision you make now for the rest of your life."

Doubt flashed in her eyes. "That confuses me even more."

"Come." Heath pushed his chair back, the social vibe of the coffee shop suddenly unbearably oppressive. "Let's walk."

Much to his relief she didn't argue, didn't demand to be taken back to Saxon's Folly. Heath tossed a bill on the table to cover the untouched beverages.

Outside the sunlight zinged off the white art deco building on the opposite side of the road. Blinking against the bright light, Heath reached in his chest pocket for his Wayfarers.

They walked in silence. Crossing Marine Parade with a group of tourists, Heath was aware of Amy's hand swinging beside his and resisted the temptation to catch it and enfold it in his. He knew what would happen if he did—she'd withdraw back into her shell and he'd have a devil of a time getting her to talk to him again. Instead, he headed for a deserted spot where a patch of parklike green grass overlooked the black-pebbled beach and, once they were alone, he swung around to face Amy.

"Just don't do anything in a hurry, or for the wrong reasons. If you decide to give the baby up for adoption, don't do it just because Roland was adopted." The words hurt his tight throat. "You can't necessarily assume he'd want the same for his child."

Amy walked past him to the edge of the rolling grass, and stared out at the blue ocean. She looked desperately alone.

After a moment she turned back to him with a sigh that seemed wrenched from her. "I keep trying to convince myself that if I can bring myself to go through with adoption it will fulfill some other woman's dreams."

She wanted to keep the baby. Weak with relief, Heath shoved his hands in his pockets to stop himself from placing his hands on her shoulders and drawing her into the shelter of his arms. He told himself that this was Amy's decision to make, not his. But, Lord, how he wanted her to keep her baby. "You need to decide what you want—not what you think might be right for some other woman out there, but what will be right for you." Then, even though he'd told himself he wouldn't pressure her, he blurted out, "If I were the baby's father I'd selfishly hope my woman would bring the child up, share it with my family after my death, let it bring happiness back to the family."

Her brows drew together. "I'm not married, Heath. I don't have a whole lot to offer a child."

"You have us, you have Saxon's Folly." His voice dropped. "You have me."

"You?" She laughed. "You wouldn't want a child."

"I'd be there for the baby—boy or girl. If it's a boy I'll take it to cricket, to soccer." Heath found himself getting fired up. He could visualise a little boy with Amy's amber eyes and dark hair. "If it's a girl I'll screen all her boyfriends—I know precisely how the wild boys think." He grinned at her, suddenly feeling elated.

She gave him a stunned look. But he got the feeling he was getting somewhere. About time.

"I thought if I helped some couple out, if the baby was adopted out, I'd never have to tell anyone." She threw him a sideways look just as the wind ruffled her hair, giving her the look of a sea sprite. "Except for you."

She'd ask him to keep such a secret for all his life, from his family? Hadn't she learnt anything from what had happened with Roland—how much Roland's sister Alyssa had been hurt by being kept from her birth brother? But there was no point in reproaching Amy now. He had to use reason rather than emotion.

"If you decide to adopt the baby out, you'll go to term and everyone will know you're pregnant. It will be hard to miss."

She tucked her wind-fingered hair behind her ears. "They won't see. I'll tell everyone I want to go and work in Auckland, or study or something. I can't stay here whatever I decide to do about the baby. Even if I keep it, it will be better for me to start over in Auckland."

"Start over in Auckland?" Her announcement came like a fist in the groin. This was a complication he hadn't foreseen. All these years he'd at least been able to see her, even if she had been pledged to his brother. "You'd run away?"

"It won't be running away. I just can't stay here."

"Why not? Lots of women get pregnant, have babies out of wedlock. No one bats an eyelash any more."

"Not me."

Steel underpinned those quiet words. With a growing sense of panic, Heath knew that on this he wouldn't be able to sway her. Whatever she decided, Amy was going to leave.

And he would lose her. Forever.

Four

"There's another solution."

Heath stood with his back to the sun, his arms folded across his chest, eyes hidden by the dark shades, his face impossible for Amy to read.

"There is?" Amy gave him an uncertain smile, relief unfurling within her. She was all out of ideas about how to get out of this horrible totally un-Amy-like mess that she'd managed to land herself in.

"You could marry me."

That knocked the breath out of her. The smile withered and she simply stared at him. Then she whispered, "Marry you?"

His mouth slanted. "Is it such a terrible proposition? Please tell me you're not about to faint again."

"No, I'm not going to faint." But his suggestion made her head spin. She stumbled away from him to where the grass met pebble and gazed out again at the Pacific. The water was incredibly blue and the moist breeze smelled of salt and sun.

An idyllic scene. Yet eighty years ago the ocean in front of her had been violently shaken by an earthquake. Right now Amy felt as though her whole familiar world had tumbled upside down. *Heath offering to marry her?*

It was insane.

"Why?" she whispered, then realised he wouldn't hear her. She turned, to find him standing right behind her. He had taken the sunglasses off, and his eyes narrowed as they met hers. Gooseflesh broke over her upper arms, and she rubbed her hands up and down them, suddenly cold despite the summer sunshine.

"Because you don't want to have a baby without being married."

"But that's my problem, not yours," Amy objected, squinting against the bright light of the Hawkes Bay and noticing for the first time that despite the upward slant of his mouth, his eyes were intense. Watchful. She glanced away from the piercing look and took in the tightly coiled stance that belied the lulling, reasonable tone of his voice.

"Roland was my brother," he said softly. "This will be his only child."

"He wouldn't expect you to sacrifice yourself for his baby." Amy had a sneaky feeling that Roland would never have done that for Heath if their positions had been reversed. She hurriedly banished the traitorous thought.

"It wouldn't be a sacrifice." There was a peculiar note in his voice.

"Of course it would! You've always said that you'll never marry—you even said it to me just a few days ago."

He nodded. "True. But circumstances have changed since then."

"What's changed?" she challenged.

"You need a husband—"

"I don't *need* a husband!" That made her sound so weak. Like some simpering female living in Victorian times.

"I mean—" Heath was scowling "—you need a father for your child. You're never going to be happy being a single mother."

Amy thought about that and nodded slowly. "Correct. I believe that in a perfect world babies belong in families." But her world was no longer perfect. It had been disrupted, turned on its head by a series of events totally out of her control.

"So marry me. We'll be a family."

He didn't move, yet Amy had the feeling he was willing her to say Yes. The strength of his power was overwhelming. "Why do you want this so badly?"

His scowl grew blacker. "I don't 'want this so badly.'"

The sudden distance between them hurt Amy in places that she hadn't thought were susceptible to hurt any more. She chewed her lip and stayed silent.

With a sigh Heath rubbed his hand over the back of his neck and said, "It seems like a way of solving all our problems."

"My problems maybe." Amy tilted her head and assessed him. Although hot-tempered, Heath had always sauntered through life with a don't-care swagger. Little seemed to matter to him. Sure, he worked hard, and the aura of success he wore with casual disregard didn't hurt. Nor did his effortless natural charm. He had lots of friends and few people cared to be his enemy—mostly due to the big-fighter, hell-raiser reputation of his youth. "*You* don't have any problems." At least none that she knew about.

"You think not?" There was that edge that made her so uneasy.

"You're successful…"

His mouth twisted. "So being rich and hardworking means I don't have problems?"

That made her sound superficial, as though she was incapable of seeing under life's surface. "You don't work *that* hard," she defended her opinion.

"Ah, so I'm just rich and lucky…maybe even a little lazy?"

"I never said you're lazy." But she'd thought it. Just as she'd thought he was incredibly fortunate. Everything he wanted always seemed to just fall into Heath's lap with little effort. Success, great harvests…fine-boned, beautiful women. Could she have been wrong about him? Amy shifted uncomfortably. "Can we change the subject please?"

She moved away, to a bench positioned to take advantage of the expansive sea view, and sank down.

Heath followed, dropping down beside her. He turned his body to face her, placing his arm negligently along the back of the wooden bench. "No, this is getting interesting. So what else do you think of me?"

"You're charming. People like you." She looked at him— really looked at him for the first time in her life. From this close up, his body was solid and compact with muscle under the black jeans and black button-down shirt. The undone top button revealed a wedge of tanned skin. Above that his jaw was granite-hard, his cheekbones high and slanted, and his eyes glittered. No wonder women always stopped to stare at him. "You're good-looking."

The last came in a rush, and to her mortification Amy felt herself flush.

"Charming. Popular. Good-looking." The dark eyes flattened with displeasure. "Hardly sterling character traits."

With a start, Amy realised he was angry. "I didn't mean to offend you."

"No matter." His lips barely moved. "You're always so polite. It's interesting to learn what you really think of me under the exquisite manners."

"You're taking this all wrong—"

"I worked damn hard to pull the vineyard out of the mess your father left it in, Amy. I planted thousands of new vines— many with my own hands. It was a day-and-night job for weeks…months." He paused. "If you didn't see me for months, that's what I was doing." His mouth twisted. "Not partying nonstop."

Was he simply underscoring how wrong her perception of him as a hell-raiser had been? Or was that a dig at the frenetic over-the-top way Roland had romanced her?

She examined him but couldn't find anything to support the suspicion. Her hand crept to the gold locket around her neck. "You know my father never allowed me to be involved with the business." He'd expected her to fill her life with ladylike pursuits. Reading. Shopping. Volunteer duties. "But the estate couldn't have been in such bad shape. Dad always—"

"It was bankrupt."

He didn't say more, but the hard line of his mouth told her that he spoke the truth. Amy glanced away. In front of her the ocean moved lazily—calm today—and to one side a territorial seagull shrieked, chasing another along the stony beach. But all she could see was the expression of dismay on the face of the bank manager when she'd gone to see him with a financial plan to run a bed-and-breakfast to help ease her father's financial burden. He'd turned her down flat. Told her that she'd need someone to stand as guarantor before the bank would even consider throwing good money after bad.

Then Heath had come in with an offer to buy Chosen Valley Winery lock, stock and barrel. She'd resented the ease with which he'd had those same bankers fawning over him. And, irrationally, she'd resented the fact that she'd never had the opportunity to save her father—and herself.

"I knew it wasn't good, but I didn't know it was that bad," she said at last, steeling herself to meet his gaze.

"You thought I'd scored a bargain?" His eyebrows shot up. "I paid more than I should've for what I got." He shut his mouth, clearly annoyed with himself for saying that much.

"If it had happened now I might have been able to help Dad save it. I've learned so much about the industry since working for Saxon's Folly." And she owed him for that job. She softened her tone, "Thanks, Heath."

"I don't want your gratitude." His hands balled into fists at his sides, his eyes seething with suppressed frustration.

"I'm sorry," she said in a small voice.

"Oh, Amy." He closed his eyes. When he opened them the heat was gone. "It's not you I'm angry with, it's myself."

"Why?"

"For the chaos I've caused."

"Your life isn't chaotic—you've got everything anyone would want."

"I caused no end of trouble as a youngster. I barely have a relationship with my father, and I know that upsets my mother."

"But they love you."

He shrugged. "Perhaps. I nearly alienated Rafaelo—I thought he was a fake. I didn't recognise my own half brother—"

"He could've been a con man."

"Thank you." He gave her the first trace of his killer smile. "And I was always far too critical of Roland when he was alive."

At this last addition to the catalogue of his sins, Amy stared blindly at the Pacific. She considered not answering, but honesty propelled her to whisper, "Maybe he deserved it."

Heath let out an audible breath. "That's why you need to marry me. When I left Saxon's Folly and first bought Chosen Valley, Dad was furious. He said a lot of things in anger—and one was that he'd never forgive me for going into competition with him, that I should never hope to come back to Saxon's Folly."

"But you are back."

"Not because my father asked. Because Caitlyn begged me, and because Joshua convinced Dad it was the sensible thing to do in the short term."

That brought her eyes back to his face. "The short term?"

"I'm on trial, Amy. And I need to get on with Dad to stay."

"Do you want to stay?"

Heath hesitated. "Yes. With all that's happened in the last two months I know now that there are no guarantees in life." Amy knew he was talking about Roland's tragic death. And perhaps even about the chasm that had opened between his mother and father with Rafaelo's arrival. "I want to heal the breach with my father."

"I can understand that." Another thought struck her. "Does that mean you'll be selling Chosen Valley?"

He shook his head. "Chosen Valley is my home now. I can be winemaker for both estates."

"Won't there be a conflict of interest?"

"No, the focus of the estates is different. I'm concentrating more on growing reds. But I need you to help me convince my father that I'm back for good, that I won't walk out again. My parents adore you—you're their favourite godchild, and they have several."

She threw him a smile, her normal cheerfulness starting to return. "It's only because my mum and Kay were best friends—and because I lived close by when I was growing up. They saw more of me than their other godchildren."

"It's not only that—you're part of the family."

Her heart warmed and her smile widened. "That's a lovely thing to say, Heath. But I'm worried they'll think less of me if they find out I…"

"Slept with Roland before the wedding?"

She gave a jerky nod, her smile fading.

Heath waved a hand dismissively. "With all the skeletons that have fallen out of their closets recently, they're hardly in the position to throw stones. And if it matters to anyone, then they're not true friends. My parents do love you."

Maybe Heath was right. Who would care? She was allowing her own scruples to overwhelm her.

He was staring at her intently, his mouth curving into a

genuine smile that made her feel like the most appreciated woman on the planet.

Amy shifted on the hard wooden bench again. Uncomfortable, but in a different way. Why had she never noticed until today how devastatingly good-looking Heath was?

Because she'd been engaged to Roland. Because she'd written Heath off as a bad boy—not her type. Because she'd been blind.

The warmth that his gaze had ignited rushed through her, coursing along her veins, pooling deep in her belly. *Stop this!* She told herself. *It's silly.*

"I'm very fond of your parents, too. It would be sad if they decided to separate."

Heath gave her a narrowed look. "If you marry me perhaps the news of the baby will help heal the wounds."

Her breath snagged in her throat. "They'd wonder why you were marrying me. Wouldn't they ask if it was your baby?" The air seemed to dry up, and distress caused her breath to escape in shallow gasps. "I couldn't bear that. I'd be so humiliated."

There was a hostile gleam in Heath's black gaze. "Don't worry. I'd make sure they never doubted that you're carrying Roland's baby, not mine."

Amy's heart started to pound. "You'd do that?"

After a pulsing moment he nodded.

"I'd hate them—or anyone—to think I betrayed Roland." She couldn't meet his bitter gaze. She stared determinedly at her fingernails. The polish on her right index finger had chipped. She needed to redo the varnish tonight.

"No one would think it, Amy. You've always done the right thing. No one would ever suspect you of sleeping with your fiancé's brother."

The savage note in his voice brought her eyes to his face. A muscle was leaping in his cheek.

A desperate need to escape closed in on her. She jumped

to her feet. "I just want to do the right thing for my baby," she said faintly.

My baby.

She closed her eyes. Oh, no. She hadn't wanted to bond with the life inside her, hadn't wanted to grow to love it—not if she was going to lose it, or give it away.

But now she had a chance to consider keeping it.

Though it would mean marrying Heath.

Did she dare?

She put her hand over her belly. The slight swelling was barely noticeable to her touch. Nothing obvious enough yet to reveal that she was pregnant. She certainly didn't feel like she was carrying a baby. It all seemed so unreal. Everything was happening too quickly.

"Marrying me will be the right thing to do, Amy." Heath had risen and stood beside her. She was so aware of his every move and the even sound of his breathing overpowered the suck of sea on the pebbles. "You'll see. Everyone will be delighted about your pregnancy."

With a gesture of bravado she lifted her chin and met those ebony eyes. "Can I think about it?"

"Take all the time you want. But remember, this baby is a Saxon and Roland was proud to be a Saxon. This is what he'd want for the baby."

Heath wanted marriage so that he could get a second chance with his family. So that his parents would forget their differences and, comforted by their first grandchild, be able to recover from the grief of losing their son.

As for her, she'd get to keep the baby…and she hadn't dared let herself think of that possibility before now.

Her baby.

A little being that was all hers that she could love with all her heart. A baby that would grow up at Chosen Valley, her childhood home. It all made perfect sense. Except…

Except there would be no love between her and Heath.

* * *

Marry Heath or move to Auckland.

It was an impossible choice. Amy glanced up and down the dining table in the Saxon's long formal dining room and the indecision that had been twisting her stomach into knots for the past two days intensified. At the head of the table sat Heath's father, Phillip, with Amy and Joshua's fiancée, Alyssa, on either side of him. Joshua sat on Amy's left with Heath opposite him.

Heath had picked her up early this evening. With Megan away for the past two days, the Saxons' usual Thursday evening gathering had been moved to Friday.

Since he'd collected her, Heath hadn't mentioned his proposal and Amy had been exceedingly grateful. *What was she going to decide?* Cutting into the chicken Maryland on her plate, Amy studiously avoided meeting Heath's gaze and pretended to listen with fascination to the three-way conversation between Joshua, Phillip and Alyssa about a Saxon Folly wine that was garnering rave reviews, while she was acutely aware of Heath sitting so silently on the other side of the table.

"Heath, I've been meaning to tell you, I had a call from the police today," said Joshua.

The police? Amy started to pay attention.

Heath set down his fork. "About the young thugs that caused Alyssa's fall? Or the fire in the stables?"

Alyssa's hand had been hurt in a fall from a horse. Joshua had blamed himself. Then only last month the stables had been set ablaze. Caitlyn had risked her life to rescue the horses. The police had suspected arson.

"Both. They've made an arrest," Joshua continued, "It would appear that the cases are linked."

"Who would do such a terrible thing?" The malice of it all stunned Amy.

"The police arrested someone called Carson Smith—turns out he's the younger brother of Tommy Smith."

"Tommy Smith?" Amy knew she should recognise the name. But she couldn't place it.

"He used to work at Saxon's Folly—Joshua fired him. And rightly so." Heath's voice was hard, his mouth tight at the memory.

Of course! Amy wanted to bang her palm against her forehead. A distressed Kay had once told her in deepest confidence that Tommy had assaulted Caitlyn…that if Joshua hadn't arrived and stepped in, who knew how far the attack might have gone.

Phillip was nodding as Joshua explained. "Young Carson blamed the Saxons for sending Tommy to jail. Now he will be facing charges for arson and assault—he admitted to knocking the guard out that night, too. He knew that Caitlyn lived in the loft above the stables, so there may well be an attempted murder charge, too."

Amy drew a deep breath. "Does Caitlyn know yet?"

"I've already called Rafaelo to update him," said Joshua. "He was ready to come back and sort the guy out himself." Joshua's mouth slanted in a wry grin. "I told him he was better off spending the time introducing Caitlyn to Spain."

That lightened the mood and the talk moved on to Spanish wines and sherries.

Amy took a mouthful of food and let the conversation wash over her. Megan hadn't yet arrived and Amy was also conscious of the empty spaces further down the long, refectory-style table. The chair that Roland always used had been pushed back against the wall, and a pang of sorrow pierced her at the sight. And there were other spaces too: Rafaelo and Caitlyn were in Spain, of course, while Alyssa occupied Kay's place now that Kay was in Australia.

If she didn't accept Heath's proposal, then soon she would

be gone, too. Amy knew she couldn't afford to wait too long to make her decision. This morning she'd noticed that the cups of her bra were tight and her breasts had developed a painful sensitivity. It wouldn't be long before the telltale signs started to show.

But it would be hard settling in a big city like Auckland after living in the Hawkes Bay all her life. She was a country girl at heart. She'd have to tender her resignation, tell the Saxons…her father…of her decision to leave. And then cut all ties for the next six to eight months.

Running away, Heath had called it. She didn't dare look at him, even though she was aware of every movement he made, the strength in his tanned hand as he buttered a roll, the grace of his movements as he lifted his glass to his lips.

What was she to do?

Amy stabbed her fork at a piece of chicken. Heath had said that her baby was a Saxon, that it belonged here. Deep down Amy knew the baby deserved to know its grandparents, to play in the Victorian homestead and roam the vineyards and hear the tales about the infamous Joseph Saxon, the first owner of Saxon's Folly.

Yet how could she marry a man she didn't love? A man with no hint of softness, a man she'd never understand?

It was a relief when Megan rushed in, cell phone in hand, her eyes bright and cheeks flushed.

"Sorry I'm late. I lost track of time. I'm still on Australian time." Megan plunked herself down beside Heath. "Joshua, can I have a glass of that, please?"

Joshua rose to his feet, uncorking the bottle, and the gurgle of the liquid filling Megan's glass was loud in the sudden silence. He moved to fill Amy's glass.

"No, thanks." She whipped the glass out of his reach.

"You have to try it," Joshua said. "It's a Riesling, sharp and drier than usual. It's superb."

"I'm not drinking wine at the moment." Dr. Shortt had been firm about that.

"You're not trying to lose weight?" Joshua said in a tone of brotherly scolding.

"Joshua!" Alyssa gave her fiancé a look that boded ill. "Leave Amy alone."

"Josh is right." Megan added her voice to the debate. "You need to add a couple of pounds—not lose more."

The weight had dropped off her slight frame in the weeks after Roland's death. But the mother-hen note in Megan's voice and all the gentle chiding made Amy want to scream. "I'm not trying to lose more weight," she said tersely.

"I mean, it's not as if you're pregnant or anything," Megan said airily.

Amy felt herself reddening.

It was Megan who tactlessly made the connection first, her gaze homing in on Amy. "Or are you?"

There was an appalled silence. Then Heath thundered, "Megan, that's enough!"

"Oh, my God." Megan's hand covered her mouth and her eyes bugged out at Amy over the top.

In utter devastation, Amy shut her eyes. She couldn't bear to look at anyone. She knew guilt must be written all over her in neon-bright colour.

Megan's timid "I'm so sorry, Amy," broke her stasis.

With a shudder she opened her eyes and faced the family she'd known all her life. "I suppose you had to find out sometime." But it didn't help the sick churning in her stomach.

"Congratulations." Alyssa was grinning at her, and Joshua stretched an arm around the back of her chair and enveloped her in a great bear hold.

Over Joshua's forearm Amy could see Phillip Saxon beaming with a joy she hadn't seen for months.

"That's wonderful news, Amy. A baby." He paused, his

eyes blurring. "Roland's baby. Kay is going to be just as thrilled as I am."

Amy gulped, her throat burning with the effort to hold back the tears of humiliation and emotion that threatened to overwhelm her. She wasn't going to cry. She'd shed enough tears in the past two months to last a lifetime. She wriggled free of Joshua's hold and gave Heath a desperate, pleading look across the table. *Help me,* she wanted to yell at him. But after one flash of unreadable emotion his features froze.

There was no hint of *I told you* so in his face. But he had—he'd told her how important this baby would be to his family. She'd simply been too dim, too shattered, to fathom why.

A miracle.

Her baby was a way to get a part of Roland back into their blighted lives.

Five

Heath floored the accelerator and the Lamborghini roared down the long lane, away from Saxon's Folly. The silence that lay between him and Amy cut into the night.

Amy had turned her head away and was staring out into the darkness, making no effort to share her thoughts about what had happened back at Saxon's Folly, but he knew her well enough to know that she would've been mortified.

Yet he had absolutely no idea how she was going to react. And that scared him.

His mouth pursed into a tight, contained line, Heath stared into the darkness beyond the headlights. He knew there was a strong possibility that his sister's tactless blunder might jolt Amy into turning his proposal down and fleeing to Auckland.

Only minutes later, Heath rolled down the narrow lane that passed through the small seaside village of Hedeby. Aside from the huddle of cottages, there was only a general dealer cum post office and a fish-and-chips takeout store. The shops were in darkness and only a few lights still glimmered through wind-thinned hedges.

The throaty roar of the powerful sports car cut out beside the white timber cottage that was now Amy's home. Already she was reaching for the door handle.

"Not so fast."

Her shoulders hunched for a second. Then she turned to face him, her face a pale blur in the night. "Yes?"

"What have you decided?"

"You want an answer now?"

Heath knew it was a mistake to push her. But dammit he didn't want to go through any more of the endless waiting that had been driving him crazy.

"I think you need to make a decision as soon as possible now that the news is out."

"The news that I'm pregnant with your brother's baby?" She made a raw sound. "It's worse than I'd imagined. I've never been so…"

"I know. You're humiliated. I could wring my sister's neck."

"It's not Megan's fault," she said with commendable loyalty.

Heath snorted. "Of course it is. She's always had a serious case of foot-in-mouth disease."

But Amy didn't laugh. "Soon everyone will know."

"Who cares?" he asked.

"I do." Amy drew a shuddering breath. "That's the difference. I'm not you, Heath. Things like this matter to me."

He sighed. It had been a long time since people's opinions mattered to him—bar a few. But Amy was wrong. There *were* things that mattered to him. The important stuff. Like Amy and her baby. "It will be a nine-day wonder, and then something new will come along for everyone to gossip about."

"Yes, but for nine days the main topic will be me." She sounded resentful. "I want my ordered life back."

"A baby's going to ruin that anyway." She'd be alone, coping by herself. It wouldn't be easy.

"It's not the baby that would ruin it." Amy put her fingers to her temples. "I always wanted a baby."

Heath had a vision of Amy holding her baby, smiling down at the shape swaddled in her arms. But the taller figure he envisioned in the background wasn't Roland…

She was speaking again. He jerked his attention back to what she was saying.

"But the babies were supposed to come after the marriage. Not like this." Amy gripped her purse and closed her eyes.

He was furious at his irresponsible brother…at Amy for not seeing Roland for what he was…and at himself for being an unwilling participant in the whole mess that had been made of Amy's life.

"So marry me." He hadn't meant to ask again but the words burst from him. "I'll take care of you—and the baby. We can go away for a nine-day honeymoon. By the time we get back all the stir will be over." He had a vision of every person Amy knew lining up to greet them on their return, eyes agog with avid speculation, and he started to laugh.

"It's not funny, Heath."

"It's not as bad as you think, either. Relax. Say Yes. I promise you, no one will dare say a word with me around. I won't let them."

"You're right. No one will dare."

He didn't want her to marry him because of his formidable reputation as a fighter, but he'd take every advantage he could. "Is that a yes?"

The faint light in the car glinted in her eyes. Heath tensed as she made a little fluttering movement with her hands.

Then she sighed. "What choice do I have? Okay, I'll marry you, Heath."

* * *

After accepting Heath's proposal, Amy found events moving at the speed of light. She'd hardly drawn a breath, and Heath was studying the calendar on his BlackBerry for a suitable wedding date and talking about arranging caterers.

Before she could beg him to slow down, give her breathing space and a chance to get used to the idea, Kay Saxon came home.

The first indication that Amy had of Heath's mother's return was the click of heels across the stone floor of the winery.

"Amy, darling." Kay burst into the space behind the counter and engulfed Amy in a lavender-scented hug. "Heath called to say that you're expecting Roland's baby…and that you two are getting married. How can I ever tell you how much this means to me?" Kay set her away, her eyes brimming with tears. "You should have told me sooner about the baby."

"I didn't know myself." A sense of being trapped closed around Amy. Leaning across her desk, she tore a tissue from the box and handed it to Kay.

"I don't know why I'm crying. I never cry." Kay wiped her eyes and stared down at the streaks of moisture on her fingertips. Then she gave Amy a brilliant smile. "They must be tears of happiness."

If Amy hadn't already agreed to marry Heath she knew that Kay's tears—and that ecstatic smile—would have sealed her fate. *She had no choice.* "You don't mind?" she asked in a small voice.

"Mind?" Kay gave her a questioning look. "Why should I mind?"

"You don't think this looks…well…bad?" Amy coloured, uncomfortable at the awkwardness of what she had to say. "That people will say that I was supposed to marry Roland and now I'm marrying Heath?"

Kay waved a hand. "Who cares what people think? It's the

baby that matters. I'm proud of Heath for doing what had to be done, and of you for recognising that it was the sensible thing. You're both behaving with great responsibility."

Sensible? How could anything about this farce be remotely described as sensible? As for responsible…if Kay only knew. The sick churning in her stomach grew worse.

"You do realise what this means?" Kay was asking.

Amy shook her head.

"It means that any thought I had of divorcing Phillip and staying in Australia is out of the question." Kay smoothed a hand over her immaculate hair. "I need to be here near you—and Roland's baby."

For a wild moment Amy thought she was going to faint again. She drew a long, steadying breath. "You can't go to Australia, Kay. You love it here."

"I could hardly stay once I'd divorced Phillip."

Did that mean Kay was no longer considering a divorce? Amy didn't dare ask. Instead she said breathlessly, "I'd love to have your help with the baby."

"I wonder if the baby will have bright red hair like Roland—or dark auburn hair like his sister?" Kay mused.

Red hair? Her heart slammed against her ribs. Oh, good gracious. She hadn't thought about what her baby would look like. "It might have my dark hair."

Footsteps scraped on the floor on the other side of the counter. Measured, male footsteps. *Oh, no! Not now.* Amy raised her head with a sense of inevitability.

Heath stood there looking oddly formal in a dark suit, watching them both, his face inscrutable. Amy couldn't help the once-over she gave him. He wore no tie, the top button of his white shirt was undone. In that brief second she took in everything about him, before giving him an awkward smile. "Heath, your mother's back—and all because of the baby."

"And the news of your engagement," said Kay happily.

As Heath came forward, the whole mood in the winery changed. There was a sudden burst of energy, of expectant excitement. Amy had never noticed how tall he was, how commanding. How could she have missed it?

"Welcome home, Mum."

Going around the counter, Kay flung her arms around his neck. "I missed you—all of you. I'm so pleased to be home. Isn't Amy's news fabulous? Your father is so pleased, too."

Over his mother's head he met Amy's gaze. He might as well have said, "See? My family *needs* this baby."

The sense of suffocation increased. Amy knew that all he cared about was the baby in her womb—and what it could do to heal the hurts in his family.

Once again, the awareness of his ruthlessness shook her. Oddly nervous, she stroked the filmy fabric of the pink dress she wore down over her hips, her hands suddenly clammy. Would she be able to retain her sense of self in their marriage? Or would she become no more than a vessel that carried a Saxon baby?

"Oh, what a good idea." Kay was clapping her hands together.

Confused, Amy stared at Heath. "Sorry? I missed that."

"Heath's going to take you out for lunch. To celebrate." For a moment Kay's eyes clouded. Amy could read her thoughts as clear as day.

Roland should be here to do that.

Guilt twisted inside her. She shoved it aside. No time for that now. "I've got work to do. I'm not sure—"

"It will be good for you to get out." Heath's tone was even.

"I'll call Voyagers, see if dear Gus can spare you a table, that's the very place where I told Phillip I was pregnant with Joshua." Kay's eyes were alight with joy. "Don't worry, Amy darling, I'll man reception while you're gone."

Amy knew when she was beaten. "That sounds lovely."
But she glared at Heath through dagger-sharp eyes.

At Voyagers the rich patina of the proprietor's Nordic ancestry clung to the light-coloured European hardwood floorboards and the linen sails that covered the courtyard outside.

Once Amy and Heath had been seated inside at a table beside enormous sash windows that overlooked the busy Marine Parade with the Pacific glistening in the sunshine beyond, they ordered from the menu of daily specials, which Gus guaranteed were made with the freshest ingredients he could source.

When the food arrived, Amy's Cajun chicken salad was to die for and Heath's steak looked equally good. They talked about the history of the Hawkes Bay and the assortment of cultures that had landed there—like Gus's family who had arrived in Napier in the late 1800s. It was fascinating. And, for once, Amy found that conversation with Heath went relatively easily with no awkward silences.

But after the meal, when his coffee and her tea arrived along with a plateful of chocolate mints, that all changed. Heath sat back and his dark suit jacket parted to reveal the breadth of his chest under the white cotton business shirt, a small triangle of skin exposed by the undone top button. Amy jerked her gaze away from that distracting bit of skin when Heath said, "There's one thing we have to talk about, Amy."

Her heart dropped through the bottom of her stomach at the unaccustomed gravity in his black-devil's eyes. Full of trepidation, she asked, "What?"

"Sex."

That single, sizzling word landed in the space that separated them like a primed-to-explode hand grenade. Amy could feel the blood draining from her face. "No, I don't want to talk about—"

"We have to." His voice was strangely gentle. He shrugged the jacket off his shoulders onto the chair behind him, as if he too had experienced a wave of heat. "We're going to be married. You can't expect me not to want to make love to my wife."

Make love.

Her body sagged.

There wouldn't be any love involved. She liked Heath. Once upon a time they'd even been friends—but love? Never. He was her extreme opposite, bad boy to her good girl. They had nothing in common.

Especially not love.

All they had was the baby, whispered a little voice. And Chosen Valley. Wasn't that more than a lot of people started with?

And there was the little fact that she was highly aware of him. He aroused feelings in her she'd never experienced. Sex with Heath would be no hardship. Amy swallowed convulsively. Animal attraction, for sure. She dismissed the irritating voice. No way was she admitting that.

"I—" She broke off. Tried again. "I don't think…" Her voice trailed away.

"You won't have to think, Amy." Heath's dark eyes smiled at her. "Only feel."

The blush took her by surprise. Wild colour suffused her cheeks, her breasts, her whole body under the candy floss pink dress, causing her to feel hot and twitchy. "Heath!"

His wicked smile faded and his expression turned serious. "I don't want a sexless marriage, Amy. And I don't want you to fool yourself that I'd ever settle for that."

Settle for…

Oh, good grief. As far as Heath was concerned he'd be settling for enough already. His brother's woman, his brother's baby. That brought up another problem. "What if you fall in love with someone else?"

"That's not going to happen."

He sounded so very certain. Amy badly wanted to believe him. "Is that why you've never married? Because you've never been in love?"

The beautiful male mouth twisted. "Something like that."

Amy eyed him, feeling as if she was missing something. But his ironic expression warned her that she might not like the answers if she forced the issue. Yet she needed to be sure.

"If you do fall in love—if it hits you like lightning—then what?"

His lips curved into what should've been a smile, if the expression in his eyes hadn't been so flat. "It's not going to happen. I'm not the susceptible type."

Amy inspected him. His chest was broad and his biceps bulged under the sleeves of the fine cotton shirt he wore. She'd seen the stream of women through his life. Petite. Pretty. Predictably interchangeable. "But you've always had girlfriends."

"I've never fallen in love with any of them."

Maybe not, but several had fallen in love with him. Poor, stupid women. "What's to stop you from having more?" A fine strand of tension wound up inside her and she watched him carefully. She didn't think she could bear it if her husband had other women. That was one of the reasons she and Roland—

"My marriage." His answer interrupted her thoughts.

"You're telling me you'd be faithful?" Amy knew she sounded disbelieving. It was more than she deserved. But if he wanted a real marriage—with sex and all the trimmings—she'd need to be sure of his fidelity.

He nodded.

"I'd expect fidelity if we were—" The flush crept over her again.

"Having sex?"

She gulped at his frankness. Her face must be as red as a beet. "Er…yes," she stuttered.

"You've got it."

Amy stared, gobsmacked. She'd expected more of a struggle to get his agreement. And that made her feel as if the rug had been pulled out from under her. Again.

Determined to regain a little ground, Amy lifted her chin and said, "And there's something else we need to talk about."

Heath raised an eyebrow.

She hesitated. If he could say *sex,* then so could she. "Sexual health."

"You're worried about your health then?"

"Me?" Amy stared. "You think I—" Words failed her.

"You slept with my brother. If he compromised his health, you were at risk."

Amy didn't like the idea that one reckless night that she bitterly regretted might have cost her so much. She'd been incredibly stupid.

"I'll have some tests done," she said decisively.

Heath's gaze dropped to her belly. "I hope it's not too late for that. My brother was a lot less discriminating than I am."

Given her doubts, that stung.

"Why should I believe that?" Amy said heatedly. "Everyone knows you're the bad boy. Black Saxon they call you."

Only the slightest flicker showed that he'd registered her taunt. "Not in that respect—you can check with Dr. Shortt. I don't take risks."

Heath not take risks? Hard to believe. He'd always pushed every boundary he could with his wild behaviour. But his gaze was level and Amy found herself believing him. Inwardly she gave a deep sigh of relief.

"I don't need to ask Dr. Shortt," said Amy.

"You should. You're entitled to a clean bill of health from a soon-to-be lover."

Her pulse started to thud. "If you give me your word, that's enough," she said a trifle hoarsely.

All Heath's attention was fixed on her. "I give you my

word. You can trust me." There was a strange note in his voice. "I've always been careful…for myself and my partners. And I've never done one-night stands."

Now that was stretching it too far. Amy snorted. "Never? Not once?"

He looked uncomfortable. "Maybe once."

"I knew it!"

When Heath started to say something Amy interrupted him with a change of subject. "What if the baby's born…starts calling you Daddy…and then you decide you want out the marriage?"

"I won't want out."

"You might get bored."

He showed his teeth in a smile that wasn't very comforting at all. "I won't get bored."

Amy shifted, uncomfortable, a little nervous, and a whole lot unsettled. She wasn't sure she understood him any more. He was so alien, so closed off. And everything he said seemed to have an edge, making her feel as if there was something that she was missing.

She hadn't liked that feeling when she'd been fourteen and the other girls had giggled about stuff that good girls like Amy knew nothing about. Stuff about bad boys and French kissing. Well, she was grown up now and pregnant to boot and yet she still had that embarrassing sense of missing half the conversation.

So she took cover by trying to look like she didn't feel stupid. She stuck her nose in the air and said in her most snooty, disbelieving tone, "You always said you never wanted to get married—so how can you say it wouldn't bore you?"

His gaze narrowed until only a glitter of granite showed. "I told you, things change. I might not have wanted to get married before, but now I do."

The feeling something was eluding her intensified. She stared back at him, trying to read what was going on behind that hard-boned face. "Because of the baby?"

After a long moment he nodded. "Yes, because of the baby."

Amy hadn't wanted Heath to agree with her. She'd wanted him to object, to argue. She'd wanted to gain some insight into what she was starting to realise was a labyrinthine mind. Heath was a lot more complex than the bad boy she'd written him off as. But she was growing weary of being nothing more than a vessel for a Saxon baby. She wanted to talk about herself and Heath…and the future. To gauge what the chances were of this marriage between them working.

With a touch of frustration she said, "Well, if we both want what's best for the baby, then I expect everything will work out."

"It won't be that easy, Amy." That edge was still there under the slight smile. "We'll have to work at our marriage."

He'd moved closer.

She felt breathless. Her skin started to tingle, and all at once the light seemed brighter, the scent of the gardenias in the gigantic glazed pots in the courtyard grew more heady. His face took up her full vision. His eyes were dark, brooding, his cheekbones forming a hard ridge under his face. He looked downright dangerous.

Blood pounded through her head. Consciously she let out the breath she'd been holding and the pounding eased a little, but the strange flutter in her stomach didn't subside.

Excitement, she realised with a sense of shock.

Amy looked quickly away, before he could read what she was feeling.

"Amy…" Heath paused.

Tension filled the air. Against her will, her eyes slid back. A small black-velvet box lay on the white linen tablecloth next to Heath's tanned hand. Amy's mouth went dry. The moment of reckoning had arrived. She stared at the dainty box, making no move to pick it up.

"Open it," urged Heath.

Six

Amy lifted her eyes to Heath's. It was no mystery about what lurked inside. An engagement ring. And she was in no hurry to see it.

In fact, she'd far rather Heath opened the box, took the ring and slid it onto her finger. That way it would be a fait accompli. She could convince herself that he'd simply swept her along, and keep telling herself that Heath was running her life for her—and keep resenting him for it.

Amy read the challenge in his eyes…and knew that he'd anticipated her. Heath wanted her to take the ring out of the box and put it on her own finger. She'd said she would marry him; now he wanted her to prove her willingness. He'd brought her here to this elegant restaurant, thrown it at her that he expected their marriage to be a real one and now he was waiting for her to get cold feet.

Did he think she was going to run away?

She glanced down at her hand. The fingers were pale and

nicely tended, her nails polished. On her ring finger there already sat a ring—Roland's ring. A sparkling, flawless, colourless two-carat solitaire in a modern platinum setting, that he'd given her on her twenty-first birthday.

Biting the soft inside of her cheeks, she sneaked a look back at the ring box on the table.

If she was going to marry Heath, she needed to wear the darn ring that lay in that little black box. With a deep breath she reached out and picked it up. The black velvet was soft under her fingers. She hesitated a moment, then lifted the lid with a burst of apprehension.

Her chest constricted. The ring that glowed against the luminescent white satin could only have been chosen for her.

A magnificent, old-fashioned, heart-cut golden diamond gleamed against white gold, surrounded by a row of smaller diamonds. The delicate filigree detail of the setting was astonishing. It didn't look like a modern knockoff. Her gaze flickered to Heath.

"This is Victorian."

"Yes." His gaze gave nothing away. "The colour matches your eyes."

She loved it. She didn't even want to think what it must've cost as she fondled it. Beneath her heart a peculiar hollowness filled her. Could Heath have chosen it by chance? Unlikely. Was she an open book to him? Could he read her at a glance? Unease stirred at that unbearable thought.

No, most likely Megan had picked it out. His sister had a stunning sense of style, and Megan knew of her love affair with Victorian jewellery. She'd often wondered if Megan had been responsible for choosing her favourite gift from Roland, the golden heart-shaped locket she loved so much. Her attention dropped back to the ring. With a note of longing she said, "It's so beautiful."

"I'm glad you like it."

Carefully she lifted it out of the box.

"You'll need to take that off." He pointed at Roland's solitaire. And started to reach for her hand.

"No!" Amy snatched her hand away, knowing this was something she had to do by herself. Without Heath's help. A flash of the conversation she'd had with Heath at the masked ball the night of Roland's fatal accident came to her like a thunderbolt.

"You're making a mistake."

It hadn't been the first time Heath had said it, but as always she didn't want to listen—mostly because she was starting to have dreadful doubts about her approaching wedding. She'd twirled the solitaire around her finger. "You don't know what you're talking about," she told him defiantly, refusing to think about the rumours she'd heard recently that Roland had a lover. It hadn't been the first time there had been whispers, but it had been the first time that she had taken heed. The suspicion that she'd been deceiving herself that Roland loved her— and only her—had taken hold. The romance she'd dreamed of since she turned seventeen was beginning to crumble.

But once Heath had moved away that night, her bravado had withered and she'd cornered Roland, demanding to know if the rumours of a celebrity lover were true. Roland had tried to laugh away her fears. But she'd persevered, and delivered her ultimatum: if her fiancé couldn't be faithful, then she didn't want to marry him.

Unconsciously Amy dropped her hand into her lap and stroked her belly beneath the feminine dress, Heath's ring warm in her palm. She didn't show yet. But she knew about the life inside her—even if no one else could see it yet. This baby of shame that she'd conceived.

The baby…the reason for this marriage. "You didn't want me to marry Roland."

Heath shrugged. "I didn't think he'd make you happy. You

ignored my warnings. And if Roland was what you wanted, then what was left for me to say?"

Amy stared at Heath. She'd had second thoughts, but she wasn't telling Heath. Not after that careless shrug. And certainly not when it might lead to too many other questions.

Defiantly, she held his gaze. "Roland was what I'd wanted since I turned seventeen."

Wanted…the word mocked her.

What had she known of wanting at seventeen? Everything she'd learned about wanting had been learned one fateful night.

Moonlight spilled in through the French doors, kissing his cheekbones, softening his wicked mouth and casting silver light over his naked shoulders. A memory of a hand stroking her hair off her face…of lips touching hers, tracing downward.

Just thinking of that night was enough to cause her body to catch fire. No, she didn't need that kind of wanting, the blazing passion she'd discovered burned inside her. *Never again.* It had been so intense, terrifying, she'd lost all sense of self. She'd done things, experienced things, she'd never dreamed of doing…of wanting. And in the process she'd awakened a passion she never wanted to experience again.

Could she marry Heath and keep her private heart untouched?

The marriage to Heath would be real. Sensual. That was clear. Would she be able to keep secret that wild, wanton side of herself she'd discovered the night her baby had been conceived? Hurriedly, she dropped the ring back into the box.

Turmoil raged through her.

Get a grip, she told herself fiercely. This was Heath. He'd offered to marry her for the baby's sake. For his family's sake. He'd never wanted marriage—clearly he didn't see himself as capable of falling in love. Knowing all that, it should be easy to restrain herself. Especially since she was pregnant, which would surely put the brakes on that unwelcome, passionate part of her.

She had her baby to think about now.

"I need to get back to work," said Amy, desperate to escape her thoughts—and this conversation.

"Oh no, you don't." His eyes glinted with annoyance. "I'm busy asking you to marry me and you still haven't put my ring on your finger."

Finally, she said, "It's funny isn't it? Ever since I was a little girl and first read fairy tales I've dreamed of a handsome guy and my wedding day—of the proposal and the ring and all the romance that went with the love and white lace." Amy pushed back her chair and the soft folds of the dress fell around her legs. "But now the stardust has been knocked out my eyes and I'm coming to realise that reality is nothing like that. It's about practicalities like an unmarried pregnancy…and making sure I still have a job."

"Forget about your damned job for today." As Heath shoved his coffee cup aside and rose to his feet, Amy realised again how big he was. "My mother is looking after reception. We might not have the romance you've always craved, but we've got today to get to know each other—and we're going to use every minute."

Heath hurried Amy along Marine Parade, oblivious to the crash of the surf to their left and the pale gold sunshine beating down on the sidewalk. His jacket hung from one finger over his shoulder, but his nonchalant manner was all fake. Inside his chest, his heart hammered and his jaw was set until it hurt, while his free hand clenched the ring box in his pocket.

All he was aware of was the woman who barely came up to his chin, but who filled such a huge space in his life.

A sideways glance revealed that she was chewing her lip in that way that she did when something was worrying her.

She was thinking too much. That wouldn't help right now. The velvet rubbed against his fingers. The bloody ring shouldn't still be in the box—it was supposed to be on her finger. He couldn't afford for her to have second thoughts.

Not now.

"Amy—"

"Oh, look." She'd stopped. Ahead of them a dark-haired toddler dressed all in pink had dropped a packet of toffees on the walkway. The little girl's face screwed up and she started to cry. Her harassed mother was trying to hold a grizzling baby, and bend to pick up the little girl's spilled candy at the same time.

Amy hurried forward. "Let me help."

The young mother threw her a grateful smile as the little girl stopped crying, her eyes fixed on Amy's pretty pink dress.

Let me help. With a wry smile, Heath shook his head and followed. It was such a typical Amy response. In a couple of efficient movements, she had the toffees back in the bag and the toddler's tears had vanished.

"Thank you."

"No worries," Amy gave the woman one of her sweet smiles—the kind of smile he'd kill dragons to receive.

Shadows flickered over Amy's expressive features as the trio made their way back to an abandoned pram, the baby settled on the mother's hip and the little girl clutching her mother's hand. Heath could've sworn Amy watched with something curiously akin to longing. A wave of tenderness swept over him.

Was she thinking about her baby?

"Come." He pulled the hand out his pocket and placed it under her elbow. "We're going to the aquarium."

"The aquarium?" She met his gaze blankly.

"Do you realise I don't even know what your favourite fish species is?" Heath looked at her in amusement as her mouth dropped open. "Or whether you're scared of sharks?"

"You need to know that?"

He nodded. "Without a doubt."

"It's been years since I've been to the aquarium," she said in bemusement.

"All the more reason to go." He linked his fingers through hers and led her toward the entrance. "Come on, Goody-Two-Shoes. Forget about work and other responsible things—have some fun."

She started to laugh, and Heath realised that he'd heard that sound far too rarely in past months.

"Goody-Two-Shoes?" she said after he'd paid the cashier. "Do you know how much I hated being called that?"

"Why? Did you yearn to be one of the Beaut-Bod Babes?" He shot her a wicked glance. "They'd never have worn pretty pink dresses and Victorian jewellery." He let his gaze linger appreciatively on her until her cheeks turned crimson.

"They were into leather and black lace," she sputtered. "Poseurs."

"Didn't stop every guy in the school from hitting on them." Heath couldn't help grinning.

"Even you," she said with a touch of acid, "although you should have known better."

He laughed until his ribs hurt.

They wandered through the glass tunnel past the pania reef tank. Unable to resist, Heath said with sly humour, "Those girls were man-eating sharks. And I only ever dated one of them."

"The pretty petite brunette." Amy rolled her eyes. "Easy to guess."

The conversation was heading for dangerous waters, so he fell silent and feigned a fascination with a mean-eyed shark, swimming lazily past behind the glass wall.

A little further on he pointed out a stingray to Amy and for the next twenty minutes contented himself with watching her wide-eyed enthusiasm. The sea horses were her favourites.

"They're so graceful," she told him.

Heath could've told her that she shared that trait. But he

didn't. Instead, he followed her upstairs to where a crocodile skulked in the bottom of a pool of water.

"Look at those teeth!"

Heath chuckled at the note of fascinated revulsion in her voice.

She peeked sideways. "He reminds me of you."

"Me?" Heath gave her a mock glare. "He's downright ugly."

"Okay, so you're not ugly." Colour rose in her cheeks as his eyebrows shot up. Hurriedly she glanced away. "But you both share a terrible reputation."

"Forget about my reputation," he advised, trying to suppress his irritation. "I've reformed."

"You'd better have."

"Anyway, crocodiles make great parents. I seem to remember they help their babies to hatch by tenderly rolling the eggs in between those evil-looking teeth." He gave the crocodile an old-fashioned look. "And don't the females put their babies in their mouths if there's danger nearby?"

Instead of smiling, Amy looked quite terrified. "It's starting to sink in," Amy said in a small voice, "that in a few months I'll have a baby, too. Hope I'll do as well as that armour-plated monster."

"You'll be a wonderful mother."

"Do you think so?" The amber eyes that met his were full of doubt.

"No doubt about it." Amy had been made for motherhood. Heath knew she'd take it very seriously—as she did everything she cared about.

"I've started to worry about that…" Her voice trailed away.

Heath slowed his steps and scanned her face. "Why? There's nothing to worry about. Take it from me, that's going to be one lucky kid."

"I wasn't sure that I'd be able to be everything that the baby needed."

"But you won't have to be." Heath drew the ring box back out his pocket and flipped it open. "I'll be there, too. Or had you forgotten?"

The hunch of her shoulders revealed her tension as she stared down at the ring. From this angle Heath couldn't see her face. A nasty sensation filled him. Was Amy considering reneging on their deal?

His head started to pound again. He wouldn't let her. Not after coming so far.

Slow down, he warned himself. *Don't frighten her off.*

"We need to talk." He shepherded her toward a seating area and waited for her to settle herself. Dropping his jacket next to her, he chose his words with care. "I'm not going to make you marry me."

She glanced away from the ring box in his hand and tilted her face up to him. The reflected light turned her amber eyes to a dull gold. "What do you mean?"

"This has to be your decision, Amy. I can't make it for you."

For a moment utter stillness surrounded her. "Are you suggesting that I actually *want* you to run my life?"

Maybe. But he had the sense not to say it as her face tightened. Amy gave off mixed signals. A mutinous expression was far preferable to the flare of resentment that he'd seen in her eyes after he'd bought her father's vineyard. To be honest he hadn't been prepared for that—she'd always seemed to appreciate Roland taking charge of their relationship. For Roland she'd always been sweet and biddable. Yet she slapped him down every time he tried to do anything for her. The difference must lie in the fact that she'd loved Roland...

She certainly didn't love him.

But Heath couldn't deny that he relished putting a spark in her eyes. He enjoyed riling her, causing her cheeks to flame with colour, so that she looked a world away from the goody-two-shoes that everyone called her.

But more than anything else in the world he wanted her to be happy. And right now she looked anything but.

He snapped the box shut. "I'm not going to force you to wear this ring. If you can't even put it on, then maybe it's not me that this marriage is a problem for—it's you."

Heath hadn't expected the blind panic that turned her eyes opaque.

"No, no, I ha—want to marry you." But before he could react to the joy that seared him, she glanced away. "It just that—"

She dropped her head into her hands. His brother's engagement ring scintillated in the iridescent light that glimmered through the aquarium. The ring she didn't want to take off— the bond she didn't want to break.

Something twisted deep inside him, putting a damper on his joy. Something dark and ugly and far too close to jealousy for his peace of mind. How low had he sunk to envy his dead brother and covet his fiancée?

Through her fingers, she whispered, "Damn, but I've made such a mess of this."

Heath did a double take. Amy never cussed. Never. A sudden burst of panic shook him. Had he pushed her too hard? He sank down beside her. "Tell me what you want me to do, Amy. And I'll do it."

Even if it meant compromising his own hopes of happiness for a future that stretched endlessly in front of him.

Her hands dropped from her face. "Will you?"

Did she have to ask? He took in the wide eyes, the quivering mouth. To be fair, she'd never known that he'd walk over burning coals for her. The seething depths of his emotions were something that he took great pains to hide from her.

"Within reason."

She held her hand out. "Put your ring on my finger, then."

The diamond already on her finger transfixed him. He couldn't bring himself to take his brother's ring off her finger.

Anything but that. Taking her engagement ring off, letting Roland go, was something she had to do herself.

He sucked a deep breath into his lungs. "First, you need to take off Roland's ring."

"I can't," she said, a suspicious glimmer of moisture silvering her eyes.

Bloody hell. This was not going to work. How could he have ever have thought there was a chance? The ghost of Roland would forever stand between them. Amy had loved his brother with her whole sweet heart. A wave of guilt flooded Heath that he was forcing her to take Roland's ring off her finger.

He deserved to be shot.

Disgusted with himself, Heath pushed himself to his feet. Letting the ring box fall into her lap, he muttered. "Forget it. Forget the whole damned thing."

"What are you—"

"This isn't going to work." He swung to face her, his hands balled in his pockets as regret washed through him.

"You don't want to marry me any longer?"

She looked unexpectedly devastated. Her bewildered expression rocked him. He gave a wretched sigh. "Hell, Amy, it's not that I don't want to marry you. It's just that—" *Roland.* Her love for Roland would always lie between them.

Amy bent her head and her graceful fingers played with the box lying in the folds of pink fabric of her dress. "What about the ring?" There was panic in her voice.

Heath resisted the impulse to step closer, to urge her, to beg her to take Roland's ring off…and open the box and put his ring where he'd always wanted it.

Instead, he shrugged. "Keep it." He didn't care about the damn ring. "I chose it for you."

Her head snapped back. The shock in her eyes had intensified. "*You* chose it?"

"Yep—who else could've chosen it?"

"I don't know. Megan, maybe."

"Megan?" He knew he sounded astonished. "Why would I have my sister choose your ring?"

"Because she's got great taste." Amy spread her hands in a helpless gesture and the velvet box tumbled off her lap. "To save you the bother."

She didn't have a clue…

"I wanted something that would suit you." His voice gentled. Like Amy, the ring had to be unique. One of a kind. "It had to be something you would enjoy wearing." Heath decided he'd said enough. But before she could ponder on what he'd given away, he glanced at the Rolex watch on his wrist.

The afternoon was almost gone. Amy must be exhausted. He reached forward and picked up his jacket and slipped it on. "Come, I'll take you home."

"I don't believe this!" Amy was on her feet, her eyes spitting sparks. "At lunch, you told me that being married wouldn't be easy—that we both had to work at it. Only hours later, you're eager to take me home and walk out on me simply because I didn't rip Roland's ring off my finger." Her breath came in little ragged bursts that caused Heath to stop dead in his tracks. "If you've had second thoughts, at least be honest—just tell me."

Her ire caused his heart to lighten. "This is not easy for me, Amy. I've never been a quitter. But I've taken this as far as I can. Now the ball is in your court."

Her expression shifted between relief, bewilderment, and something curiously like apprehension. "Heath—"

A group of Japanese tourists bustled passed, giving them curious looks. When they'd gone, Amy grabbed Heath's arm. "I know you've said you never had any intention of marrying, Heath, that you proposed because of the baby, out of a sense of obligation. So I can understand if you feel trapped and if you want to—"

"Change my mind?" He gave her a hard look as he finished the sentence for her.

If she only knew...

"Well, maybe you should. I mean, I know you said you wouldn't but that doesn't mean that you can't." After that bit of garble, Amy was looking anywhere but at him.

Heath rather liked this deliciously flustered, at-a-loss-for-words Amy. But the time had arrived for some straight truths. Heath squared his shoulders. "If you can't even bring yourself to take Roland's ring off your finger, you're not ready for this. That's the reason I'm walking away—it's for your sake."

Her forehead puckered. "But I don't want you to go. I'd rather you married me." And then she spoilt it all by clapping her hand over her mouth and looking utterly horrified.

It didn't get any better.

"My baby's going to need a father. We agreed on that."

Heath let out his breath in a soft hiss. The baby. Of course. This wasn't about what Amy wanted. It was about what Amy thought was best. For her baby.

Amy was already tugging at her ring finger.

Heath watched in speechless disbelief as she shoved Roland's sparkling diamond into her purse.

She'd done it.

His legs felt unaccountably weak, as if he'd run a marathon. Suddenly, he had an overwhelming need to sit down. He ignored it and rocked back and forth on feet planted hip-width apart.

"There." Lifting her chin, she gave him a challenging stare and presented him with her bare hand. "Happy now?"

It started to sink in that Amy was determined to marry him. If the set expression on her face was anything to go by, she wasn't going to let him walk away.

He let out the breath he'd unconsciously been holding. "Not yet," he said hoarsely, not daring to consider whether what would make him happy was within his reach.

"Okay." She bent to pick up the ring box where it had fallen. The golden diamond winked in a ray of sunlight. Beautiful. Seductive. Perfect for her. Poised, holding it between her fingers, ready to slip on, Amy let out her breath and said, "Will this make you happy?"

"Give it to me." Heath discovered he didn't want her angry when she put his ring on her finger. To his surprise, this feisty Amy obeyed. "May I have your left hand… please?"

She held out her hand with a delicate grace that caused his chest to tighten. Taking her slim fingers between his broad calloused ones, Heath slid the ring onto her finger, slowly, with great ceremony. It fitted as if it had been made for her. Suppressing a sigh of immense relief, he bent his head and kissed the finger on which the ring rested, a sliver of gratitude slicing through his heart.

She could have made it so much more difficult. But, by taking his brother's ring off, she'd met him halfway. Roland's ring had formed an impenetrable barrier between them. He couldn't have removed it. There would have been too much baggage. But she had done it—and her action gave him hope that maybe this marriage would work. Hell, it would work. It *must* work.

Despite the warm day, her fingers were unexpectedly cool between his. Heath lowered his head and pressed another kiss to her soft skin, reluctant to release her hand. The pale fingers trembled slightly under his lips and Heath suppressed a surge of triumph.

She did want him.

Amy was every bit as aware of him as he was of her. He parted his lips against her skin, a hot lingering gesture. Above his head he heard her breath catch. Satisfaction warmed him.

There would be no problem with the physical side of their marriage.

"That finger is supposed to lead straight to the heart."

Her unsteady voice washed over him, and he raised his head to stare into eyes the colour of summer honey.

Refusing to think about the past, or the future, Heath focused on the tension that simmered between them. It had to count for something. She desired him. Relentlessly, he held her gaze. The instant the amber eyes melted, Heath knew what he was going to do. All the talk about sex and marriage and the path to her heart had been too much.

It needed only one small shift of his feet for him to reach her. Then Heath covered her mouth with his.

He heard—tasted—her gasp.

His tongue swirled past the soft barrier of her lips, filling her mouth. He claimed her mouth with a calm deliberation that almost went to hell.

Closing his eyes, Heath forced himself to focus on the moment, on each breath, on every sensation. She tasted faintly of chocolate and mint. The inside of her mouth was hot and sweet and a sharp stab of desire pierced him.

"No!"

The lips uttering the inexplicable refusal moved beneath his and her hands shoved at his shoulders. Shaking himself, to get hold of his reactions, Heath ended the kiss.

"This is a public place." She pulled away and stared up at him, her eyes stretched wide with shock…and something more. Her pink tongue slid over her bottom lip causing his stomach to clench. Heath ached to press his mouth against that moist, plump lower lip. But the uncertainty in her face held him back.

"That's the only reason you said no? Because it's a public place?" He could take care of that.

"And there are kids around."

"Not right now." That space surrounding them was empty. But that wasn't all that was worrying her. Heath sensed her hesitation. "What else?"

"Heath, I don't want this."

"This?" His brows drew together. The power of his passion made him impatient. He knew what wanting tasted like. And there was no doubt that Amy wanted him. "You don't want to kiss? Not even if we find somewhere more private…someplace with no kids?"

He knew he sounded disbelieving. But, hell, he hadn't been mistaken. Amy wanted him. And her need had awoken a driving hunger in him.

She gave a little nod. "That's right."

"You don't want to kiss, but earlier at lunch you agreed that you'd make love with me once we're married." Heath shook his head. It made no sense.

Amy looked wretched, trapped. She opened her mouth and closed it again. He waited, refusing to make this easier for her. This was her last chance. She had to make up her mind; once they were married there would be no going back.

"It's not that I don't want…" She stopped, flushing. "Okay, maybe it is. Heath, I don't *want* to feel like this." The jerky words sounded ripped from her.

And he finished the rest of the sentence silently. *I don't want to feel like this…about you.* A flash of pain sliced through him, followed by sympathy for her plight.

Guilt. It must be eating her alive.

And she was alive—very much so. Her response to him proved it. She hadn't—he prayed—buried her heart with his brother.

But guilt gnawed at him too. For a different reason. He felt bad because he was pretty pleased that she was confused— it meant that however much she'd loved Roland, at least she still wanted him, Heath, the bad boy she'd always given a wide berth. That meant that he wouldn't have an emotionless cardboard cutout in his bed. Heath didn't want a sacrifice in his bed; he wanted a flesh-and-blood wife.

"Don't worry about it," he said gruffly and shoved his hands into his pockets to stop himself from drawing her close. "Once we're married, everything will be easier."

She flicked him a little glance. "That's what I've been trying to tell myself, but I'm scared—"

"Scared?" He pounced on that. The last thing in the world Heath wanted was a terrified bride. "Of me? But why, for God's sake?"

Her straight white teeth closed on a bottom lip kissed to fullness. A fresh blast of want shook him. And shadows instantly flickered in her eyes.

"Not of you. Not really. I'm scared that if I let this happen…" Amy covered her face. "Oh, I can't tell you."

Heath frowned at her as he tried to work out what the hell was going on inside that feminine brain. This was about more than guilt.

But what?

"Amy." He withdrew both hands from his pockets and reached to cup her face between his hands and tilt it up. The eyes that met his were full of reluctance. Doing his best to look reassuring, he said, "Don't hold back. This is Heath, I've known you most of your life. There's nothing you can't tell me."

She gave a shattered sigh. "You're wrong. There's plenty that's impossible to tell you." Her gaze slid away, then returned a split second later. "As for knowing me…you don't know this me. I don't even know *this* side of me—it's embarrassing!"

Relief flooded him. Amy was talking about desire… about her ravenous response to his kiss, about wanting to make love with him.

The laugh that escaped him came from deep within his stomach. It was full of relief. His fingers slid along the silky skin beneath her jaw, under her ears, and cradled her nape.

"Believe me," he said huskily, "I very much want to get to know this side of you."

"Heath!"

Her scandalised whisper had him saying, "So we'd better get married quickly. Because, make no mistake, ours will not be a passionless marriage."

"You promised to give me time!"

The plea was accompanied by an apprehensive glance that Heath had no power to resist.

"Ah, Amy—" He reached for her.

"No!" Her lashes swept down before he could read what lay hidden there.

A flare of fear shot up his spine. But she didn't move away and Heath took heart from that fact, dismissing his fears as unfounded. She'd agreed to marry him. She'd removed Roland's ring. She wore his ring on her finger.

All that remained was to get the wedding arranged as quickly as possible. He'd involve his mother and his sister and get the ball rolling. Amy wasn't the kind of woman who would jilt a man. Her sense of right wouldn't allow it.

Nothing would go wrong.

His lips curved into a smile that was intended to reassure her. "And I will give you time. But make no mistake, we will be lovers. Don't think that this is going to be an empty shell of a marriage."

This time when he dipped his head, Heath was confident she knew what was coming. And that she would respond.

He was right. Her ribs rose and fell against his chest as her breathing grew shallow and she inched closer. Heath's hands closed around her waist. The filmy pink dress she wore presented no barrier. Her flesh was warm and soft under his fingers.

Need shook him.

This time there was no demur. She was ready for him, and her lips parted before he touched her.

This time his kiss was explicit, possessive, full of warning and dark desire. It was time for Amy to accept that she would be his woman—his wife—in every way.

Seven

The wedding date had been set for the coming Saturday.

Five days. That was all she had, Heath told Amy late on Monday afternoon as he leaned over the wooden counter above her desk, effectively cornering her. Most of the winery staff had already finished for the day. Amy was aware of the silence in the huge reception area…and that they were alone.

Despite the drumming of her pulse in her temples, she wanted to protest at the speed with which everything was happening. Kay had already been by to talk about the choice of food that the caterers would supply; less than an hour ago Alyssa had offered to call and invite everyone on the guest list that had been whipped up; and Megan had bombarded Amy with demands to go into town to choose a dress. The Saxon family had embraced the idea of her marrying Heath with wholehearted enthusiasm and everyone had flung themselves into rapidly putting together the wedding between her and Heath. And Amy found herself simply agreeing to everything.

Yet how could she object? Amy didn't dare risk Heath calling everything off. Not with the joy and hope that this hasty wedding had brought the Saxons. Not with Kay looking happier than she'd looked in a long time…her godmother had abandoned all talk of staying for a while with her family in Australia. The wedding—and the baby—had given Kay a new lease on life.

Now Amy gave Heath a glance from under her lashes as he towered over her. Understandably his features showed strain, his cheekbones spare, hardly the picture of the deliriously delighted groom.

No, Heath was doing the best he could. For her. For his family. For everyone.

There was another reason why a quickie wedding brought Amy relief. *The baby.* It wouldn't be long before she started to show. It might be cowardly, but Amy knew that she would be happier if she were married before that happened. Even though that meant all sorts of other endless complications. Like the fact that she'd be marrying Heath instead of Roland…and everyone would be speculating about which Saxon brother's baby she was carrying in her womb.

She rolled her chair back to put some distance between them and said, "I'll be glad when this hullabaloo is all over."

He didn't smile. If anything his eyes grew darker than ever. Devil's eyes. Yet he'd been so kind. This was no devil, this was Heath, and she'd known him all her life…

His eyes intent, he rested his folded arms on the top of the polished wooden counter and asked, "Where do you want to go afterwards?"

"Afterwards?"

"After the wedding. For a honeymoon."

Honeymoon? Liquid heat melted through the bottom of her stomach at the idea of going somewhere all alone with Heath. She had a vision of them sharing a candlelit dinner in velvety dusk. Just the two of them. She swallowed. "Uh…we don't need a honeymoon. No one will expect us to—"

"I think we need one." There was no room for negotiation in those five words. "It will do us good to have some time away to get to know each other."

Spend time alone with Heath? Even though she'd known him forever…being alone with him was something else.

Amy gulped in a mouthful of moist evening air, suddenly overwhelmingly conscious that they were the only people in the winery. The silence weighed heavily on her.

Her words came in a rush. "Heath, I know this isn't going to be a platonic marriage." He'd made that clear enough. "But we don't need a honeymoon. This isn't going to be that kind of marriage."

His eyes narrowed dangerously. "That kind of marriage?"

Amy's heart fluttered at the intensity in the dark depths.

"Uh…" She started to stammer. Blood rose in her cheeks. Her stomach plunged and a sense of her whole world shifting shook her. "I just meant that it's not a love match. No one's going to believe that. Not with Roland dead a little over two months."

A muscle moved in his jaw. "People will believe that grief brought us together."

She stared at him, her mouth dry, her throat suddenly tight. In that instant no one existed other than the two of them. "That's what you're going to tell everyone?"

"I won't need to tell them. That's what they'll assume. As long as you don't tell anyone anything to the contrary." He was frowning now.

"And what else are they going to assume?" she asked, because she had to, but shuddering inside, her every sensibility recoiling. Amy still didn't know how she was going to handle the speculation. "Everyone will be counting on their fingers, wondering if the baby is Roland's—" through her lashes she could see his jaw tightening "—or yours."

His features looked like rock. Hard. Implacable. "Everyone knows you have always loved Roland. There will be no reason to gossip about the baby's paternity."

Her lover moved, his body sliding over hers. A beam of moonlight revealed the stark lines of his face. A side of him she'd never seen. A moment of sanity—too brief—caused her to hesitate, then he kissed her, openmouthed, erotic kisses that turned her limbs to water and the moment passed. Never to return. With a sigh of delight she succumbed.

Staring into Heath's face, adrenalin surged through her. "What if they do?"

"No one will dare speculate."

The implacability in that hard face convinced her. Heath looked terrifying. And somewhere inside her, warmth stirred at his protectiveness. That warmth was worrying, too. What if she did something to make him think she wanted him? Because she did. Even though she wasn't ready to admit that yet. Not to herself…and certainly not to him.

All the more reason to stall a honeymoon.

"But what about the summer festival?" Amy scrambled around for excuses. "I'm supposed to be helping arrange that. Things are crazy around here right now." She grabbed a to do list off her desk and waved it in his face. "I can't just take off."

Nothing changed in his expression. "I think you can. It'll be our honeymoon. Everyone will understand."

Uh-huh. His face was filled with purpose. There was going to be no getting around this.

"How long?" Amy finally caved in.

"Five days—that will give you plenty of time to help with the festival when you get back. I'll help, too." His gaze raked her. "Better prepare me some to do lists, too."

That didn't reassure her one iota.

* * *

As the days hurtled past and the wedding day rushed closer, the tension within Amy rose to the breaking point. Her control over her own life was being eroded away. She'd had no say in the date of the wedding, or the decision to go on a honeymoon. She was starting to resent Heath's ruthless purposefulness…and beginning to feel increasingly pressured.

But there was one thing that was within her control…her decision to marry Heath—only she knew the real reason why she was doing it. She'd never believed that knowledge was power. And she knew she shouldn't be holding out on him. The guilt was killing her. Heath deserved to know.

She tried several times to talk to him—she really did—but every time, at the last minute, her courage gave out. Coward. But she promised herself that she wouldn't marry him—not without telling him what she found so hard to talk about.

But every day it became harder and harder to confront him. Until, on the eve of their wedding, all Amy's good intentions of telling Heath exactly why she was marrying him flew right out the window.

The evening started well enough. Heath had planned a dinner at Chosen Valley. Just her father and the two of them. It was a casual evening—no one dressed up; Amy wore a pair of jeans that had grown tight around her waist teamed with an Icebreaker top. Heath, as usual, wore his signature black jeans and T-shirt. But for once she saw past the bad boy wear.

His consideration had touched a chord deep within her that he'd known she would want to spend a last quiet evening with her father.

The meal was fantastic. Afterwards, all three of them moved to the sitting room, where dim sconces bathed the room in a soft glow. Josie, Heath's housekeeper, brought a cup of hot chocolate for Amy while the two men sampled a selection of ports. Much to Amy's embarrassment, her father had almost turned maudlin as he recounted tales of Amy's childhood and Heath let him ramble. In fact, apart from the odd, indecipherable glance, Heath appeared to have forgotten that she was there.

Finally, he seemed to recall her presence.

"Have you taken your iron and vitamins today, Amy? It's going to be a long day tomorrow. You'll need all the energy you can get."

All her resentment at his high-handedness coalesced. She forgot about what he'd done for her. Forgot about what he was doing for her baby.

"Stop telling me what to do!" Amy discovered she was breathing hard. "Despite what you might think, I'm no longer a child."

The words were overloud in the gracious room. She faced him, her heart pounding. Deep inside she knew she was being unfair. But she couldn't stop the childish resentment that overwhelmed her. Ever since he'd bought Chosen Valley, this had been simmering inside her.

"Calm down," said Heath.

"Then stop trying to take over my life." Amy felt like she was losing control of hers.

"Amy!" Her father's groan increased her remorse. "Heath saved me. Can't you understand that? I know you wanted to save us, Amy-girl—but it wouldn't have worked."

"What do you mean, Ralph?" Heath intervened quietly.

Ralph Wright looked at Amy, apology written over his still-handsome face. "I know you wanted to help, but I was in too deep. I left the harvest too late…the rains came—" he shook his head "—there was no other way."

"Dad, it's okay." Amy rested a hand on her father's shoulder, wishing desperately that her father had never started this conversation.

Heath's gaze settled on Amy and his voice gentled. "What were you planning?"

"I'd met with the bank…I tried to extend our credit. They weren't interested." The memory of her humiliation spread through her. "I'd planned to start a bed-and-breakfast venture. It was something I'd always dreamed about doing. I delivered a business plan."

"You should've told me."

As she held his gaze, she read his intention there. "What, so you would've bullied them into giving me a loan?"

He gave a slight smile. "You credit me with too much power. I couldn't have talked the bank into giving you a loan—but I might have been able to stand as guarantor for the loan. Or I'd have advanced you the money—"

"No." Amy shook her head. "That was the last thing I wanted."

"But why?"

How to explain? Reluctantly, she admitted, "I didn't want to feel indebted to you. I'm a grown-up, I didn't want you sorting out my problems as you always have." As he had when she'd been a schoolgirl. Except it hadn't stopped there. He'd bought her home. He'd arranged a position for her as PA at Saxon's Folly. She'd felt like a puppet on a string.

There was a strange expression on his face as he set down his port glass and said with fixed intensity, "Amy, I haven't thought of you as a child for years." Something about how he looked at her left her breathless. Before she could reply, he added, "You'd just started dating Roland back then. Did you turn down his offer of help, too?"

He hadn't offered. And she hadn't asked. In fact, she and Roland had argued about her plans. Careful to keep all expression from her voice, she said, "I discussed it with Roland. He travelled so much, he said that in the future I'd be going with him—he thought a bed-and-breakfast business would tie me down." They hadn't been engaged back then, but Amy had known Roland's intentions were serious. He'd known she was the marrying kind, and he hadn't wanted his wife to work. Period. He'd been with her father on that. A wife's position was to support her husband and make his life easier.

The plan she'd drafted for the bank had been filed away, and she'd shelved the dream. Roland had said that once they were married there would be enough to keep her busy helping him with the entertaining he did in his role as marketing manager.

She'd finally managed to convince Roland that while they were dating she needed an income, her independence. He hadn't liked it. But he'd gone along with her working at Saxon's Folly. She'd turned down his offer of an allowance— worried that it came with strings attached. Amy had wanted her white wedding to be exactly that.

She touched her belly where her baby lay.

Her pure, white wedding was yet another dream that had been shattered. After all those years she'd spent refraining from intimacy before marriage, wanting to keep herself pure for her husband—her wedding gift of love—she'd lost even that.

A memory of a mouth against her neck, of hot words whispered in her ear caused a frisson to run through her.

Amy shivered with delight as his very male fingers lingered against her bare skin that glowed like white rose petals in the moonlight. It was wrong, this ecstasy, so very wrong. But she couldn't bring herself to tell him to stop. The burning, the hunger, that his touch had ignited consumed her.

Now, in the presence of her father and husband-to-be, she ruthlessly suppressed the wanton images. She should never have given in to the temptation. She'd broken her chastity pledge to herself. She was as bad as Roland.

During the two years they'd dated, and the year they'd been engaged, she'd never considered that Roland might be unfaithful. That had been part of her vision of true love. She'd believed they would spend that time getting to know each other—building a delicious romance between them.

But Roland hadn't shared her beliefs.

When she'd confronted him about the rumours of another woman, and issued her ultimatum, Roland had blamed her unrealistic chastity vow. He'd argued that if she'd slept with him rather than insisting on an archaic white wedding and a virginal wedding night, he wouldn't have needed to stray. He'd made her doubt her values—her beliefs—that night. She'd felt pressured, upset. She'd started to believe it was *her* fault that he slept around with other women—that it was *her* fault that he'd been less than faithful to her.

It had made her doubt everything.

Her feelings. Her values. Even who she was. Her head had been a mess.

And now Heath was watching her every move, as if he were trying to see inside her head. Amy flushed. And found she had to glance away. Before he read exactly what she was thinking.

The darkness hid the hectic colour that his caresses had seared her skin in a hot flood. A dreamy lassitude assailed her. She could pretend this was a beautiful dream, that the nightmare world of earlier tonight had vanished forever. That she'd waken in the morning in her beloved's arms and everything would be right...

Avoiding Heath's gaze, Amy told herself that Heath couldn't possibly know what she was thinking.

Heath stared hungrily at the high colour that stained Amy's cheeks. She wouldn't meet his eyes.

Did she know that he wanted to kiss her, taste her lips, leave them coloured with the same rosy flush that suffused her cheeks? She had a ripeness to her that suited her. Even in casual wear, she managed to look sultry. So sexy. So incredibly tempting. Nothing like the good girl that everyone thought her to be.

And his secret knowledge left him wanting her more than ever.

Ralph had moved onto everyday talk about rain and weather forecasts and Heath heard himself reply, even though all his attention was focused on Amy. Only Amy. At last she turned her head and glared at him, telling him without words that she knew exactly what he was thinking. Heath suppressed the wild, joyous grin that almost spread over his face.

Sweet, innocent Amy.

If only it was that easy…

It would take a lot more than a glare to stop what he was feeling right now. He'd always wanted her with this ache that never left. She pursed her mouth in that delightfully disapproving way that made him want to kiss her until that tight pink rosebud mouth blossomed under his. He winked at her. She glared harder, no hint of amusement in her eyes.

Maybe he wasn't playing fair. He stretched his legs, wishing he could whisper at her not to worry, it would be okay. He'd promised not to pressure her.

Ralph was looking at him, too. Heath felt himself flush at being caught staring like a lovestruck idiot at the man's daughter.

"Are you ready?" Ralph asked.

Heath blinked. Ready? Hell, yes. He gave his father-in-law a reckless smile. He'd been ready years ago. "Yes, I'm ready for tomorrow."

Lifting the small glass of ruby-coloured port, Heath took a sip of the rich sweet liquid. He couldn't believe that it had gotten this far, that Amy was finally going to marry him tomorrow. Euphoria rushed through him.

"I never dreamed that Amy might one day marry you," Ralph said with a fond glance at his daughter, who was cupping her mug of chocolate between her palms. "Can't think why I never thought of it before. It makes sense. You two fit well together."

"I was engaged to Roland," Amy said, setting down the mug with a clatter.

"I think Heath will be better for you."

"Why do you say that, Daddy?"

Heath tilted his head back against the top of the chair, confident that his emotional response to Amy was his closely guarded secret, but more than a little interested in his future father-in-law's take on the situation.

The older man swirled the dark port around his glass and took a sip. "Just that you've always been a homebody and Roland was never here. He was always off gallivanting."

"But that was his job," Amy protested. "I accepted that. He'd even told me that after we were married he wanted me to go with him, help him entertain."

Her father shook his head. "It was more than that. Roland was restless…never satisfied. You would've hated being dragged around in his wake."

Ralph was more perceptive than he'd dreamed, Heath realised. He'd had Roland pegged. His adoptive brother had always been a rover—with a roving eye to match. Not that Amy knew about that.

"You think he would've found me unsatisfying? That I would've bored him?" Amy's eyes flashed at her father, and Heath suppressed a smile at the ridiculousness of the question.

"Amy-girl, it's not a criticism of you…it's the kind of man he was. Wild. Restless."

Amy gave a little laugh, but her fingers played with the folded linen napkin. "You're confused, Daddy. Wild and restless describes Heath exactly. Look at him."

The inspection that Ralph gave him through narrowed eyes didn't miss a thing. Not the monochrome black shirt and jeans, not the strain around his mouth. Suddenly, Heath was sure that his future father-in-law had seen more than Heath wanted. Tensely, he waited for Ralph's assessment.

But all Ralph said was, "I don't know about that, my girl. Never believed all that rubbish myself. Heath has always been where he's been needed, always worked hard, he's always there." He set his glass down. "But it's not for a father to tell his daughter about the man she's marrying."

Slowly, Heath let out the breath that he'd been holding. His secret was safe. But the knowledge that someone had questioned the acts he'd been blamed for, warmed him.

"What do you mean?" Amy was asking her father.

Ralph gave Heath a conspiratorial smile. "I've said enough. It's time for me to leave."

That smile told Heath everything he needed to know. Ralph was not going to say more. Relaxing a little, Heath pushed his chair back and rose to his feet.

Amy came with him to the door to see her father out, but Heath saw that she had no intention of leaving. Her hands clenched and unclenched, revealing her inner tension. She looked like a woman with a lot on her mind.

After Ralph had driven off, Heath rested a courteous arm around her waist and ushered her to the sitting room.

"You're upset."

She shrugged his arm off. "A little." Amy opened the glass doors and stepped out onto the wooden deck.

Flipping the verandah lights on, Heath followed more slowly. Outside the night was warm, and the air held a tang of salt from the distant ocean. The light from the full moon spilled across the landscape, giving it an eerie, fairy-world quality.

"Are you angry with me?" Heath wanted to get a clear handle on her state of mind, so that he could assess what needed to be said.

She turned to face him, her arms wrapped around her middle. "I'm angrier with myself."

Heath started to smile. "Why?"

"Because I'm a coward."

He did laugh then. But she gave him a reproachful look that told him this was no laughing matter. Heath restrained himself with difficulty. Anyone who knew Amy knew that she never shied away from doing what was right. If something needed telling, she could be trusted to say it.

"I wouldn't let it worry you."

"But it does." Her bottom lip jutted out and he longed to kiss it, take it between his teeth and play with it. Perhaps not quite yet. Soon…

His gaze lifted and in the harsh moonlight he met the rebellious golden eyes. The laughter left him. Instantly, his body hardened. One glance. That was all it took.

He drew a steadying breath, controlled the rush of emotion and centred his attention on the discussion they were having. No mean feat. "It's not just yourself you're angry with. You're a little mad at me, too. Right?"

She didn't reply.

Heath stepped closer and ventured into forbidden territory. "Because I'm alive and Roland isn't?"

Her eyes stretched wide with shock. "No! Never that."

Heath's breath escaped in a slow hiss. There was no reason to feel guilty for the deep emotion she stirred in him. His brother was dead. Amy was his.

Even though she didn't love him.

She would learn to love him. Heath wasn't conceited but he knew women cast him little glances all the time—imagining his prowess as a lover, measuring his strength as a man, his excellence as a provider.

After the wedding tomorrow, they would have all the time in the world, starting with their honeymoon. She would learn to love him. *She had to.*

Thinking about her claim earlier that he was both wild and

restless, he asked, "Why do you persist in thinking I'm still the wild, restless teenage boy? Does it make it easier?"

"What do you mean?" But her rapid prevarication and the flash of vulnerability in her eyes told him she knew exactly what he meant.

"I suspect it's because that way you can tell yourself that I'm the bad boy—that I've got nothing in common with you, the good girl."

"That's not true. I don't think that." But her eyes slid away from his. After a moment she looked back at him. "But you did some wild things when you were young."

"Some," he conceded. "But not as many as everyone blamed me for."

"But those that you did were awful."

"Not all were my deeds. Sometimes I just copped the blame."

Uncertainty flickered in her eyes. "Is that true?"

"Sure."

"So who did you cop the blame for?"

He shrugged. "That's a no-brainer. And it's ancient history."

"Who?"

"My brothers. Their friends."

"They wouldn't have done that."

He laughed at her naiveté. "They were boys. I was the youngest. It's perfectly normal. And sometimes I even liked copping the blame. It made people forget I was the baby."

"Megan was the baby."

"Yes, but she was a girl."

Amy rolled her eyes. "Oh, good grief!"

"You still talked to me in those days." He could remember one incident clearly.

"I knew my mother would've wanted me to be your friend." Her arms unfolded and dropped away as her eyes grew dreamy with long-ago memories.

Amy had always been aware of the right thing to do. Ye

her friendship had ignited his awareness of the girl with grave golden eyes and her prim rosebud mouth. He remembered the day that he'd first noticed the curve of her breasts under a snug white singlet and how it had affected him. He could remember wanting to kiss her…but deciding she was still a kid.

He could wait.

The bad boy and the good girl. They'd grown up on neighbouring vineyards; she was the daughter of one of his mother's best friends.

And they'd been friends.

Almost.

Until she'd turned sixteen and it had become apparent that she idolized Roland, and he'd started to put space between them.

Roland. Always Roland. And now she was pregnant with Roland's baby. The swollen mounds of her breasts pulled the T-shirt tight and announced her fertile condition quite clearly. But some things never changed. He still couldn't keep his eyes off her.

"I think she'd be happy."

"Who?" He'd lost track of the conversation. Heath looked guiltily away from her lush shape.

"My mother." A little crinkle formed between her eyes as she gave him a puzzled stare. "I always knew she'd be happy married one of Kay's boys."

"Is that why you decided you were in love with Roland?" Incredulity hardened his voice. "Because you thought your mother would've wanted it?"

She hesitated. "Don't be silly. I'd never have married Roland for that reason."

But Heath wasn't so certain. She must've missed her mother dreadfully. An only child. Kay's goddaughter. "Are you sure?"

"Yes! Of course, I'm sure."

"Ever thought that you could've decided that it was me you loved not Roland?"

"Heath!" She gave a little laugh. "But it was Roland."

"Why? What made him so special?"

"I don't know…" She lifted her shoulders. "But when I opened his present on my seventeenth birthday, I knew…" Her voice trailed away.

A pang of dismay pierced right through him. "Knew what?"

"That he was the one. He gave me this." Her fingertips brushed the locket. "It was so romantic, so perfect."

The gold heart could've been made for Amy. He'd known the moment he'd laid eyes on it. Just as he'd known the ring would be right. The smile he gave her was barbed. "So if I'd given you a romantic Victorian locket studded with diamonds, would you have decided I was the one?"

Her eyes studied him in puzzlement. "It wasn't about the gold or diamonds."

"I know. It was about connecting with what you liked."

"Yes." Her eyes flickered. "And you didn't."

"No, you're right, I didn't. But you're marrying me, and my mother is certainly happy enough about that." He gave her a smile. But he found he couldn't let it go. Stretching forward he placed a hand on her stomach, felt her start. "Just think, it could have been my child."

For a moment she looked at him and time seemed to stand still. Shadows shifted in the golden eyes. She licked her bottom lip nervously and started to say something.

The sight of that slick bottom lip caused his stomach to tighten. All the desire he'd felt over the years, pooled between his thighs. Reckless with want, he said, "God, I can't wait to make you mine."

"You promised me time." Her expression shifted, her eyes growing blank in the moonlight. She crossed her arms over her breasts. "It's getting cold out here. Time to go in."

Heath hadn't noticed a difference in the temperature. He tipped his head sideways. "There's no wind."

"Well, then, maybe it's just me. I'm cold."

He couldn't stop thinking about how she would feel in his arms. He needed to hold her, touch her, make sure this was real. Perhaps he was being too optimistic. Perhaps her love for his brother would always be a wall between them and she might never learn to love him.

But it was worth taking a chance.

Eyes filled with determined purpose, he moved to her. "Then let me warm you up."

Eight

"Oh, God!"

He hadn't warmed her, he'd set her on fire. Amy's fingers touched her lips. They felt swollen where Heath had just kissed her with pulverising thoroughness. Sensitive. Tingling. She lifted her lashes to find Heath watching her through narrowed eyes that did nothing to stem the turbulence...the aching...that rolled within her. She despised herself for it.

"Amy, don't."

He must have read her self-loathing in her eyes. He stood there, strong, magnificent, his eyes full of an emotion that she didn't recognise. Pain? Passion? She didn't know any more. He confused her so. She confused herself. As for the feelings he aroused in her...

"Amy, don't look like that."

But even as he reached for her, she shut her eyes to block out the sight of him. Amy folded her arms tightly around herself to fend him off.

How could she be feeling like this? It made no sense. Yet she couldn't stop thinking about how his lips had moved on hers, how her heart had jumped and twisted over as desire flashed through her. For one blinding instant it had felt utterly, heart-stoppingly fabulous.

Until reality had set in and she'd remembered…this was Heath.

"I'm sorry. I promised you time." His voice was low, repentant. This time the arms that came around her were gentle as he pulled her to rest against the vibrant heat of his body. Amy tried to resist. But it was unexpectedly good to be in his arms. In the coolness of the moonlit night, his flesh was warm against her, his heartbeat solid. Instantly, her body was on fire, even though she knew that he had no intention of kissing her again, that this time he was offering nothing but comfort.

He'd comforted her before…and where had that ended?

In desperation Amy shut the little voice out and let her hands creep up his chest. His T-shirt was soft under her fingertips and his chest lifted under her palms as he sucked in a deep, shaking breath. Good. At least she knew that he wasn't finding this easy…that he couldn't just switch on and switch off like a robot. It made her feel a little better, a little stronger to know that this…this…wildness wasn't confined to her alone.

There was a certain insanity in what she did next. Afterwards she told herself she'd been testing him…trying to see if he was as in control as he always seemed. If she was the only one being jerked about like a puppet on a string. Linking her fingertips around his neck, Amy followed her mad instincts. Just then, tipping back her head, planting a kiss on his jaw seemed like the right thing to do.

But it didn't stop there.

The night was filled with the sound of denim rubbing against denim as he stepped closer and yanked her to him. She gasped. And Heath gave a deep moan that shook his tall frame and his mouth took hers in a kiss that made her knees go weak.

His mouth ravaged hers. His hunger ignited her own unruly desire. She squeezed her eyes more tightly shut and allowed herself to be towed along by the uncontrollable force, her hands clinging to his neck.

By the time he lifted his head, Heath was panting. As Amy cracked her eyes open she caught a glint of triumph, too.

Despair set in.

It was always going to be like this.

He'd kiss her, caress her, send her up in flames, and she'd lose all willpower. And, even worse, now he knew that she was vulnerable.

She simply couldn't understand what was happening to her. It wasn't as if she loved Heath. She'd loved Roland. How could she lust after Heath like…like a bitch in heat? The image didn't sit well with Amy. It didn't fit with the person she'd always considered herself to be. Whatever he said, Heath was a wild one. He didn't even believe in marriage… why should he, when he could have countless brief affairs? Heck, he'd told her himself that he'd never even *wanted* to marry.

How could she let herself sink to such depths where she became one of a legion of many? Where was her self-respect? Why did he have this horrible power over her body? How could she go against everything she believed in about love…about marriage just for the sake of this overpowering carnal hunger?

Feeling sick and utterly disgusted with herself, Amy wrenched herself out of his arms. The desperate need to escape him forced the words out of her, "*I can't do this.* I can't marry you."

He grabbed her as she rushed past. "It's too late to pull out, Amy."

Terrified that he'd kiss her again—or cradle her against his heart—she broke out of his grip, her breathing ragged. "It would be wrong for me to marry you."

"You're going to jilt me, then?" The dark eyes glittered in the reflected light that spilled from the house, revealing a wariness that made her want to weep.

Steadying herself against the doorframe, Amy hauled in a deep breath. "We can call everyone now…tonight…let them know that there won't be a wedding." The words tumbled over each other. "That way no one will be jilted."

"But I haven't decided to call it off." He said it so softly that for a long simmering second Amy thought she'd misheard.

"*We have to.* Heath, I can't—"

"Why?" he interrupted her, his voice harsh in the night. "Answer me that one question, Amy. Why don't you want to marry me?"

She barely understood herself. All she knew was that she feared the wild passion he aroused within her. Grasping at straws, she said, "You don't even believe in marriage."

"How can that be true? I'm marrying you, aren't I?" he said with incontrovertible logic.

Only out of a sense of family obligation. "But you don't believe in love," she flung at him.

"That's it?" The tension in his face eased and he took half a step toward her. "That's the only reason you won't marry me?"

Amy recoiled. "I don't love you, either. Marriage vows should be sacred. I can't lie in a church. Vowing to love, honour and obey you will be a lie. Don't ask me to do it." It would haunt her for the rest of her life.

Heath froze and his mouth twisted. "Then we'll get married on the beach."

"Don't be facetious!"

"I'm not going to let you back out of this—"

"I'm not going to vow to love you. You can't want me to marry you," she interrupted, "not if I don't want to."

"Oh, yes I can." His gaze scorched her, leaving her feeling branded. "There are good reasons for this wedding. Reasons better than love. You're pregnant. Our families are close— our mothers were best friends. You get to return to your family home."

Amy had to admit that it was a formidable list of reasons why this marriage would be a good one. But it wasn't enough. Not any more. Not without telling him the truth. "I can't—"

"I'm sick of hearing that you can't!"

His eyes snapped in the silver light, his body coiled and tense. Amy could sense the frustration and rage radiating from him as he said, "It's too late. You can't *not* marry me. My parents are happier than they've been in months. You will marry me in the morning. Because my parents want it."

A rush of her own anger filled her at his hardheadedness. "Well, go to the church tomorrow and wait. You can't force me to show up." She turned away, ready to leave. Inside she was trembling from the bitter exchange.

She hadn't wanted this.

From behind her he murmured, "If you don't arrive tomorrow, Amy. Then I will leave Saxon's Folly."

Shock made her freeze. But she didn't turn around. "What do you mean?"

"I will be winemaker of Chosen Valley and I will never again bring in a harvest at Saxon's Folly."

At that she spun around and she met his relentless, flat, black gaze. "You can't do that to me."

"Try me." Heath spoke through lips that barely moved.

Panic flooded Amy. She sensed that he would not back down. "You'd force me to marry you—even though you said it had to be my decision?"

He hesitated. For an instant she thought he was going to soften his stance, then his shoulders squared. "Yes, I would. It's too late to have second thoughts now, Amy."

Forcing herself to ignore the pulse drumming in her head, she scanned his face, taking in every stony feature. He would do it. And Amy knew that it would forever drive a wedge between him and his father. She couldn't bear for that to happen. She couldn't bear to know that she might have prevented it.

Would it be such a hardship to be married to Heath? Amy placed her shaking fingers against her temples, struggling to think clearly. What she decided now would shape the rest of her life—and Heath's…and his parents' lives, too.

Her instincts urged her to run as far away from him as she could. The powerful emotions he aroused in her terrified her. Could she give herself up to such a crazy passion? Could she marry a man who'd been a serial dater? A man incapable of committing himself to loving one woman?

Heck, it wasn't as if she was in danger of falling in love with him.

So why was she making it into such a big deal? Heath never intended to marry anyone; it wasn't as though she was ruining his chance at finding true love.

And she'd forgotten the reason for marrying him in the first place.

Her baby.

Their baby.

The baby needed a father. And who better to marry than the baby's real father?

"We'll be married tomorrow." Her baby's father spoke from behind her rigid back. Not soft words of comfort. Or whispers of desire. These words were ice-edged, as hard as the man himself. "There will be no more doubts. Understood?"

A swift glance at Heath's face had her quaking in trepidation. Her throat was too tight to reply, so she nodded slowly.

But even that didn't soften the frown that darkened his face.

She couldn't tell him the truth tonight. He was so angry. And she was too mad at him to make sense tonight. It wasn't the right time. It would lead to recriminations…bitter words better left unsaid. It would have to wait.

Until they were married.

Amy knew she had no choice but to marry him. Heath was right. Their baby was going to draw a splintered family together.

But she wished it could've been different. Her shoulders slumped. "I really despise you, Heath Saxon, for forcing me into this."

The fragrance of flowers—orange blossoms and freesias—filled the stone church in the seaside village as Amy entered through the open wooden doors on her father's arm. Against the stone walls the light from hundreds of slim white candles danced. And despite the smallness of the church, the pews were packed with people.

The intimate gathering wasn't the wedding she'd imagined—or planned. Yet the atmosphere was friendly. Joyous even—despite the fact that the Saxons were still in mourning.

Heads turned and faces lit up as Amy drifted past, doing her best to smile widely. But the heavy knot inside her stomach grew tighter with every step that she took. What would they all say if they knew the man good little virginal Amy had planned to marry had not fathered the baby in her womb? That the Saxon waiting for her at the end of the aisle was her baby's true father? Cold shivers rippled across her skin and shame curled inside her. It didn't bear thinking about.

And, most disturbing of all, was the man waiting at the altar.

The man she'd sworn that she despised last night.

Another lie. The powerful emotions Heath stirred in her might not be love, but nor were they hatred. They were linked to more basic feelings, instincts that it shamed her to possess.

It was herself she despised.

He stood at the end of the aisle alone, legs hip-width apart, his back to her. Tall, straight, clad in a dark suit that fit those shoulders without a wrinkle, he seemed remote, powerful. The filmy lace bridal veil had been folded back from her face, over her dark hair, and Amy could see him clearly. This wasn't the teen she'd known as a child…or the wild youth of her high school years. Nor was he the winemaker everyone called Black Saxon.

This was someone else altogether.

A powerful man. A saviour who had comforted her and held her in his arms through the worst night of her life. A lover who had made her forget her agony and taken her to heights of ecstasy she'd never known.

Memories of him had haunted her for the past two months. Making love with him would be no hardship. Just thinking about his touch caused her to turn to liquid…

Her lover drew her close, comforting her at first. Then, in a flash, it all changed. His mouth was cool against her hot flesh. Her head went back and a wild, keening sound escaped from her throat. He'd ripped away the ladylike veil to reveal someone she didn't know.

She reached the altar, the ivory silk taffeta whispering against her stockinged legs. Heath turned his head. The eyes that met hers were dark, serious, intent. He wasn't taking this marriage lightly. Her father placed her icy hand in Heath's, then he was gone, sliding into the first pew on the bride's side of the church, abandoning her into Heath's care.

The touch of Heath's fingers was hot against her cold hand. A slow warmth filled her. That uncanny connection. Amy swallowed.

Her lover shifted, a stab of pain followed. She flinched and tensed. He stilled and the tight tearing abated. "Don't stop," she whispered in a tone she didn't recognize as her own.

He moved again and pleasure buffeted her along, pain forgotten, as he wrapped her in strong arms. He moved against her…within her…with slow deliberate thrusts that caused the

wildness to unravel within her. And she rushed headlong into
the white heat that waited. It terrified her, this untrammelled
passion. He'd turned her into someone she didn't know.

Heath had chosen to marry her and make her his bride. For
the sake of a baby that he didn't know was his. She'd misled
him. Deliberately. Her impulsive words came back to haunt
her. She'd been in such turmoil….

"I'm pregnant, Heath."

She would never forget the expression on his face when
she'd told him.

"You're sure?"

And then she'd given the answer she bitterly regretted.
"Three months pregnant."

She had to tell him the truth. He would understand why she
had misled him by adding an extra month, Amy thought. Heath
knew her, Goody-Two-Shoes. He would realise how impossible
it had been for her to confess to anyone that Roland was not the
father of her the baby in her womb. And she hadn't wanted him
to work out that he was the father of her child. Heath would
never have suspected that she'd deliberately deceived him. She
would tell him the truth—make it right.

She clung to his hand, drawing a startled glance. He gave
her a quick wink and his serious expression dissolved.

The priest started to speak. Amy tensed. This was it. A
squeeze from Heath's hand caused the clammy, disoriented
sensation to recede and she started to feel a whole lot more
upbeat. No one leaped out of the woodwork to demand that the
ceremony be stopped, and the priest's familiar words washed
over her. A choir of sweet voices sang one of her favourite arias,
and a dreamy feeling of well-being seeped into Amy.

For the first time she started to believe that everything
might work out.

When the time for the vows came, Heath passed her a card.
She glanced at it and stiffened. Heath had written out new

vows. There was no mention of love. Only sharing, caring... cherishing.

She glanced up at him, her eyes dewy with gratitude. Her gaze lingered on the cheekbones that sloped sharply away from those wicked eyes and the black-as-night hair. The hard, rocklike features softened for an instant.

She'd told him how she felt about lying before God. Had he changed their vows for her? Of course, it gave him an out, too.

Now he didn't have to lie, either.

Afterwards, in the sunlit gardens of Saxon's Folly, in front of the old white Victorian house where he'd grown up, Heath played his part as the proud-new-husband as guests showered both him and Amy with congratulations and wished them many years of happiness together.

His mouth slanted at the irony.

If Amy'd had her way last night, today's wedding would never have taken place. With his arm slung possessively around Amy's shoulders, he led her to where a jazz ensemble played smoky music from a rotunda set back between the Nikau palms.

"Would you like to dance?" he asked.

Amy hesitated. Not giving her a chance to demur, he took her hand and hustled her into the grassy space, which posies of white roses staked into the ground and joined by white and silver ribbon marked out as the dance floor.

As he swept her into a waltz, the guests crowded closer. Amy tensed in his arms and clutched his hand in a deathly grip.

"Relax," he murmured, smiling down at her. "Today's supposed to be your day. Enjoy yourself."

"How can I?"

The late afternoon sunlight filtered through the fronds overhead, casting gold splashes over her face. "Ignore everyone. Pretend it's just us."

"That scares me even more." But she smiled as she said it, and her grip on his fingers eased a tiny bit.

Other dancers joined them. Keeping his attention focused on her, he expertly threaded a path through them. "Listen to the band. Aren't they great?"

She nodded. "I thought so, too. They're one of the bands booked to play at the summer festival." After a beat she said, "There's so much to still do."

"I forbid you to think of work for the next five days." He softened the order with a smile, but he had every intention of making sure that Amy took it easy. It was about time someone pampered her a little; she'd been through so much.

She gave a soft sigh. "Easier said than done, but I'll do my best."

"Don't even consider packing a to do list. Or a pen."

That made her laugh. "I promise. And I won't even bring a laptop."

"I should hope not," he said darkly.

Amy giggled. She was moving fluidly now, graceful in the feminine wedding dress. Heath was astounded to discover that the bridal look turned him on. He wished he hadn't promised to wait. He would've loved to have peeled the ivory dress off her and revealed her naked skin and stockinged legs.

The fantasy made him grow all hot. By contrast, Amy seemed to have forgotten about her earlier tension. A burst of possessiveness rushed through him. She was his now. He would take care of her—and her baby.

She didn't even object as he drew her closer—ostensibly to avoid a pair of enthusiastic dancers. He didn't ease his hold, keeping her against him, enjoying the whiff of tuberose, her feminine softness as his thighs brushed hers under the gauzy wedding gown.

Bending his head, he asked, "Have I told you how beautiful you look today?"

Her head came up, her eyes startled. "No."

"You do."

Emotion flashed through her eyes. "Thank you."

Before he could say anything more, Ralph tapped him on the shoulder. He surrendered Amy to her father and watched as she danced away. This courting stuff was going to be hard on him, he suspected.

One step at time. Baby steps.

The rest of the day's festivities passed in a rush. The cutting of the cake. The tossing of the bouquet—which his sister caught—and the throwing of the garter to a pack of prowling males. Heath cast them a glare that warned them to keep their distance. They backed away, the tallest jumping up to snatch the prize when he flung it. Heath glared as the winner roared his triumph.

"Time to leave," he murmured to Amy.

The violet shadows under her eyes revealed the toll the day had taken on her. "Where are we going?"

It was the first time she'd shown any interest in their destination. He gave her a reckless grin. "You'll find out soon enough."

By the time she'd changed out of her wedding dress into a white pantsuit over a silk top and retrieved the bag she'd packed earlier, the helicopter was ready for them. For a moment Amy baulked on seeing it. "We're going in that?"

He nodded. "Of course."

"But—"

"Come," he knew he sounded impatient. But he was done going slow. He wasn't giving her any cause to refuse to go with him. "We need to leave now. I don't want to fly in the waning light."

"You're flying?"

He flashed his most devilish grin. "Yep."

"Oh."

But after that little breathy exclamation, there was no objection. She clambered in without another word. And her silent display of trust made Heath feel ten feet tall.

"Sit beside me."

She put on the headphones he gave her without argument. At first Amy was silent as he went through the preflight checks.

"Flick the switch."

She gave him a puzzled stare that turned to understanding as he gesticulated to the headphones she wore. She turned the switch and he could see her relief as the thumping noise of the rotors dulled.

"All set?" He said into the mouthpiece, and she nodded.

Once the helicopter lifted and swung, she gave a gasp. Beyond the bubble windows, their guests were waving.

Out of the corner of his eye, Heath watched her raise a hand and wave back. As they gained height, he saw that her hands were placed tightly over her harness, over her stomach.

The significance of that gesture hit him and his gut turned to mush. "Relax. Everything's going to be all right. Nothing will harm you—or the baby. I'd never take that risk."

The flight passed quickly. As Heath prepared to land, Amy said, "I always said I'd never fly in one of these contraptions."

"I remember." He'd offered her a trip many years ago.

"I valued my life." But he thought he detected a note of wistfulness. Had Amy wanted to fly with him back then when he'd first gotten his licence? She'd certainly never shown any desire to fly that he'd noticed. "I thought this thing would be the death of you one day," she added.

Heath didn't laugh. "I'm very careful."

"Good!"

He laughed then, amused by how much she managed to convey in that one word. Prim disapproval. He suppressed the urge to lean sideways and plant a kiss on her provocatively pursed lips and concentrated on bringing the bird down safely.

After the rotors had slowed, Amy said excitedly, "Oh, this

is Mataora. I can see the welcome sign. It's part of the Meitaki Islands, if I remember my geography right."

"You do. But we're not staying in the main resort," Heath said. "I've booked a bungalow on the beach."

As they stepped out, they were surrounded by well-trained staff who promised to secure the chopper, took their suitcases and led Amy and Heath to the open SUV that waited.

The drive to the bungalow didn't take long, and once they'd been settled, the welcoming committee departed after Amy refused their offers of elaborate alcoholic cocktails.

Suddenly the air felt very charged. In an effort to refuse the tension that had sprung up between them, Heath said, "You take the main bedroom, I'll take the other."

"There are two?"

He tried not to be insulted by the relief in her eyes. It was hard. "I thought you'd be more comfortable."

"Thanks, Heath."

Her gratitude grated. He'd much rather receive thanks with a husky note of satisfaction after lovemaking, than under these circumstances.

He sighed. They had five whole days together. Heath was determined that by the end of that period Amy would be at ease with him—and with the attraction that simmered between them. The hardest challenge of his life faced him: to convince Amy to fall in love with him.

Nine

When Amy emerged from her room the next morning, there was no sign of Heath in the luxurious sitting area or in the state-of-the-art galley kitchen. Hesitantly, she pushed open the door to his bedroom. It was empty.

A strange sense of desolation swept over her. Then she forced herself to rally. They were hardly the traditional honeymooners. They weren't even in love. This was a practical marriage, underpinned by practical considerations. So why was she feeling abandoned?

Heath wasn't seated on the sheltered deck outside the bungalow that overlooked the sea. Had he gone for a walk… without her? Or had he ventured to the main resort in search of entertainment that his wife could not provide?

Amy's shoulders had just sunk dejectedly when the call of her name made her straighten.

"You're awake." Heath came toward her, wearing dripping board shorts that clung to his thighs. The droplets of moisture on his water-slicked chest gleamed in the morning sun. And his black hair lay seal-sleek against his head.

Oh, my.

Amy didn't know where to look. The pleasure in his eyes made her forget all about her dejection of seconds ago. Flustered, her skin suddenly tight and hot, she couldn't think of a single intelligent thing to say.

Heath had no such problem. He flashed her a smile, his teeth white and straight in his tanned face. "The water's crisp and clear. Put on a swimsuit. I'll wait for you."

"I don't think I brought a swimsuit." Amy felt utterly foolish. She was usually so prepared. "I won't swim, I'll just watch." Then she blushed at how that sounded, and heat spiked through her at the notion of watching Heath in the water. "Uh…I'll bring my book."

Heath shrugged. "Whatever makes you happy." But Amy noticed the glow that had been in his eyes when he'd first greeted her had dimmed a little. Perhaps she could've been a little more enthusiastic. It made her feel like an utter killjoy. Yet she had no intention of joining a practically naked Heath in an ocean frolic.

Not while he roused such flames within her.

Good girls simply didn't play with fire.

There were worse ways to pass the morning than lounging in a deck chair on the beach reading, Amy decided an hour later. The only problem was that the book she'd packed was a sexy romance she'd been reading—and somewhere along the line the dark, sexy hero became Heath. It was inexplicable. It was discomforting.

Snapping the book shut, Amy shoved it back in her tote and shifted restlessly in the deck chair. Heath kept drawing her gaze like a magnet. His broad, bare shoulders gleamed like polished bronze in the sunlight whenever he stood full height in the shallows. Occasionally he would turn to face her, hesitate, then wave. Each time she felt just a tiny bit guilty at being caught looking, like a kid with a hand in the cookie jar. Finally, in danger of becoming mesmerized, she forced herself to look away. Adjusting her shades, she closed her eyes and fell into a half-dozing, half-dreaming state.

She started when cold droplets splashed onto her arm.

Heath stood beside her. Too big. Too naked. And far too close.

Amy's heart started to hammer. "Are you finished?"

"Mmm…it's not much fun swimming alone. There's sure to be a beachwear shop in the resort—we'll go buy you a swimsuit after lunch."

"Maybe." Amy wasn't sure that she was that keen on swimming alone with Heath. "But I'm not sure that I'll swim while we're here."

"Why not? I remember you being a very good swimmer when we used to splash around at the waterhole at the vineyard." He paused concern in his eyes. "Or did your doctor suggest that you give up swimming?"

"No, nothing like that." On the contrary, Dr. Shortt had said that swimming was a good form of exercise during her pregnancy. Cornered, she said, "Okay, we can look for a swimsuit."

The first thing that Heath discovered in the aptly named Splashes, the resort's boutique, was that he and Amy had opposing ideas on the nature of the swimwear she required.

"I can't possibly wear a bikini," she said in a scandalised whisper. "I'm pregnant."

"It's barely noticeable." He eyed her full breasts appreciatively, the only place where clear changes had taken place. "Try this one."

"Not that one. It's barely decent. And if it gets wet…" her voice trailed away.

Imagining the skimpy white fabric wet, clinging to her full breasts, was enough to make Heath grow hard. "That could be interesting," he said huskily.

"Heath!"

"Our bungalow is at the end of the beach. Pretty private." He shot her a simmering look. "Only I would see."

"That's one person too many. I'm not wearing it. Finished." The prim tone was back. And her colour was high.

"Fraidy cat," he murmured so softly that only she could hear. He took wicked satisfaction from making her blush. It delighted him. And meant she had to be aware of him.

She didn't answer back.

"What about this?" This time he took an outfit with a Lycra top in shades of pale rose pink and grape-coloured swirls with black piping and a black bikini bottom off the rack. Heath knew she looked good in romantic pinks and purples… and, more importantly, she wore them often.

Relief flooded her face. "The magenta is a bit bright. But much better than that," she said with a dark glance at the bikini before snatching the bits from his hands and heading for the fitting room.

Heath bit down on the urge to laugh. He'd forgotten how much he used to enjoy teasing Amy once she'd turned sixteen. He'd delighted in her wide eyes and her frowns of disapproval. It appeared that nothing had changed.

Except when she opened the doors, his breath snagged in his throat.

Everything had changed. This was no sixteen-year-old girl standing in front of him with curves in all the right places and defiant eyes. This was a woman. A woman he wanted. Badly.

"Don't you like it?" Amy asked when the silence stretched too long.

Heath almost choked. Like it? Hell, he loved it. "It'll do," he said instead. But he couldn't resist jerking her chain one last time. "If you're sure you don't want the white bikini?"

He could've sworn he heard a snort. But that wasn't

possible. Not from Amy Wright. Amy Saxon, he amended hastily. Hell, how could he have gotten that wrong?

"You get changed, and I'll meet you up front." Without waiting for an answer he made his way to the front of the boutique. He collected a wide-brimmed straw hat, a straw beach bag with a beach mat and a tube of sunscreen on the way. If she hadn't brought a swimsuit, she'd need those, too.

A dress that shimmered like liquid sunshine caught his eye. Somewhere between bronze and gold, the shade reminded him of Amy's eyes. He added the silky garment to the growing pile.

By the time Amy emerged with the swimsuit in hand, he'd already paid and was waiting in the front of the store, a large silver bag in his hand.

She stopped dead. "I was going to pay for that myself."

He waved a dismissive hand. "It's done."

Her mouth pursed.

"A gift for my beautiful bride. Put your purse away and thank me instead," he said, while the shop assistant looked on with an indulgent smile.

"Thank you," Amy said far more sweetly than he expected. He'd expected gritted teeth at the very least.

He leaned toward her. "And my kiss?"

Heath knew he was being deliberately provocative. He was pushing her buttons. He wanted a response; he wanted to see her precious eyes shooting sparks at him. But he knew it was highly unlikely. Amy always behaved perfectly.

No reason to expect anything different this time.

Even if he was taunting her.

Her expression didn't change. The first indication he had that not all was as it had always been was the way she swayed toward him, her lashes lowered. Instead of the hesitant peck on the check that he'd expected, her lips puckered into a sultry moue and landed squarely on his mouth. Soft. Sweet. Heath's heart started to pound in his chest.

Her mouth was soft and her lips moved just enough under his to give him an idea of what he was missing out on by giving a promise to give her time.

A long moment later she stepped away, her eyes flicking to the shop attendant, revealing that she was as aware as he of their audience.

"Thank you, my darling," she murmured throatily.

Touché. Amy taking risks was a very dangerous woman. To Heath's utter disgust he found that he was sweating.

That evening the air was heavy with the distinctive fragrance of frangipani from the shrubs that grew in lush profusion around the bungalow. Amy sat in one of the cane armchairs grouped on the wooden deck and tried to appear relaxed as she leaned back against the plumped-up cushions, no easy feat with Heath towering in front of her, his back to the ocean as he leaned against the wooden balustrade.

Holding her gaze, Heath raised his glass.

"To my bride."

The words resounded in the velvety dusk. A melting sensation rushed through Amy. She hadn't forgotten the way his eyes had skimmed her swimsuit-clad body in Splashes boutique earlier. In fact, odd tingles shot through her every time she thought about it, even though she tried very hard to avoid thinking about it at all. Yet she couldn't seem to help herself. She couldn't forget how his eyes had been dark one moment then bright with carnal desire the next. The transformation had taken her breath away. It had been shocking…but exciting too. And it had awakened worrying wanting feelings in her.

She didn't *want* to want Heath.

"Thank you," she managed a husky response to his toast and took a quick sip of the mineral water she'd opted for in place of champagne from the elegant tulip-shaped glass, then wondered what to say next.

Despite the fact that the resort felt like a place for lovers, honeymooners, she didn't feel like a bride. But she couldn't confess that. It wasn't his fault. It was hers. Perhaps he expected a toast in return? She shot him a furtive little look from under her lashes.

"To—" She broke off awkwardly. *To my groom.* No, she couldn't bring herself to say it. He wasn't the groom of her heart. "To our marriage," she offered instead, a little lamely.

"To our marriage," he echoed, his voice deep.

The glow of candles spilled through the large picture windows from the bungalow and suffused his features with a golden cast, highlighting his bottom lip, throwing his eyes into deep relief. All gold light and dark shadows. A sexy, brooding stranger.

A frisson rippled through her.

Stop it, she told herself. This was Heath. No stranger. She'd known him all her life. There was no reason for her heart to be fluttering in her chest, no reason to be apprehensive about the *a deux* dinner he'd arranged. They weren't even alone, for heaven's sake. A chef was preparing their meal in the kitchen. A few minutes ago a waiter clad in white, except for a striped butcher's apron, had appeared armed with a bottle of champagne, the champagne that Heath was drinking, and that Amy had refused, conscious of the life within her.

But Heath was staring at her, unsettling her.

"Your hair suits you like that," he said.

She smoothed her hand over the tousled locks. "It's a mess." She'd taken a shower and changed into the gauzy bronze dress that Heath had bought for her. It had seemed the perfect choice for the balmy night. Then Heath had knocked on the door to advise her that the catering staff would be there in five minutes. She hadn't had a chance to blow-dry her hair into its usual bob. Instead she'd focused on a quick fix—a dab of hair mousse, moisturizer on her cheeks, a brush of mascara and a soft pink lip gloss.

"I like it."

A thrill of pleasure rushed through her at his compliment. Followed by something else, something infinitely more dangerous.

He moved closer. She stiffened and quickly drained her drink.

"Here, let me take that."

For a moment she held onto the empty glass, reluctant to surrender it. The glass gave her something to hold, sipping the water gave her something to do, creating a barrier between them. With the glass gone, he would be even closer.

Reluctantly, she released it. He set her glass down on a glass-topped table and turned back.

Amy was on her feet, a strange cat-on-a-hot-tin-roof edginess making her say hurriedly, "Let's walk to the water's edge."

He gave her a strange look. "There isn't enough time. Dinner will be ready shortly."

"Oh." He had her there. She tripped toward the railing and, resting her hands on the wood, stared across the pale beach at the sea glimmering in the waning light.

"Do you really want to walk now?" He was right behind her. "Perhaps after dinner?"

"It was just an idea," she said, her voice suddenly husky. Not a brilliant one. But then escape had been at the forefront of her mind, driven by the need to protect herself from the restless edginess his proximity evoked.

And what had it gained her? He was closer now. Even though he wasn't touching her, she felt crowded, trapped between his body and the balustrade. Her heart leaped. He was too close. There was no escape.

Yet it was strange to be thinking of Heath trying to besiege her. She was hardly his type. The bad boy never dated good girls. But he'd been her friend, kind of, once upon a time. And now he was the father of her child, she reminded herself.

Her husband, too.

Her hands gripped the wooden railing. The fact that he was her husband should have made it easier to cope with the disturbing feelings he aroused in her. It didn't. It only made it worse.

This kind of pervasive desire was supposed to come parcelled up with love. It devastated her to realise it wasn't. She certainly didn't love Heath.

But she wanted him. It was disturbing—shocking—to feel this way about him. It was as if her body had been taken over by a force she did not recognise. And she didn't like it one little bit.

It was wrong to feel this way about him.

She'd loved Roland—

"I don't want to go anywhere," he whispered against the exposed skin behind her ear, causing shivers to riot down her spine. "I want to stay right here."

Amy whirled around. "Heath—"

His arms came around her. Amy's breath left her in a whoosh of air. Then she realised that the focus of his attention lay beyond her, behind her. She stilled. When his hands returned to in front of her, he held a spray of frangipani between his long, blunt fingers—winemaker's hands—and the night was full of heady tropical scent.

"Stand still."

The command was not necessary. Amy couldn't have moved if she'd tried. Her knees felt weak. Her senses were overpowered by him, holding her captive. She hoped desperately that her ragged breathing wouldn't betray her. His fingers touched her ear. Amy started, and adrenalin exploded in a rush into her veins as he slid the frangipani blooms into her hair.

"There," Heath stepped back and suddenly Amy could breathe again. Until he smiled. Her heart twisted and for a moment she swayed toward him.

Heath was safe. As long as she could keep it straight in her head that desire had nothing to do with love, as long as her mind didn't start playing tricks on her, and have her imagining she was falling in love with Heath…everything would be fine.

She'd be safe.

Her silly, trampled-on heart would be safe, too.

And she and Heath didn't need love to bind them together. They had the baby. The baby he believed was his brother's.

Her stomach rolled over and a sick sensation assailed her. She needed to tell him about that…

But not now.

Not when his head was coming toward her with that mellow gleam in his hellfire, bad-boy eyes and an irresistible smile turning up the corners of his mouth. But the sound of a footfall gave him pause, and they both turned to find the waiter indicating that dinner was served.

Dinner was done, and the resort staff had departed.

Heath lounged back on the sofa in the living room and his smile widened as Amy's throat bobbed as she swallowed.

She was nervous. Good. He wanted to keep her off balance. He didn't want her starting to harbour brotherly thoughts of him.

"Come to me," he whispered softly. For a brief instant he thought she was going to say something, refuse even, then with a sigh she came.

She stood before him, her eyes lowered, and even in the subdued glow of the candlelight he could see that she was trembling.

Heath frowned.

"What are you afraid of?"

Her eyelids shot open and her wild, golden gaze met his. The impact made him shudder. Heath's breathing quickened as he scooped her onto his lap, her thighs straddling his hips. Her scent enveloped him, she smelled of roses and raw passion.

It wasn't fear that was causing her to tremble. It was desire.

He was already hard, his erection straining against the front of his trousers.

Before she could object to the intimacy of the close contact, he threaded his hands through her silken, tousled hair and pulled her close. Her lips met his, lush and soft, and he groaned aloud.

Their mouths met, kissed, parted and returned to kiss again. An erotic dance. One that left Heath aching for more.

Cupping her head between his work-worn hands, he eased her closer to taste the sweetness of her mouth…again and again.

"I will never tire of this," he whispered against her lips.

Amy made a soft, satisfied sound, almost a purr of delight.

In response, Heath freed her hair and stroked his hands over her bare shoulders, which shimmered in the candle glow and down her back, over the sleek fabric of the bronze dress.

Then, one-handed, he yanked his shirt from his trousers and impatiently undid the buttons so that the shirt fell open, baring his chest.

Amy's gasp of awe, followed by the stroke of a lone fingertip along the centre of his breastbone caused his erection to leap in response.

"Touch me," he demanded, wrapping his arms around her, drawing her a little closer and letting his fingers play along the indent of her spine.

Both her hands came down on the bare skin of his torso and traced the straining pectoral muscles before sliding down to explore the ridges of his abdomen.

He closed his eyes and hissed through clenched teeth, a sound of suppressed delight.

When he opened his eyes, he stared straight into golden ones glinting with curiosity and hunger.

"I didn't see you last time." A hectic flush coloured her cheeks.

Last time they'd been surrounded by night. Heath's hands stilled. Last time…

He'd brought her to Chosen Valley, shocked and shaken after surviving the car accident that had injured his brother. Barely bruised, she'd shivered with reaction. Finally, he'd given her a mild sedative and crawled in beside her, holding her until she warmed and her teeth stopped clattering, until she eased into a restless sleep.

Long before dawn he'd left her sleeping under Josie's supervision and gone to the hospital to see how Roland was faring in intensive care. His brother had passed away while he was there.

Distraught, he'd driven home, dismissed Josie and broken the news of Roland's death to Amy.

Her grief had been palpable. He'd held her in the predawn darkness…and then the raging grief had exploded into something else. Instead of comforting her, he'd loved her under the cover of darkness.

It had been the only way to stanch their grief.

He would never regret making love to her.

"Look all you want," he murmured now.

The smile she bestowed on him was confident…sensual… intensely womanly. "You bet I will."

Heath's fingers slid beneath the shoestring ties of the bronze dress and worked them loose. The dress fell away, pooling around her hips. Leaning forward he kissed the smooth, white-marble skin, the dark tips of her full-blown breasts, revelling in the throaty moans she made.

She was so sensitive, so responsive. His arousal skyrocketed, and he knew that if he didn't act soon it would all be over before it had even started.

Loosening his zipper he slid his pants down over his hips. Then he drew Amy close. He felt her start as his rocklike hardness nestled against her secret places.

He stroked her bare back with his palms. She was quivering with expectation. And Heath's tight control gave.

"Look at me," he said hoarsely.

Her eyes clashed with his, glazed with passion. Staring into the molten-gold depths, Heath slid his hands under the hem of her dress.

When he discovered the minuscule thong she was wearing, his heart nearly gave out. She gave him that tantalizing, slow smile again and his pulse thundered. He ran two fingers under the barely decent strings and found her slick wetness.

His breath caught in his throat and his body surged forward. The thong snapped. Her eyes went wide.

Heath held her hips, lifting her, positioning her. The catch of her breath made him shudder. And an instant later her hot heat closed around him.

Heath groaned. And then she was sliding against him, the motions causing silver bursts of sensation to explode through him even as the rippling shivers took her over the edge.

Ten

Heath woke through slow degrees.

His first thought was for Amy. He turned his head. She was still sleeping. In the faded pink of the morning light, her dark eyelashes fanned down against her pale skin and one of her hands rested between the pillow and her cheek.

After they'd made love last night, she'd been silent and had avoided Heath's gaze.

He'd tried to draw her out, to no avail. She'd delayed going to bed and had finally fallen asleep on the sofa. He'd carried her to bed.

Had Amy regretted being swept away by the passion that simmered so hotly between them? Had she felt as though she'd betrayed Roland…for a second time?

He'd promised Amy time.

And had broken that promise. Two nights after making their vows he'd taken her. Taken her…

Just thinking of what his hunger—what he'd done—caused

him to tense in shame. Yes, she'd responded to his loving. Carnally. Voraciously even. That was not the point.

"As for knowing me…you don't know this me. I don't even know this side of me—it's embarrassing."

The point was she didn't want to feel this hunger for him. Her words came back to haunt him. She'd feel ashamed. And he'd done that to her. All because he was too damned impatient to wait. Because he wanted her. To brand her as his. And in doing so he might've risked losing her.

He'd given no quarter last night. He'd taken her, intending to imprint himself on her, so that she would never forget.

Pure male possessiveness.

Mine.

How could he expect her to ever trust his word again?

Later, after an English breakfast complete with fried eggs, bacon, toast and marmalade, they drove to a beach that was supposed to be magnificent. With the straw beach bag Heath had bought for her slung over her shoulder, Amy followed him down a narrow pathway. The moment they came through the trees Heath stopped dead.

Amy bumped into his legs and instantly felt a flutter of heat at the unexpected physical contact.

"Sorry," she muttered.

"Don't apologise." Heath turned his head, the tanned skin drawn tight across his cheekbones. She couldn't read the expression in his eyes behind the dark lenses of his Wayfarers.

This stilted discomfort had been there since they'd woken up. There had been a distance between them. And Amy had known she'd missed the chance to tell him that the baby was his. It would be much harder now that they'd made love.

Breathlessly she asked, "Is this the right beach?"

He stared at her unblinkingly until she started to feel uncomfortable.

"Oh, yes, this is the right beach."

So what was the problem? Amy glanced past him to the deserted strip of golden sand and dark turquoise sea. "Then why are we stopping?"

"I'm not sure this is a good idea."

"Why?" Amy frowned. The beach looked like a still from an advertisement for paradise. "Is it unsafe?"

"You could say that."

Amy narrowed her eyes against the morning sun glittering off the water looking for flat sections of water, that might signal a riptide or something equally ominous. "I can't see anything wrong, it looks idyllic to me." She turned worried eyes on Heath. "What's the problem?"

He took his time answering. "Not enough people." He looked at her from under hooded eyelids.

And then it hit her. He didn't want to be alone with her. The first thing she felt was hurt. She shrugged it off. Did he regret making love last night?

Pretending that she hadn't gotten his point, she strode forward. "Well, we don't need to swim. The concierge was right, it's beautiful," she flung over her shoulder. "We can just soak up the sun and the peace away from the crowds."

Halting at the edge of the sea, Amy pulled a straw mat out of her bag, unrolled it, and laid it down. She was aware of Heath behind her, but she pretended not to notice his presence.

Slipping off the loose-fitting, crinkled-cotton pink dress with shoestring ties to reveal the bathing suit Heath had bought for her, she slathered on sunscreen, then she stretched herself out on the mat.

There was dead silence from behind her.

At first it rattled her nerves, and she fought the urge to peer through her lashes and see what Heath was doing. But as the silent seconds stretched into minutes, she began to relax.

If Heath thought there was safety in numbers, she'd prove

to him he was perfectly safe on this deserted beach with her. She certainly wasn't going to fall all over him.

It wasn't her style.

So Amy lay with her eyes closed, her hands behind her head, absorbing the sun's heat. She must have dozed a little, because a while later she stirred at the sound of Heath's voice asking whether she needed more sunscreen.

"Mmm," she murmured, more asleep than awake.

The shock of his hands on her legs woke her with a start.

"What are you doing?"

He gave her a barbed smile. "Putting sunscreen on you. You asked, didn't you?"

"I thought you meant to pass me the bottle."

"My hands were already oily. No sense in two of us getting sticky," he said with horrible logic.

"I suppose so," she said, reluctant pleasure creeping through her as he applied the lotion in long, lazy strokes. "That's far enough," Amy objected when his slippery fingers skirted the high-cut legs of the bikini bottoms.

"If you say so." His eyes glittered. "These bits of skin often get overlooked and burn badly." His fingers swept under the edge of the stretchy fabric and she leaped to a sitting position as if she'd been electrified.

"Give me that cream."

He surrendered it, and Amy knew his black-devil's eyes would be laughing behind the Wayfarers, damn him!

He lay back, his elbows propped in the sand behind him, tanned skin gleaming in the sun, and watched her through half-closed eyes.

Self-consciousness rippled through Amy. Her fingers hesitated for a moment then she forced herself to rub cream into her arms and shoulders with brisk circular movements.

"Careful you don't rub your skin off. You sure you don't

want me to do it for you? I'll be much more gentle." There was amusement in his voice.

She ignored him and squirted more cream into her hand with unnecessary vigour. Peeling the bottom hem of the tank top up, she slathered on cream across the strip of skin above her black bikini briefs. The cream was cold against her sun-warmed stomach. Amy caught her breath. She heard Heath gasp, too.

When she looked up, Heath sat upright, his eyes blazing. "Did the baby move?" he asked hoarsely.

"No, the cream was cold." She rubbed the last remnants in as she offered the humdrum explanation.

"Oh, I thought—" For a moment he looked uncertain, then he dropped back into the lounging lazy position in the sand. "I thought it was the baby. Have you felt it move yet?"

She shook her head. "I saw it move on the scan at my last appointment. But I haven't felt it yet. It's kind of strange. Dr. Shortt says I will in a couple of weeks."

"Tell me when it happens."

Amy let the high-handedness go. He cared. He really cared. And that warmed her more than she'd ever expected. He was complicated, her husband. He never did quite what she expected.

"You missed one spot."

"What?" She stared at him blankly.

"You need some sunscreen on your—" he broke off "—on your chest." His voice had gone all raspy.

She glanced down at the pale bare skin that the neckline of the magenta-and-pink tank top framed.

"I suppose." She wasn't wildly keen to touch the sloping flesh of her breasts—not with Heath watching. Not with last night's wild lovemaking still so fresh in her mind.

"Do you want me to do it for you?"

Amy glared at him. Those darn sunshades. She couldn't read his expression. But from the way her breasts tingled, she suspected that was where his gaze was fixed.

"Heath, stop it! You're making me feel self-conscious."

"Sorry." Instantly he was contrite. "I promised you time—and I broke my word."

Broken his word? He was talking about last night, Amy realised. He felt guilty. That he'd pushed her too soon. Didn't he know it took two to tango? That she'd been as guilty—if that was the right word—as he was?

Before she could say anything, he'd pushed himself to his feet, his taut stomach muscles rippling in the sun.

"I need to cool off."

Amy suspected that he meant that in more ways than one. Perhaps this was exactly what he'd feared when he'd realised the beach was deserted. Perhaps she'd been mistaken when she'd thought he hadn't wanted to be alone with her. The ache of hurt she'd experienced vanished.

Amy watched as Heath loped into the shallows and sank into the lapping wavelets. Driven by a fresh sense of energy, she jumped to her feet and ran into the water.

As his head surfaced, she swept her hand through the salty water sending up a spray that hit him squarely in the face. He sputtered.

Amy laughed.

"I'll get you for that!"

Just before she started to swim, she called out, "Catch me if you can."

That set the tone for the rest of the day. They laughed and joked and Amy found herself looking forward to the night to come. There was no doubt in her mind that they would be making love again tonight.

There was an electric awareness between them, a sense of waiting. Heath would look at her with heat in his eyes when he thought she hadn't seen, and glance away when her gaze caught his.

It cut two ways. Because every time she scanned his long lean body and remembered the sleekness of his naked skin against hers last night, heat would sear her and her breathing would quicken. The strength of the physical thread between them held them both equally ensnared.

Amy had never imagined anything like it.

But nor had she imagined enjoying time alone with Heath this much. They laughed. They talked. He listened to what she had to say and treated her opinions with a respect that she'd never received from Roland. The silent admission felt like treachery, but it was true. Heath exhibited a caring, a respect, toward her that was enormously seductive.

That night, he arranged to take her out for an early dinner to a popular restaurant on the island.

Amy was wearing the bronze dress again. It was so comfortable, but so liberating too. She'd never owned anything as sophisticated. Other than her gold locket and the ring Heath had given her, she wore no jewellery. But the dress didn't need more. Heath's eyes told her that as his gaze stroked over her.

"You're beautiful, Amy."

She felt the colour surge in her cheeks. "It's the dress you bought," she bubbled. "I'd never thought of wearing this colour before."

"Oh, no." He was shaking his head. "It's you, Amy-love. You're beautiful."

The blush intensified. Not for the first time, she wished she could control it. That her skin wasn't such an obvious barometer of her every emotion. No one had ever called her beautiful before. Pretty, yes. Feminine. Well-groomed and stylish. But never beautiful.

But there was no doubt that Heath was sincere—it radiated from him. He truly believed she was beautiful.

And she wasn't disabusing him of that belief.

"The car is here," she said with relief as an engine purred beyond the bungalow windows, breaking the quiet of the island evening.

The evening passed too quickly. Amy glowed under Heath's attention, hardly noticing the staggering array of seafood on the buffet, picking at morsels of oyster and squid, barely tasting a thing.

A dreamy state encapsulated her. She felt as if she'd stepped into someone else's body for the night. Until she met Heath's gaze and felt the desire bolt through her.

Reality crashed in. There was no doubt that this was her body. She was becoming accustomed to the hunger that he aroused in her sometimes with only a look. The shame was finally starting to recede.

She was married to the man. He was her husband. She was pregnant with his baby.

All day she'd been putting off telling him, not wanting to spoil the unspoken truce that hovered, so fragile, between them. *Just give me tonight.*

That's all she wanted. One more night. A little more time to cement the accord that was slowly building between them. Until that awful night of Roland's death, she'd never done anything wrong in her life.

Since then, it seemed she'd done nothing right.

Sleeping with a man she wasn't married to the night the man she loved had died. Agreeing to marry a man she didn't love. And omitting to tell him that the baby she carried in her womb was his. The catalogue of sins was serious. So serious that she'd borne them all alone.

"Just one more day, please," she prayed hoping that a higher power would give her the time. "I'll never do anything wrong in my life again."

The bargaining appeared to work. The accumulated years of good deeds must've held up. Because Heath kept watching her with smiling, approving eyes and listening to her with his full attention. Heady stuff. Amy could've sworn that the fruit juice she'd drunk had gone to her head. She felt light-headed, a touch dizzy with delight.

It was when she rose to her feet that the pain hit her.

"Heath!" She grabbed his sleeve as she doubled over.

"Are you okay?"

"I'm not sure," she gasped. The spasm passed. She straightened cautiously. Another piercing pain surged through her. And panic followed. "No, I'm not okay."

"Where's the pain?" he asked urgently.

"My stomach."

He blanched, his lips paling. "The baby?"

Heath voiced the words she hadn't even dared think.

"I don't know!" A worse wave of dizziness shook her as another spasm hit her. "Heath, I want to go home."

"I'll get you home."

Turning his head, he summoned a waiter. Within a minute he had her in the car.

Misery consumed Amy.

The baby…

She hadn't wanted it. She'd resented its presence—tangible evidence of the mistake she'd made. And now her belly was full of pain. She didn't deserve to keep her baby. A sob broke from her throat.

Heath's arm steadied her. "There's no doctor on the island at the moment, Amy. But there's a nurse. She's meeting us at the airfield."

"The airfield?"

"As long as she says it's safe, I'm taking you home. I'll do everything in my power to see that you don't lose your baby."

* * *

Dr. Shortt folded up his stethoscope and straightened from examining Amy on the large bed in Heath's navy–and–dull gold bedroom back at Chosen Valley.

"The island nurse was correct. It *is* food poisoning. Amy will need rest and plenty of fluids over the next few days."

"And the baby?" Anxiety balled in Heath's chest. The baby was her last connection to his brother. Even though she hadn't wanted to be pregnant, Heath had no doubt that losing the baby now would devastate Amy.

Dr. Shortt gave a sigh. "It depends on what bacteria caused it. There are some nasties out there that can affect the fetus. I'll take samples and the lab will do a culture. It will be a couple of days before we have a result."

"A couple of days?" said Amy faintly from the bed. "Do we have to wait so long?"

"Yes," said the doctor.

"It must have been the buffet dinner," said Amy.

"Unlikely," replied Dr. Shortt. "The bacteria had probably already been in your system for at least eight hours before you started to feel ill. More likely breakfast."

"I had eggs over easy and bacon," said Amy.

"That's a possibility." Dr. Shortt nodded. "Now don't forget to drink plenty of fluids—and call me if the cramps return or grow more severe."

"Could I still miscarry?"

The doctor hesitated before saying very gently, "If it's a bug like listeria, that's possible. Miscarriage usually occurs within twenty-four hours."

"Oh," Amy fell silent.

Heath spared her a glance. Her face was pasty, her skin dewy with perspiration. She'd been running a fever earlier. That, along with a headache, nausea and vomiting had made the trip in the helicopter back from Mataora a nightmare journey for her.

He hurried to her side, tenderness overwhelming him. "You just take it easy, Amy-love."

She gave him a wan smile. "Thank you for taking my worst fears so seriously."

"Always," he vowed, holding her gaze for a long moment. Then he turned his attention to the portly figure of the doctor. "Thank you for coming out."

"I'm sorry it was under such circumstances. Call me if you have any concerns. Otherwise I'll pop by in the morning to check on Amy." He made his way out.

When the doctor had closed the door behind him, Heath closed his fingers around Amy's. He wanted to tell her how worried he'd been about her, how the nightmare flight back had seemed to take forever. Instead, forcing a cheerful note, he said, "A few days and you'll be as right as rain."

"And my baby?" Her gold eyes held terror.

"We'll take that one day at a time. For now let's concentrate on getting you well and back on your feet."

Heath didn't voice his own fear: that if she lost this baby, then the whole reason for their marriage vanished, too. Heath clenched his fists.

There would be no reason for Amy to stay married to him. None at all.

He would do everything in his power to make sure that her baby survived. Without the baby, he'd lose her for sure.

Eleven

Three days later Amy felt weak and washed out, but the debilitating nausea and vomiting had finally passed.

She began to fret about wrecking the honeymoon that Heath had seemed to want so much, about missing work, about the approaching summer festival. But it didn't matter how much she fretted or what she said, Heath would not allow her to rise from the big bed in the master suite at Chosen Valley.

For once his take-charge behaviour didn't grate. Amy was silently relieved to be told to take time off for her weak-as-water body to recover.

There wasn't even the opportunity to get bored. Over the past three days she'd had plenty of visitors. Her father. Heath's parents. Alyssa and Joshua. And Megan. Everyone was so concerned about her, despite her constant reassurances that she would be fine. Although, to be truthful, her stomach still ached and she was sure that she must have lost at least ten pounds.

The tests came back confirming that she'd been infected

by salmonella bacteria and Dr. Shortt popped in on the fourth morning to check her over. After he'd checked the tympanic thermometer and declared her temperature normal, he carefully explained that there would be no risk to her baby.

Joy and relief flooded Amy.

"You're sure?" she asked, desperate for reassurance.

He nodded.

Amy felt as if a gigantic weight had been taken off her shoulders, as if she'd been granted a reprieve from a sentence too awful to think about.

After the doctor had left, Amy fell back against the plumped pillows and stared out the window across to the green hills in the distance and counted her blessings.

At what point had the baby become so important to her? Her teeth gnawed her bottom lip. When had she stopped wishing that she wasn't pregnant and started to accept the life growing within her body? She laid a hand on the burgeoning bump of her stomach. Somewhere along the way, she'd started looking forward to the birth. Had it been on the day that Heath had given her that exquisite engagement ring and taken her to the aquarium? Maybe.

Her musings were interrupted when the bedroom door banged open and Megan burst in.

"How are you feeling today, sister?"

Amy beamed at Heath's energetic sister. "Wonderful. Dr. Shortt assures me that there will be no lasting damage from this bout of food poisoning. I'm so relieved."

"Oh, great!" Megan came and gave her a hug. "I'm thrilled for you and Heath. When's the baby due?"

"End of June." Amy touched her tummy. She couldn't seem to stop. "I've even got a baby bump to prove it."

Delight spread over Megan's face. "We'll have to go shopping. I've never shopped for maternity clothes before. Or cribs. Or strollers." Megan rubbed her hands in glee.

Amy started to laugh helplessly. "I hadn't even thought about all that." Heath wouldn't want to come. By telling him she was three months' pregnant instead of two, she'd effectively caused him to believe that the baby was Roland's. There'd be no reason for him to want to come. "I'd love to have your help. I'm glad you're here, Megan. All my life I wanted a sister."

"Me, too. Although I love my brothers, believe it or not."

"What's not to love about your brothers?" Whenever she'd spent time at Saxon's Folly, Amy had gone home wishing she'd had siblings.

"Now you're part of the family," Megan said generously. "We're all glad for you and Heath. He's so happy."

That startled Amy. She hadn't noticed a difference. "Heath's happy?"

"Walking on air. He's so in love with you it's sweet."

Megan believed Heath loved her?

Amy gave Megan an uncertain smile. "Glad you think it's sweet."

Megan placed her forefinger over her lips. "Don't let my brother hear I described him as sweet. He's gotten far too used to his Bad Saxon image." Megan wandered over to the dresser and pinched a dab of Heath's Eau Savage cologne. "We couldn't believe it when he broke the news that you were getting married."

Amy waited tensely.

"Mother was worried. Heath assured her he'd only asked you to marry him because he loved you."

Heath loved her.

The rest of Megan's visit passed in a blur of chatter that Amy didn't even absorb. Megan finally rushed off and Amy stared at the white plastered ceiling, her brain working overtime.

After the first shock wore off, Amy discovered that Megan's revelation had caused a huge shift in her thinking. It cast a whole new complexion on Heath's behaviour. She thought about the attention he showered her with on Mataora, his concern during her illness. She remembered the way he smiled at her, the tenderness that sometimes glowed in his eyes.

That was love.

A lightness came over her. Suddenly the future seemed brighter. She liked the idea of Heath loving her.

When the door opened again a little later, Heath stood there, tall and dark and so gorgeously male that her hormones went into overdrive. Amy's heart twisted over and she sent him a smile full of tender joy.

"You're looking better," he said, his eyes lightening as he scanned her features, his inspection warming her. "Would you like me to carry you downstairs? The sitting room is pleasant and sunny. I can open the doors to let some of the summer in. A little later, when it gets dark, we can put on the Christmas tree lights."

"That sounds lovely. But honestly, I can walk."

His black eyes sparkled. "You don't need to."

Advancing on her, he swept her up in his arms and Amy gave herself up to his strength. Nestled close to his heart, surrounded by the lemon-and-oakmossy masculine scent of him, she clung to his broad shoulders as he headed down the stairs. Once in the living room, he lowered her onto the plush velvet sofa. Shafts of December sunlight fell in broad golden bands across the Kelim rug, giving the room a glorious warmth.

"I'll get you a mohair throw for your legs."

"I'm fine," she protested, "honestly."

But he disappeared into the hall and she heard him rummaging in the hall cupboard.

Amy was starting to realise that Heath looked after his own and would never let her down. Her father had been right when he'd said that Heath was always where he was needed, solid as an ancient oak. She'd been blind to that side of him.

What else had she missed?

Heath had once joked that she could have picked him to be the man she loved. She'd dismissed it. Now she couldn't help considering whether, in the blinkered way of youth, she'd chosen the wrong guy.

Roland had been older. Glamorous. She'd been blinded by his sophistication. In love with the notion of being in love. And she'd been wary of Heath's bad boy image—and he'd already been gaining a reputation as a love-'em-and-leave-'em type. Not quite what she'd wanted with her naive dreams of a princely groom and white wedding night.

So maybe Heath hadn't given her the virginal wedding night her young heart had fantasised about. But he'd made her first time something special—even though it had been at a time when her world was falling apart. He'd given her something to cling to in the days—weeks—that followed Roland's death.

They'd conceived a child.

When he came back, he covered her legs and sank down on the sofa set at right angles to the one where she sat.

"Dr. Shortt called to tell me that he'd visited you this morning and gave you a clean bill of health."

Amy nodded. "Yes, he says it was salmonella."

"He told me—and he said that the baby would be fine."

Amy gave Heath a beatific smile. "It's such a relief. I'd started to feel like every way I turned things were going awry. Everything seems to be coming right again." Like the discovery that he loved her. She paused, wondering how best to broach that. Finally, she said, "Your sister came to visit this morning, too."

Heath raised his eyebrows. "I suppose she showered you with gossip about the summer festival and got you all fired up about getting back to work?"

"Well, it *is* only a five days away now."

"Don't worry about it, *Amy-love,* it's all under control. Alyssa and Mom and I have all been tying up the final loose ends."

Amy hesitated. But the endearment Amy-love spurred her on. "Megan told me something very interesting."

"What was that?" Heath didn't sound particularly interested in what his sister had to say.

A silence. Then Amy said softly, "She told me that you're in love with me."

For a moment Heath's expression didn't change, then all the emotion drained out, leaving it devoid of all expression.

After a moment he said, "And you believed her?"

Her heart thudded in her throat. Megan was often tactless, but she was also brutally honest. "She was very convincing."

He didn't look like a man in love. The sinking sensation in her stomach confirmed that Megan must've had it all wrong.

Amy swallowed desperately. Had she made a terrible mistake confronting him with his sister's opinions? No, she hadn't. They were married. She deserved the truth. "Are you denying it?" she asked bravely.

"I'm certainly not admitting it." There was an angry edge to his tone. "Amy, you shouldn't believe everything my family says. Of course, they think I love you. I've made damn sure they believe that. What other reason could I give them for marrying you?"

All the joy and confidence escaped Amy like helium from a child's balloon. "Didn't they believe you were doing it for the sake of Roland's child?"

He shot her a bitter look. "That's what you believed. They would've hated that."

"What do you mean?"

"Oh, Amy, that would've worried my mother to death. She would've been so concerned for both of us. I can see her trying to talk us out of the marriage. At least this way, by thinking I loved you and that I was going to help you through the grief of Roland's death, it gave my family hope that this mad marriage would work."

Mad marriage? Her heart sank. "But it can work." Amy felt as though she were wading through quicksand. Every way she moved, the situation became worse. "It has to work."

"For the baby's sake. I know." His voice was flat, his eyes empty of all emotion. "Don't worry, Amy, I'm not going to desert you."

"I know that. I trust you, Heath."

Emotion leaped in his eyes like flame. Then it went out like a doused candle. "Do you? Really?"

"Yes." She sucked in air. "I was wrong about you in the past when I thought you were wild and reckless and unreliable. I didn't see the real you."

"But you do now?" There was a twist to his mouth that she didn't much like. "Because my sister told you I was in love with you?"

"Okay, I shouldn't have believed it. It's rubbish, I accept that."

"It's not love that ties us together, Amy-love. It's something a lot more basic."

She flinched at the mocking use of what she'd considered an endearment until a few minutes ago.

When he came toward her with swift, panther strides, every muscle in her body tensed. The kiss he bestowed on her surprised mouth was ruthless and by the time he'd finished Amy was breathing hard.

"That's what binds us together. It's not called love. You'll never love me and—"

"Don't say it." Amy covered her ears. She didn't want to hear him denigrating the tenderness that had grown between them during their honeymoon, didn't want to hear it labelled by some crude word.

It hurt to hear the edge in him. Clearly he didn't love her—had never loved her. Desperate to bridge the chasm between them, Amy said, "Don't let's fight. And don't let's forget that there's the baby, too. A baby that will always bind us together." Her hand dropped to her stomach, while she held Heath's bitter black gaze.

"Roland's baby—a Saxon baby." There was weary acceptance in his words.

"No! Not Roland's baby. Your baby."

Amy waited with baited breath.

"My baby?" His eyes still flat, revealing none of the burst of emotion she'd expected. "Why are you telling me this now?"

Did Heath think she was lying? She tried to read his inscrutable gaze, and failed. Surely he couldn't think that. Except for leading him to believe the baby was Roland's by changing the length of her pregnancy, she could never remember consciously deceiving anyone in her life.

"Early Christmas present?" She hid her fear beneath a veneer of flippancy. Then instantly regretted it when his eyes lit up—and not with the love she'd deluded herself that she'd glimpsed previously. "Wait. That came out badly. I'm sorry."

The flare of hot anger subsided. He drew a deep breath. "What made you decide that the baby wasn't Roland's?"

What to say now? She couldn't tell him that she'd always known. She felt ashamed at the idea that he'd know she lied. This was so tough. If only he'd soften a little…

But he didn't.

His gaze bored into her until she felt like a bug on a pin. Amy began to fidget. She hated that feeling, as someone who had striven to be good for most of her life, she wasn't accustomed to it. "Quit staring at me like that."

"Or did Dr. Shortt make an error?"

She couldn't let the doctor take the blame. "It was me— and it wasn't a mistake."

His gaze narrowed to black cracks. "It wasn't a mistake?"

"Okay, I lied," Amy confessed baldly, and stared back at him.

Heath blinked. Whatever he'd expected her to say, clearly it hadn't been that. *"You lied?"*

He sounded thrown.

"Yes, I lied. Me, little Miss Goody-Two-Shoes." Her self-mockery hurt.

"I never referred to you as that when you were young."

"Then you must've been the only one." She sighed.

A gleam flashed in the depths of his eyes. "But then perhaps I saw a side of you that no one else ever did. I saw fire."

Horrors. Had he suspected the passion she hadn't even known lurked inside her? She threw him a wary glance. "Fire? That sounds dangerous. I think I prefer to be thought of as boring."

"Goody-Two-Shoes didn't mean everyone thought you were boring. People liked you, Amy. They considered you to be a good example to others. You were kind. Always helpful. Always trustworthy," he finished.

"Sounds boring to me."

He inspected her. "It's those characteristics that have always made you so special."

She swallowed and wished that she'd never lied to him. Even by omission.

"So if I lie, I suppose that means I'm no longer special?"

An emotion she couldn't identify flared in his eyes, then just as quickly it was gone.

"You're still special." It was so soft that she had to strain her ears to hear. "But this changes things."

"How?" she demanded, suddenly very scared.

He shook his head. "I don't know…but believe me, it does. I need to think about it." He rose to his feet.

"You're going out?"

"I need to clear my head. I need to walk."

Amy watched helplessly as the man she'd married, the man she'd known most of her life but only just started to value, walked out on her.

A sick feeling heaved her stomach that had nothing to do with salmonella. She hoped frantically that he would come back. She'd waited too long to tell him the truth…

A hard walk through vineyards and a hike up The Divide failed to ease the turmoil that raged within Heath.

Amy had lied to him.

Three hours after he'd set out, Heath decided only alcohol would cauterise the pain that seared his innards.

Jock, the whiskered barman at the Roaring Boar, welcomed Heath like a prodigal son. "Long time no see."

A glance around revealed that the pub was as popular as ever on Friday nights. "Good to know you're still here, Jock." Heath clapped the barman on the shoulder. Jock had witnessed much of his youthful stupidity and had never said a word.

That's probably what had drawn him back to the Roaring Boar all these years later.

"Aye, I'll be here till the day I die." Jock gave him a wide grin. It faded with his next words. "Terribly sorry to hear about your brother."

"Thanks." Heath hadn't come to talk—or to reminisce. He'd come to get quietly, seriously rip-roaring drunk. "Double bourbon, please."

Jock shot him a hooded look, but held his tongue as he turned to the glass shelving filled with bottles of all shapes and colours behind him.

Heath found a lone seat at the end of the crowded bar counter and wedged himself in between a giant of a man and the panelled wall of the pub. Seconds later a glass landed in front of him with a thud.

Heath picked it up. The glass felt curiously cold and smooth between his fingers, and the amber colour of the bourbon reminded him of Amy's eyes.

Damn, he couldn't even escape her here. Better he moon

over her like a lovesick puppy in the safety of the Roaring Boar rather than in his home.

Her home.

Chosen Valley was *her* home. She belonged there. He couldn't go back. Not until he'd decided what to do.

The baby was his.

Heath still couldn't absorb it. The revelation had shaken him to the soul. Not Roland's child. But his.

The night he'd spent with Amy—the worst and best night of his life—had resulted in a new life.

He raked a shaky hand through his hair and with the other hand raised the glass. The strong smoky smell of the bourbon filled his nostrils.

Heath set the glass down, undrunk.

Amy had known he was the father of her baby. She'd confessed that she'd lied about the dates. Miss Goody-Two-Shoes had lied to him. She'd known the baby had been conceived the night they spent together.

An unwelcome thought struck him. That's why she'd been so devastated at finding out she was pregnant. Roland's reckless, wild younger brother was the last guy she would've picked to father her child. So why the hell had she agreed to marry him?

It certainly wasn't to give Roland's child a chance at a Saxon life.

The answer came in a blinding flash. In Amy's world, marrying her baby's father would be the only thing to do. *The right thing.* He pushed the bourbon away, repelled by the uncompromising odour of raw alcohol and sank his head in his hands. Somehow, there was a profound difference in knowing that she married him because the child was his—not his brother's.

It took away her element of choice.

"No, no, I ha—want to marry you."

Her panicked statement the day in the aquarium came back to haunt him. *I have to marry you.* In her own mind Amy would've had no choice but to marry him. He shut his eyes.

She'd never loved him. Hell, he'd done his best over the past weeks to court her and she was still no closer to falling for him. He opened his eyes and stared blindly at the scarred wooden counter in front of him. Sure, Amy wanted him. But she resented the molten desire that bonded them together.

Groping for the glass, Heath slugged the bourbon back. The heat of the fiery liquor tasted sour in his mouth and he fought the urge to spit it out.

The guy beside him chose that moment to shift his large mass on his stool and jogged his elbow, knocking the rest of the bourbon over Heath. Accepting the man's embarrassed apologies, Heath resisted the urge to swear.

What the hell was he doing here? He had a wife at home. A wife who was pregnant, who'd been ill. A wife who believed he was out taking a walk. He was behaving with the wild, reckless irresponsibility she'd previously accused him of. Getting drunk tonight wasn't going to convince Amy to fall in love with him.

A night spent drinking would only give him a devastating hangover that he didn't need this close to Christmas.

At least Amy no longer believed he loved her. He could've wrung his sister's neck when he'd heard what Megan had revealed to Amy.

Pride and fury had given him no choice but to dissemble when Amy had put him in a corner by questioning whether he loved her.

A man deserved his pride. He wouldn't have Amy pity him. Right now his damned pride was pretty much all he had.

And Amy.

And the baby.

Heath straightened. That was a helluva lot more than he'd

had only a few months ago. Resolution filled him. Despite
Amy's lie, his marriage wasn't over. Fate had dealt him a
lucky card. He—not his brother—had fathered Amy's baby.

Rising to his feet, Heath dropped a twenty dollar bill on the
counter before heading for the door with newfound optimism.

He loved Amy. This baby was his. And he was not going
to walk away from that responsibility. Amy would learn
that he intended to be beside her for every minute of his
child's life.

A walk?

Heath had gone for a walk? Amy paced up and down the
living room. A walk that lasted for over five hours? She
stopped and peered out the window. It was pitch dark outside.

She had expected him back within an hour. At first she'd
practiced what she'd been going to say to apologise for not
telling him sooner about the baby. Then she'd grown mad that
he'd taken so long. Finally she'd grown worried.

He hadn't answered his cell phone. He hadn't gone to
Saxon's Folly. No one there knew where he was.

And that's when she'd grown more mad than before. *Where
was he?* The Lamborghini was missing from the four-car garage.

What if…

No, she wasn't letting her mind go down that terror track.
She padded back to the hall table and picked up the phone and
hit the redial button. It rang and rang. Just as she was about
to give up, Heath answered.

She'd never felt so relieved to hear his voice. Hunching her
shoulders, she demanded, "Why didn't you answer your
phone?"

"I left it in the Lamborghini."

"Where are you?"

There was a burst of static. "I'm just leaving The Roaring
Boar."

"The Roaring Boar?" Amy discovered she was crying. "I thought you'd been in an accident, that you might be dead. But you're only drunk!"

"Amy?"

He shouldn't be driving. She was so angry that she couldn't speak. *How dare he do this to her?*

"Amy? Are you there? Are you okay?"

No, she wasn't okay. She was furious. She was terrified. "Yes," she mumbled. "I'm okay."

"I'm not drunk." His voice grew clearer as the reception improved. "I didn't even finish the one drink I ordered. But if you had to smell me now, you wouldn't believe that."

She fished in the pocket of her dressing gown for a tissue. "Why?"

"Someone spilt bourbon over me. My drink."

Good grief. "Did you get into a fight?" That would be typical of Heath–the–hell-raiser. And far worse than getting drunk…or reeking of alcohol.

"No fight. Nothing happened." Another burst of static. "…home."

"What did you say?"

"I'm coming home."

The line went dead.

Heath was coming home. Amy liked the sound of that. She liked it very much. The misery of the past hours drained away, replaced by a blossom of hope. She wiped the tearstains from her face with the crumpled tissue and considered why those few words—*I'm coming home*—had brought the comfort that she'd desperately needed.

Her hand rested on her stomach as she made her way back to the living room and dropped down onto the sofa to await Heath's arrival. She could've sworn she felt a tiny flutter as she finally made sense of why she'd been so upset by Heath's extended absence.

Amy's breath caught in her throat as the knowledge sank in. She'd been so worried—not just because she feared for his safety. It was more than that. Much more…

She'd fallen in love with Heath Saxon.

Twelve

Heath strode into the house and dropped his keys on the intricately carved chest in the hall. The heavy wooden front door thudded shut behind him. The fresh clean scent of lemon and beeswax lingered, overlaid by a hint of tuberose. Quickening his step, he made for the living room.

It was empty.

Not even the flickering of the Christmas lights on the tree could fill the void that opened inside him.

Of course Amy hadn't waited up for him. Why should she?

She'd told him that the baby she carried was his. He'd been so shaken he'd told her he needed time—a walk to clear his thoughts.

How had his desertion made her feel? He remembered how horrified she'd been to discover she was pregnant. No wonder. The wrong Saxon brother had fathered her child.

Then a memory of the hesitant, hopeful expression in her eyes when she'd told him flashed through his head. And the despair that had followed when he'd said he needed to think, that he was going for a walk.

He gave a groan.

Had Amy imagined he was leaving?

Because he had walked away from her—and he hadn't come home. No, instead he'd gone to the Roaring Boar. Now he stank of bourbon.

Selfish!

Heath gave a groan of self-disgust, his nose wrinkling in distaste at the alcoholic odour that clung to him.

He needed a shower. Then he needed to apologize to Amy. For not listening when she'd needed him to hear her explanation. For walking away. For causing her to worry. And perhaps once he'd apologized, he'd be able to salvage something from the mess he'd made of everything tonight.

Because Amy and the baby meant the world to him.

Swiveling on his heel, Heath exited the living room and headed upstairs. But when he entered the master bedroom, he came to an abrupt halt. Amy wasn't there. Yet the bedside lamps had been switched on, and they cast a gold glow over the rich colours of the bed cover. Amy's dressing gown lay slung over the end of the bed, and her distinctive tuberose fragrance hung in the air.

A noise from the adjoining en suite attracted his attention. His heart quickening, Heath made for the bathroom.

Amy stared at her reflection in the wide mirror. The discovery that she loved Heath had shaken her. She thought about the surprise and joy that had filled her when Megan had said Heath loved her. Why hadn't she put two and two together and realized what he meant to her then?

If only Heath actually loved her in return....

Heath wanted her, that much she knew. She scanned her features in the mirror. Despite her recent illness, her skin glowed. Pregnancy suited her. Maybe they could build on the attraction that sizzled between them…and on the protectiveness and tenderness he displayed toward her. Maybe Heath could grow to love her.

She slid her hands over the silken nightdress, measuring the changes in her body—her full breasts, the curve of her stomach. Heath's baby had made her beautiful.

A sound behind her caused her to turn her head. She met Heath's hooded gaze.

"You're back," she said after a charged moment, hastily dropping her hands from her body.

Heath moved forward with swift grace. "I'm sorry I caused you to worry."

His gaze held hers and she read the sincerity there. "I thought…" Her voice trailed away.

"I know what you imagined." There was an intensity in his eyes that caused her pulse to quicken. "I should've realized you would worry I'd crashed the Lamborghini when I didn't come home. I have no excuse."

"Apology accepted." She owed him a much bigger apology for her behavior—for her failure to tell him the truth. Her gaze fell beneath his piercing regard. Only then did she notice the stains on his shirt. She inhaled deeply.

"Yes, I smell like a bar. I need a shower," he said and reached to turn the faucet on.

The sound of rushing water broke the sudden silence that stretched between them.

Heath turned his head, his eyes blazing with emotion. "Amy, I'm so glad that our baby is okay."

Our baby.

Hot emotion balled into a tight knot above her heart. Her throat tight, she murmured, "Me, too."

Heath stripped off the bourbon-soaked shirt and dropped it on the marble floor, revealing his gloriously muscled torso. The rest of this clothes followed as he shed them in economic movements.

Amy found she could no longer breathe.

Heath quirked an eyebrow. "Coming?"

Amy blinked to snap herself out of the thrall that held her. Slowly she shed her night dress, and by the time she stepped into the shower cubicle it was hot and steamy.

Heath's hands, slick with soap, closed on her upper arms. He stroked her flesh with long, smooth movements.

"So beautiful," he whispered.

Her nipples pebbled under his touch and pleasurable sensations rippled through her as his strong hands massaged her and the hot water sluiced over her.

Too soon he ushered her out the shower and wrapped her in a thick white bath sheet before swinging her in his arms.

"Heath, you don't need to carry me."

He shot her a grin. "I enjoy it, indulge me. You're such a little thing."

She froze as he set her down beside the vast bed and rubbed her dry. Little thing? "I never realised. I'm a petite brunette."

"You forgot pretty."

She flushed. "So by marrying me you're acting true to type."

"Amy-love, you're the pretty, petite brunette prototype."

"What do you mean?" The breathlessness was back.

But he stood in front of her, nude and magnificent. "We're talking too much." Then he was kissing her and her mind cleared of all thought. All she could do was feel.

He stripped the bath sheet away and tumbled her naked onto the bed before following her down.

His hands touched her belly, his palms moulding the gentle rise where the baby was starting to make its presence known.

"This is more than I ever hoped for." Heath kissed the soft skin of her stomach, and Amy dug her fingers into the corded muscles in his upper arms.

"What do you mean?"

"You…" another kiss and then he raised his head "…and our baby."

"You hoped?" She groped for the words.

"Oh, yes, I hoped. And prayed. Every day of my life. But I never believed it would happen."

"You mean us?"

He didn't answer. Instead, he ran his hands over her thighs, parted them and traced the intricate folds between her legs.

Amy gasped.

His head dipped to follow where his fingers had touched and in the minutes that followed Amy's breath grew ragged.

Finally she pushed him away. "My turn."

He resisted for a moment. But she wouldn't allow him to stop her. When her mouth closed over him, he shuddered, every muscle in his lean frame taut.

She licked and sucked at his hard flesh with an avid curiosity that almost drove him mad. Once. Twice. He fought to stop himself from coming in hot tangy blasts.

When he could take no more, he groaned and flipped her on her back. He planted a gentle kiss on her pouting lips and slowly, his weight propped on his arms, he sank into her.

With slow deliberate strokes he drove the ever-increasing spirals of pleasure higher and higher. Watching her, he waited until the moment that her lashes fluttered over those incredible, glowing eyes.

One more slow thrust and they both came apart.

Afterwards, Heath reclined back against stuffed continental pillows and held his wife in his arms. For a long time they both lay quietly under the covers. Finally, he turned his head and met her sated gaze. "There's something you need to know."

She tensed and her eyes grew wary. "What?"

"That I'm never going to walk away from my child." He slipped a hand under the cover and rested it on her stomach.

"Or you. This marriage truly is for better or worse, even though I rewrote our wedding vows."

She didn't speak, simply held his gaze.

He didn't like the silence. He found he wanted to know what she was thinking. So he lifted his hand from her belly and brought it out to brush her hair behind her ears, then asked, "How could you be so certain that the baby was mine?"

The smile that she gave him was bittersweet. "That's easy. I never made love with Roland."

Shock slammed through him. "What?"

"There was only ever you."

"Only me? But why?"

Curled into him, Amy watched as the glazed expression in the ebony eyes slowly cleared. "Because I wanted a white wedding night."

"Why didn't you tell me…stop me?" Horror filled his face. "I would've stopped. Even though it would probably have killed me, I would never have taken that precious gift from you if I'd known."

"What was the point?" She shrugged and her bare skin rubbed against him, arousing frissons of awareness. "I'd guarded my virginity…it caused terrible grief between me and Roland…and then he died. It hardly seemed worth prizing any longer."

Heath swallowed, his Adam's apple moving. "I appreciate that. Thank you for telling me."

"Okay, my turn to ask a question." Amy glanced up at him through her lashes. "What did you mean I was the prototype?"

Heath grinned at her. "I knew you'd ask that. You're the love of my life. The woman I searched for in every other female I dated. The woman I believed would never be mine."

"You're joking? Since when?" Amy pulled away from him, her eyes wide with disbelief. Then, more subdued as she took in the pain behind his grin, she said, "You're not joking. You're serious."

He pulled her back to where she'd rested before she'd drawn away. "Since you were sixteen." His mouth slanted. "I thought you were too young. I intended to wait for you."

Amy covered her mouth with her hands. "And I fell for Roland. Told the whole world on my seventeenth birthday— after he gave me the gorgeous locket that convinced me he was my soul mate. Stupid child."

Heath's eyes dimmed for an instant. She got the impression he was hesitating, then he said, "I told myself all I wanted was for you to be happy. I lied. I wanted you for myself."

"Oh, Heath. And Roland and I were going to get married."

"That's one of the reasons I made myself so scarce. My fight with Dad wasn't the only reason I stayed away from Saxon's Folly, except for the odd dinner. I didn't want to hear about the wedding arrangements. I'm a sinner, sweet innocent Amy. Every wicked thing you've ever heard about me is true."

"You won't scare me, Heath." She planted a kiss on the side of his neck.

He suppressed the urge to grab her and haul her beneath him, and start loving her all over again. "I should," he growled.

She lifted her head and gave him an indecipherable look. "You couldn't have done anything worse than what I've done."

"You?" Heath shook his head in denial. Not Amy. "You're as near to perfect as it gets."

"I'm not. I'm—" she broke off, averting her face. Then she said, "So what have you done that's so terrible?"

"I coveted my brother's fiancée!"

Her breath caught with an audible gasp. "Heath—"

"And then I—"

"Stop. You tried to warn me that Roland wouldn't suit me…"

"That wasn't wholly self-motivated. He'd always had girl-friends you never knew about. I was worried about you."

"But no one ever told me."

"I couldn't. Roland was my brother. I owed him some

loyalty. And I was in the worse position. If I told you…and it came out how I felt about you, I'd look like the world's most dishonourable jerk."

Amy wriggled along his body until she rested as close as she could get. Gazing into his eyes she said, "I can understand that. So you tried to warn me off. But I refused to listen. Until that final night. I broke up with Roland—did you know that?"

Heath shook his head.

"I'd heard he was having an affair. I confronted him. I told him that I wanted fidelity from the man I married…that I didn't want someone who cheated on me." She glanced away from his perceptive eyes for a brief moment. "That's why I felt so guilty when he died. I'd promised to marry him and I broke that promise. If we hadn't fought, he might not have died."

"Oh, Amy!" Heath gathered her close. "Never feel guilty. He breached the promise of trust and fidelity first. You had every reason to end your engagement."

"He didn't want to break up. He was upset. Much more upset than I expected." She hauled in a deep breath. This was so hard. Living with it had made her miserable for months. "But I insisted. It was my fault. I caused the accident. I broke his concentration."

"You can't blame yourself. You didn't want Roland dead. Nor did I." He sighed. "I loved my brother." He cupped her cheek with his calloused fingers. "And I loved you. It was a hell of a place to be in."

"You know what I don't get?" Amy paused. "Why did Roland want to marry me if he couldn't give up other women?"

"Who knows? Maybe he loved you as much as I did, despite the other women." Then Heath snapped his fingers. "He knew about your virginity pledge?"

"Oh, yes."

"Perhaps that was it. Roland always loved a challenge."

Amy considered that. "It's possible, although we'll never know."

"What's important is not to forget the parts of Roland that we all loved. His energy. His generosity. His enthusiasm." Heath's eyes were gentle. "And always remember that I love you."

"Oh, Heath, I love you, too. I'm so lucky to have found you."

He grinned, a happy carefree grin. "Amy-love, you had to look a long way to find me next door in the house where you grew up."

"Let's just say I missed the obvious. But now that I've found you, that's it."

"I'm not going anywhere. I chose you a long time ago."

He pulled her toward him and kissed her gently, and Amy knew that was a promise he would never break.

Christmas Eve, the day of the Saxon's Folly Summer Festival, dawned fresh and bright. By midafternoon the rhythmic sound of jazz music echoed through the vineyard and over the surrounding hills.

People streamed through the curved gates and by three o'clock the grassy expanse around the bandstand was covered with picnic blankets as couples and families ate and listened to the melodic strains as one band followed another.

"Would you like some cotton candy?" Heath asked Amy as they walked past a row of food stalls which had been set up for today's event.

She eyed the pink candy. "I think I'll pass until I've had some real food. And then we have to find the family."

All the Saxons were here today. And Amy's father, too. Earlier in the week, Joshua and Alyssa had been away in Auckland, necessitating a delay in telling the family the truth about the baby's parentage. But they could delay no longer.

"We'll round everyone up." Heath scanned the swelling

crowd. "Though I'm starting to have my doubts about getting everyone together at the same time. It's a madhouse today."

A few stalls along, Heath bought a platter of hot fresh rolls and roasted vegetables, and they returned to where he'd set up chairs under a large oak tree on the perimeter of the grassy clearing. The vegetables tasted sweet and the bread was crusty on the outside and soft when she broke it open.

"Feeling okay?" he asked.

"Completely." She drew a deep breath. "Thank you for looking after me for all those days that I was ill."

"In sickness and in health," he said, his eyes intense.

"We didn't say that. You changed the vows, remember?"

"But those go without saying…and to love." His eyes glowed, and warmth suffused her.

Before Amy could respond, a burst of laughter broke the mood between them.

"Heath Saxon?"

The woman who stood beside the picnic blanket was confidently stunning, her face known in every home throughout New Zealand. Kelly Christie. Uncertainty pierced Amy. Had the beautiful Kelly been one of Heath's conquests? For a brief instant, every fear that Amy had ever had about falling for Heath returned. Then she shoved the crazy doubts away.

Heath had married her.

He loved her. Only her.

Her nerves steadied. Heath had never done anything to make her doubt him. He'd been steadfast and caring. How could she doubt him now? The tall, leggy blonde television goddess wasn't even his usual type. No pretty, petite brunette. Amy started to smile as the momentary doubt and uncertainty evaporated.

"It's wonderful to meet you, Heath," Kelly simpered. "If you don't mind, I'll bring the cameras over and film you for a little while and then I'd like to ask you a few questions for our midday Christmas show tomorrow."

Heath revealed no pleasure at the prospect of cozying up with the TV hostess for millions to see. Kelly wasn't an ex, Amy realized. And judging from his frown, Kelly had failed to impress.

Already Heath was shaking his head. "Not today, Kelly. It's been a busy week. My wife and I are taking private time out to enjoy the concert."

"Of course, your wife. Emily, isn't it?"

"Amy," she corrected. All animation vanished from the blonde's features and her pale blue eyes turned to slowly inspect Amy.

This woman hated her.

Why?

Amy didn't even know her, could've sworn she'd never met Kelly. Instinctively, Amy shifted closer to Heath to escape the venom.

His arm came around her, warm and solid. Kelly didn't miss the gesture. She laughed. "So how does it feel to be the fortunate woman to have snared two of the gorgeous Saxon men, Amy?"

Then Amy knew.

This woman had been Roland's lover, the celebrity she'd heard rumours of and confronted him about. Had his mistress loved Roland? The hurt lurking below the rage in those azure eyes suggested that she had.

Amy looked at her with pity.

Kelly had beauty, a fabulous career, but she'd fallen for another woman's man. A man engaged to be married who showed no sign of abandoning his hometown fiancée.

How that must've stung.

Roland had cheated both of them. By a tragic turn of fate, Amy had escaped marrying him. She'd married Heath instead. Tender. Protective. Fiercely loyal. A man worthy of her love.

She could afford to be generous.

"Kelly, if you call after Christmas, perhaps we can set up a time for you to interview the Saxon family as we look forward to the next harvest." Amy gave the other woman her sweetest smile. "You and your cameramen would get access to the wineries on both sides of The Divide, Saxon's Folly and Chosen Valley. An exclusive, if you like."

Kelly looked startled. Then her composure returned and she gave Amy a suspicious narrow-eyed look.

Amy held her gaze, refusing to be intimidated.

Finally, Kelly smiled, a genuine smile that glowed with charisma and revealed not an iota of resentment. "I'd like that very much, Amy Saxon. Thank you."

She turned to go.

Amy sneaked a glance at Heath. His eyes glittered a warning at the TV hostess. Dangerous. Confidently, Amy linked her fingers through his.

"Kelly," she called.

The TV hostess swiveled on her white high heels.

"Feel free to announce that Heath and I are expecting a baby on your Christmas day exclusive." The woman's eyes widened in stunned amazement. "The first Saxon grandchild," Amy added. "And you're the first to know. Please give us a chance to tell the family—so keep it confidential until your show at noon tomorrow."

Kelly shook her head, her eyes disbelieving. "You don't mind?"

Amy turned her head and met Heath's incredulous gaze. "Everyone's going to find out sometime," she told him. "Kelly might as well get the first break on the news."

"Amy, it's not hard to see why the Saxon men adore you. Thanks again." And with a wave and a flash of that famous white smile, she was gone.

"I'm not sure that was a good idea." Heath's hand tightened around her fingers. "I may get Alyssa to contact Kelly's station to cancel that interview."

"I should have checked with you first." Amy's heart dropped. "I thought the publicity might be good for both wineries—her show is very popular." And how could she explain that her heart had ached for Kelly?

"Kelly Christie can cause a lot of trouble."

He wasn't annoyed with her. He was concerned for her. This was Heath in protector mode. The certainty solidified. She squeezed his fingers. "If you're referring to her affair with Roland, then I have to say I think you're wrong."

"You know about that?"

For the second time in minutes, Amy saw that she'd shocked him.

"I told you I knew Roland was having an affair shortly before he died. Until just now I didn't know the identity of the woman."

"But Kelly didn't say anything—"

"She didn't have to. I knew. She was jealous…and upset. The pain and unhappiness were in her eyes."

Heath fell silent. Tugging her hand, he pulled her close and said, "That was an incredibly classy—and gutsy—thing to do." Heath nuzzled her hair. "I think you have a fan for life."

"I'm sure she won't step out of line."

"She won't get the chance," Heath said darkly. "No one will harm you while I have breath in my body."

Amy basked in the glow of Heath's possessive words as dusk fell and the stage lights came on, suffusing the estate with a glow.

Heath's brother, Joshua and Alyssa joined them and a little later Megan made her way over, too.

"Where are the parents?" asked Heath.

"They left," said Megan. "Mom said they had some serious stuff to discuss. But they were holding hands."

"Dad has a lot to make up for," Joshua said. "But I hope that Mother forgives him."

Heath and Amy exchanged glances. Their news would have to wait another day.

"It's been a wonderful day," said Amy dreamily.

"Now the work starts on next year's festival."

Alyssa rolled her eyes at Joshua's droll observation.

"Hey, don't look like that," her fiancé said, "I know you loved every moment of it."

"Actually, I did," said Alyssa. "I love being part of the Saxon family."

Joshua leant over and gave his fiancée a lingering kiss. "I'm so glad I found you."

Pleasure spread through Amy at their clear love for each other. Absently, she touched the locket around her neck. She'd have to get a picture of Heath to put in there. She'd removed the image of Roland the night before the wedding. It had been the right thing to do. But Heath was her love now. She wanted his image close to her breast.

"That's a lovely piece of jewellery," Alyssa said, leaning forward to get a closer look. "Victorian, is it?"

Amy nodded.

"Roland bought you that for your birthday," Joshua recalled. "I remember. Was it your eighteenth birthday? He dragged us all along to help him shop for your present, do you remember?"

"It was Amy's seventeenth. He wanted my opinion because I was a girl." Megan was laughing.

Amy's fingers stilled. All these years she'd cherished the locket, believing Roland had chosen it for her. "You mean you chose it?" she asked Megan.

Megan shook her head. "Not me. Heath did. I would've

gone for something art deco–inspired. Heath pointed out that you loved lace and old-fashioned fripperies. He found the Victorian heart. He wanted to buy it for you, but Roland paid for it before he could. I think Heath sent you flowers instead."

"Yes, he did." She'd almost forgotten about the lovely bunch of long-stemmed white roses.

"So if I'd given you a romantic Victorian locket studded with diamonds, would you have decided I was the one?"

Amy's eyes met her husband's as she remembered his words. He'd known. And she hadn't.

"Didn't you know, Amy?"

Megan's uncanny question brought her back to the present. "No, Heath never breathed a word."

"Oh, dear!" Megan covered her mouth with her hand. "Have I put my foot in it again?"

"Looks like it." Joshua unfolded himself from where he was sitting. "Should we go dance, darling?" he asked Alyssa.

"I think I'd better go, too." Megan weaved her way into the crowd.

Amy didn't look away from Heath. There was nothing she needed to say. He must've read it in her eyes.

"Roland was wrong for you."

"I was so young." Too young.

"He should've known better." Heath's eyes were steadfast. "He was my brother, I loved him. But he wasn't capable of committing to one woman."

"You love me." It was a statement, not a question.

"Always and forever." His intensity was palpable.

"I must be the luckiest woman in the world." Amy fell silent when a group of children dressed as angels wearing long white robes with big silver wings and holding candles filed past. At the base of the rotunda, they formed a circle. The band burst into a funky version of "Joy to the World" and the dancing crowd swayed and sang along.

"I hope there are angels where Roland is now."

Heath chuckled. "If there are, I'm sure Roland will find them."

Amy shook her head even as she laughed. "I suppose you're right."

"Tired?" asked Heath.

"There are still two bands to play," she said.

"I know. But I thought you might have had enough."

She caught the concern for her in his eyes. Something softened, and heat flared inside her. "Perhaps it's time to find a different party."

The skin across his cheeks grew taut. Amy could feel tension winding through his every muscle.

"What are we waiting for?"

Epilogue

The Christmas bells sounded joyous to Amy as she and Heath exited the stone church hand in hand after the early morning sermon.

The sun had already risen over the sea and the sky was suffused with shades of pink and orange, and a golden glow heralded her and Heath's first Christmas together.

Amy glanced sideways at her husband. "Thank you for coming with me this morning."

His hand tightened around hers and she knew without words that the service had moved him as much as it had her. The message of love that the priest had delivered had been so right for her and Heath, it had brought tears to her eyes. And it made her feel closer to the man beside her. Amy was no longer afraid that she'd failed to live up to her good girl reputation. More importantly, she'd found love. Real love. Heath was her match, her mate, her equal.

She'd said a silent prayer for Roland, too, resting his memory in peace. She suspected Heath had, too.

Her husband held the passenger door of the Lamborghini open and she ducked in. Within minutes they were roaring down the long, tree-lined drive of Saxon's Folly.

The house came into sight, a white Victorian homestead tucked in against the hill covered with rows of vines. The great wooden front doors were already open.

Their arms filled with gaily wrapped gifts, Heath and Amy found the family in the sitting room and added their offerings to the enormous heap of wrapped gifts under the evergreen tree.

Across the room, Ralph Wright rose to his feet and gave Amy a kiss on the cheek before shaking Heath's hand. "Merry Christmas to you both."

"Oh, it is." Amy smiled at her father.

Megan shut the cell phone she'd been texting on and came over to give them both an enthusiastic hug. Alyssa and Joshua were more circumspect, but Amy could feel their love and affection.

"Heath, dear," said Kay Saxon, "Rafaelo and Caitlyn just called to wish us a Merry Christmas—they send their love. Rafaelo says we must all go visit. Maybe we should consider visiting next Christmas."

"There will be their wedding too," pointed out Alyssa. "Speaking of which, Joshua and I have finally set a date: Valentine's Day falls on a Saturday next year. So make sure you note that down."

Kay perched herself on the arm of the leather chair where her husband sat and gave him a loving smile. Returning the smile, Phillip put an arm around Kay's waist, and his face softened with love.

Amy exchanged a pleased glance with Heath. It looked like

the rift between his parents had been mended. From the corner of her eye, Amy saw that Alyssa had noticed it, too, and was whispering something in Joshua's ear.

Heath led Amy over to his parents. "Mom, Dad, we've got a gift for you." He looked across to Amy's father. "And you, too, Ralph."

Kay and Phillip broke out of their self-absorption and looked at them with interest. Ralph came closer.

"You've decided to stay at Saxon's Folly, I hope?" said Phillip.

Heath nodded. "Yes, I'd like that, Dad. But that's not the gift we came to tell you about." Heath drew Amy closer. "We want your blessing."

"For your gift?" Phillip frowned.

Kay looked puzzled. "Our blessing?"

"I'm the father of Amy's baby," Heath announced into the waiting silence. "Our baby will be due in June."

"I'm not surprised," said Ralph.

Then everyone started to talk at once. There was laughter and tears and hugs and when it had all settled back to normal, Heath grinned at Amy and mouthed, "I love you."

With a soft smile she responded by tugging his hand and kissing him sedately under a sprig of mistletoe.

At last the family all made their way to the Christmas tree where the gifts awaited.

"Next Christmas there'll be a new member to add to the family circle." Heath smiled down at Amy and she knew that he was thinking that their marriage, their child, had hastened the healing in the family. "The first grandchild."

"The first of many from the Saxon brides," concluded Kay as she handed a wrapped gift to Megan. "Be happy, all of you. Love each other every day of your lives."

Her eyes glowing with joy, Amy looked around the circle

of familiar faces. "It's wonderful to have a family Christmas together."

And everyone heartily agreed.

* * * * *

A sneaky peek at next month...

By Request

RELIVE THE ROMANCE WITH THE BEST OF THE BEST

My wish list for next month's titles...

In stores from 18th January 2013:

3 stories in each book - only £5.99!

❏ Undressed by the Billionaire – Susan Stephens, Amanda Browning & Susanne James

❏ A Very Personal Assistant – Jessica Hart, Margaret Mayo & Nina Harrington

In stores from 1st February 2013:

❏ Platinum Grooms – Sara Orwig

Available at WHSmith, Tesco, Asda, Eason, Amazon and Apple

Just can't wait?

Visit us Online

You can buy our books online a month before they hit the shops! **www.millsandboon.co.uk**

0113/05

Special Offers

Every month we put together collections and longer reads written by your favourite authors.

Here are some of next month's highlights— and don't miss our fabulous discount online!

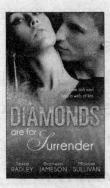

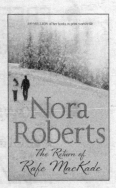

On sale 18th January　　On sale 1st February　　On sale 1st February

Find out more at
www.millsandboon.co.uk/specialreleases

Visit us Online

0213/ST/MB399

The World of Mills & Boon®

There's a Mills & Boon® series that's perfect for you. We publish ten series and, with new titles every month, you never have to wait long for your favourite to come along.

Blaze®

Scorching hot, sexy reads
4 new stories every month

By Request

Relive the romance with the best of the best
9 new stories every month

Cherish™

Romance to melt the heart every time
12 new stories every month

Desire™

Passionate and dramatic love stories
8 new stories every month